Paper Chasers

Black Print Publishing
289 Livingston St
Brooklyn, NY

Black Print Publishing
289 Livingston St
Brooklyn, NY 11217

Copyright © 2003 Mark Anthony

ISBN 09722771-7-X

Printed in Canada

In Memory Of Richard Jones Jr.
a/k/a Richie

Acknowledgements

I want to make sure that I take the time to thank all of those who believed more in my ability to write than I did. I am always flattered and amazed that I can touch people with words. Without your encouragement my ideas and dreams would not have had the fuel to move forward.

A special thanks goes to Carl Weber. Your passion for books causes you to reach out and help those who are striving to be where you are.

And a very special thanks goes to my wife, Sabine. Sabine thank you for all of your support and understanding during the hours it takes to accomplish the stories that I write. You are in my corner and you give me confidence and help me believe that I can achieve and accomplish anything that I set my mind to.

Author's Note

As an author, I fully understand that entertainment has impact and has always played a big role in any society. Entertainment, whether it is movies, music, television, or books, very often gets at the root of our emotions and can therefore pull from us either a negative response or a positive response. I have seen and heard many forms of entertainment that was labeled as "glorifying violence," "explicit," "graphic," and so on. So when I set out to write this book, I wondered what kind of message I would be sending out. Would my message be the same old run of the mill garbage that people would cast aside and label as glorifying violence?

It is a fear of mine that my work will be viewed as having a negative impact on its readers. That fear caused me to present the subject matter in a tasteful manner. My hope is that readers from all walks of life will be able to connect with characters in this story. Because without an emotional connection, people can't relate to those that are outcast, and if they can't relate they will be less inclined to help those who are outcast.

If the readers of this book are able to connect with the characters in this story, hopefully that connection will lead to dialogue or simply a better understanding of what a very small fraction of urban males have lived through and continue to live through.

So as an author and as a father I understand that I must be responsible in what I contribute to the public. If this book is viewed as glorifying violence then I apologize for using my talent in a negative way. But I will honestly say that this book was written in order to put a human connection to some of the ills that we see and have seen in society. This book was also intended to show the grave spiritual reality of what will happen if people don't have the courage to change their negative lifestyles in spite of all the obstacles.

Lastly, I want the readers to realize that this book represents the reality of the times in which I grew up. And although it may not be the present reality, we all know that life goes through cycles and history has a way of repeating itself. Hopefully that history of drugs and violence will never again have to be lived through by anyone. The setting of this book is New York City in the year of 1991. During 1991 there were 2,571 murders and 112,342 robberies in New York alone! Those are real numbers and some of the highest crime numbers that New York has ever experienced, and those numbers were fueled by drugs, and crack cocaine in particular. To me, those statistics were and still are more than just numbers on a page. There were real people and real events attached to those numbers and it is with that in mind that I wrote this book.

All Readers: Be sure to refer to the glossary in the back of the book if you are unsure of the meaning or the context of certain slang words.

The Funeral

Not ironic at all was the fact that it had rained for the past three years on the same day that Dr. Martin Luther King, Jr. was murdered. It also rained on the day that marked the death of Malcolm X.

It was June 8, 1991, and again it was pouring rain outside. It was only 7:15 a.m., and usually at that time I would have been asleep, but not today. I felt like pulling the covers over my head and sleeping until eternity. I was never one to be lazy, never loved to stay in the bed, but today was different. Still, as much s I wanted to hibernate, I knew I had to get up and get dressed.

I was wishing this was all just a bad dream or something. Unfortunately, I knew that was not the case. Couldn't I just go back to sleep, and when I awoke everything would be different? Since I had to deal with reality, the answer was no.

Reality was staring at me from across my room in the form of a neatly pressed black suit. That reality made me feel grim. The rain outside my window wasn't what had woken me. The fact that I had to attend a funeral in three hours is what had kept me awake, tossing and turning throughout the night.

Richie was dead. I had just walked and talked with him five days ago, and now he was dead. How would his casket look? What would he be wearing? Would he look the same dead as he did alive? Would everybody be able to see the cut on his throat? The same cut that allowed every ounce of blood in his body to shoot out like a water fountain. *Oh my God!* I thought to myself. I couldn't believe it. Another one of my homeboys was dead. And for what? For no reason at all.

There was no time to dwell on the many thoughts that were racing through my head. It was time for me to peel myself out of the bed and get dressed. Why was I moving so slow? Maybe because I was thinking of a way to bring Richie back. But I just simply couldn't think of one.

"I'm sorry, Richie. I'm sorry. You know I'd bring you back if I could," I announced to my room. I knew Richie could hear me.

Maybe it was Richie slowing me down, making me take twenty minutes to brush my teeth. I knew he didn't want me rushing to see him lowered into the ground with all the worms and maggots. The same ground that gets cold and as hard as a rock in the winter months, and the same ground where Richie's body would return to dust. Yeah, I didn't want to see Richie like that no more than he wanted to be murdered.

My thirty-minute shower was finally coming to an end. Ten-thirty was approaching faster and faster. My black suit looked good, but it had seen better days. I guess that this was about my tenth time wearing it. Sadly, every time I wore it was to see one of my homeys put to rest. And this present day in time was no different. Or was it? I guess it was different simply because it was Richie's funeral that I was going to. Richie was my niggah. The most jacked up part about him dying was the fact that he had just graduated from college. Yeah. He had his B.A. in Criminal Justice. And only two weeks after getting his degree, he was dead. As the saying goes, shit happens.

Richie was a young black man. He was the type of person who wore gold teeth, let his pants sag below his butt and drank forties. I guess you would call him your stereotypical hoodlum, only he knew what time it was. His mind was always focused. Half of the world would look at him and think he was definitely not college material. But that was just a stereotype, one that he didn't fit.

I'll never forget what he told me one day. He said, "Holz I'm gonna change the minds of society so that we won't all be stereotyped like we are. Stereotyped just because of the way we look." He added, "See, I'm gonna finish college, not so I can come out and make a lot money, because anybody can do that. I could do that by just standing on the corner slinging dope. See Holz, I want to finish school so I can better myself. Once I better myself I'll be able to better the people around me. That's what an education should be all about. It's about bettering yourself as well as the people around you." Richie always talked about ending black on black crime in New York. Little did he know, as fate would have it, that he too would be killed by a brother.

I was finally dressed. My father was going to drive me and some of the other cats from Fourth Crew to the funeral. That's the same crew that Richie was a part of. We picked up Randy, Dwight, and Tee. They were down the block at Tee's grandmother's house. The next stop was Kwame's house, to pick him up. We got Kwame and we were ready to roll to the funeral. The funeral was being held in a church on Linden Blvd.

On the way to the church we passed the spot where Richie had been killed. As we drove past the spot, the vision of his throat being slashed replayed in my mind over and over again, like a scene from a movie.

Everything had happened so quickly that day. On the day of his death, Richie and I had just gotten haircuts. We went to pick up his girl, Elizabeth. Elizabeth was the older sister of my girlfriend, Sabine.

You could tell that Richie was excited about the fact that he had finally graduated from college, because that's all he conversed about. I was happy for him because, I mean, who actually thought that he would make it? The truth was, nobody did except us who were a part of Fourth Crew.

"I'm glad you got your degree, 'cause now your gonna be making mad money and I wouldn't let myself marry you if you didn't get your college degree." That was all his girl Liz kept telling him. Richie kept trying his hardest to explain to Liz that the reason why he'd pursued his education had nothing to do with dollars. Liz didn't understand. She just thought it equated to dead presidents.

After leaving Elizabeth's house, which was located in Hollis, Queens, we caught the number five livery van to my house. Sabine was supposed to come by my house after she left work. Then we were all going to go out to the movies that night. Too bad we never made it.

Liz had on these turquoise biker spandex shorts and this black spandex tank top which revealed her belly button. It was the type of outfit that showed off every curve and accentuated the gluteous-maximus. She had a slammin' body, so you know she was looking good.

When we reached our stop we stepped out of the van. All of the guys who were on the corner hanging out were clocking Liz. They were all scoping her big bootie. I wasn't worried about any niggahs out there that day trying to play us by flirting with Liz, because I knew just about every head that was on the corner.

Richie and I went into the bodega on the corner. Liz stayed outside and waited for us. But after a couple of minutes she came into the store looking irate. She told us that one of the guys outside had squeezed her butt. Richie, who had a quick temper, stepped outside.

"Yo! Who the hell squeezed my girl's ass?" he yelled.

There was silence. No one said a word. Richie looked annoyed. He huffed loudly and repeated his words in a more stern, serious, parent-talking-to-a-bad-group-of-kids kind of way.

"YO! WHO THE HELL SQUEEZED MY GIRL'S ASS?" Again there was silence. Nobody said a word. The heads on the corner just kind of lamped and twisted their upper lip as they sniffled a fake runny nose.

Then Richie said, "Yeah, all y'all fake-ass punk niggahs is playing like girls now and ain't saying nothin'. That's ah'ight though, 'cause y'all can't do me nothin' anyway."

Finally Liz pointed out the guy who'd felt her butt. I had never seen him before, or maybe I had seen him once or twice, but I knew for a fact that he wasn't from our part of town. But after a moment or so it finally hit me. I did know who he was. His name was Cory. He was from South Jamaica, Queens. He would come to Laurelton every now and then to knock off some work, A.K.A sell drugs.

Richie stepped up to Cory and asked in a screw-faced kind of way, "Yo Money, did you touch my girl?"

"Yo Potnah!" Cory put his hands in Richies's face. "Get out my face. Don't try to play me in front of your boyz, 'cause I ain't having it!"

"If you disrespect my girl then you're disrespecting me, and I ain't tryin'a hear that. POTNAH!" Richie threatened.

"Don't try to play me," Cory said again. "I'm not the one. Now get outta my face, ah'ight?" Then Cory just swung from outta nowhere and snuffed Richie. He clocked Richie in the mouth. Richie stumbled back a little, regained his composure and went buck wild, throwing a barrage of punches. In an instant he was whipping Cory like he'd stole something valuable.

It seemed as if all of the people on the corner were magnetically drawn to the fight. They converged on the fight, making a jagged circle, leaving just enough room for two people to get at each other. Everyone watched and jeered as Richie proceeded to whip Cory's black behind.

Then suddenly, like a flash, Cory pulled a knife and slashed Richie's throat. He did it so quick that I didn't even see if it was an actual knife or if it was a box cutter. After he cut Richie's throat, he took flight like Carl Lewis. He hauled ass down Merrick Blvd. Nobody tried to chase him because everyone was in shock, myself included, that Richie had been cut.

The knife had hit his jugular vein. There was blood everywhere. The blood was literally shooting out of Richie's neck like the Fountain of Youth. I had seen niggahs get split wide open in street fights before, but I had never witnessed anything like I was witnessing with Richie. Richie grabbed his throat and staggered around in a panic. Every time his heart would beat, another stream of blood would literally shoot out of his neck. It was chaotic. Females were screaming and guys were howling in disbelief.

Before I knew it, Richie had collapsed. I ran over to him and put my fingers on his wound. In seconds my hands were slippery from all of the blood, too slippery to hold his neck. There was so much blood, I just couldn't believe it. My shirt, pants, and sneakers were red from all of the blood.

Richie, well forget about it. He was soaking in his own blood. It was one of the worst sights a human being could possibly witness. He was literally drowning in his own blood. I was doing the best I could to slow down the rush of blood. As I sat on the concrete and cradled Richie's head in my arms, I heard Elizabeth in the background screaming hysterically.

"RICHIE! RICHIE! RICHIEEE!" Each time Elizabeth screamed his name, her voice would echo in my head. Tears rolled out of her eyes as she helplessly watched Richie's blood roll along the curb and into the sewer. Her man was dying a senseless death right in front of her eyes and there was nothing that she, or I, or anyone could do to help Richie. All we could do was hope for the best. I pleaded for someone to call an ambulance

Finally someone grabbed Liz and tried to calm her down. By this time, the whole block was filled with onlookers. Traffic on Merrick Blvd. was stopped in both directions. All eyes were on Richie. Richie's eyes were open and he was silent. He had such fear in his eyes, fear that I'd never seen before in any man. Then again, that was the closest in physical proximity that I'd ever been in terms of a dying man.

Richie's eyes stayed glued on Elizabeth. Wherever she went, his brown pupils followed. He didn't even look at me when I told him that he was going to be alright.

I kept saying, "Richie, you're gonna be ah'ight. Just try to relax. The ambulance is coming for you. Just hold on, Richie."

People were everywhere.

"Where is this ambulance? My man is bleeding to death!" I yelled.

Finally, after fifteen minutes that felt eternal, I heard sirens blaring. Sirens were coming from all angles. By this time Elizabeth had gotten lost in the sea of people and Richie's eyes shifted away from the crowd. With the sound of sirens blaring in the background, Richie looked at me. He was struggling to talk. All of the life was just about drained out of him by now.

He said, "Yo Holz." He was talking in a real slow and low tone. Again he started to speak.

"Yo Holz. Don't… let me die…. Please, man…."

"I won't, Richie," I promised. "Richie, come on. Just don't die on me! Man, I won't let you die, but you gotta help me out! Rich, be strong and hang on! Reach inside, man. Hang on. I know you can do it! Richie, if anybody can do it, you can definitely do it. Just like you're always telling me. You can do anything that you put your mind to!"

At that point, police came busting in.

"Everyone get back! Back the hell up! Give him room, please. Back up!" they yelled at the dazed crowd.

I felt like I was hyperventilating as I screamed, "Officer, officer, he's been cut, he got slashed, help him!

Y'all have to hurry up, 'cause he ain't gonna last much longer!"

The cops and paramedics started working on Richie's neck. The paramedics cut all of his blood soaked clothes from his body, leaving him in his underwear. After working on him in the street for about five minutes, they lifted him on to a stretcher. His neck was packed with mounds of white gauze and all kinds of Band-Aid looking material. As they prepared to lift Richie into the back of the ambulance, he looked at. His eyes locked into my eyes as if to say, "You promised I'd be alright."

The moment they lifted the stretcher, I put up four fingers across my heart, indicating the Fourth Crew sign. Richie just looked at me. Then his eyes closed. That was June third at around five p.m. That was the last time I saw Richie alive. Unfortunately, after his funeral, which inevitably was gonna come to an end, I knew that I'd never see him again. All that would be left would be the memories.

Again and again, the entire tragic incident kept replaying itself in my mind. I just kept wishing that I could have done something to have prevented Richie's death. Why did we choose that day? That time? That route to go to the movies? He asked me not to let him die. He asked me, and I couldn't help him. That was the most jacked up thing that kept racing through my head. It was as if I could still hear him asking for my help.

We finally reached the church where the funeral was to be held. You could tell that Richie was well liked because there were so many people going into the church. Black limousines draped with flowers were parked all along the street. Some were parked on a grass lot that was located nearby. For as far as the eye could see, people and cars were everywhere. Everybody had come to pay their last respects to Richie.

The moment I stepped foot inside the church I heard the sound of an organ playing that same sad funeral song that I hear at every black person's funeral. I also heard the extremely loud wailing and sobbing for Richie. People were fainting. Some had to be restrained from grabbing the casket. I guess when someone so young and with such potential dies so suddenly it's a great shock, because the funeral was definitely emotionally charged.

My head suddenly began to feel very light. From that point on I stopped noticing anyone that was around me. It was like I had slipped into another world. I heard people saying a bunch of that funeral mumbo jumbo such as, "Hi, how are you doing? How are you coping with it?" I would answer them, but my glossy eyes never made contact with the person to whom I was speaking.

My girl, Sabine, who was very emotional, came next to me and escorted me to my seat. Elizabeth was already sitting down. I couldn't bring myself to look at Elizabeth. I sensed she was tearing a little bit. There was just no way that I was gonna look at her.

I took my seat next to the girls. Randy, Tee, and Kwame also came and sat in the pew with us. My body was getting numb. I was totally out of it. Someone was preparing to deliver the eulogy. I heard the speaker speaking but I wasn't even being a gentleman. I mean, there was my girl crying right next to me, and I didn't even put my arm around her or help wipe away her tears.

Time was moving so slow. Then came time for all of those who wanted to look at Richie's body one last time to do so. Almost everybody got up and formed a line. One by one, people walked past his coffin. The coffin was money green, Richie's favorite color. Elizabeth couldn't get herself to walk past the casket. She said it was just too much for her to handle.

Others stopped and stared at Richie's lifeless body. Some shook their heads in disbelief while others kissed and touched his lifeless body. This, by far, was the gloomiest part of the funeral. It was marked by observers who just couldn't bear the grief and had to be restrained and led away from the casket.

All of Fourth Crew walked past Richie and said good-bye to him. I stopped at his coffin and I stared at his body. I felt him looking at me. Although music was playing I no longer heard it. My world was in total silence as I looked into his coffin.

Without blinking I stared at him. Then I reached out and touched his hand. It felt somewhat cold and hard. I knew he could feel my hand. I kept my hand on his, then I remember starting to break down. I thought to myself, *Ah man. Ah man, ah man.* I had never cried at a funeral before. I'd never even cried in front of my girl. Sabine was right behind me. She just stared at me, but she didn't say a word.

As I cried, I said very quietly, "I'm sorry, Richie. Are you still my man? We still boys, right?"

Why wouldn't he answer? When was he gonna answer me? I waited for as long as I could for an answer, but I never got one. I prepared myself to leave the coffin. Before I left, I kissed Richie on his forehead and I said, "Richie I love you man. I'll see you, kid. I'ma see you."

Sabine held my hand and followed behind me as we made our way back to our seats. I was still crying. Sabine hugged me.

"It's gonna be OK, honey. He's going to a better place. He's with God right now. It'll be alright." Then she wiped my tears away.

I was beginning to come back to reality a little bit, but not totally. We sat for a little while longer, and before long, people were going to the microphone and speaking about the good times that they had spent with Richie. After the last person spoke, someone sang *Amazing Grace* and

I'll Fly Away. Then people started slowly filing out of the church.

Everyone piled into their cars. Relatives and close friends got into limousines. Fourth Crew had two limos parked in front of the church, waiting to take us to a cemetery out on Long Island.

The ride to the cemetery wasn't too long. As a matter of fact, it was pretty quick. But when we arrived at the cemetery, I just couldn't get out of the limo. While everyone else went to go see Richie lowered into the ground, Sabine and I stayed inside the limo. I was just about fully back from the shock that I had slipped into when I first walked into the church.

I remember smiling and saying, "Yo... I cried, Sabine."

She replied, "It's alright, baby. There's nothing wrong with that."

I paused and thought for a moment. "Yeah, there isn't," I answered.

"Sabine, I can't watch them put Richie into the ground. I just can't watch that."

Sabine reassured me. "It'll be alright, Mark," which was my real name. "I'll be with you."

Again I started to cry as Sabine gestured for my hand and helped me out of the car. Together we walked across the grass toward the spot where everyone was standing. A cemetery service was taking place for Richie.

Because of the rain, everyone was forced to stand under this tent that had been erected. The coffin was decorated with all types of flowers. A few people spoke and then I realized that they weren't going to put Richie into the ground right away, at least not until all of the rain had completely stopped. The electrical equipment which was used to lower the coffin might have gotten wet and caused problems.

So as everyone started to disperse back to their cars, I took one more long look at the coffin, shook my head and turned to walk back to the limo. Once inside the car and out of the nasty rain, I plopped myself into my seat. I panicked as I remembered that I hadn't written a poem for Richie. I didn't have the time to write what I'd wanted to, but I asked Sabine for a piece of tissue and a pen. Then I scribbled this poem:

To Richie
Look into the world,
Tell me what you see.
Maybe you see hope,
Maybe you see me.
I certainly see fear,
I certainly see despair.
Despair is sure to be me.
Definite is hope,
Hope waiting to be set free.
I know the better of these,
But which one will I find?
Maybe, just maybe, it'll be hope.
Only if you help me Richie,
Help me find the grace of God.
Love, Mark

I stepped out of the limo and tossed the pieced of tissue, watching it softly float near the spot where the casket would be set into the ground. That way it would be waiting for Richie when he got there. I looked back at the coffin.

"Richie, you're with God now, so don't worry about a thing. You'll be ah'ight. We love you." I told him, then I yelled as loud as I could, "FOURTH CREW!" as I jogged back to the car.

The limo ride back home was slow because it started to rain very hard. It was raining about as hard as it did on the night Richie was killed. I remember thinking how it was a good thing that it had rained on the night he was murdered, simply because the rain helped to wash away the blood stains that were left on the concrete from Richie's wound.

The Elements

The funeral was finally over. I'd taken off my suit and put on my baggy jeans along with my hi-top, green and white Nike Airs. Then I placed my gold caps into my mouth and clipped my beeper to my pants.

"Paula! If ma is looking for me, let her know that I'll probably be at Randy's house, or I might still be over Richie's crib eating dinner, ah'ight?"

My sister hollered back, "OK. Be careful." With that, I walked across the street to Randy's house and knocked on his door.

I called out for him, "Yo Randy, open the door. It's me. Holz." Randy had been slow at everything he'd ever done in his entire life, so finally after about five minutes of knocking, he opened the door for me.

"Yo man, you ain't change your clothes yet?" I asked as I went into his basement. Randy still wore the clothes he'd had on at the funeral.

"Yo, hurry up, man! Everybody's already at Richie's house. His family cooked dinner for us. We gotta bounce."

As Randy switched outfits he said, "Holz, I can't believe Richie is dead."

"Word! I know what you mean," I answered. See, death for us was nothing new. We all knew people in the past who'd been killed, but Richie was the first one from Fourth Crew to be exterminated.

The crew was so close that we might as well have been family. There were so many of us. We even had peoples in Virginia who were down with the crew. But there was still a group of us that was the main members.

First there was me. My government name is Mark Holsey. However, for years everybody has called me Holz. Kinda like on the TV show Happy Days, when nobody called Arthur Fonzarelli by his full name. See, the same way he was called Fonzie or Fonz, I was called Holzie or Holz.

Also in the crew was Randy, whose birth name was Randolph, and Latiefe, whose nickname was Tee. And there was also Dwight, who went by the alias Dee, or Big Dee, or Godfather Dee. There was Kwame, Xavier (a.k.a X), Donnie, Erik, and Claudius – the six-foot-five-inch, more-hops-than-Mike-Jordan basketball man-child. Rounding out the crew were J.P. and Reggie. Reggie stayed in Virginia. His dumb jackass joined the Marines after high school and he got shipped to Virginia like a slave.

We all grew up together. All of us lived on the same block, either right across the street or down the block from one another. We hailed from a town in Queens, New York called Laurelton, or L.A. for short. More specificly, we grew up on 234th street, one of many perpendicular streets and avenues that ran through Laurelton, dividing it into rectangles on a map. The main street that ran through all of Laurelton was called Merrick Blvd.

Merrick Blvd. was where all of the action took place. It helped New York earn its reputation as a fast-paced, crime-filled city. All kinds of dirt went down on Merrick, everything from drug dealing to killings to numbers running to prostitution and more. Merrick Blvd. had literally, although illegally, made millionaires out of a few brothers.

We named our crew after the last digit of our street. We became Fourth Crew from 234th street. We pronounced it "Forf Crew," because saying "Fourth" sounded too proper and white. Basically, by pronouncing it "Forf," we gave it that street swagger.

As a crew, we were mixed up in all sorts of things, including crime. But we weren't a gang, because usually gangs were and are of negative mentalities from their origin. Fourth Crew was basically about positive actions. Everyone in the crew had roots of a positive mentality.

Yeah, we got mixed up in wrong doings, but so did almost everyone else in America, including the government and its officials.

On occasion, we have been compelled to bring it to a niggah. Yes, we'd definitely stomped out many other crews and gangs. We'd gotten into a lot of beef in our day, but no one in the crew had ever been murdered, not until Richie was killed. I guess you could say that it was bound to happen sooner or later. But even with Richie's death, it was not like the crew was just gonna dismantle. We would continue on as a crew, no doubt about it.

In the past, Kwame had flirted with death on a number of occasions. Latiefe had been slashed on the back of the head and neck and needed almost one hundred stitches to close the gash, which left a permanent, nasty scar on his head. But death, never. Not in Fourth Crew.

Randy was finally ready. We walked down to Richie's house and when we arrived, we mixed in with the rest of the crew members who were already there. My sister was there, as was her best friend Nia. Sabine was there with Liz, and everybody, including Richie's family, was all packed shoulder to shoulder inside the house. We ate the typical Black Sunday meal of cornbread, black-eyed peas, collard greens, and ribs drowned in bar-b-cue sauce.

As we ate we shared memories of Richie. I didn't say anything out loud, but the memory that stuck out most in my mind was Richie's common sense. I guess that in and of itself is not really a memory of a past event, but that's what I was remembering.

Richie and I always discussed things, like what it was that we thought led blacks to kill one another. Or why there were so many drug dealers and things of that nature. We constantly rapped about the problems of the black community. We would also discuss the different stereotypes that went along with being an inner city black male.

We would discuss all kinds of topics, including things like the New York City public school system, college, religion, the thought of 'really knowing' yourself, and things like that. Just about anything that you could name, I'd bet money on it that we had discussed it. We both used to have theories on the negative and rising statistics relating to black males. You know, things like why were so many black males in jail, or why was there so much black on black crime.

Richie always said that the reason for the rising negative statistics was because of one or more of the elements gone bad in a black man's life. He even had a name for his theory: *The Elements in a Black Man's Fist.* According to him, the black man's fist represented anger. Usually that same anger was used to kill someone, pull a trigger, or knock someone out.

Richie theorized that the same fist could easily be opened up into a gentle hand, a hand used for a warm handshake, or used to grip a pen or grasp a book. I remember how frustrated he would get with society.

"Society," he would say, "could stop the negative statistics from rising. They could do this by identifying the specific elements in a black man's life that need fixing and help to fix it."

He believed that the prevention, detection, and correction of a cancerous element was the difference between disaster and prosperity in a black man's life.

As I sat in Richie's house that day eating food and celebrating his passing to the other side of life, I said to myself, One day I'm gonna tell the world about those elements so that they'll be able to help us. That way Richie's death won't be in vain.

As we highlighted Richie's life, his mother kept herself busy by serving food to everyone. I felt for her, because I saw her as an innocent victim of a senseless reaction, which was caused by a huge social problem. She'd lost someone precious, someone who she helped to create, someone that she carried inside her for nine months, someone she'd been patient with, nurtured, trained and raised. She was a tough, strong lady, though. She'd make it through somehow.

All of the food was just about gone. We had been there for nearly an hour and a half. Latiefe was saying that he thought it was time for us to leave. One by one we thanked, kissed, and hugged Richie's mom. As she thanked us for coming, her eyes looked as if she was saying goodbye to us forever. I told her to stay strong. I also told her that if there was anything she needed she shouldn't hesitate to ask.

Most of the crew went back to Randy's house. That was usually where we hung out. If we weren't at Randy's crib we would all pile up at Latiefe's grandmother's crib. While at Randy's house, Dwight started talking about how it was imperative that we kill Cory. We all joined in and added our input, trying to come up with the perfect murder plot. We visualized that this would serve as a payback to Cory and in honor of Richie.

As we plotted, I remember thinking to myself that Richie wouldn't have wanted that. If we were to kill Cory, it would have just added to society's misconception that all black men are nothing more than a bunch of hoodlums. I was willing to bet one hundred dollars that Richie was probably turning over in his grave as we plotted to kill his murderer.

"Word is bond! When we see that niggah Cory we're gonna empty a whole clip on him and then put one in his head to make sure he's dead!" Dwight shouted. "He's gonna be so Swiss-cheesed-up that his moms is gonna have to have a closed casket funeral!" We all agreed with Dwight.

It was getting late, so some of us started getting ready to bounce home. After a few minutes everyone had left except for Randy and me.

"Holz, man, it's only June eighth," Randy said to me when we were alone. "The summer is practically just starting, and look at how it started. It started with Richie's death."

"Yeah, I know. It's just ill, man. Real ill. But Randy, every year it gets worse."

Randy replied, "I know. You're absolutely right. But Holz, man, you better get used to it, 'cause mad heads is gonna fly this summer. Just watch." Randy meant that a number of people would die this summer, and I knew that his grave prediction would most likely be right on the money.

"Holz, remember last summer and how wild it was around here? I'm surprised we even made it to 1991. I just hope I make it through the summer, 'cause once the summer is over, things start to cool down, you know? I'm only 20 years old. I don't wanna die yet. I ain't ready."

"I know what you mean," I answered. "I'm only 17, and I definitely ain't ready to go."

"Holz, it's getting too wild, though. I probably will get killed or something. Man, I ain't gonna even front. I'm scared of dying. Word is bond! I'm afraid of it. I mean, I have my whole life ahead of me, and I'm sayin' I want the kids, the house and a car. All of that American Dream stuff. But POW! Just like that, in a split second, it could be over. One bullet to the temple is all it takes." Dwight shook his head. "I would hate for my family to see me in a coffin, for them to be sobbing and losing sleep over me after I'm gone. Plus, where do you go when you die? Will anybody remember me? Holz, I'm scared of that. Word! I'm scared. But I tell you what. If I do die, I bet you it'll be at the hands of a black man."

"Randy," I told him, "listen, man. That's just the way it is for us. What can we do?"

Randy replied, "Yeah, I know. But things have to change, Holz. Things have got to change."

I told Randy that I was the one who was going to change the mentality of everybody from black thugs to white conservatives and anyone else in between. All I needed to do was to tell the world about the elements.

"What elements?" Randy asked. "What are you talking about?"

"Just watch. Soon everybody's gonna know about the elements to a black man's fist."

"Holz, man, you sound like one of those church folks that's speaking in tongues. What the hell are you talking about, man?"

I ignored his question and got ready to leave. "Yo kid, I'm outta here. I'll get with you tomorrow. I gotta get some sleep, kid."

"But Holz, what was you talking about?" Randy asked again.

Without answering him I walked out of his basement and went across the street to my house. I was exhausted from the day's activities. I couldn't wait to get some sleep. When I got home and hopped into bed I prayed, just like every other night.

"Dear Lord, although today was a sad day, I still want to thank you for life and for loving me. Please watch over me, my brother Ronnie, my mother, my father, my sister Paula, and my future wife Sabine. Please protect us. I thank you for everything. Please let Richie's soul be OK. Oh yeah, please watch over everybody in the crew as well. Make sure that we're all OK. Lord, I love you, and it's in Your Son's name I pray. Amen."

I opened my eyes. I was staring into space, trying to think of a way to tell the world about the elements. Then it hit me. All I had to do was print out on paper, in detail, exactly what each element was about. Then I could just simply get the phone book and mail out the elements to different addresses. Yeah, that was it. This killing had to end. I had to do my part somehow. And this was the only means that I had of reaching people.

My plan was that each week I was going to write out one element and mail it. Then I would wait and write out and mail another element, and so on until all of the elements were on paper and in people's hands.

Savages

My birthday was two days ago, on June fourteenth. I'd turned eighteen years old. Finally, as the world would say, I was legal. Huh? Legal to do what? Vote? Don't make me laugh. It wasn't like politicians gave a damn about people that looked, dressed, and talked like me. Anyway, turning eighteen was no big deal. I certainly didn't feel any different.

My birthday celebration was two days belated, but it was fun. All of us in Fourth Crew went to this park in Queens called Roy Wilkins Park, named after the Civil Rights leader. There was a step show taking place at the park, presented by many different black fraternities and sororities like the Q-Dogs, the Alphas, the Sigmas, the Deltas and the AKA's. Certain Rap artists also performed. The whole affair, which was called a Greek Picnic, was similar to the Freeknik in Atlanta or the Greek Fest at New York's Jones Beach. The event was guaranteed to attract Black people from all over, and we knew that. That's why we'd decided to go.

People came from Washington D.C., Atlanta, Maryland, you name it. We just couldn't wait to get to the park. Just thinking about the vast amounts of thick shorties that would be there was reason alone for all of our anticipation.

Transportation to the park was not too big of a problem since we lived just five minutes away. The problem was our pride. Nobody in our crew had a nice car. Xavier had a car, but we would have looked pretty stupid if we all piled up in that one car. The car only sat four people comfortably, and if we had tried to get more than that in the car we would have looked like a bunch of Puerto Ricans. They were famous for cramming into one little car.

On the other hand, I could have driven my father's station wagon. But there were two reasons that I wouldn't. Number one, I didn't like playing myself, and number two, I didn't like playing myself. Not to mention the humiliation we would have felt if someone had seen us stepping out of that car. It wouldn't have been worth it, not one bit.

We knew that walking to the park was definitely out of the question, even if it was a better option than a station wagon. I mean, nobody walked anywhere in today's day and age, at least not in New York City. Erik came up with the idea of taking a cab. Even though we needed more than one cab to fit all of us, once we split the fares it would only be about a dollar per man, and it was well worth it to save our pride.

While we were in the cab, though, even that dollar was something we just didn't want to spend. Latiefe, Randy, Erik, Donnie, and I were in the same cab, and we all had the same thought. We weren't gonna pay the fare. As soon as we reached the park we all jumped out of the cab and ran. The cab driver couldn't do a thing because we managed to get lost very quickly in the sea of people.

Dwight, Kwame and the rest of them paid their cab fares like a bunch of Herbs. We all laughed at how we didn't pay for the cab. It was funny because we hadn't even planned our actions. We hadn't told one another that we weren't going to pay. But with a crew as close as ours, acts like that became second nature, sort of instinctive. Just like whenever we'd hear gun shots, we'd drop to the floor or duck behind a car quicker than you could snap your fingers. It was all street instinct. Bang! We'd drop to the ground.

As we waited to get into the park we went and bought forties of malt liquor. Kwame already had some Vodka, some Bacardi, and all kinds of hiccup juice. Donnie had the weed and the Phillies, so he rolled the blunts. We were all getting high like birds and planes.

We started noticing people we knew so we started shouting to them, "Yo Big Tuse, what up kid? Yo what up Baby Pa? Ah'ight dog, I'll catch y'all later. Peace out."

We were rappin' to girls that we didn't know. "Hey baby, can I walk with you? Pssst, hey sexy, what's wrong? Cat got your tongue, or do you want my tongue to get your cat?"

Music blared in the background while we kicked it to the ladies. The park had it going on. Yeah! Things were starting to set off a little taste. There were people everywhere but the crew held close by one another. Punk niggahs knew what time it was. They knew that we were representing, so nobody tried to play us by stepping to us. They were clocking us, but they didn't say nothing. It was a smart move on their part, because our crew was rolling about twenty niggahs deep, and that's not counting the other people who had joined our entourage as the day went on.

I could have cared less about those stupid ass fraternities and their step show. I was there to create my own fun. My head was feeling real nice from the forties and the blunts. The blazing sun made me get drunk even quicker. Matter of fact, all of us were drunk by this point. We weren't sloppy drunk or anything like that. We were more like happy, feel-good type of drunk.

We were all acting the fool and continuing to meet females left and right. I felt sorry for the girls who didn't give us their number or the time of day for that matter. Dissing us like that was like committing the ultimate sin against us, 'cause whenever we got drunk it was like the rest of the world was at our feet. The females who didn't acknowledge our come-ons got badly dissed. Randy had said hello to some girl and she played him by ignoring his advance. So he dissed her out loud for the whole world to hear.

"You horse-hair-wearing, weave-havin, skanky whore!" I know she must've felt embarrassed, because all the people in that vicinity started laughing.

The day was rolling along good. Everyone was having fun. This was exactly what black people needed more, events that brought us together where we could all just have fun. We watched and danced as the rap stars performed. It was like the whole crowd was sweating our crew. Large crowds of people had formed a circle around our entourage and watched, cheered, and jeered as we did our dance. Our dance was called The Fourth Crew Two-Step. We definitely had it going on, and we were loving every minute of the attention.

As the music blasted we continued to party. All of us by now were past high and all eyes were on us. We felt like we were top billing. Unfortunately, ugliness was about to take place. I could just sense it.

As rap star Chubb Rock's hit song blared into the park's air, Randy, who was by far the drunkest one of all, quickly approaching sloppy drunk status, started screaming, "Go New York, go New York, go!" As Randy chanted, the rest of us were partying like we'd lost our minds. Before long, a small group of people that we didn't know started chanting along with Randy. Before we knew it, it seemed as if the entire park was in harmony and everyone began chanting, "GO NEW YORK, GO NEW YORK, GO! GO! GO!"

Guys in the park who weren't down with our crew stared at us. It was obvious that they were starting to get jealous because we were stealing all the female attention. From out of nowhere and for no apparent reason, some guy came up to Randy.

"Fuck New York!" the brother screamed in Randy's face. I guess the guy was from Chicago or D.C. or somewhere. He obviously wasn't from New York.

There was a brief, awkward pause and then he said it again, real harsh and loud. "Fuck New York!" As he shouted his words, spit flew from his mouth and landed splat on Randy's face.

"Fuck New York!" he yelled again as Randy wiped the spit from his face.

Randy yelled back, also in a very loud and vulgar kind of way, "NEW YORK! NEW YORK! NEW YORK! WHAT! WHAT! WHAT!"

The short, stocky guy pushed Randy backwards then hauled off and hit him. Wrong move. It was on, and we had to bring it to 'em. The joyous day of music, beer, weed, and girls was about to turn into a violent and chaotic disaster. After Randy got punched, he continued to be the recipient of punches and kicks from about three guys that we didn't know. They were pummeling the hell out of Randy. In mob fashion, Fourth Crew went wild, hitting anybody and everybody that we didn't know. We managed to get Randy back to his feet and he helped us do work.

We were kicking butts and taking names later. Dwight, who was the biggest of us all, hit somebody so hard that I thought he had paralyzed the kid. Seriously, I really thought the kid was damaged for good. But there was no time to dwell on that, 'cause I had to get mines off. And I can tell you that it was a good feeling to have punched someone flush in the face and then watch that person writhe and grimace in pain. That is exactly what I did to this kid that tried to step to me during the melee.

The fight went on. It lasted for about two minutes. But when there's chaos like that, two minutes feels more like thirty. Two minutes had been more than enough for me. I was ready to get out of the park. In fact, I knew that I had no choice but to get out immediately. Hands, fists, and feet were flying everywhere. I knew that the gun shots and knives were soon to follow. They were probably only seconds away.

See, there are some major rules that you have to follow when you're involved in violent street brawls like the one we were in. One of those rules is that you get the hell out of dodge when you can, and not when you have to. You gotta get yours off quick and then get up outta there, because in the chaos the odds are stack against you that something will go wrong. I mean, I don't care how big you are, in a free-for-all fracas you could easily get whacked over the head with a bottle, shot, or stabbed. Anything could happen, so you gotta stick and move.

Being that the park was so big and there were so many people, only those who were in the immediate vicinity of the melee actually knew that a fight was going on. In fact, at the two-minute mark of the fight, security was nowhere to be seen. Things were definitely wild, but it was fun and crazy at the same time. I mean, we were acting like savages or crazed Pit Bulls. Who cared, though, 'cause it was fun and we were loving every second of it.

I looked around and saw Xavier on the ground getting housed. I mean, he was getting straight up waxed! I also saw Reggie on the ground getting pummeled and stomped. I desperately wanted to help out the both of them, but at that point in time the best thing for me to do was to keep my guard up and keep moving. I don't know how X and Reggie wound up on the ground, but all I knew was that if they didn't get up quick, they were looking at a possible death. X and Reggie both looked like they were in pain and I was praying that they'd get to their feet as quickly as possible. See, they were violating another one of the major rules of street brawls. Never allow yourself to get knocked to the ground.

Fortunately, Reggie got to his feet, but X was still on the ground getting rocked. I saw him get clocked over the head with a huge, boom box style radio. I thought for sure he wouldn't live to see another day. Like I said, although I wanted to help, I couldn't. But Latiefe was fighting two people and I was in closer proximity to him. So in a crazed-dog fashion, I ran up on one of the two guys that Latiefe was fighting and I sliced his head open with a razor blade. I heard the guy scream in pain as he quickly vanished from the fight. It was such a satisfying feeling. I had put a long, thin gash on his head. Nothing life threatening.

Latiefe and I then proceeded to beat the lone stander of the two guys that he had been fighting. I should have sliced him open as well, but I didn't. I took a quick glance around to analyze the situation.

"Yo, Latiefe. It's time for us to get the hell outta here!" I announced frantically. I couldn't see anyone else from the crew and I didn't know what to think. Latiefe and I were both beginning to feel a bit hopeless and helpless.

Latiefe shifted into the psyche of a crazy man. Even I couldn't believe it when he pulled out a semi-automatic weapon.

"Back up! Move! Move! Move! Everybody back the hell up! Move!" he screamed. He let the gun off and started lickin' shots. It sounded like fireworks. In succession, one bullet followed another. *Clack clack clack clack clack clack clack.*

Latiefe just kept firing bullets into the air like he'd lost his mind. People started running and scrambling for cover. Some people just dropped to the ground. Others ran for their lives. Some ran and never looked back. They might still be running to this very day.

The brawl, which had been an isolated incident or a small, sort of organized confusion, was no longer such. After the gunfire erupted, the music abruptly stopped. Whoever was performing at the time, I forget who, jumped off the stage in a panic.

By now, someone else in the park began shooting. Before you knew it, the whole park had turned into a human tidal wave. People were literally trampling each other trying to get to safety. An entire sea of people would run one way, then gun shots would ring out from a new direction, causing the whole crowd to shift its momentum and run in a totally different direction.

Dwight had managed to find me and Latiefe, so at this juncture it was just the three of us. We were running like everyone else, trying to make it out of the park alive. Tee kept shooting into the air while we ran. I loved Fourth Crew, but it was no time to pause and try to figure out where everyone else was. It was time to think only about surviving. Survival of the ghetto-est.

Fortunately the three of us were able to make it out of the park. Every thug in the park must have had a gun, because by the time we'd safely made it out of the park the scene was totally out of control. Gun shots were breaking out from all over the place. We heard everything from little .22 calliber hand guns to .45's to Mac 11's being let loose. It was like a seen from a Vietnam movie.

Tee had finally run out of bullets, so he was somewhat forced to put the gun away. Being that Tee had the gun, we couldn't just hang around to watch. On the low, I also had a gun on me and I definitely was not trying to get bagged for no gun charge. The spot was just way too hot with police. Mounted police officers as well as police on foot were called in to try to restore order. They came in with their riot gear. Ambulances were starting to pile up all over the place. So the three of us jogged just about all the way back to 234th street and we waited at Tee's grandmother's house for the rest of the crew to return.

We waited for about two hours or so, but there was no word from anyone else in the crew. We didn't know what to think, but at the same time we weren't too concerned. I went home to try to sleep off the headache I'd developed from all the chaos, not to mention the beer and weed. I was able to crank out about an hour and a half worth of sleep. When I woke up, I told my sister about all that had transpired in the park. To my surprise, Paula told me that she had been at the Greek Picnic and had almost been trampled to death when everyone rushed the park exit at the same time.

I wanted to stay and kick it with my sister but I had only stopped at home in order to sleep off the headache that I had. I had to check on my crew. I quickly left the house and went over to Randy's crib to see if everyone had made it back. I was relieved to see that most of the crew was already at Randy's when I got there. We decided to walk to Tee's, 'cause no one was there and we all wanted to be alone, without any noisy little brothers or sisters, and no nosy mothers or fathers.

J.P., Donnie, Erik and a few others were still missing, but we sensed that nothing bad had happened to them. We all sat and kicked it about the details of the melee. Some guys from 229th street were also present during our conversation. They too had been to Roy Wilkins Park earlier in the day.

As Xavier iced his jaw, which was swollen from the blow he received from the boom box, we all took turns talking, laughing, and describing in detail exactly how many punches and kicks we all threw, how many had landed and where they landed. Dwight and Tee both were getting on me, calling me soft because they knew that wherever I went I always carried my small .22 caliber handgun in my pocket.

Dwight kept saying, "Holz you shouldn't have cut that kid in his head. That was a sucker move." Dwight's wish was that I had shot and killed the kid.

Latiefe thanked me and called me his man for helping him fight off the two cats, but he sided with Dwight. His reasoning was that the cat had his back to me when I slashed him. I could have easily shot him in the back of the head and stepped off. No one would have known a thing.

Their words definitely made me think. I mean, I always carried a gun to events similar to that of the Greek Picnic, but I had never used it on anybody. I guess I didn't have the guts to actually kill another human being. I would only fire shots into the air in order to scare people and cause a panic. I would wave it in a person's face just to bring a hell like fear to that person. In essence, I was a cowardly punk, hiding behind a trigger. I used that trigger to make myself into this fierce hooligan. But I was just imitating.

"Man!" I screamed, "I could have killed that cat! I should've shot 'em point blank in the head. That could have been my first body and probably the easiest."

Randy, who just this past winter had shot someone, not fatally, said to me, "Holz, man, in a situation like that, you gots to kill! Listen to me. If the roles were reversed and that whore-jack niggah had a gun, you, Mark Holsey, would be up there with Richie right this very moment. No doubt, just like in poker, you and Richie would have been two of a kind, or a dead flush!" At that, laughter filled the room.

Being that Donnie and myself were the two youngest in the crew, everyone always tried to school us on the ways that things went down on the streets. They often told us how we should handle certain situations and why. It was as if we were in some sort of an apprenticeship. The room, which by this time was at its capacity, was beginning to take on the feel of a university auditorium with many different lecturers.

Someone said, "Yeah, you gotta get before you get got."

After sitting and thinking logically I said, "Man, come on with that! I'm glad I didn't kill him, 'cause then I would be walking around cotton-mouth and worried about getting locked up."

"So the hell what?" someone yelled. "Jail ain't nothin' but a thing."

Although I knew that just about half of the heads in that room had at some point in their brief lives been nothing more than inmate number bla-bla-bla, I still wasn't willing to concede to their so-called street knowledge on this subject. And I proceeded to disagree.

"What do you mean jail ain't nothin'?" I inquired. "Who in their right mind wants to be caged up for five years, or twenty years, or for the rest of their natural life? Being told what to do, being told when to eat, being told when to sleep, being told when to use the phone, being told when to take a shower. Even a dog would hate to live under those conditions. My brother is in jail right now and I know from visiting him and from speaking to him that prison ain't no joke.

Yeah, granted, y'all have been to the joint, but for how long? Thirty days? Overnight? Six months? See, that's why yall are sayin' it ain't nothin'. But try being in that piece for a three-to-nine. Three to nine years of getting poked in the butt by some big, muscle-bound dude, while some cat on the outside that you hate is doing your girl."

When I was done talking, I noticed Dwight looking at me with a look of disbelief.

"Holz you just don't get it do you?" He stared at me and shook his head, which was slightly tilted to the right. His lips were semi-twisted to the right side of his face.

"Don't try to get off the subject," Dwight continued. "The point is, the gun you have ain't that loud, so you could have easily shot that niggah and stepped off without anybody even noticing. Without any consequences. Period!"

Dwight continued in an attempt to expand on a moot point that he thought he'd made with his self-proclaimed 'infinite street wisdom.' "Remember this: Life for us ain't about living, 'cause we rarely do that. Life for us is about surviving. If you have to go to jail, then you go. Besides, sometimes jail is the safest place to be. But while we're out here doing our thing, don't even think about jail, because you don't have time to think. You only have time to survive.

You can't care about nobody. Once you start caring about this or worrying about that, you are out of the game. You lose that instinct to survive on the street.

Holz, there is a way around everything in life. Everything except death. Once you go, pssst, that's it. Bye. See ya, and I wouldn't wanna be ya. You ain't coming back. That's why you have to survive. It's about survival baby. Listen to me! I know what I'm talking about."

I sensed that life for us in the crew was changing drastically. We weren't murderers or criminals. I knew we weren't. We were better than that. Then why were we starting to think so negative, as if there was no hope? Maybe it was because we were subconsciously afraid to live. When you're scared, you do some weird things.

Yo, somebody had to help us get rid of the frame of mind that we were starting to develop. Our frame of mind was starting to affect our actions and our speech. What went wrong? Maybe something went wrong when we were still playing with G.I. Joes and riding dirt bikes for fun. All I knew was that we were beginning to get caught up in a terrible set of circumstances. But I guess I should have just gone with the flow.

I have to finish those elements quick, I thought to myself as I sat amongst misguidance.

"Holz…Holz…Holz!" Dwight screamed.

"Yeah, yeah, what?" I replied. "What the hell are you screaming for?"

"See, that's exactly what I mean. Holz, you always daydreaming. What the hell are you always thinking about? You don't have time to think. Just react to everything. No conscience. Live for today." Dwight started pacing. "If Richie had thought like I do, he would be alive today. But he was just like you, always thinking and analyzing things.

And for what? Look, he's dead, right!? Dead 'cause he started caring. Think about it !"

Dee shouldn't have said, that because it caused a disorderly outburst in the room. Talking about Richie like that wasn't going to be tolerated. It was like blaspheming the Almighty. Even though Dee was the oldest and the biggest and the Godfather of the crew, dissin' Richie wasn't going to be tolerated.

"Don't mess with Richie! Dwight, man, I'll go to jail tonight for murdering you if you don't leave Richie alone and let the niggah rest in peace!" I yelled, and I knew that the rest of the clique would back me up.

Tensions were getting extremely hostile and the tone in everybody's voice was raised to the tilt. We were all upset. In my heart I knew that we weren't actually mad with each other per se, because yelling and dissin' one another was commonplace in our crew. On occasions we'd even come to blows, but we would always make up.

Why at times did we get so hostile with one another? I really didn't understand it. The crew reminded me of little kids who throw temper tantrums when they're caught up in a situation that they don't want to be in. For example, when it comes time for them to clean up their room, they get mad at someone close to them, like their parents. The same thing existed in our crew. The only difference was we would get vexed at one another. See, we didn't want to kill our own brothers or go to jail for some nonsense crime. Yet we continued to make our own mess.

We would try to justify our actions by convincing ourselves that our way of life was normal. When we would get upset with each other, it was probably because subconsciously we knew that eventually we were going to have to pay for our actions one way or another. Just like those little kids all eventually have to clean their rooms or suffer some type of consequence. The difference between the two situations was that those little kids weren't facing a jail sentence or a toe tag like us.

Emotions in the room were still hostile but they were beginning to calm down. Everyone had spoken and vented their feelings. Then Xavier, who could hardly open his mouth due to his sore and swollen jaw, started screaming for everyone's attention.

"Look! Look!" He screamed in a muffled tone. "Look at the TV!"

We all turned our necks like pigeons and stared at the tube. We found ourselves watching the eleven o'clock news. The lead story was about the events that had transpired at the Greek Picnic earlier in the day. We all gawked intensely as the anchor man relayed to all of New York what had taken place.

"Disaster struck at a Queens park today, as a crowd estimated to be as large as 25,000 came out to the annual Greek Picnic, where big-name rap acts were slated to perform." He went on to say, "Ironically, an event that was supposed to spur on unity in the black community turned fatal as thousands trampled over one another in a desperate search for safety. They were fleeing the hail of gunshots that erupted from within the crowds. No one knows what sparked the gunfire, although one eyewitness that I spoke with claims that it was just a case of too many people at one place. She went on to say that something as trivial as a person getting his shoe stepped on could have caused the ruckus."

The television camera scanned the park to show the aftermath of the riot-like area. All you saw were people laid out on the ground. There probably weren't enough ambulances in New York City to attend to the carnage that was being displayed on the television. On camera, people were screaming hysterically and pleading for help as many of their friends and relatives lay on the concrete and in the confetti-filled grass, waiting for medical attention.

The reporter ended his report by saying he couldn't remember a more tragic local event in all of his eleven years of journalism. Then he gave the numbers. Twenty-seven critically wounded and four dead. Latiefe leap-frogged out of his crouched, intense listening position and turned off the television.

"Yes, boyee! We set that off! Fourth Crew ain't no joke. They got us on the news and all that. Lead story at that!" he yelled victoriously.

All of us in Fourth Crew were happier than pigs in slop. We had sparked something like that of hell-fire. It made the news and we felt good about it. We were giving hi-five's, low five's, jumping in the air and bumping chests. This was a celebration.

As long as no one that we knew had been hurt or killed, we really didn't care about the less fortunate ones. Who cared about the victims' families? Families that would now have to live with the memories of a senseless, savage tragedy.

We all celebrated and talked for a little while longer but we had to cut the celebration short. We knew that we all had to depart in order to get dressed and go out to this party that was taking place in Brooklyn. We were planning to leave for the party at around midnight.

I trotted home to put on some fly gear. As soon as I walked in my door my mother questioned me on my attendance at the picnic.

"Yeah we were there," I said as I ran up to my room. "It was buck wild, Mom, real wild."

"Did any of you all get hurt, Mark?" my mom asked. After I didn't respond to her question, I heard my mom in the background yelling, "Mark, I don't want you going to any more things like that. You better start staying in this house. You hear me? Boy, do you hear me talking to you?"

"Mark, did you see the news?" my sister and her friend Nia asked when I got upstairs.

"Yeah, I caught it," I replied.

"See, that's why black people can't have nothin'. Black people don't know how to act. They're always killing and shooting each other. Now watch the media blow up the spot and blame everything on rap music. Black people make me sick to my stomach," Nia said. Nia, by the way, is black.

"Yo. Y'all know what? We set that whole thing off. We had to represent for the crew. And Nia, why are you so pissed? I mean, it's not like you or Paula got hurt."

My sister looked at me with disgust.

"Yeah we sparked it," I barked.

"See, that's exactly what I'm talking about. Mark, is all Fourth Crew a bunch of ignorant thugs or what? Y'all ain't about nothin'!" Nia yelled.

"Shut the hell up, Nia. You're just jealous 'cause you ain't down with us. And what difference does it make, anyway? I mean, if we didn't set it off, somebody else would've sparked it. So tell me, what difference does it make who sparked it? And don't stand there and act like that's not true."

Nia simply stood and stared at me in disbelief while she shook her head.

"Oh yeah, by the way Nia, you're right. Black people don't know how to act." I gave a sarcastic laugh and then I simply walked away.

As I was getting geared up to go to the party, I said to myself, *This is sad, we started that whole thing and not one of us cared about the seriousness of it.* Again I wondered what was happening to our minds. How did we let our minds get to this point? Better yet, what exactly was it that had caused our minds to become so corrupted?

In my head, I managed to scream for someone to help me. Then I thought very calmly to myself, *No conscience. No conscience, baby. No conscience. You can't let yourself have one.*

Not Guilty

The New York City Police Department. Five-O. Blue and White. The Fuzz. Or as they have arrogantly proclaimed themselves, New York's Finest. Whateva.

I'll grant that it must be particularly tough to be a police officer in any one of New York's five boroughs. To boot, the police force seems to always be outgunned. They carry little thirty-eight caliber six shooters while the opposition carries guerilla warfare type artillery; sixteen shot semi-automatic weapons, AK-47's, AR-15's, Glocks, Forty five's, and believe it or not, hand grenades. To go along with that, there are many people in the hood who flat out hate cops with a passion just because of the uniform they wear. In the hood, even if a cop happens to be a good cop, he's bound to be hated more than he's liked.

There will always be racist cops. There will always be good cops. And of course, there will always be the Robo-Cop. Better yet, the Robo-Cops, plural. Robo-Cops are the ones who spoil it for the good cops. Robo-Cops, be they white or black, are the type of people who shouldn't have any type of authority. Robo-Cops are just like the security guards and store owners who follow me around, gawking my every move from the time I enter a store. You know, the ones that assume I'm there to steal something. Authority goes to their head and they abuse it. Their badge makes them feel super-human, God-like.

I personally hate cops for a number of reasons. But the main reason I hate cops is because of their preconceived notion that all black men are guilty. If we were standing on a street corner, we must be guilty of selling dope. If we had a hood on our head, we must've been wanted by the police for something. But the thing that we were most guilty of was when we legally and legitimately had nice material things, like gold or fancy cars. Yeah, I know those are not crimes, but if you're a black man, you better believe that it is indeed considered a crime. If it wasn't a crime, then why was cops always pulling us over, assuming that the car we were riding in was stolen?

I mean, it literally never failed. Whenever we were riding in Erik's father's Jeep or J.P.'s father's BMW, we would get pulled over. When I say every time, I mean every time. Off the top of my head I could describe seven incidents when we were pulled over. I remember them vividly, because all seven times were in the same month! Seven times for absolutely nothing. I guess that's what you would call DWB; Driving While Black.

On each occasion, it was always the same scenario. We were simply driving along our merry way and before we knew it we would see flashing lights from the rear. The flashing lights were always followed by that *Woop woop* of the sirens. Then, of course, that sound was always followed by the voice of a Robo-Cop on a PA system. "Pull over to the side of the road!" The cop was always loud enough for the entire neighborhood to hear.

Mind you, each time we were pulled over we were never speeding and if we switched lanes, we were always sure to signal. We always kept our seatbelts on. We were never so stupid as to drive with a broken taillight. That would have been just asking to get pulled over. But frankly, all of our actions were always strictly legal. Robo-Cops just liked harassing us.

Aside from the time when we got pulled over seven times in one month, I remember a more current and typical harassment episode. It was a time when five of us were in the BMW. J.P. was driving, Latiefe was in the passenger's seat and Dwight, Randy, and I were seated in the back. Two Robo-Cops gave us their legendary signal to pull over. After we pulled to the curb, one cop came to the driver's window while the other cop came to the passenger's side.

The typical Robo-Cop routine. It was dark outside, so of course they had to shine their bright, four-cell flashlights into our eyes to blind us.

The white Robo-Cop who'd come to the passenger side was a tall, doofy, lanky guy. I could have easily whipped him if he didn't have that badge or that gun. He identified himself as police officer Gary Spath. He came to the window with his gun drawn. He tilted his flashlight so he could see into the car.

"I want to see everybody's hands. Put your hands in front of you where I can see them!" the officer yelled.

"I didn't do it. I'm innocent. Please, don't arrest me. I didn't do it. Please officer, don't whip me," J.P. said sarcastically.

"Shut up," was the order that came from Officer Sarney, whos tood by the passenger window.

"Do you have a reggie?" Officer Sarney asked. In plain English terms, he was asking for the car's registration papers.

J.P. replied, "Yeah, I know a Reggie. He stays in Virginia. Yeah, that's my homeboy." All of us in the car burst out in laughter.

You could tell that this Robo-Cop didn't like J.P.'s joke. His pale face turned blood red. "Let me see the got-damn registration, the insurance card and your license right now or I'm taking all of yous in!" he yelled.

J.P. deliberately paused.

"Now! I want to see the paper work now! As a matter of fact, not now, right now!" the officer insanely and impatiently yelled.

"Officer I just want you to know that the paper work is in my wallet which is in my front right pocket. So I will be reaching in my pocket to get it. OK? I am not reaching for a gun or any weapons or anything like that." J.P. spoke very calmly now.

He moved very slowly to get the papers, and then finally handed the paper work to the officer.

The officer went back to his patrol car and keyed something into his computer. I guess he was checking to see if the car was stolen, which it wasn't, probably to the officer's disappointment.

After giving back all of the documents he asked, "OK fellas, where are the guns? Where are the drugs? I know you guys are running something illegal."

"Come on, man. We ain't got no drugs or no guns! We're only trying to go home," J.P. replied.

Officer Spath, who had been relatively quiet up until this point asked, "Where are you guys coming from?"

Randy yelled from the back seat, "None of your damn business!"

The officer shone the light in Randy's face and stared him down. Randy wasn't afraid and he didn't back down from the cop. He intensely stared right back at the officer with a look to kill. Even with the bright light shining in Randy's eyes, he purposely did not squint his eyes or even blink.

"Alright, everybody out! Get the hell out of the car right now!" Spath demanded. As he snatched us all by the head and threw us out of the car he hollered, "Come on! Hurry up!"

The cops lined us up on the car, frisking each of us. They checked the insides of our mouths. They checked in our socks. They checked everywhere. All they had to do was have us bend over and check our butt holes and it would have been a complete and illegal search.

The cops quickly separated us and asked us the same questions. They made sure that we were not in ear shot of each other. This was one of their oldest tactics in the book, trying to determine if all of our stories were matching up. If any of our stories were conflicting then they would have just probed harder, trying to find something. After that separate-and-question tactic didn't work, the cops seemed to become even more infuriated.

Randy, the indirect cause of this search, was ordered to get face down on the concrete. He was frisked a second time. I was praying that they didn't plant a gun or drugs on him. Fortunately, they didn't. After they didn't find anything on him they kicked Randy two or three times in the ribs.

"Alright. Get up, punk, before we really smash your head in."

Dwight, who also hated cops, asked, "Why did y'all have to kick him?"

The tall, doofy cop rudely and arrogantly replied, "Because we felt like it. We needed a little exercise. Why? What is it to you? Do you have a problem with it?"

I was praying that Dwight would stay tight-lipped. Luckily for us, Dwight did remain silent. The cops then began rummaging through the inside of the BMW. They were looking for some sort of contraband. They didn't find any, because we knew that we couldn't ride in such an expensive car and keep drugs or guns with us. That was just asking for some jail time. Besides, Donnie was the only one in our crew who was hustling. And he wasn't with us at the time. So we knew that there was no chance of them finding anything illegal, unless of coursed they happened to frame us, and in the hood, that was highly probable.

The thorough check of the car was completed. Officer Sarney simply said, "Alright, everything seems to be OK. Sorry for the inconvenience. You fellas make sure you get home safe."

Just like that, it was over. J.P. ran over to the patrol car and asked, "Officer, can you tell me why you pulled us over in the first place?"

The officer just looked at J.P. and didn't say a word. Usually they lie and say that they pulled us over because we were speeding or we fit a certain description. The same old tired lines that they've been running for years. Their lines were older than the pick up line, "Don't I know you from somewhere?" But these two cops uncharacteristically kept silent.

But it was obvious to us why they'd pulled us over. See, just like I mentioned before, they pulled us over because of DWB. They called themselves protecting the public, because as far as they were concerned, five black men in a BMW must be up to something illegal. In actuality, this was just another form of harrasment. They didn't actually have anything on us, other than the color of our skin. The only thing that any cop ever wanted to do was to get lucky and catch us with drugs in our possession. Or they wanted to catch us in a stolen car so that they could get some sort of commendation or promotion.

J.P. got back in the car and we drove off. Although we had told the cops that we were going home, we were actually on our way to visit some chicks. So as we continued on our way, Randy who was beyond vexed, started screaming.

"I hate cops! Why won't they just leave us the hell alone? People wonder how cops get killed in the line of duty. They get killed 'cause niggahs get tired of being harassed! One day before my life is over, I'm gonna smoke one of them pigs. Mark my words. I'm sick of this harassment!"

Randy was right. After a while, it did get to you. But hey, what could we do? We just had to take it. They were the ones with the power, not us. Whatever the cops wanted to do to us, we had to simply sit back and take it. The feelings that we'd get from being harassed were probably just as bad as the feeling a woman gets if she is raped.

But then again, playing the devil's advocate, I had to ask myself, could we really blame the cops? Maybe not, 'cause I'm sayin', I've been in many a stolen car in my day. I've carried many illegal guns in my day as well. So hey, when we did those things, weren't we making DWB a justifiable reason for cops to profile us?

At times I had to ask myself, was that verdict of guilty that we seemed to have pasted on our foreheads warranted by our actions? And at the same time, didn't somebody say we were guilty until proven innocent? Or was it innocent until proven guilty? All I knew was that when you're a black male in New York City, it's innocent until proven black.

Uptown – Harlem – 125th Street

June 19th, 1991. A Wednesday night, and Fourth Crew had made plans to profile in Uptown, Harlem. 125th street, to be exact. 125th street was our Wednesday night tradition. Like any street in New York City, 125th street is very large. In fact, it's long enough to allow ten or more avenues to cross through it at different intersections.

The world famous Apollo Theater is located on 125th street. Years ago, 125th street was the stomping grounds of greats such as Redd Foxx, Joe Louis and Malcolm X. But in 1991, 125th street was the current stomping grounds for Fourth Crew.

For someone who's never visited New York City and plans to do so, they should definitely make plans to visit Harlem. Harlem, New York should be a separate state. Despite all of the visible poverty, Harlem is filled with zestful life. There's so much ethnocentricity, nostalgia, history, culture, and tradition related to Harlem.

Wednesday night was always amateur night at the Apollo. However, on many Wednesdays, amateurs weren't the only performers to perform. In fact, some Wednesdays at the Apollo featured big name performers. Performers such as A Tribe Called Quest, Leaders of The New School, Ice Cube, LL Cool J, and Queen Latifah. June 19th was one of those nights. Amateurs were performing, but so was the mega rap/movie star Ice Cube. There was sure to be crowds of people coming to see the show.

Dwight, Xavier, Randy, Latiefe, and I decided to drive to the Apollo Theater in Xavier's little Toyota. We in Fourth Crew rarely ever missed a Wednesday night at the Apollo, but as funny as it may seem, we never went to amateur night with the intentions of going inside to see the show. We always timed ourselves so that we would arrive in Harlem just as the show was ending and everyone was being let out.

Let me tell you, as foolish as this may sound, we definitely were not the only native New Yorkers that did this. As a matter of fact, people would come from as far away as New Jersey, Connecticut and parts of Pennsylvania to do exactly what we did. Before, during, and after the show, 125th street would always be jammed with cars and people. And just like us, the majority of the people there would be there for one reason, and that was to profile.

Just as the saying goes, New York is truly the city that never sleeps. It would be nearly 2 a.m., yet there would be more people on 125th street at 2 a.m. than there were at 2 p.m. And always, after the crowds of people from 125th street began to disperse they would make their way further uptown to a spot called Willie Burgers. Willie Burgers was a little corner-food-stand set up that had no dining area. But let me tell you, the food from Willie Burgers knocked McDonald's, Roy Rogers, Wendy's, Hardee's, Denny's, Burger King, White Castle, and any place else out of the box when it came to burgers, fries, shakes, or whatever.

But Man! The scene in front of Willie Burgers would always be mobbed with people. People who wanted to grab something to eat before going home, people who wanted to get their last bit of 'Mac' on, or people who wanted to do both. The majority of our quests uptown were usually by way of Xavier's Toyota. But no matter what kind of car we drove in, our routine was always the same. We would drive to any spot on 125th street that was within at least two blocks of the Apollo. Usually we had to double park due to the large volume of cars. Then we would get out and stand in front of the car and parlay and watch as hundreds of cars drove by.

The cars that drove by would be packed with girls or packed with niggahs, it was either one or the other. Rarely did you see a mixture in the same ride. Every now and then we would spot a celebrity or two driving by in a car or a limo.

Many other people also parked their cars in the middle of 125th street just to lamp and clock everybody that passed by. After profiling, we would hop back into the car and drive up and down 125th street repeatedly, just to see everything and everybody. We would pass vendors selling Muslim oils, T-shirts, snap shots, bootleg video and audio tapes, and the New York original street Dee Jay tapes by Dee Jays such as Dee Jay Kid Capri.

Whenever any guys went to Harlem they would expect to see some beautiful honeys. But on Wednesday night, it was off the hook with women. I mean, on a Wednesday night women would be everywhere. Not just run of the mill females, either. I'm talking major beauty queens, the thick Janet Jackson types.

To Fourth Crew this was tons of fun. We were always either drunk, high off weed or both when we visited Harlem. The atmosphere of 125th street on a Wednesday night was always slammin'. Listening to the sounds of loud music blasting from the cars, talking to pretty young ladies, or just marinating was what I and just about all of Fourth Crew lived for.

June 19th was a smooth night in terms of no clashes breaking out. Of course, that night, like any other Wednesday night, we heard gun shots going off here and there, but those random gunshots had become commonplace. In fact, it was to the point where even cops on foot patrol were used to the gunshots. When the shots would ring out, most of the cops would usually remain at their posts and not even investigate where the shots were coming from.

Surprisingly, with as much as we visited 125th street, we never got into any beef. Even Five-O would always be cool and just let us do our thing. Fourth Crew always came simply to chill and have a good time. Actually, we knew that we had better come to Harlem in peace if we wanted to make it back home in one piece. We knew that if we tested the wrong people uptown that we were liable to get killed at the blink of an eye. See, cats from uptown were ruthless. Uptown cats were the type that dealt with beef by literally cutting your head off and leaving it on your doorsteps along with the daily newspaper. Your severed head would be a gift from them to your Moms. So needless to say, getting into any fights uptown was out of the question. Unless of course we were to get totally played to the point where we'd have no other choice but to fight.

Wednesday was also the night you could find out who had the best car in the Tri-State area. We stood and watched mad fly whips drive by. Top of the line BMW's, Mercedes', Ninja Bikes, Lamborghini's, Lexus'. You name it, we saw it. There were so many chromed-out cars, custom fitted with ragtops, spoilers, sunroofs, different color leather interiors, which were made available by way of legendary Harlem entrepreneur Dapper Dan, neon-lights, everything you could imagine. Some cats had even bit the West Coast style and put hydraulics on their rides to make them bounce up and down. Fourth Crew's biggest and only shortcoming as far as we were concerned was not having a phat ride. No one in the crew had a spanking car that they could claim as their own, and definitely not one that could match up with the expensive whips that we would see uptown every Wednesday night. In fact, it wasn't just cars. It was gold chains and all of that materialistic crap we didn't have. And boy did we wish we did own the gold chains and the phat cars just so that we would have been able to impress all the females in the street.

It was always a few ladies that who would give us some play and kick it to us for a little while, but it was never the Janet Jackson types. The Janet Jackson's wouldn't dare to talk to us because they were always on some trip like What-can-you-do-for-my-image-and-can-you-help-me-maintain-the-way-I-look? We didn't have that Mercedes or those diamond-studded medallions and rings. To put it in street lingo, our pockets weren't fat. Something however was different about that June 19th Wednesday night. Due to the fact that we looked like we didn't have much loot we got dissed by females. Usually we didn't let the chicken heads that dissed us override the fun we would have. Personally, I could have cared less, 'cause see, my girl Sabine treated me real good and she wasn't into all of that materialistic garbage. Besides, if those girls out there did ever talk to me or to anyone in the crew, all we would be after would be a piece of nah-nah. So getting dissed never hurt my ego too bad. We were just kicking game to them anyway. After all, the whole player process is like one continuous game.

Latiefe and Randy, gigolos number one and two respectively, always let the disrespect bother them. I guess it was their egos playing insecure tricks on them. Latiefe's hurt ego was probably what sparked off criminal conversation later on that June 19th night. Rather, I should say, early that morning of June 20th because by the time we returned home from Harlem it was technically a new day.

Just like every Wednesday, that Wednesday also eventually came to an end. And in doing so, so did our fun come to an end. That night we swayed from our normal routine. We didn't visit Willie Burgers. We all just drove home. Xavier had driven us all back to the block. He went to his crib and the rest of us stood out in front of my house and talked until the sun rose.

I was glad that Xavier had left us for his bed. See, we started talking about conducting illegal ways to get paid, and I definitely wouldn't have wanted to see Xavier getting caught up in anything illegal. That would have been like asking for another Richie type situation all over again, being that Xavier only had one more year of college to complete. It made me damn proud to see Xavier going straight through college in the manner in which he was, with no interruptions at all.

As we talked, Latiefe was like, "Yo, we gots to get paid this summer! I'm talking about big time loot. No nickel and dime nonsense. Y'all see how every week those chicken heads be sweating those punk niggahs just 'cause they got dough? Every week it's the same thing. And if it's not at the Apollo then it's somewhere else. But all I'm sayin' is the only thing that them cats be havin' over us is the fact that they have more chips than we do, and that's why they be flossin' and we don't."

"Word," Randy agreed. "And half those cars out there are from drug money. You know cats ain't working nine to five's to pay for those rides. You can't! How the hell is a twenty year old gonna be driving a 500SL? What job is paying dough like that?"

Tee went on, "That's exactly what I'm sayin'. Yo, we're gonna be out there soon. Real soon. This summer we ain't gonna be poor, broke, and pitiful. Nah, not like last summer. We ain't gonna be sitting around looking at each other and pulling our penises. To hell with that! We're getting paid this summer. Watch! Ninety one is gonna be the summer we really have fun."

By now it was nearing five in the morning. The sun was still rising. I was tired as was everyone else. I was ready to put my head on my pillow and be out. "Yo, I'm outta here," I informed.

Before I departed, Latiefe asked, "So Holz, what's up? You wit' it or what? You wanna get paid?"

"No doubt," I responded. "You know I'm wit' it kid."

Tee replied, "Ah'ight bet, then we have to really discuss this. We have to sit down and map everything out. I know we gotta get some sleep, but before this week is over we have to talk and we gotta get started. Every year we talk all of this and all of that about how we should do this, that, and the third, and so on and whatever, and it's always just talk. But that's over with. I'm dead up serious!"

"Alright, bet," we all replied as we gave each other pounds and departed our separate ways to our beds.

As I lay in my bed that morning just staring into space, I thought about all of the cars and women that I'd seen uptown. Man! It was the beginning of the summer, so that's probably why there was such an abundance of heads out that night.

Man, nothing but fly cars, I thought. I wanted one of them cars, but the drug game scared me a little. Honestly, I didn't think I had the heart for it. I was intrigued by the profit potential, and I knew for a fact that it could bring me all of the material things that I wanted, but maybe it was a dead end. Most of the time it's either a cell or a grave. In the past, as a crew we had discussed the idea of selling drugs, and fortunately all that it had ever amounted to was talk. Now though, for some strange reason, maybe it was fear, but I could sense that our desires for material things was about to lead us beyond just the conversations of illegal ways of getting paid. If I was gonna be in it, I couldn't have a conscience. I just had to be down for whateva.

I stared at the wall in my room for a little while longer. All sorts of crazy, chaotic thoughts filled my head and raced back and forth. I got up out of my bed and I rammed my fist into my bedroom wall. I was feeling extremely frustrated. I could feel that I was about to get caught up in too much nonsense. What could I do? What should I do?

I heard my father moving around the house as he prepared to go work. I thought about just going downstairs and speaking to him. Unlike many black males, I actually had a father, and he was a daddy at that. Maybe he could add some direction and just help me see things in their proper perspective.

I was about to make my way downstairs to talk with my father but I changed my mind as I reminded myself once again, *no conscience.* I tried to relax and slowly made my way back into the bed. Before I fell asleep, I prayed:

"Dear Lord, please let me, my mother, my father, my brother, my sister, Sabine, and everyone else that I love, like, and respect be OK. Thank you Lord, for letting me have such a wonderful day that just passed. Please Lord, continue to let me have nice days. Thank You for life. I love You so much. Oh... P.S. Lord, please help us that are in the crew. Watch over us Lord, please. In Your Son's name, Jesus Christ, I pray. Amen."

Kingpins

"Mark, the telephone! Mark! Mark! The telephone!" my sister yelled.

Like a grouch, I responded. "Yeah, ah'ight. Paula, why couldn't you just tell whoever it is that I'm sleeping? Can't you see that I'm tired?... Man!" I went on to angrily explain that it was Saturday morning and that I never woke up until at least one in the afternoon on Saturdays.

"Mark, just pick up the damn phone and shut the hell up!" Paula sounded very disgusted.

I picked up the phone. "Hello? Who the hell is this?"

"Yo Holz, it's me, man. It's Latiefe."

"Latiefe, what do you want this early? It's like eight o'clock in the morning."

"I don't care what time it is. All I know is that you better get up, niggah, 'cause at ten o'clock we're all meeting at my grandmother's house."

"For what?" I asked as I finally began to wake up.

"You know for what. I'm sayin', remember what we talked about this week?"

"Oh, you mean…"

Latiefe quickly interrupted me. "Yeah kid, that's what I mean. It's on. Ah'ight? We're all going out to breakfast like big time Mafioso."

"Ah'ight bet," I said. "I'll be there, no diggidy. Peace."

Before Latiefe hung up he sternly warned me to get dressed and to not go back to sleep. At ten o'clock we were to discuss how we were going to build an empire of illegal activities that were gonna get us paid during the summer of '91. I was very tired. I knew that the meeting was important, but the bed was calling my name. I rolled back into bed, pulled the sheet over my head and before I knew it, I was knocked out, sound asleep.

When I finally did wake up, I realized that it was five minutes to ten. I couldn't believe it. I lost total control as I scrambled to get up and out of the house. I darted to the bathroom, brushed my teeth, hopped in and out of the shower, raced back to my room and threw on some clothes, and I was out the door.

By the time I'd finally made it out the house it was about ten fifteen. I jetted to Tee's grandmother's crib. Most of the crew was already there and waiting. Donnie, Erik, Randy, Tee, Dwight, Kwame, J.P., they all were there. Earl and Wiggie were also there. Although they were from 229th street, you might as well have considered them as part of the crew. See, Earl lived in the same house as Dwight and Latiefe because he was the father of Latiefe's aunt's baby. Latiefe's aunt was named Audrey. They all lived with Tee's grandmother. Confusing, right? Even I sometimes got confused trying to explain all of the relationships of the inhabitants of that house. But to make it simple, Earl and Wiggie were blood brothers and they chilled with us all of the time, so basically they were down with us.

"Holz, what took you so long?" Latiefe asked. "Even Randy was ready before you."

Smiling, I said, "Yo, I fell back asleep. But I'm here, so what's the deal, fella?"

Randy suggested that we go to IHOP. We all jumped into cabs and headed for the IHOP on Hillside Avenue, in Jamaica, Queens. Once we got there, we all sat down and waited to order. Although no one had given us permission, we pushed three tables together so that we could all eat at the same spot.

Everyone ordered food except for Earl and Wiggie. They held some superstitious theory that eating breakfast caused them to have bad luck. Whatever that meant. But to hell with that, the rest of us weren't holding back, because the food was good and it was filling.

Latiefe, after sipping on his orange juice said, "Yo y'all, we didn't come here to eat. We came here to discuss this narcotics thing." Without waiting for a reply, he started explaining his plan. "I've been here and there the past couple of days, trying to get everything situated and set up. I've been talking to some people, trying to figure out just how we're gonna do this. And I got it figured out, so check it. This is how we're gonna do this.

Donnie, you're the only one of us that's out there hustling already. You ain't big time yet. I mean, you're selling drugs hand to hand for that cat Montana. And you know Montana is paid, but you, you're making out ah'ight. Enough loot to buy you some new clothes or whateva, but come on, tell me, don't you want that big loot? That 850 BMW loot? Big time, baby. That's what I'm talking about! Big time! We don't have time for that hand to hand, nickel and dime, watch out for Five-O nonsense." All eyes were on Latiefe as he continued sharing his ideas.

"Montana, Fat Cat, Supreme, all of those big time hustlers are already out there and established with a firm grip on their spots. They're paid, and they plan to keep getting paid. They have spots sewn up, and those niggahs don't want no extra competition. It took them too long to get to the top, and they plan on staying there. But you know what? They never really had to worry about competition until now. And no, before y'all even ask, I ain't talking 'bout us trying to knock one of them off. 'Cause that drug-war-slash-turf-war violence ain't necessary. We can save that for the movies. And even if we did start a war, there are mad heads waiting in line ready to take their places, so if we started a drug war we would be fighting that war forever."

Randy asked, "So Tee, how are we gonna get out there? We can't just start off boom! Straight to the top. Everybody in the drug business started off low level like Donnie, going hand to hand on the street. Then they worked their way up until they controlled blocks and became kingpins."

Eyes shifted from Randy and back to Latiefe as he answered. "Randy and everybody else, listen. Montana, Supreme, Fat Cat and all them niggahs are paying their workers twenty dollars for every one hundred dollars worth of drugs that they sell. See, money goes to money. Hand to hand kids don't understand economics, and that's why Montana is so paid. Now listen, that's what we have to take advantage of. We have to play with the economics.

See, we go buy some weed, coke, heron' or whateva', and bag it ourselves. Then we give it to those niggahs going hand to hand on the corner. We could hit all of Merrick Blvd., all of Laurelton, all of Far Rockaway, all of Montana's territory. See, we'll have Montana's workers working for us on the low."

I butted in and said disrespectfully, "Latiefe, you know what? We should go into the candy store, play Lotto and hope that tomorrow we'll be millionaires, 'cause we probably have a better chance of hitting Lotto than we have of doing what you're sayin'. I mean, I don't know, but your plan sounds too easy, and things just don't click like that on the street."

Tee barked and raised his hand as if he was gonna smack me. He snapped back, "Holz what the...Yo, you think I'm stupid or what? I know what I'm doing! Now let me finish. Damn!" He shook his head and sighed before he addressed the crew again.

"Ah'ight, see now, if we pay Montana's workers forty dollars for every one hundred, they'll sell for us on the low. I'm telling y'all, they'll do it for that kind of money. Money talks and everything else walks. I guarantee you that they'll pump for us. We'll just tell them to keep pushing Montana's garbage for him and at the same time they'll be knocking off our work. The only thing is that they would have to keep it on the low. Donnie what do you think?"

Donnie was deliberately slow to respond as he thought about the question. He looked toward the ceiling, he bit a piece of his bacon and then he replied. "It could work, but peep this. You own a business and you're grossing a hundred thousand a week consistently. Then for no reason at all you start grossing twenty thousand a week. Yet your store has the same number of customers coming in as you did before your drop in sales, and there's no shortage of inventory. How do you explain that? And if you're the owner of that business, what do you do?"

Tee paused, then he said, "Yeah, I see where you're coming from. But yo, life ain't perfect and there's drawbacks to everything. Doctors work bad hours, Priests can't have sex, and we just have to deal with Montana making less dough. But hey, everybody knows that the greater the risk, the bigger the return on your investment. Y'all feel me on this?"

We all agreed as we started to see where Tee was coming from with his John Gotti-like mastermind plan. He went on, "Now Donnie, you gots to get like twenty workers who you know that would do this for us and wouldn't open their mouths and rat us out. 'Cause I'm sayin', a kid could easily front like he's down with us, then out of hopes of getting promoted to lieutenant go back and tell how we're scheming. So when you approach them cats you gotta come at them with mad game and sell this idea like it's surefire. In your pitch, make sure you remind them how Montana has been jerking them for all of this time and how they could literally double their earnings overnight. And oh yeah, make sure you remind them of what they could do with all of the extra loot that they've long deserved to be making."

Donnie replied, "I see where you're coming from. Don't worry, kid. I got game, no doubt about that. If I can get a person to try crack for the first time with them fully knowing how addictive it is, then you know that I got game. 'Cause I'm yo' pushaaaa."

After a brief second of laughter from the crew, Donnie went on to say, "But for real though, I know mad dealers, myself included, that Montana has been jerking. Sometimes he'll give us five dollars for every hundred, you know what I'm sayin'? So niggahs be like 'what the hell am I risking going to jail and getting shot up and all of that for got damn McDonald's and Burger King type wages?' So Tee, all we gots to do is get the work. Knocking it off ain't gonna be a problem. We know the risks, so what's up? Whatcha waaant niggah?"

"Ahhh! We gon' get paid!" we all happily said in unison as we clasped each other's hands.

"Hold up. Hold up," Latiefe said. "Don't get too excited yet. We ain't finish mapping this thing out. My man Gangsta runs a little something in Far Rockaway. He promised me from an old solid that he would give us a spot out there in the projects. So all we have to do if find some boyz to go out there for us and pump the work."

Earl informed us that his cousin had spots uptown and in Brooklyn. Spots that he would be willing to give to us for a certain kickback of whatever we made. We all agreed that we would hit Brooklyn, but we weren't going to mess with uptown because we unanimously felt that the niggahs out there were just too ruthless.

I went on to pessimistically tell everyone that it wasn't going to be as easy to come out like we were planning to do. Besides the fact that we would be stepping on toes, we were risking not only our own lives but the lives of those who we would recruit to work for us. Plus we had to start from square one with absolutely no cash. We needed loot, and a lot of it, to kick off the operation. Purchasing kilos wasn't like purchasing Cheerios. Kilos cost big dough and we had no money whatsoever.

Montana and the rest of the big time hustlers and players all had crazy cash coming in, so they, with one phone call, could go out and buy weight, a.k.a large amounts of drugs, like it was nothing. Our crew didn't have any money, nor did we have any money coming to us. It would be tough for us to get started.

Dwight suggested that we only deal with crack and marijuana. The true heart of the crack era had reached its peak probably during the summer of '87, but there was still a faithful enough remnant of crackheads to make us rich. Marijuana seemed to be making a resurgence, so to speak. Every time I turned around I heard someone talking about smoking weed, or smoking Phillies, or puffing on L's. The latest term that I'd been hearing to describe the use of marijuana was the saying 'smoking trees.' I even saw brothas walking around with pictures of marijuana plants on their T-shirts. We couldn't have passed up that kind of free promotional marketing. We just had to execute a plan to profit from it.

Dwight was on point with his suggestion. He went on to say that on the streets of Queens, marijuana and crack sold the fastest, so that's what he suggested that we concentrate on. See, if we were dealing in Washington Heights, a section of Manhattan known as Spanish Harlem, the drug of choice would be Heroin, a.k.a. heron', and we would have to concentrate on pushing that. Just your classic case of what you learn in economics 101 about supply and demand.

Dwight added that if we were planning to have a spot in Far Rockaway, a spot in Brooklyn, and heads working for us all over Montana's territory we would need at least four pounds of weed and 20 eight balls of cocaine. We all figured that we could get the four pounds of marijuana for about $7,500 and the 20 eight balls of cocaine for about $2,500. In all, we estimated that $10,000 would be a good amount of money to get us started.

See, one pound of weed went for about two grand. But we'd get back three grand in return, or a fifty percent return on our investment. One eight ball of coke could be cooked up into crack rocks and sold on the street, netting us somewhere in the neighborhood of five hundred dollars on a two hundred dollar investment. A one hundred and fifty percent return on our money. It didn't take a Wall Street genius to figure out that if you could make those kinds of flips with cash within a week's time and pay no taxes, that it wouldn't be long before you'd have a house on the white sand beaches of St. Thomas if you wanted it.

The thing with the drug trade, just like with any investment, was the more money you played with, the more you stood to make. Or the higher your risks, the greater potential of your returns. Like if all went well with our plans, we stood the chance of making close to a two hundred percent return on a ten thousand dollar investment. Just imagine if we made that kind of return on a one hundred thousand dollar investment. And see, that was our plan. But we'd have to start small. In this biz you could be large overnight. If we played our cards right, before we knew it, we could have one hundred grand to play with.

Erik, who had been quiet all along, came up with the idea of us dealing with 'weight out of state.' That meant selling pounds of weed and ounces and kilos of coke, very large volumes of drugs. His plan was that we could be wholesale suppliers to drug dealers in states like Virginia. Selling weight out of state was quickly becoming a growing trend. What it did was cut out the retail portion of the drug business. We would have dealt strictly on a wholesale scale with drug kingpins from other regions.

Like I mentioned earlier, dealing with large quantities definitely meant larger profits. And for that reason, selling weight out of state was becoming commonplace amongst New York drug criminals. Many dealers paid females five or six hundred dollars to get on a bus, ride to D.C. or wherever on the East Coast with drugs in their suitcase. They would have them make a drop, get the cash and head back north to New York on I-95 with a pocket full of cash and no hassles from state troopers.

I-95 was a drug dealers' and gun runners' highway to riches simply because state troopers didn't pull over buses and check each and every suitcase and every carry-on piece of baggage. Some drug dealers were bold enough to drive out of state with drugs in their car, but I personally wouldn't have done that because it would have been like pressing your luck. With a commercial bus, the only real risk was not getting paid or getting robbed when you got to your destination and attempted to make the drop. I guessed it was that fear of getting jerked that led drug dealers to drive armed in a regular car to close deals themselves.

Erik's idea was a good idea, considering Reggie already knew some heads that were in the drug game down in Norfolk, Hampton, and Virginia Beach. Even the crew, although we didn't live in Virginia like Reggie, knew people who had relocated from Queens to Virginia for the sole purpose of selling dope.

Latiefe agreed that dealing with weight was a good idea. But our main focus, he said, would be to come up with the ten thousand in order to get things rolling in New York. He predicted that after we started, and if things went well, it would be about a month or two before we would be ready to sell weight out of state.

So that was it. Fourth Crew was going to be one big conglomerate of dope pushers, or better yet, one big drug kingpin. We had to set the operation off fast, but at the same time slow enough as to not make any mistakes. We, as a crew, had to keep everything on the low and amongst ourselves. Whoever worked for us would have to be kept in strict check. If necessary, we would have to literally control their lives. We couldn't, for the sake of what we were trying to achieve as a conglomerate, have workers coming up short with our money. And we couldn't have them opening their mouths and singing about our cutthroat way of doing business.

We kept this vital business meeting going. We moved on to what I call the cash flow segment of the meeting, where basically we discussed how we planned to stay in the black. The plan was, after paying our workers we would throw all of the profits back into a pot. That way our business could flourish and grow. If we were to consistently do that, and if things went according to plan, we would be able to purchase kilos with ease.

Latiefe was sure to remind us that although we would be making what would seem like a lot of money, it would take a little time before we really started flipping loot and seeing the Pablo Escobar type dough. "If we do things right, we'll be living fat before we know it. One thing we have to do is promise to live by our mission statement which is, *FOURTH CREW BEFORE CASH.* Our mission is to be the most dominant drug hustlers in the Northeast. Yo, we're in this together, so that means that no one or no thing is bigger than the crew! Ah'ight?"

"No doubt," we all agreed in unison.

Randy began to speak. He said, "All of this talk sounds good. Matter of fact, we sound like we're some Fortune Five Hundred executives and all that. But how in the world are we going to get ten grand to set this off? How? Big executives, tell me where do we get the start up capital from?"

Latiefe attempted to put Randy at ease. "OK, OK, see, me and the Godfather already discussed that. And the most logical conclusion that we came to was the fact that we gots to become strictly ruthless, all out illegal criminals to get the money we need in order to pass go. This is the deal. We're taking anything and everything that we want, from whoever we want, when we want. Anything valuable that we see, we're taking it, housin' it, taxing it, whateva! We ain't stopping until we get the ten grand that we need." Then with the most satanic look in his eyes, Latiefe finished, "We'll be robbing cats, and if we have to, we'll be murdering cats!"

I was amazed at the conviction in which Latiefe spoke with. He kept on. "We have to be slick and we have to be smart. If we do that, we have nothing to worry about. We're all in this together. No rats! If one of us gets caught and goes down, that doesn't take us all down."

Latiefe paused. He slowly looked everyone in the eyes and said, "I don't think any of y'all is soft, but if any of y'all are soft, and y'all feel yourselves starting to get shook, tell me now."

Everyone looked at around as if to challenge each other, but not a sound was heard, which indirectly gave Latiefe permission to continue.

"We gots to go on a crime spree to get this cash that we need. Then we're gonna blow up on the drug scene. So again, whoever is down now, is down. If you don't want to be down with this, tell me now. But word is bond, when we blow up and if you wasn't with it from jump, don't try to hop on the wagon when the getting is good. I mean, we're homeboyz and cool with each other and all of that, but I won't be trying to hear that."

Again, no one said a word. You could hear a pin drop amongst the crew as everyone seemed to be deep in their own thoughts. The silence ratified everyone's decision to be down with the plan. We were in this thing together.

Dwight, the Godfather, took over from this point. He discussed tactics. He said, "All of us has some type of gun, and we're gonna need them, with bullets. Get your hands on as many guns as you can because after this crime spree is over we'll need them for the drug trafficking. We're also gonna need ski masks, gloves, all that. Y'all know what y'all need to rob with, right?"

Dwight commanded that since there was ten of us, during our crime spree, each day we were to go out in teams of three's, rotating amongst ourselves everyday. There would always be one team with four members.

"Monday," he said, "we're gonna start our rampage. Monday morning the rampage starts and it won't end until that following Friday. It has to end by that Friday because by then the cops and detectives will get hip or we'll slip up and get bagged. Ten G's, y'all. That means a lot of work has to be done. We're going to be working from sun up to way beyond sun down. From now on, we're gonna be a bunch of ruthless hooligans! We can't care about nothing! If we die in the process, we die. We can't even care about our own life. That's the kind of mind that we have to have. No conscience.

But hey, yo, I know y'all know the tricks to this game, or should I go over them? Y'all know the simple things like don't commit crimes in your own neighborhood. Or, if you're going to use a stolen car, don't steal a nice flashy one, and make sure that it has gas in it. And yeah, make sure that it's fast enough to at least outrun the cops if needed."

J.P., sounding very insulted interrupted and said, "Yeah, yeah, we know all of that. We ain't stupid!"

"Ah'ight," Dwight said. "Just checking up."

J.P. asked, "Shouldn't we keep this crime thing going until Saturday night? That's the night that we could get the most loot. Saturday night is party night."

"No, got damit!" Dwight yelled as he banged his fist on the table. "I already told y'all Friday is the last day! Remember, I'm the Godfather. We're gonna do this my way or no way at all. We need a shorter time frame so y'all will see the urgency and work harder toward what it is that we're after."

After a short pause, Dwight successfully displayed his authority by rhetorically asking, "Now, anybody else got something to say?"

Silence swept across the room.

"Well then," Dwight replied to the silence, "Let's bounce."

Latiefe informed us that we had the rest of the weekend to think about what we were getting ourselves into. He then added that Monday was showtime. "Monday morning at seven thirty we'll all meet up in front of Kwame's crib and take off from there. Ah'ight?"

The whole crew responded, "Ah'ight."

"Let's be Audi five thousand," Latiefe said to end the meeting.

Dwight interrupted our exit from the restaurant by saying, "Oh yo, next Saturday, we're having breakfast at the McDonald's near our block over in Rosedale. By then we'll have the loot and we'll need to lay down the solid plan about the drug distribution scenario. Ah'ight. Yo Earl, go call a cab."

"Yeah, ah'ight Dee," Earl replied.

Stick Up

When I know that I have to wake up early for something, I prepare myself. I tend not to sleep as hard as I normally do. A light sleeper, that's what I become. Last night I didn't really sleep at all because I knew that soon it would be Monday morning and our crime wave would begin.

Yeah, I was up early that Monday morning. I woke up at about six-thirty. I took a shower, got dressed and waited for the phone to ring. My nerves were running rampant. I felt like I was going to a new job for the first time. In a way I guess I was, because that morning marked my first day on the job as a stick up kid. Yeah, I knew that would make my parents proud. What was it that made me stop chasing those dreams of becoming a stockbroker or a doctor? At least those professions didn't have a guilty conscience or a jail sentence attached to them. Stick up kid, now that profession had many negatives associated with it.

My palms were sweaty and my heart was beating a little faster than normal. The picture of Jesus Christ on my desk seemed as if it was watching my every move. I glanced at the picture then I quickly glanced away from it. But it seemed as if something magnetic made my eyes keep wandering back to His face.

My palms continued to sweat. In the background the telephone rang and it startled me. It sounded more like a fire alarm. I was really beginning to think that I was paranoid.

I shakily answered, "Hello."

"Yo Holz, it's Kwame. Man, you ready?"

"Yeah… Um, I'm ready."

"So come down to my crib right now."

"Ah'ight. I'm coming."

I slipped on my black Nike Airs then I reached my hand under my bed until I got a hold of a gray metal box. I reached in and pulled out a black 9mm handgun. I inserted a clip into the gun and placed it on my bed. I thought about bringing my .22 automatic, but I decided against it because it was too small. It wouldn't be intimidating enough. I put the box, which was full of back-up

That picture of Jesus kept following me. I tried to ignore it as I grabbed my gun and my ski mask. I tucked the ski mask into my back pocket and stuffed the nine into the front of my pants, pulling my shirt over it to cover the bulge. Before I left my house, I spoke to the picture on my desk. "Lord, please watch over us."

Randy and I were leaving our houses at the exact same time. As we walked to Kwame's crib we saw that everybody was already outside waiting. By then it was seven-thirty a.m. When Randy and I reached Kwame's gate, Dwight didn't waste no time. Without giving us a pound or asking what's up, Dwight immediately started to give out instructions.

"Ah'ight, this is how we're gonna do this. Me, Wiggie, and Holz are going together. We'll be FC1. Kwame, Latiefe and Donnie, y'all go together, and y'all will be FC2. Randy, Earl, J.P. and Erik, y'all four will be with one another, and y'all will be FC3."

Dwight reminded us to stay out of Laurelton and Rosedale. For one, we lived in Laurelton and the town of Rosedale was too close to our neighborhood. Dwight's words were, "Yo, we gots to go out to Long Island, 'cause that's where the money is at. If y'all do stay in Queens make sure that y'all go to towns like Bayside, or Rego Park, the white areas. But remember, try not to stay too long in white neighborhoods, 'cause we'll stick out like a stiff dick in a pair of swimming trunks."

We all started to walk toward Rosedale. Latiefe guided us to the Long Island Railroad. The LIRR stopped in Rosedale to take passengers either into the city or in the opposite direction, which was further east on Long Island. At the Rosedale stop on the LIRR there was a tremendous parking lot. Every morning commuters would drive their cars to the parking lot and board the train. They'd leave their cars in the unattended parking lot until they returned from work.

Most of those commuters worked in the city. And just like most New Yorkers, the act of parking their cars and taking the train to work was an unwanted necessity, simply because the city was so congested with cars, leaving drivers who ventured into Manhattan with either no place to park or stuck in traffic jams. Stated simply, most commuters found the train much more convenient. Unfortunately for the commuters, we planned to capitalize on that convenience.

Once we made it to the parking lot, Latiefe quickly stated, "Ah'ight. Each group pick out a car, and let's be out."

Our three-man posse, FC1, picked a Pontiac Grand Am. FC2 picked out a Toyota Celica. FC3 decided to ride in a Pontiac 6000. Like amateurs, we broke the driver's side window of each car, unlocked the doors, got in, popped the ignition, and in less than five minutes we had ourselves get-away cars. We knew that the cars wouldn't be reported stolen until after 6 p.m., when the unlucky owners returned from work. But by that time we would have been rid of the car.

At that point there was no more planning. We had to rely only on our instincts if we wanted to figure out where the members of each separate posse were during the day, and what exactly they were doing.

Wiggie was the driver of our car. Dwight sat in the passenger seat and I sat in the back. Of course we had to ride with all of the windows down, being that the passenger window was broken. That way we wouldn't look suspicious.

Out of habit or some type of unwritten street law, brothas always tried to look cool when they rode around. Yes, even in the stolen car we tried to look cool. Both of the front seats were reclined all the way back. All three of us sat slumped down, as if we didn't have backbones, but that's how you did it if you wanted to Mac.

Dwight asked us where we wanted to go. I suggested that we head out to a town on Long Island, called Freeport. So that's where we went. It was bugged, because from the moment that we'd left the front of Kwame's house and walked toward the train station's parking lot, we didn't talk at all to one another. No one said 'peep.' What was also unusual was the fact that none of us was in a joking mood. Although I sensed fear in the hearts of us all, I just wasn't man enough to stop the madness. I thought that I was acting hard. In essence, I was the biggest coward for not speaking against what we were about to do. Fear was still in my heart while the three of us rode in the car toward Freeport. But I knew that I had to transform my mind into that of a psychopath. I had to lose all fear. I silently hoped that everyone else in the crew was also transforming themselves.

The frame of mind of a psychopath was definitely the mindset that we needed to help us commit crimes. I knew that if I was gonna rob someone that I had to strike total fear in that person's body. How could I strike fear into someone if I myself was also afraid? There was no way I could have done that.

I was beginning to psych myself up good. The fear was starting to leave my body. Adrenaline was beginning to work on my brain. *Yeah*, I was thinking, *let me see a punk with some gold on!* I was ready. Ready to walk up on anybody and convince him by my actions that I was indeed downright crazy. Adrenaline was taking over my mind, soul and body. I was actually starting to believe I was crazy.

"Yo, yo,yo! Wiggie, stop the car. No! No! Drive. Drive around the block. I got a victim. I got somebody!" I frantically informed. Our first robbery was about to take place.

Dwight inquired, "Holz, what's up, man?"

"That automatic bank teller over there. That cash machine. I'ma get somebody coming out."

"Ah'ight," Dee said as he began to breathe a little heavier. "OK, OK. We're gonna let you out here and we'll wait for you right down the block near that bus stop. Just go jack the first cat you see and then haul your ass back into the car and we'll be out."

"Yeah, OK," I said. "Let me out." I immediately walked across the street and followed a woman inside the ATM cubicle. See, the cash machine wasn't exactly located inside the bank. It was portioned off from the main part of the bank where you would go to apply for a loan and stuff like that. I guess it was set up that way to cause less confusion to the customers.

So I followed the lady as she walked toward the bank. I continued to walk right behind her as she made her way to the ATM. I wouldn't have been able to gain access to that part of the bank unless I too had an ATM card, which I didn't. So I had to stick to the lady like glue.

Once inside, I saw a line of about five people. I got on the end of the line and acted as if I were a regular customer. I didn't know who to rob, but I knew that I had to wait for somebody to withdraw a good amount of money before I made my move.

My heart thumped as I nervously waited for the right moment to strike. I was so nervous that I thought I was going to un-psych myself and not follow through with the robbery. Man I wasn't cut out for this. I was two seconds from bouncing and punking out when an angry voice inside of me tempted me and said, "Holz, just do it!"

I was getting antsy. I noticed this tall, heavy set white man at the machine taking out money, but I couldn't see how much money he was getting. That same angry voice inside of me sounded like an attack dog as it whispered into my ear, "Holz, get 'em!"

There I stood, all six feet and 170lbs of me, scheming on some white dude who looked to be about six four and 215lbs. I knew that if I was gonna successfully rob him that I had to get him to respect me, and I had to gain his respect quickly. One thing that I learned from the 'hood was that almost anyone will respect you if they're in fear of losing their life.

As the white dude stepped away from the cash machine and was about to open the door to leave, I darted toward him and whipped out my 9mm.

"Gimme your damn money! Run the cash right now!" I yelled as I pointed the gun underneath his chin, pushing it into his skin.

My heart was pounding a mile a minute as the victim looked more shocked than he did afraid. With the gun pressed with my full strength underneath his chin, he mumbled, "What's… What's going on?"

I thought to myself, *Holz, playtime is over. Hurry up and get this fool's money and get the hell outta here!* As I repositioned the gun to his forehead I screamed, "Yo! Gimme all of your got damn money right now or I'll murder you! Give it up! NOWWW!"

As the other customers realized what was going on they began screaming and scrambling. The place was in a state of chaos. The white man shakingly said, "OK, OK, just don't kill me."

"Did I ask you to talk? Shut up and give me your money!" I yelled.

He reached in his pocket and gave me all of his cash and his wallet. I snatched it and burst out of the door like a lightning bolt, heading straight for the car.

When I reached the car I yelled, "Come on! Come on! Come on! Come on! Let's go! Let's bounce!" I jumped in the back seat of the car and continued to yell, "Drive! Let's go! Get outta here!"

We peeled off and headed straight for the highway. We were barely a block away from the bank, yet Dwight and Wiggie began interrogating me with questions. "Yo, how much you got? Holz, how much did you get?"

My heart was still pumping a million gallons of blood per second. Sounding out of breath, which I was, and gasping for air I replied, "I don't... I don't know... Let me count it. Just let me catch my breath."

When I'd finally counted the money I realized that I had made off with $360. "Yes! Yes!" I screamed pumping my fist in the air, "I got $360 from that white cat!"

"Yo Holz, you the man!" Dwight cheerfully exclaimed.

"No, you the man," I replied.

Jokingly, Dwight again replied, "No, you da man. You are da man! My man, big Holz!"

We all proceeded to laugh as Wiggie asked, "Yo, how did you rob him that quick?"

Playing it off as if I was the most hardened criminal in the world, I sucked my teeth and said, "Yo, I just ran up on him, pointed my gun in his face and told him to run his loot."

"That's it? That's all you did?"

Careful not to mention how terrified I was and how I almost didn't follow through with the robbery, I continued to play like a fat cat. "Yeah, that was it. It was easier than taking candy from a baby. Here Dee, take this money," I said as I handed Dwight the dough.

I slumped back into the seat of the car. I was beginning to come down from my crazed high and I couldn't believe what I had just done. I had just robbed someone! But yo, that's not what scared me, though. The scary part was what if the man had hesitated one more second? If he had, I would have popped a cap in him, probably killing him. I was also scared 'cause I had made too many mistakes during the robbery.

That voice in my head that had been sounding angry and tempting me to actually commit the crime, returned to my head, only this time the voice sounded more compassionate as it said, "Well, at least you got the first one off your chest." I ridiculously nodded my head in agreement with that voice because I knew that there would be many more robberies to come.

As I sat and tried to play reverse psychology tricks on my conscience, Dwight instructed Wiggie to exit from the highway. We had driven far enough from the first crime scene and we weren't in any clear and present danger of getting caught. After exiting from the highway, we realized that we weren't too far from our point of destination. We found ourselves in a town called Hempstead, which was also located on Long Island. We drove around Hempstead for about twenty minutes just looking for our next victim.

"Oh, whoa! Look at those honeys over there!" Dwight exclaimed. "Wiggie, hurry up and catch up to them."

Wiggie hastily made a U-turn and pulled up alongside these two fine black females. "Excuse me. Hello, hello. How y'all doin'?" he asked the two young ladies.

At first the women weren't to responsive, but before you knew it, Wiggie, with his smooth words, was able to get a conversation going.

"I'm sayin', can't a brotha at least get a hello?" Wiggie asked.

One of the females seemed turned off by the unwanted attention that they were receiving from us. With an attitude, she twisted her head and stated, "First of all, we don't even know y'all. We can't just be speaking to anybody."

The other female had a completely opposite demeanor as she first responded to her friend and then she acknowledged us. "Nah, chill. They seem cool. So what's up? How y'all doing?" she asked.

From that, a conversation began to flow. As the two spoke to us we found out that they were both nineteen years old and were attending summer school at Adelphi University. Adelphi was near Hempstead. It was located in the adjacent, affluent town called Garden City. We also found out that their names were Lisa and Kim. Lisa was the more friendly of the two.

Wiggie asked Lisa for her phone number and she gave it to him. These stupid, non-street-smart women didn't even realize that they were about to get robbed. They played right into our hands when they asked us for a ride.

"Why don't y'all do us a favor and drop us off on campus?" Lisa asked.

"Yeah, no problem. We'll drop y'all off," Wiggie calmly replied.

So the two got in and we drove toward the campus. As we were driving, Wiggie continued to converse with Lisa. Kim was also starting to loosen up as words began to flow out of her mouth. While we were all engaged in conversation, Dwight slowly turned his body around so that he could face the back seat of the car. He was smiling a nice, big Kool-Aid type of smile, and as shrewd as a cobra he pulled out his gun. He too had a black 9mm.

"I'm sorry," he told them, sounding as if he was amusing himself with his actions, "but y'all gots to give up all y'all money, jewels, and whatever else."

The two young ladies were sitting right next to me, with one on my left and the other on my right. They both hesitated and looked at each other as if they were dumbfounded. They had good reason to look confused. I mean, five seconds ago Dwight was asking them about their GPA's, and just that quick he had a gun pointed in their faces asking for their goods.

Dwight appeared to have slipped into a rage as he screamed, "Yo, this ain't no game! Now both of y'all run the jewels!"

With a gun to their heads, Lisa and Kim were left with very few options, so they wisely complied to Dwight's demands. They briskly followed his orders to the letter.

Wiggie pulled the car over to the curb and very calmly said, "Thank you, ladies. And uh, y'all make sure y'all have a nice day, ok?" As the girls got out of the car, Wiggie purposely tried to sound as if he was a shy nerd or something. "Uh... Uh... Lisa? Can I still call you?"

With that, the three of us burst into laughter. As we drove away, Wiggie yelled out of the window, "This better not be a fake number either!" Wiggie's last comment really caused us to double over in tear-jerking laughter. Lisa and Kim were left standing on the corner, crying and in shock.

We managed to take from them: four gold rings, one bracelet, a gold chain, two sets of gold earrings and thirty dollars in cash. All of which wasn't too bad, considering how easy it was. It was just something inside of me that made me feel very cowardly as I realized that we had just jacked two defenseless women. Needless to say, I felt like a real punk.

Fortunately, I wasn't the only one with a pulse. Wiggie's conscience spoke up and said, "Yo, we shouldn't have jacked them. I mean, they were ladies."

Dwight rudely and abruptly interrupted him. "I don't care if they were ladies. I'm gonna tell y'all again just like I've already been preaching to y'all. We're robbing women, we're robbing men, we're robbing anybody and everybody. What!"

Neither I nor Wiggie replied. We both just sat and let Dwight's words marinate in our minds. After driving in silence for about two whole minutes, Wiggie managed to finally break the silence by suggesting that we step up our game and rob the next niggah that we saw. I guess his reasoning was that it would make all of us feel more manly.

So after having driven deeper into Long Island we decided to stop in a town called Massapequa. We were all feeling hungry and we decided to dip into some of the money that we had stolen and buy ourselves something to eat. A hamburger spot called White Castle was what we all agreed upon.

After we'd finished eating the Murder Burgers, as they are commonly referred to in New York, we sat for a bit, just to let our food digest. We talked, burped, farted and kicked it for about twenty minutes. Then it was time to get back to work. I guess you could have called that our lunch break.

"Come on y'all, let's be out," Wiggie dictated.

The three of us departed. We had work to do, so we immediately resumed driving in the quest for yet another robbery victim, one whom we all agreed would have to be a black male.

It seemed as if it had taken less than a minute after our lunch break for us to pick out a new victim. He was a black male, about twenty-one years old. He looked as if he could have fit right in with our crew. However, he did have that Long Island look about him. That sissy look. One big difference about coming from Queens or any other borough in New York City and going out to Long Island was the contrasting looks. The city look was a much tougher, slummish look. The Long Island look was more punkish and suburban.

The victim that we had selected was standing next to a white Volkswagen Jetta. He was talking on a pay phone. We parked alongside the curb, right behind his car. Dwight got out of the car, went to the adjacent pay telephone and pretended like he was using it.

Wiggie and I sensed that the guy knew what was up. He knew that we were plotting evil. The guy was wearing a thick, gold herringbone chain with a nice gold medallion. He kept putting quarters into the phone in order to keep his conversation going. As he was talking on the phone, he nonchalantly tucked his chain inside of his shirt.

After five minutes or so, Dwight had stopped pretending as if he was talking on the phone and he made his way back to our car.

"Yo Dee, he knows what's up," I said.

Dwight answered, "Yeah I know, I know. I'm just trying to bait him."

As Dwight was talking to Wiggie and I, the guy finally hung up the phone and walked toward his car. Dwight made his move.

"Yo money, you got another quarter? I ran out of change," Dwight asked.

The kid quickly responded, "No," and he briskly kept it moving.

Dwight got closer to him and pulled out on him. "Don't move, money! I know you already know what's up, so just run that chain."

The guy hesitated as he glanced at his surroundings and pondered his options.

"Yo, money, take off that gold right now or word is bond, I'll murder you!" Dwight screamed that command as he simultaneously got closer to the kid's face and attempted to intimidate him. He came across very convincingly and the kid wisely listened. He took the chain from out of his shirt, pulled it over his neck and held it out.

Dwight snatched the chain and patted the kid down to see what else he had on him. He took all that was in his pockets and said, "Oh, I thought you didn't have a quarter. You lied to me!" With that, Dwight slapped the kid upside the head with the gun.

"Now turn around!" Dwight screamed. "Turn around and start running as fast as you can."

Like a flash, the kid took off running. Dwight fleetly walked back to our car and we bounced. As we were pulling away, I pulled my gun and I shot out one of the windows as well as one of the tires on the Jetta that the guy had been driving. I did that just for extra precaution.

"You didn't have to do that, Holz," Dwight said, sounding a bit perturbed.

"Why not?" I asked.

" 'Cause I took that niggah's keys, so he ain't going nowhere no time soon."

Dwight also had the guy's gold nugget watch, fifty-five dollars in cash and his wallet, which had his driver's license and some credit cards in it. But undoubtedly the most surprising thing that Dwight had snatched was a chrome 380 handgun. One just like Randy always carried.

"Yo, that cat had heat on him!" Dwight informed.

"Say word!" I said, sounding as if I were shocked.

"Word. But yo, it's ours now."

Wiggie decided that we should head back to Queens, so that's where we headed. While we were driving, Dwight said, "Y'all see how easy that was? And yes, it was a dude that time."

Dwight started to school us as he enlightened, "Don't ever sleep on anybody when y'all are jacking them. If I had jacked that kid the wrong way or if I did it like I was scared, that kid would have blown me away with his burner! But I did it right, and now I got his biscuit, the same biscuit that could have killed me, and the same biscuit that probably could have killed all of us."

Again, that made me think I had to be insane to be doing what I was doing. Dwight's stick-up reinforced in my mind that I indeed had to keep my mind transformed into that of a crazed psychopath.

Dwight continued to advise, "From now on, don't take anybody for granted, because they just might be packin' heat. Even ladies carry tiny handguns and mace. If we make one mistake too many, it could cost us our lives. If y'all tell a cat not to move and he flinches, pop a cap in him! Don't waste no time. If y'all tell a cat to give you his joints and he hesitates, pop a cap in him! After y'all get whatever it is that y'all want, make the kid either turn around and run, or make him lay face down on the ground. Once he's down on the ground, fire a shot into the air. That way he'll think you shot him. We have to do one or the other, that way we'll be protecting ourselves."

Wiggie asked, "Yo, why don't we just start frisking everybody we rob?"

Dwight answered, " 'Cause we might not always have the time to frisk, so if we frisk or not, still make the muthas turn around and run, or make them get on the ground."

The lesson on how to jack somebody was over and we'd made it back to Queens. We decided to go somewhere secluded, park the car, sit in it and just chill. Robbing that guy had sparked many new ideas. We had his credit cards, but we all agreed that wouldn't have been wise to try and use them. We discussed how we could have taken his car if we'd wanted to.

We discussed carjacking, which Dwight thought was a great idea, but first we had to find ourselves a chop shop. There, they would take the car apart to sell the parts, and in return we'd get money for the bringing the cars in. Depending on what type of car we could get our hands on, the reward was sure to be high. If we got our hands on, let's say, a 1991 Mercedes Benz, we could probably get two thousand dollars for it. But again, we would first have to find a chop shop, so taking cars would have to wait.

"We got his driver's license," Dwight said. "Why don't we just wait until tonight and break into his house?"

I adamantly opposed. "Nah, I ain't doing that. No way!"

Wiggie agreed with me. "Dwight, that's too risky, 'cause we don't know what somebody has inside their house, or who's liable to be inside. For all we know, there could be a man on the other side of the door with a shotgun, waiting to blow our heads off as soon as we step in."

Dwight said, "Ah, man! Yo, y'all niggahs is soft! It don't matter who's inside the house, 'cause whoever might be in the crib ain't gonna know who they're dealing with."
Dwight paused and then he continued to ramble on. "Man, I don't care who's in the house or what kind of weapons or dogs or whatever they may have. Nobody is iller than me. Nobody! Besides, I thought we were supposed to be a bunch of ruthless hooligans. What's up with y'all?"

I didn't care. Call me soft or whatever, but I wasn't gonna be a cat burglar. I didn't have it in me.

Dwight added, "Look. If we do it, we're doing it in the daytime, ah'ight? Besides, we don't have to go back to that kid's crib if that's what y'all are thinking, because maybe y'all are right. It probably won't be worth it. But yo, how about this? Why don't we just pick someone's crib at random, break in and rob it?"

"Are you crazy, Dwight?" I asked.

Dwight looked at me as if he was indeed crazy, but he didn't say anything.

"Listen to this," Wiggie schemed. "Instead of us breaking into people's houses, why don't we get them to let us in?"

"Come on now, Wiggie. Ain't nobody gonna open their door for any one of us," I replied.

"I know that," Wiggie said as he started up the car and we drove off. "I got a plan. Just hear me out. See, lets go out to Amityville."

As we drove out to Amityville, Wiggie laid out his plan. "This is how we gonna do this. We're gonna drive around until we see a delivery truck or something like that. Any type of work truck. When we find one, we'll follow it, because eventually it's gonna go to someone's house for a delivery. We'll just wait for that someone to open their door, then boom! We push our way in. It'll work. I'm telling y'all."

With eagerness to sin, Dwight quickly responded, "You know I'm wit' it."

I guessed that the two of them automatically assumed that I too was going along with the plan. So I did go along with it, even though I didn't like it. Again, I caught myself starting to regain a conscience. I had to remind myself, *No conscience, Holz, none whatsoever.*

Wiggie continued, "Once we get inside a house, Dwight, you head straight for upstairs. Holz, if they have a basement, you head straight for the basement. If there's no basement then go with Dwight. I'll take the middle floor, the one we enter on. We have to gain control of everybody that's in the house. If somebody tries to be a hero, we'll let 'em have it, no questions asked. After we get control of everyone, we're gonna bring them all to one floor in the house. Dwight, you'll watch them and make sure nobody moves. Me and Holz will ransack the place. We're only taking money, jewelry, and expensive stuff that we can carry out easily. We have to be in and out, no longer than ten to fifteen minutes."

After driving for more than forty minutes, we had finally reached Amityville, and before we could blink we had spotted a telephone truck.

"Ah'ight," Wiggie said. "Here we go."

We followed the truck in a manner that didn't seem obvious. The truck pulled in front of a two-story frame house, on a block with twenty or so such houses. We pulled right in back of the truck.

The truck, which was actually the size of a van, only carried a driver, no co-worker. The driver, who was a black man, got out and made his way to house number thirty-two. He rang the bell, and after a minute with no answer, he left. He got back into his truck and continued on his route. Off to another house he went, and we followed. We followed in the exact same manner as before.

The telephone man turned onto Atlantic Street. His truck started to slow down. At first we thought that he'd spotted us following him. But he hadn't. He was only preparing to pull in front of house number 14, which he did. The driver, who hadn't figured out that he was being followed, again got out and made his way to the front door of the house.

"Lets go!" Dwight instructed. We got out of the car and hastily walked to the house next door, number 16. We had to be careful, making sure all of our movements were crisp and precise. The driver still had not noticed us as we ducked behind some shrubs.

"Put your masks on," Dwight whispered. We did as he said. Then the front door opened. A white lady answered.

"Are you the repairman?" she asked.

"Yup, that's me," the man replied as he smiled.

"Come in. I've been waiting for you."

It was at that point that we sprang up like jungle bunnies from behind the shrubs and ran to the lady's front door, catching it just as it was about to close. We pushed the door open and ran in with our pistols drawn. The white lady screamed frantically.

Wiggie instructed the lady and the repairman to both keep quiet and get on the floor. I checked to see if I could find stairs that led to a basement. Apparently there was no basement, so I darted upstairs to see what Dwight was doing.

When I reached him, Dwight said, "Here, here. Take them downstairs." He was talking about a white teen-aged boy who looked to be about sixteen years old, and a cute little baby girl who looked like she was maybe a year and a half. I guessed that the two were brother and sister.

"Hurry!" Dwight yelled at me. "Take them downstairs so I can see what's up here." I proceeded to bring the two downstairs. While carrying the little girl in my left arm, I pointed my gun at the white boy's head and instructed him to walk.

"Is that everybody that's in the house?" Wiggie asked when I got downstairs.

"Yea," I nervously answered.

"Ah'ight, Holz. Watch them. I'm gonna go see what I can take. If they even flinch, you blast 'em."

I couldn't believe that Wiggie had called me by my nickname. That was all I needed was for the cops to have something to pin this whole robbery on me. But there was no time for paranoia, because I knew that's how a mistake on my part could happen.

So while I held the lady, the repairman and the two young kids at gunpoint, Dwight and Wiggie ransacked the place. Those that I was holding at gunpoint appeared to be incredibly frightened as they sat side by side on the waxed parquet floor.

The white lady was still screaming and crying. She kept repeating, "Let me hold my baby. Please just don't hurt my baby."

"OK lady!" I shouted. "Shut the hell up!"

In the background I heard all sorts of ruckus going on. There was rumbling and bumping along with the sound of furniture being moved.

"What are they doing to my house?" the lady inquired.

"I already told you to shut the hell up, lady!" I screamed.

Just as I finished screaming at the lady, Wiggie came back into the living room where I was located.

He notified me, "We got everything. Let's get up outta here. Yo, Dee! Come on, let's go!" Again I couldn't believe that Wiggie had slipped up by calling Dwight by his nickname, butit was too late to worry about it now.

As Dwight came downstairs, he asked what we were going to do with the occupants of the house. He got no reply from me or Wiggie. There was a pause of inexperience.

"Lady, where's the rest of the money at?" Wiggie yelled. "I know y'all got more dough!"

She didn't say anything. She just kept crying. Dee told Wiggie that he had already found some cash upstairs in the medicine cabinet.

"No!" Wiggie said. "I know this rich white chick has some more money somewhere in this house. Lady, where is the money?" Wiggie insanely shouted.

"I don't have anymore money," the lady said as her voice cracked from fear and from crying. "Why are you doing this to me? Please just leave us alone."

Wiggie tapped me with his gun and told me to check them to see if they had anymore money on them. One by one I went through each of their pants pockets. I took the repairman's wallet. The young white boy didn't have anything on him. When I got to the white lady, she screamed.

"I don't have any money on me. Here. Take my rings, but please just don't hurt my baby." So as she bear hugged the innocent-looking, tiny baby who was dressed in a pink and white dress along with little white dress up baby shoes, Wiggie became enraged.

"What?" he screamed. "What did you say? Yo, ain't nobody gonna hurt your baby!"

The lady screamed and sobbed even stronger. I guessed she was feeling a bit more insecure.

"Oh, so you're calling me a killer?" Wiggie asked.

"Put the baby down!" Wiggie instructed her.

The lady clutched tightly to her baby.

"Lady, put the damn baby on the floor right now!"

The lady wouldn't listen, not until her son said, "Mom, listen to him."

The lady placed the little girl on the floor next to her. Wiggie then proceeded to immediately kick the little girl. He literally punted the baby as if she were a football. The baby began screaming and her mother continued to cry, helplessly reaching her arms out in an attempt to grab her daughter.

Bang! That was the next sound I heard.

Oh man! I said to myself as my heart raced and my eyes opened as wide as they could possibly open. Wiggie had just shot the little baby. I couldn't believe it! The one slug from Wiggie's .45 caliber handgun was so powerful that it had literally ripped the baby in half. The baby's whole right side from her shoulder up had been blown away.

As I looked as the baby's jagged, lifeless body lay on the floor in a pool of blood and watched her brains trickle down the living room curtains. I was in total shock, disbelief, numbness, you name it. My eyes stayed widened, my heart continued pumping fast and I was breathing hard. The type of breathing where you can see your whole diaphragm rise then fall, rise then fall. I scanned the room and stopped after focusing on Wiggie. Then I heard the repairman screech the words, "Oh my... No! No! Noooo!" Then I heard *Boom! Boom*!

Wiggie had shot the repairman. What in the world was going on? I began to think of a way to stop this satanic episode.

The white lady, who was on her hands and knees frantically trying to scoop up her daughter's insides, had her back turned and didn't even notice that she was about to get whacked. *BOOM!* Was the sound I heard from Dwight's gun as he shot the lady once in the back and watched her plop face down next to her dead little girl.

As the repairman and the white lady lay bleeding and motionless alongside the dead little girl, only one person remained. That was the white, teen-aged boy. He curled his body up into a big ball, cringing and preparing for the worst to happen. And the worst was what he received as Wiggie let off his gun. *Pop! Pop!* Two bullets entered the kid's body, which caused his curled-up body position to slowly unfurl.

Unlike the other three victims, the young white boy was still alive after having been shot. He'd momentarily escaped death by surviving the first two rounds. His eyes were open and he was breathing very anxiously. You could sense the fear that he had inside of him.

"Holz, kill him!" Wiggie instructed.

As if to say, *No, I can't,* I hesitated.

"Holz!" Wiggie screamed. "If you don't shoot him, I'll kill you right now! Word! Now shoot him!"

Again I hesitated. But I knew that Wiggie was dead-up serious about blowing me away if I punked out on the execution. I slowly walked over to the teen-aged boy. I remember looking at him as if to say, "I'm sorry." I was so scared and I felt so much compassion for the kid. I mean, I literally felt like crying. What was I to do? I mean, I knew Wiggie wanted me to pull the trigger for the simple reason that if we ever got busted, then all three of us would be going up for murder one.

The scared look that the boy had on his face reminded me of the look Richie had on his face when he realized he was about to die.I cocked my gun and aimed it right at his ear lobe. I held my arm stiff and steady because I didn't want to miss my target and have to repeat the grueling process. Then I squeezed the trigger.

It was so weird, because I didn't even hear the gun go off. I just heard thin air. The sight of the boy's blond hair flying up as if he had been electrocuted was all I needed to see to know and confirm to myself that enough damage had been done.

I had just caught my first body. And it was literally the most sickening feeling that I had ever, ever, ever, ever felt in all my life. Hollywood had always made it seem so easy and effortless, but that was as far from reality as the ground is from the moon.

The rest of that day became a numbing mystery to me. I honestly don't remember a thing that happened after that moment. I don't recall leaving the house that we'd robbed, I don't even recall going to sleep or saying my prayers that night. All I remember was the very graphic and gory details, which depicted before and after pictures of innocent people's lives. Here one minute and gone the next.

Oh yeah. There is one more thing that I remember, and I know I will never forget it, because it's like the sound is branded into my brain. I remember the "Ha ha ha ha ha ha," sound of laughter from Dwight and Wiggie after they'd watch me murder someone. Yeah, their laughter etched deep into my mind.

Ain't No Stopping

It was already Wednesday. I still couldn't remember what happened after I'd murdered that teenager on Monday. However, Tuesday was still very vivid in my memory bank. The act of me walking in on my mother and father as they spoke about current events was the start of a very remorseful day in my life. Not to mention the suspicion and anxiety the day brought me.

When I woke up Tuesday morning, my plan was to not read any newspapers. Watching the news was also a no-no for me, because I feared that I would have to relive what I had done the previous day. My plan folded from the time my mother, who worked the grave yard shift, came home from work at around 8:30a.m. The first words out of her mouth the moment she stepped in the door made guilt ripple up and down my spine.

"That's a shame what happened to that family out on Long Island. I tell you, people in this world are sick." Those were the words that my mother spoke to my father.

My father gazed into the newspaper and calmly said, "Yeah honey, it's getting bad out there. I bet you those were some niggahs who killed those people out there like that. I bet you."

Right then I knew that they were talking about the killings in which I had starred in and won an Oscar for Best Supporting Murderer.

"Mark, did you hear about this?" my father asked.

"No, what happened?" I asked, trying to sound very concerned.

"Herem read this," he said.

I looked at the front page of the newspaper. The headline, fittingly in bold letters read, *Amityville Horror.* Underneath the headline I saw a picture. The house we'd robbed was in the background. The forefront and the most capturing part of the picture displayed a worker from the county morgue. The worker was carrying a tiny, black body bag, a body bag that contained the corpse of Michelle Fisher.

Michelle Fisher, I read and learned was the name of the little white girl whose life Wiggie had eliminated. The newspaper story said that police suspected there was a robbery attempt at the house. The paper also indicated that police had no suspects and there were no eyewitnesses. I learned that everyone except for the mother had died. The mother was in critical but stable condition with a single gunshot wound to the back that narrowly missed her spine.

No suspects, no witnesses. *Yes,* I said to myself. The cops had no leads, so we probably wouldn't get caught. Still, even if we managed to elude the police, I was certain that eventually all of us were going to pay a price for what we did.

The guilt that I was feeling that day seemed to be non-existent in the rest of the crew. We had told the others of our murderous doings. They all seemed shocked, but at the same time, they all gave us praise. Arrest and prosecution was the main concern of everybody in the crew Randy mentioned that if anyone had gotten the license plate of the stolen car that we were in, then there existed a slight chance of us getting knocked. If not, we would be home free.

See, he figured if the cops obtained a license plate number they would figure out where the car was stolen from. The police department would simply try to pin someone from either Laurelton or Rosedale in connection with the murders.

I knew if we all kept our mouths closed and gave things a chance to die down, so to speak, that we would be in the clear. Besides, there were no witnesses, at least up until that point anyway.

Even with the murders hanging over our heads, we still went on with the same old plan. Again on Tuesday we had filled the day with robberies. No murders this time, thank God. However, we did change up as far as who we worked with, and again our means of getaway were stolen vehicles.

Financially, everything was right on course. For Monday and Tuesday combined we netted approximately $3,000 in cash and gold. We were still $7,000 short of our goal. Fortunately we still had three days left to reach that goal. Although we had three G's, three murders and one attempted murder, as well as a double kidnapping in our front pocket, there was no stopping us. We were determined to put $7,000 in the other front pocket.

The dreams of cash, fancy cars and fly women were held in our back pockets. That must have been the force behind us. It woke us up every day with kicks in the butt. Those kicks would carry us through to the night, getting us into all that was wrong and tempting us to do all sorts of evil.

Anyway, Wednesday we decided to use the same stolen cars that we'd used on Tuesday, a very risky move. The reasoning was that we would be pressing our luck if we had gone back to the LIRR to steal cars, because undercover cops were bound to be staking out all LIRR parking lots.

Donnie had managed to come through big-time for all of us. He found a chop shop. It was part of a junkyard near Liberty Avenue in South Jamaica, Queens. Rumor had it that a big time Mafia boss was connected to the chop shop. The owner of the chop shop, Donnie said, wanted only 1991 cars and nothing else. Of course the cars had to be top of the line. Big brand names like Jaguar and BMW.

As each three-man crew went their separate ways, our goal for that day was to continue robbing people. We also had to be on the lookout for opportunities to steal a car that we could take back to the chop shop. Actually, trying to find a fly car became our most occupying thought. See, with chop shops, every day they were getting busted by the Feds. Therefore, they kept moving. A chop shop would be here today and gone tomorrow.

On Wednesday I was working with Randy, Kwame, and Latiefe. Latiefe was our designated driver. We decided to drive to different restaurants and snatch people's valuables as they were preparing to enter the restaurants. For obvious reasons, we were to have nothing to do with Long Island. If we went to Long Island, the cops would definitely have been on our tails the moment we stepped foot in there. Our territory now consisted of anywhere in any of the five boroughs.

The first stop for us was a high scale restaurant located on Queens Blvd. in the Rego Park section of Queens. We parked our car on the corner of 63rd Drive and walked along the busy boulevard. The empty side streets were usually where people parked their cars before walking to the restaurant. The atmosphere was reminiscent of a busy Manhattan street.

Five minutes was all it took for Latiefe and Randy to pounce on a rich-looking couple who had just parked their car. Kwame and I played lookout as Randy and Tee gobbled up the dough.

Once back in the car we discovered that we had made away with $400 in cash and a diamond ring that the lady had been wearing. That was it for the day for us, as far as robberies were concerned. We quickly left the Queens Blvd. area because we knew that in a matter of minutes there would be an APB out on us.

After that quick robbery, we wanted to concentrate our efforts solely on getting a car for the chop shop. After filling our stolen car's tank with gasoline, we cruised everywhere. I'd taken over the wheel, because if we happened to find a car that we could steal and the situation called for quick action in stealing it, Latiefe would have had to handle it, simply because he was the best at stealing cars. Also, if the car that we wanted to jack turned out to be a stick shift, that also catered to Latiefe's talents. That's what he drove best.

We drove around for a while, just bugging out and trying to relax. We cruised all over town and before we knew it we'd found ourselves in Brooklyn. Like comedians, we continuously snapped on one another, but our laughing and horsing around had almost cost us an opportunity. Fortunately Kwame's sharp eagle eyes saved us.

"Kwame, what's up?" Randy asked after seeing the hunger in Kwame's eyes.

"Over there, across the street, that 735 BMW. The one that black girl is about to get in. Holz, hurry up! Get over there now!" Kwame hollered.

No sooner than that was said and my foot was on the gas pedal. I swung the car around, causing a screeching sound, not to mention the illegal U-turn and the red light that I'd run.

"Let me out here," Latiefe instructed. The car came to a screeching halt as I slammed on the brakes.

"No, no, stay in the car!" Randy cautioned. "Don't run up on her, 'cause she might get scared. Play it smooth. Yo Holz, drive up to her real slow."

As I drove alongside the young lady, Randy rolled down his window and said, "Um, excuse me sweetheart, but can I talk to you for a second? How you doing?... Oh you're doing fine? That's good, 'cause you look fine. But you probably already know that though, right?...Ah, I see I got you laughing, so before I mess things up, let me ask you, do you have a name?... Ayesha?... That's a pretty name, you know. It's like it's not too white and it's not one of those over-exaggerated African names like Shaniqua... Oh you laughing at that, too?... I know that you don't have all day Ayesha, but this is my friend Mike, that's Keith, and oh yeah, my name is Willie. And that guy over there, that's my man Steve."

Ayesha returned the crew's hellos. At that point, Latiefe opened his door and got out. He walked over to Ayesha and said, "Ayesha, nice to meet you. Yo, that's a real nice car. Word!"

She must have sensed something, because she immediately started to make her way back to her car as she said, "Yeah, this is my man's car."

"Well," Latiefe said, while pulling out his Mac-11, "it was your man's car, but it's my car now. Give me the keys or you'll be laying dead right hear on Atlantic avenue! You wouldn't want your man to see you like that, would you?"

Faced with the choices of life or death, Ayesha grudgingly handed over the keys. She also admonished us for being suckers who had to use a gun in order to car jack a female. We didn't fall for her reverse psychology tricks. Latiefe grabbed the keys and we were out with a spanking ride. We headed straight for the chop shop. Kwame, Randy, and I followed behind Latiefe.

Coincidence had it that once we arrived at the chop shop we saw Dwight, Earl, and Wiggie. They had made off with a plush, money-green Jag. While we discussed the intricate details of our separate jackings, Latiefe, who had con artistry in his blood, hunted around the junkyard for a man named Sal.

It took him a while to find Sal, but when he found him he quietly explained that we were friends of Donnie and that we had just grabbed two late model cars. He told Sal that the cars had been snatched less than an hour ago. Such a quick time frame had to give Sal some reassurance, because the last thing that a chop shop wanted was merchandise that was simply too hot to handle, such as a one-week-old stolen car.

Sal was real cool about the whole situation. As he spoke, he used a lot of hand gestures. He said to Latiefe in an Italian slang type of way, "Tell your friends to get outta here. I'm dealing with you and only you. This is not a social club. When I do business I only speak to one person. You know what I'm saying? You make money, I make money, y'know? So if you want to talk business, let's talk." After speaking, Sal rudely walked away as if he were disgusted.

Latiefe instructed us to wait around the corner or wherever. We argued with Latiefe because we all wanted to be in on the intricacies of the deal. Latiefe seemed a bit heated by our sinister eagerness to be in on the deal-making. He gave us two options, which were either we could let him and Sal do their thing so we could get some loot or we could be hard-headed and let our efforts go down the drain. Needless to say, we all understood the point that Latiefe was trying to make. We reluctantly left him alone with Sal and we patiently waited around the corner for everything to unfold.

How could someone kill a two-year-old? I asked myself as we waited. *'A little baby who had everything to live for. How could it happen She couldn't have ratted on us to the cops. Man! A two-year-old baby. She probably just learned to talk.* All kinds of thug-less thoughts ran through my head as we waited for about twenty minutes.

Finally Latiefe came back around the block and joined up with us.

"Let's go," he said. "Come on. Let;s go to my mother's crib."

"Latiefe, what happened?" we all asked.

"I'll tell y'all when we get to my mother's crib. Now let's bounce."

"Latiefe stop acting like a homo!" Randy agrily shouted.

Latiefe didn't respond. He just smiled. So we quietly but eagerly drove to his mother's house, which was on 171st, right off of Baisley Blvd. While in the basement apartment where his Mom's lived, Latiefe pulled out a bank roll of money.

"Oh, my man! Oh my! Ohhhh my penis is erect! My penis is erect!" Kwame yelled. "Latiefe, how much cake is that?"

Latiefe explained that Sal had told him that the cars we had snatched were worth at least eight thousand a piece. But since he didn't know us and being that we were black and not Italian, he was only willing to give us twenty two hundred for both cars. He claimed that the chop shop had to keep the rest as a mark-up to protect against possible unforeseen incidentals.

For some reason I didn't believe Latiefe. I knew in my heart that Latiefe had taken some of the loot and put it in his pocket. I was guessing that he'd probably taken two to three thousand dollars for himself and pocketed it on the low. He probably had the cake tucked in his underwear as we spoke. I mean, why would Sal give us a figure like $2,200? To me, a more rounded figure like $2,000 or $3,000 would have sounded better. I mean, heck. Even $2,500 would have sounded better than $2,200. I didn't say anything, but having full knowledge of Latiefe's fiendin' nature and his love for money, not to mention the fact that he probably would have stabbed one of us in the back if given the chance, I just knew that he had pocketed some of the money. He was a con artist in disguise even though he was our man.

So Wednesday turned out to be a heck of an easy day for us. Depending on how much loot Donnie, Erik, and J.P. came up with, we were sure to be damn near only two thousand dollars away from our goal. I decided to spend the rest of that day with my girl Sabine. I needed real bad to make love to her. That would be a real good way for me to release some of the tension that went along with the activities of the past couple of days. No way was I going to tell Sabine what we were up to, 'cause I knew that she wouldn't have approved. But at the same time, it was for that very reason that I should have told her.

See, my rationale was that if I had told her then she would have gotten so upset with me that she might have left me. And with the way Sabine had me whipped, if she had even hinted that she was going to dump me, I would have gone crazy trying to find any way to please her. Yes, if she found out and told me to stop all of the robbing and to rid my mind of the senseless thoughts about dealing drugs, I definitely would have ceased with all of the negativity because that's how much I cared for her.

I often daydreamed about buying Sabine a nice car and new clothes. I even daydreamed about buying her and myself a house of our own and starting a family. All that could happen, I told myself, if this drug thing worked. It was funny, because Sabine would never have wanted any parts of me if I was in the drug game. Yet I had convinced myself to stick with the robbings and the drug plan because I figured that eventually I would be able to give Sabine whatever she wanted. Now, was I weird or what?

Later that night we found out that Donnie, Erik, and J.P. had netted $560 dollars for the day. I didn't want to calculate it, but I knew that we were only about $1500 dollars away from our goal.

Before I slept that night, I made a point to have a meeting with God. *"Dear Lord, please let us all be O.K., especially my family and Sabine. Lord, forgive me and the rest of the crew for killing those people. Lord, you know that killing and crime is not in our hearts. Please forgive us. Lord, give the families of those that we murdered the strength to move on with their lives. Thank You, Lord. I love You. In Your Son's name I pray. Good night and Amen.*

Finally it was Friday. TGIF. Our crime spree was behind us. Yesterday, we'd gobbled up three more cars and brought them to Sal. He gave us about $900 a piece for the cars. The cars weren't that expensive. They were two American-made Jeeps and one Honda Accord. I have to say that although Sal had only given us $2700 dollars, we still made off good. For the week, we'd made more than what we intended to make. Best of all, we were all still alive and free from jail.

We decided to go to the park and play some basketball. The exercise benefited us all. As I laced up my sneakers and prepared to play, I found nothing wrong with what I was about to do, maybe because I was transforming into an athlete and not a murderer. All I wanted to know was, how on Earth did I let myself and my friends who I'd claimed to love, get to the point where we would kill innocent people and have no remorse? Or to the point where we wanted to get involved in something that ultimately was either going to get us killed or get the people around us that we loved hurt? I guessed the love for cash was controlling us.

Maybe it was not my fault for behaving like a heathen. It was bugged, 'cause man, I just hated what we were getting into. I hated it, but at the same time I loved it. I mean, I was a rationally thinking human being, so there was no way for me to justify my actions. The guilt and anxiety inside of me was what would make me feel like I was gonna go crazy. The guilt and anxiety were there because I knew full well what the right thing to do was, but I just didn't have the courage to do it.

Could my lack of courage be the blame for all of this nonsense? I didn't know. But I did know two things. In a quest for riches and paper chasin', I had come very far along the path of destruction, and there was definitely no stopping. The second thing that I knew was that I had to get *The Elements to A Black Man's Fist* out to the rest of society very quickly, because something just wasn't right.

That night, I planned to write about one of the elements and to stop procrastinating. I felt that writing about the elements would probably wake me up to the realities of what I was doing. But again, I felt bugged, because I mean, if I didn't have the courage to stop myself from doing what I knew was wrong, then how on Earth was I going to have the courage to hold the world accountable for helping to stop black on black crime?

"Yo Randy, pass me the ball. Hurry up and pass me the rock, kid. Holz cathes the pass. He sets. He shoots. For three. At the buzzer... The shot... Swish!... It's gooooood! It's gooooood! The crowd goes wild!"

The Purchase

Fourth Crew's second pre-planned breakfast was scheduled for Saturday June 29th. Being that we had accumulated so much money during the week we decided to splurge and live it up. No more small-time Rooty-Tooty-Fresh-And-Fruity breakfast from IHOP. We decided to play like Big Willies and take a cab to City Island. Everyone in the Metropolitan area knows just how expensive food is at City Island. But when most people think of City Island, they think about expensive seafood dinners. What many people sleep on is the breakfast that is served up at the many City Island restaurants. The breakfast at City Island is off the hook! And since we were rollin' just a little taste, we had to splurge.

We arrived at City Island at about ten in the morning. Once we were seated we took a look at the menu and we knew that we didn't belong. Ten dollars for one scrambled egg, six dollars for seven ounces of orange juice. When it all boiled down, though, we really didn't care how much the food cost. We had cash and we were there to discuss how we were gonna make more cash. We pulled out all the stops. After looking at the menu, I was estimating at least a $300 bill.

All eyes in the restaurant were on us. Fourth Crew always attracted attention wherever we went. We were always making noise and cracking jokes, showing no class at all. Yeah, we had class, street class. The simple way that my pants hung off of my butt, that right there was in a class by itself.

The pretty white waitress, who had taken our order amidst cat calls and propositions for sexual favors, finally returned with our food and we dug in right away. We attacked our food as if we were a pack of deranged lions. When the feverish pace of eating had slowed down, we continued talking and laughing. Our conversation was based on a recap of all of the robberies that we had committed during the past week. Randy and I, for whom an obsession with the Mafia has lingered throughout our lives, suggested that we start our own Mafia. A black Mafia, one in which all of the members would have to be Afro-American. No Haitians or Jamaicans unless they were born in the United States.

"Yo, we could really do it, y'all!" Randy emphatically said. "All we need is a little more organization, just like the real mob."

I jumped in and reminded Randy that the real Mafia didn't like to deal with narcotics.

"Yeah, whateva. We'll still deal with drugs because we'll be a black Mafia. A black La Cosa Nostra, that's what it'll turn into!" Randy screamed, sounding as if he was auditioning for a role in the Godfather movie.

"Y'all gotta understand," I said, "even being illegal, black people will still never have anything. Why doesn't the real Mafia deal with drugs? Because they know that with drugs they'll get too much friction from the cops and too many disputes from within the organization. The mob's reasoning is exactly right. I mean, look at the illegal black people. All of the big time drug dealers eventually get pinched or their organization eventually falls apart because of the little people in the organization. The little ones get greedy and be wanting all the glory. They cause the whole organization to crumble.

Even with the legal things in life, black people won't ever really have anything, simply because no one is willing to accept their role. Everyone wants the spotlight. Everyone wants to lead our people. If they're not the leader, instead of trying to help out in another way, they belittle the one who is trying to lead. That's why black people in this country won't ever have nothing. Because on a whole, black people's egotistical and materialistic attitudes always cause a breakdown in their intentions."

"Holz, shut the hell up!" Latiefe shouted, annoyed with my analysis.

"I know," Erik added. "Who do you think you are? Martin Luther King?"

"Nah, nah," Dwight said while laughing. "He's, um, a new Spike Lee or um, Malcom X. Holz, just please shut the hell up, you Crispus Attucks lookin' buffoon!" When that was said the crew burst out into laughter.

"Alright, I'll be quiet," I said. "But watch, even in our crew, as close as we are, this drug thing is gonna cause something negative to happen from within. Watch. I'm sayin', it happened to the Gambinos when they brought drugs in and it's gonna happen to us."

"Yeah, yeah. OK, Holz. Now shut up niggah, please!" Latiefe shouted.

"Earl, you got all the money counted up, right?" Latiefe asked.

"Yeah. We have eleven or something close to that."

Dwight took charge as he said, "Ah'ight. Eleven G's is what we have. Now do y'all just wanna split the loot and forget about this whole paper chasin' thing? I mean, we'll each get a little over a G."

"What!?" Randy barked. "Hell no! We going through with this. I'm in it to win it. All y'all still wit' it, right?"

"Come on man..." everybody rhetorically stated in an effort to show compliance. "Of course we're still wit' it."

"That's what I thought," Dwight replied. "Now it's time to really get this paper. As for any of y'all who still doesn't understand how we're gonna get paid, I'll explain it. See, anytime that you have a business your objective is to make a profit. We're not in the service business. We're in the retail product business. When your business sells a product, no matter what kind of product, certain principles are usually followed. One of those principles is purchase your product wholesale, then simply sell it above wholesale prices for a profit.

Now, what do you do with the profits? Number one is, you pay your expenses in order to keep the business going. Number two, the rest of the profits are yours to keep and spend however you choose. Smart business people save most of their profits and reinvest those profits back into the business. And that's exactly what we're gonna do. We're gonna buy our drugs wholesale, package it ourselves, put it on the street and sell it at a profit. It's as simple as that. Tonight we're going uptown to buy the work. I know y'all heard of the crew called Mob Style, right?"

"Yeah we heard of them cats," we all intently replied.

Dwight went on to say, "Well, my cousin Bunny knows a lot of the kids that are down with Mob Style. She already told some kid where to meet us tonight and he's gonna have some work for us to move when we get there."

Contrary to our inventory plans of a week ago, Dwight suggested that we step it up and buy a quarter of a kilo of cocaine and three pounds of weed.

"Yo Dee," Earl interrupted. "We shouldn't even mess wit' the cocaine and the cracks. I'm telling y'all we should just deal wit' the weed. Think about it. Marijuana is damn near legal in New York, and in some states it is legal, kna'imean? Plus, if we get busted with weed the cops ain't gonna do nothing. And if they do, all we'll get is a slap on the hand, probation at the most. But we won't do no time."

"Nah, nah, no," everyone voiced disagreement to Earl's suggestion.

Dwight responded, "Yo Earl, I hear what you saying, but all I'm saying is cocaine moves much quicker and it makes you much more loot. So if we're gonna do this, we're gonna do it right. We're dealing with both."

Dwight went on to say, "Bunny told me that the kid will sell us a quarter of a kilo of coke for about six. And for three pounds of weed he only wants thirty-five. We'll buy that and still have a little bit of cash left over. We'll be starting off in the black."

So that was it. Time to get paid. I started thinking big. I was thinking about all of the new clothes and jewelry that I was gonna buy. *Yes!* I was thinking in my head, *Yes!* My orgasmic-like feelings were warranted, and very much so. Just think, we were about to purchase a quarter of a kilo of coke, which was the equivalent to a little more than a half of a pound of coke, for $6,000 dollars. If we cut it up right and sold it correctly, which was what we were planning to do, we easily estimated getting back $20,000 to $24,000 dollars. Easily! Even the three pounds of weed, that alone was guaranteed to make us 10 grand. Rich, rich, rich! That's what we were gonna be; young, black and rich.

Latiefe asked Donnie if he had spoken to any of Montana's boys and all of the other cats that were gonna sell for us.

Donnie replied, "Yo, I been took care of that. All y'all gots to do is give me the packages and I'll give it to them, or y'all can give them the packages yourself. They been ready to knock off the work. They already know who y'all are, so it ain't nothing to it but to do it."

"One question," I interjected. "They know us, but who are they? Donnie, give us some names so that we'll know who to go to."

Donnie proceeded to spit the names of those who he'd recruited. "Now y'all know who they are," Donnie added. "So just give them the packages or whatever, and check with them every now and then to see if they knocked it off or not. If they did, just take the loot, give them their cut, and y'all take the rest."

Latiefe mentioned that he had spoken to Gangsta. Gangsta was Latiefe's big drug dealer friend from Far

Rockaway, Queens. "The spot in Far Rock is waiting for us," Latiefe said. "Gangsta has cats set up and ready to work for us. So as soon as we get the drugs we have to head straight out there before somebody else comes and tries to set up shop on our block."

"So Earl, what's up with the spot in Brooklyn?" Dwight asked.

"I didn't speak to my cousin yet," Earl added. "I didn't wanna ask him for anything because we wasn't ready. I didn't want him to think that I wasn't for real, you know what I'm sayin'? But yo, I'll just call him today and get everything organized. Don't worry, that Brooklyn spot is definite, and it's a definite money maker."

"So yo, how are we gonna get uptown tonight?" I asked.

"Why don't we just get X to drive us in his ride? It's small and it's not flashy, so it won't attract any cops," Randy answered.

I reminded the crew, "Xavier is in summer school at his college. He ain't trying to take us uptown. He probably has to study or something. Plus if we tell him that we're going to pick up drugs you know that he's definitely not gonna roll with us, much less take us in his whip."

"Yo, all we gotta do," Randy said, "is tell Xavier that we're going to see Latiefe's cousin Bunny. You know he'll go then. Everybody loves Bunny and her fat tail."

"Yeah, that's a good idea," Dwight said, " 'cause it's not like we'll actually be lying. But the only thing is that all of us won't be able to go. We can't all fit into that car. So me, Holz, Latiefe, and Xavier will ride."

Dwight explained that once we got there, all of us except for Dwight would stay in Bunny's apartment while he and Bunny would go downstairs to the kid's apartment and purchase the drugs.

Randy imparted, "Yo, that'll work, word. But either Holz or Latiefe, one of y'all should actually go with Dee and

Bunny to the apartment when they go to make the purchase. Don't let Dwight go into that kid's apartment by himself. I'm just sayin', we gotta be smart and we gotta be safe, kna'imean?" Randy paused and then he quickly continued on, "Yo, matter of fact, y'all better make sure that y'all are strapped, just in case those niggahs try to flip."

"There ain't no way, yo. I'm sayin', them niggahs uptown ain't stupid," Dwight said. "They're gonna frisk us before they even let us in the apartment. So we ain't tryin' to go up in their piece with heat. Forget about it. We can't take no gun. If they frisk us and find the gun then they'll think that we had plans on snaking them. It's our first time buying from them so we don't need that kind of first impression. I mean, we can take guns, but we're gonna have to stash them in Xavier's car. Randy, I'm telling you, it just won't look right if we try to go up in there with guns on us. Besides, Bunny will be with us and she knows them, so they ain't gonna jerk us."

For some reason I sort of agreed with Randy. But I didn't say anything. I mean, going into a major drug dealer's apartment uptown, with no heat in our waistbands, I didn't know about that. As wild as those Harlem cats were, they were liable to kill Dwight and Bunny. And it wasn't like our crew had a reputation throughout New York, a reputation that carried some weight and would help to protect us. Aside from our family and friends, nobody had really heard of our crew. As far as street thugs were concerned, the illest crews in Queens at the time were The Supreme Team and The Lost Boyz. If Mob Style sensed that we weren't really live, they would more than gladly take all of our loot and then take our lives and wouldn't lose a night's sleep in the process.

"Let's get up outta here," Dwight commanded. We paid our bill and departed from the restaurant.

Holz," Dwight said as we were driving home in a cab, "when we get home, you call X and get him to take us uptown tonight."

"Nah, let Latiefe do it," I said. "Latiefe is more convincing than I am."

Randy replied, "Yo, if Latiefe does the asking, X is gonna know that we're up to something no good."

"True," I said. "Ah'ight. I'll ask him."

Once we reached our block, some of us departed and went our separate ways. The rest of us, including myself, went to parlay at Randy's crib. As we sat and watched music videos, Dwight said, "Yo Holz, Xavier's car is outside. Call that niggah right now before he leaves or something."

"Yo Randy, where's the phone at, man?" I asked.

"It's under that pile of clothes over there."

"Got damn. Randy, why don't you ever clean your room? This place is nasty!"

"Holz, go to hell! I'ma clean it! But matter of fact, I should make one of y'all big-greasy-farting-ass-burping-forty-ounce-drinking-weed-smoking-no-dough-having
niggahs clean it for me! Y'all are always over here like y'all live here or something, so I'm sayin', that's why it stays looking like this." We all laughed.

"Be quiet, be quiet. The phone is ringing," I said.

"Hello," someone on the other end answered.

"Hello. Can I speak to Xavier?"

"Hold on a minute."

"Hello."

"Yo, what's up X?"

"Who is this? Holz?"

"Yeah man," I replied.

"Yo, what's up?"

"I'm chillin', kid. Yo, where you been at, X? We ain't seen you in a minute."

"Yeah, I know. I've been studying. This school work ain't no joke. All these damn calculus equations, nonsense like X to the Z hypotenuse over the IA perpendicular coordinates to the 2,9,7, parallel lines! Yo, it ain't no joke."

I laughed and said, "Yeah, I know what you mean, kid. Just stick with it, though, 'cause you're almost finished. It'll pay off in the long run. Plus, this is your last year, right?"

"Nah, I was supposed to get out in May, but I messed up in my freshman year. So I probably won't graduate until December."

"Yeah, that's right. You got skipped in junior high school just like I did. Man, X, I finished high school when I was sixteen years old. I could have had my degree by the time I turned twenty if I hadn't stopped going to college. I'm sayin', I could have been a doctor by the age of twenty four. That's ill, right? I could have been like Doogie Howser, you kna'imean? But X, you're doing the right thing, 'cause you'll be twenty- one when you get your degree. And yo, make sure you get that degree, kid! Word is bond. We need more educated brothers. Like I said, the studying that you're doing right now, it'll pay off in the end."

"Yeah I hope so," Xavier said. Then he asked, "Yo Holz, you going back to school in September or what?"

"I don't know X, 'cause I can't concentrate and go straight through school like I want to. You know? I mean, I can't do like you're doing. There's just always too many interruptions and distractions in my life."

"You can do it Holz, I'm telling you," Xavier encouraged.

"Yeah, I'm gonna finish. No doubt about that. That's if I don't get killed or something ill like that," I said as I started laughing. "But yo, before I forget, what are you doing tonight?" I was trying to change the subject and get to the point of my call.

"I'll be in the crib, just chillin'," X answered.

"So yo X, since you won't won't be doing anything, why don't you drive us Uptown to Bunny's crib? All of her sisters and her friends are gonna be there. Yo X, cuties with booties are gonna be everywhere, kid!" I added that in an attempt to gas the situation.

"I'll go, but I can't stay that long 'cause I have to wake up for church in the morning," X replied.

"Yeah OK, no problem. We'll leave about eightish and get there at about eight thirty. We'll bug out with them for a little while and we'll be back home by like eleven tonight, twelve the latest. Ah'ight?"

"Yeah, I'll go. Just come get me when y'all get ready," Xavier instructed.

"Bet. Good lookin' out, X. One love."

I proceeded to tell everyone that was in Randy's crib that Xavier had cooperated and he was willing to take us to Manhattan. At that point it was around two in the afternoon. We weren't planning on leaving until eight, so that meant that we all had free time to ourselves. Of course, any and all free time that I had, I would try to spend it with Sabine, or at least talk to her on the phone. I called her and we talked for a very long time. She wondered why I hadn't been spending as much time with her lately.

"Mark, are you cheating on me?" she asked.

"Nah, come on with that," I said with a chuckle. After I chuckled there was a brief moment of silence. I broke that silence as I said, "I mean, yes. Sabine, as a matter of fact, I am cheating on you baby. That's right. I have a new love in my life. Two new loves, at that. You wanna know their names? Their names are cocaine and marijuana. And they can give me what no other woman can. Lots of money."

"Mark, I know you're joking, right?" Sabine said sternly. I tried to explain to her, but she wouldn't even let me get a word in edgewise.

"Sabine..." I said as I was angrily cut off.

"Mark, are you serious?"

"Yeah, but..."

"But nothing! I don't wanna hear it! If you're involved in that... Mark, all I'm sayin', if you are, then you know I'm gone, right?"

"Yeah baby, but I have to do it," I said, trying to sound desperate. "I wanna make some money."

Speaking slow, sharp, stern, and pronouncing single words as if they were whole sentences, Sabine said, "Mark!... What!... Is!... Wrong!...With!... You?... You're not even thinking about your future! So if you won't think about it, I'll think about it for you. I love you. You say that you love me, but..."

"I do love you, Sabine!" I rudely interrupted her.

"No you don't! You probably lust for me, that's about it."

"What the hell are you talking about?" I asked. "I just wanna make some money. Damn! What's wrong with that?"

"What about college?"

"What about it? Forget school!"

"Mark, you know what?"

"No, let me tell you what!" I said angrily. "Sabine, I'm doing this. I don't care. I'm getting into the drug game no matter what! Besides, there's no way that I can get out of it now even if I wanted to."

"Mark, I love you, and you know I'll always love you. But your head must be screwed on backwards, because you seem to be straightforward about what you wanna do. I'll tell you like the Bible says, 'Warn a decisive person once, warn them twice, and then have nothing to do with them.' See, Mark, if you're gonna be stubborn about what you want to do, then fine. But from this point on, it's over. You have your mind made up and I can't be with you if you're gonna be doing something negative with your life."

After saying that, Sabine sounded as if she was beginning to cry. "Mark, don't be a fool. Don't waste your life away."

I didn't respond. Although I knew she was only trying to lookout for my best interests, I had to play like a hard rock tough guy.

Sabine broke the silence, "Mark, you better call me to let me now how you're doing." Then there was more silence. And before I knew it, Sabine started crying a little bit harder. She added, "I hope that I won't have to come to your funeral, 'cause I love you too much. OK, baby? I'ma go, 'cause I can't talk when I'm crying like this. Take care," she said as she passed a kiss through the phone. Then she gave me one last reminder, "Please, please be careful, Boo."

After she hung up the phone, I stood in shock with a cordless phone in my hand. I couldn't believe what had just transpired. For the first time in two years, Sabine and I had just had our first disagreement. I had actually let my girl just walk. After two years I gave her up at the blink of an eye for the greed that was inside of me. As much as I loved her, I had just let her walk away from me with no qualms. I hoped that this wasn't an indication of what the drug game would bring; separation from my loved ones.

Drugs...Money... What was happening to me? I decided to just lie down and relax. But before I knew it I was knocked out. Sound asleep. When I woke up, I was in a daze. I felt like I had hibernated or something.

Yo! What time is it? I didn't mean to get that comfortable, I thought as I groggily woke up. It was seven o'clock and I decided to call Dwight and Latiefe so that we could get ready to bounce.

We got a hold of Xavier and in a flash we were ready to roll. To Xavier's complete unawareness, I had a 22-caliber handgun on me. Tee had a snub nose 32 and Dee had close to eleven thousand dollars in his pockets. Off to Manhattan we went. We took the Van Wyck

Expressway to the Grand Central Parkway, which took us over the Triboro Bridge, then finally we reached Harlem. We navigated through the streets of Harlem until we reached East 110th street, the street where Bunny lived. We parked the ride, got out and entered Bunny's building.

We got on the elevator and went straight to Bunny's apartment. We rang the bell and waited. While we waited for someone to open the door I wondered if Latiefe and Dee were feeling as nervous and as anxious as I was. If they were human then they had to be experiencing the same feelings that I was.

As Bunny opened the door she cheerfully said, "Hey, what's up, what's uuup?"
She then expressed her love as she gave us hugs.
"Xavierrr!" she screamed as she hugged him. "I haven't seen you in a while."

"Yeah, I know. I've been layin' in the cut a little something. But Bunny, you know I'm always thinking about you."

"X, please. Don't try to run that game on me," Bunny said as she laughed.

We all sat in Bunny's living room and talked and bugged out with each other. Bunny's sisters and her friends had all joined us as we sat and conversed. Bunny nonchalantly pulled Dwight to the side and they began talking privately. After about five minutes they returned to the rest of us and continued in on our conversation.

Dwight and Bunny's departure from the apartment was soon to follow. No one knew where they were going and it wasn't like their exodus caused a problem. In fact, it was basically unnoticed. Besides, no one noticed because our conversation was so intense. We talked about music, school and sex. All types of weird and wild questions came up as we talked.

Before I knew it, I looked at the kitchen clock and it was nearing a quarter to ten. Dwight had been gone for about forty-five minutes. I was praying that nothing had gone wrong. I mean, I sensed that everything was OK, but I was just a little concerned. After all, forty five minutes was a long time to be buying dope. Not to mention that they only went to an apartment two floors below.

Relax Holz, just relax, I kept saying in my head to convince myself that everything was in fact OK.

As time passed, our conversation started to lose some of its intensity. I was growing tired and restless and I found myself dozing off. With my neck real limp, my eyes would close then my head would fall either to the side or to the front, then it would snap back into place. After my head would snap, my eyes would pop open. I didn't know why I was so tired. Maybe it was because of the liquor that we had been drinking and the weed that we were smoking.

Finally, at about ten minutes after ten, Dwight and Bunny returned. Dwight was carrying a brown paper bag.

"Yo, where were y'all at?" Xavier asked.

"Oh, we went to the store to buy some soda for the Bacardi. We would have been back sooner but we stopped to see my friend Linda," Bunny replied.

"Well yo, I don't mean to be a party pooper or anything like that but I'm ready to bounce," Xavier stated. Little did Xavier know that his timing for departure was more than perfect. Hopefully Dwight had made the purchase and was carrying the drugs in the brown bag that supposedly had sodas in it. If he was, then we too were ready to leave because we had acquired what we came for.

"Word," Latiefe said. "Lets leave, 'cause I'm getting kinda tired myself."

Bunny's sisters and her friends, who also didn't know that the only reason that we came to visit them was so that we could buy drugs, said, "Man, y'all niggahs from Queens is butt. Y'all can't even hang! It's not even eleven o'clock and y'all are ready to go home and sleep. That's why Queens is the soft, quiet borough."

"We'll be back up here soon," Xavier stated to my surprise. I guess he was trying to defend his manhood or something.

"When?" they asked.

"Oh, in a couple of weeks, after I'm done with summer courses."

"Ah'ight. Just make sure y'all come back. We'll be looking out for y'all," they replied.

"No doubt," we all said in partial unison as we kissed all the girls on their cheeks and gave them good-bye hugs before leaving.

In the elevator, X was acting real excited about our visit. I guess you could tell that he didn't get out much. "Yo Tee," he blurted. "I love your cousin. Yo, I mean I wanna marry her. Word up! I ain't joking."

We all laughed. Then X said, "We have to come back up here again soon."

As we were driving back across the Triboro Bridge toward home, I looked out of the car window and I saw the New York City skyline. It was beautiful to look at, especially at night when all of the tall, exquisite buildings and the bridges were illuminated.

I said out loud, "I want one of those condos over there."

"Holz, keep dreaming," Xavier said pessimistically. "The rent in those buildings are like two thousand a month for a one bedroom apartment."

"That ain't jack!" I said.

X just laughed and said, "Yeah ah'ight."

I had figured, along with Latiefe, that Dwight had in fact made the purchase. Being that Xavier was in the car with us, we all knew not to discuss what it was that Dwight had in his hands. We didn't discuss anything, because none of us wanted Xavier to think that we had used him. We also didn't want him to get nervous, because nervous driving would have attracted the police. So our mouths stayed zipped. Although I must admit, I caught myself one time. I almost let it slip. I was so anxious.

"Dee what did you...?" I started to blow up the whole script, but fortunately I caught myself and stopped speaking in mid-sentence.

As we arrived on our block Xavier asked us what were our plans for the rest of the night.

"We'll probably just chill at Randy's crib or something like that," I informed.

After X parked the car we got out and slapped and clasped X five before bouncing.

"Y'all be cool," Xavier instructed.

"Ah'ight. Chill, X," we replied.

As we approached Randy's house, Latiefe and I were both filled to the brim with excitement, but Dwight displayed no emotion whatsoever, nor did he say a word. He wouldn't budge on the subject of what he'd purchased. In a classic Italian Mafia Godfather kind of way, Dwight said, "Call everybody down."

Latiefe hustled to the phone and started sending for everybody in the crew.

"Yo, Donnie, what up? This is Tee. We got it. Yeah. Look, don't worry about all of that. Just come down to Randy's crib right now. And yo, try to find Erik and the rest of them," Latiefe instructed.

More phone calls were made and after about thirty minutes or so Randy's basement was filled to the brim with Fourth Crew members. At that point, Dwight was finally ready to budge as he continued to speak in Godfatherly tones.

"Ah'ight. Everybody stand around the table," Dwight commanded. We all stood around as Dwight sat at the clear glass dinner table. Like hawks, we watched Dwight's every move and we saw him unroll the brown bag. Our eyes were locked on him. It was as if everything was happening in slow motion. He reached his hand inside of the bag and pulled out what looked like a white brick. After placing the brick on the table, he again reached inside of the brown paper bag. He pulled out what looked like three Ziploc bags filled with green-looking, dirty crap. Actually, it was marijuana packed in clear wrappings.

Dwight placed the weed on the table right next to the white brick. Then he proceeded to turn the brown bag upside down, spilling the rest of its contents on to the table. Hundreds of tiny glassine envelopes poured out, as did a giant Ziploc bag filled with empty crack vials. There were plastic-coated wire ties and much more paraphernalia.

The room was totally silent. None of us wanted to disrespect the Godfather by speaking out of turn. Dwight then crumbled up the brown bag, which was now empty. He folded his hands together and placed them behind his head, folding his right leg on top of his left knee. "This is it fellas...Dig in!"

Instantly we all started jumping around going crazy. "Yes!" We were shouting and hollering like women. "We're gonna get paid. Fourth Crew! Fourth Crew! Roof roof roof!" We shouted and barked like dogs. We sounded as if we were in the studio audience at the Arsenio Hall show.

"Calm down," Earl said, as he tried to restore some type of order in the basement.

"Dwight, what's up? How much did they charge you?" Earl questioned.

Dwight said, "Well, for a quarter of a ki I paid six-five, and for the three pounds of weed they charged me four thousand. All of the empty vials and empty nickel, dime and twenty bags, he gave us all of that for free."

Dwight explained that Mob Style had informed him that if we became regular customers, then they would give us better deals and cheaper prices.

"Bet," we said. "So from now on, we'll just try to deal only with Mob Style when we buy our work."

Dwight stated, "Tomorrow we're bagging this up. Oh yeah. We need a triple beam scale. We also need some baking soda, but were not touching anything until tomorrow."

"Here," he said as he proceeded to peel off $40 for each of us. That's what was left over from the money we'd gathered.

Earl said, "Yo, I spoke to my cousin in Brooklyn, and when we're ready to roll, they'll be ready. Everything is set up out there."

"Ah'ight, cool. So tomorrow we'll get this ready to sell," Dwight stated. "But as for now, let's all relax and go do whateva tonight. Lets hang out, chase some tails. I don't know."

I really don't remember exactly where everyone went that night. Erik and Randy probably spent the night at some females' house. The rest of the crew probably went to a club in Manhattan called Bently's. As for me, I went straight home to try and call Sabine. I tried unsuccessfully for an hour to get through to her. Her line constantly stayed busy. I always thought to myself that her house had to be the only house in Queens without call waiting.

After taking a shower I laid in my bed. I placed my right hand just above my eyebrows and slowly moved my hand back towards the top of my skull. Looking towards the ceiling I gazed into my dark bedroom. What in the world was happening to my life?

I thought, *Lord, why am I letting this happen? What am I doing with my life?* I continued to lay with my eyes wide open. I would blink once every three minutes or so. I guess my brain and my body were exhausted from all of the recent going-ons. I finally closed my eyes and said a silent prayer before going to sleep for the night.

The Delivery

Sunday morning, the last day in June. How did Fourth Crew spend that day? Working. We worked all throughout the morning and afternoon. What exactly were our jobs? Well, there were many different jobs that needed to be carried out. I, for one, was a bagger. All I did was sit and wait for Dwight, the cook, to finish cooking up the crack rocks. After he finished I would place the crack into vials, with some vials being worth $10 and some worth $20 After I put the crack into their vials I set up packages. I made packages of $200 in value. For example, I took twenty $10 vials of crack and put them into one bag. That one bag would be a $200 package.

I also made packages that contained cocaine in the powder form. For that I would get the cocaine that Latiefe or Earl had cut and measured out into half ounces and grams and even half-gram measurements, which is known simply as a halve. One gram of coke sold for about $100 and a halve would run about $40. With the halves and the grams I would do the same thing in terms of making up packages of $200 or more. But before I actually made the package, I would carefully place the small amounts of white powder into what is known as a twist. A twist is basically a snipped-off corner piece of a plastic bag that could hold grams and halves of powder cocaine. Then it was bound with a plastic-coated wire tie.

With a completed package, all one of the members of the crew had to do was take the package and deliver it to one of our dealers. After the package was delivered, we would just sit back and wait for our dealers to push it. We planned to pay our workers $40 for every $100 that they sold. So calculations on a $200 package were simple to figure. When we were ready to collect the money from our workers to whom we had given a $200 package, they in turn had to give us $120. Or we would take the whole $200 from them and then pay them $80. Either way, it didn't make a difference. See, no matter what the gross worth of the package was, we would always receive 60 percent and our workers would get 40 percent.

So bagging was my job. Latiefe, Randy and Earl's job was a bit more complex. They cut the cocaine and placed it on a scale. Being very precise, they would weigh out ounces or grams of coke. Those ounces and grams of coke were actually less than ounces and grams, because it was laced with something such as flour, soap powder or baking soda. They would water down the coke, so to speak. We had to lace the coke with something, because straight, pure coke was liable to kill someone, which of course would have been bad for business.

Lacing the coke also allowed us to stretch our supply, which in turn would generate larger profits. We had to be careful not to lace it with too much garbage, because we didn't want to diminish the power of the coke. Basically speaking, lacing it with too much garbage would produce a weaker high. A weak high would produce unhappy drug users. Unhappy drug users would produce a loss in sales, which would mean a drop in profits. Lacing was a tricky thing and it required some skill, because you had to realize chances were that when we purchased the coke from Mob Stlye they had already laced it themselves. It was safe to assume that we only had about 70 percent coke when we bought it from Mob Style, so to lace it some more had to be carefully done.

Anyway, those ounces and grams of laced coke were later bagged and were ready to be sold. The net worth of one ounce of powder cocaine was about $2500. But keep in mind that if we converted that same ounce into crack rocks we could easily net $3000 or more, because one ounce of coke could cook up 200 or more rocks.

Donnie and Erik were in charge of bagging nickel bags and dime bags of weed, which sold on the street for five dollars and ten dollars respectively. Kwame and Wiggie put together combined packages of crack and weed. A package of weed and crack consisted of twenty nickel bags of weed and twenty dime vials of crack or more. Some packages were worth over a thousand dollars. In all, I would say that Latiefe, Earl and Randy had the toughest job of all. The art of cutting and weighing out cocaine took a lot of skill.

J.P. cleaned up after us, making sure we didn't make too much of a mess. Every now and then he reminded us to go outside to get some fresh air. We needed fresh air more than anything, because the smell of the narcotics, especially that of the crack that was being cooked, was enough to make anyone in the room feel high and drowsy. If we were to get high and drowsy it was sure to hamper production and diminish quality control.

The breaks were also used so that we could air out Randy's basement. We didn't want that smell getting trapped into the carpets and the walls. Plus, we didn't want the smell of drugs to build up to a point where the neighbors might possibly smell it. If any neighbors on our block had become alarmed to the smell of the drugs they would have definitely sought the assistance of the police. And believe me, a police presence was the last thing our crew wanted to see. There were enough drugs in Randy's basement to send us all to jail for a good amount of time. I mean man, two ounces of cocaine was a mandatory 15-year jail sentence. Mandatory!

Our hard work had finally paid off. After hours of working in the basement, our drugs were ready to hit the streets. It was pretty late now. I guess it was close to 7 PM, But we had finally finished. We all assisted J.P. in cleaning up the basement. We restored the basement to a spit-shine, clean image. Cleaning up didn't take us long at all, since there were so many of us.

"We're finished. Tomorrow morning this hits the streets!" Dwight emphatically said. He also informed us that in the morning he and Donnie would deliver packages to our workers on Merrick Blvd. They would deliver it at a time when he thought all of our workers would be out on the street.

Donnie advised him that our workers would be out bright and early and ready to hustle. "Probably at 6 AM they'll be out there hustling," Donnie said. "Hustlers are always up before the sun, getting their hustle on."

Being that my father was off from work on every Monday, Latiefe asked me would I be able to borrow my dad's car in the morning. I figured it would not be a problem, especially with him being off and everything. The plan was for me to drive, escorted by Latiefe, Earl, and Randy to our other two drug spots to make deliveries. We had nothing to worry about as far as getting pulled over, because my father's station wagon wasn't flashy.

"First we'll drive to Far Rockaway," Latiefe said. "Then we'll hit Brooklyn."

Even though the members in Fourth Crew weren't very important people, we all had beepers. For about the past two years we had all carried beepers just to keep up with the fad. But now with this drug thing we finally had a reason to get some real usage out of them.

Latiefe reminded us to make sure that all of our workers had at least one of the crew members' beeper numbers'. That way if they ever ran out of drugs and needed to be replenished, they wouldn't have a problem contacting us. If they ever contacted us with the need for more drugs, we then would arrange somehow to get the drugs to them.

Latiefe also appointed himself as treasurer. Every three days or so, he would start going out to Far Rockaway and Brooklyn to collect our money from our workers. Donnie was put in charge of collecting the money from our twenty workers that we had stationed along the corners of Merrick Blvd. However, once he collected the money he would have to see to it that it was funneled back to Latiefe. Latiefe told us that he would then count up the loot, divide it equally amongst those in the crew, and pay us accordingly. So every three days we expected to see dough in our pockets.

Personally, I felt that the job of treasurer should have been appointed to me. Not only was I better in mathematics, but I was least likely to snake my boys by not dividing the money equally. Not trying to sound like I'm self righteous, but I really feared that with Latiefe handling the money we all wouldn't get our fair cuts.

Dwight reminded us that we had to flip our profits from the first week of upcoming business. It was all to be injected back into one big pool of money. That way, he said, we could purchase more drugs and purchase larger quantities of drugs, which in turn would mean more loot in our pockets.

Fine, we all agreed that the first week we wouldn't make any money. We were going to just pay our workers, and with the rest of the loot we were going to use it to 're-up', a term which meant buy more drugs to replace the old supply.

Latiefe, the treasurer, said that after the first week he would start automatically deducting some money from us every three days. That money, he said, was to be set aside so that we wouldn't have to worry about needing enough money to re-up. In a sense it would be like a forced savings or getting taxes taken out of a paycheck every week.

So that was it. All was said that had to be said. The drugs were ready to be sold. Everyone knew exactly where he stood and we all knew exactly where we wanted to go with our business. After tomorrow, we would just sit back and wait for the money to roll in.

Dwight made one final point. "We have to remember not to let our drug supply get too low. If it gets too low and our demand is high, we'll lose money. The moment we notice our supply getting low we have to make a drug-run to re-up." We all promised that we wouldn't get so wrapped up into the money that we would forget to keep a watchful eye on our supply.

■■■

July 1, 1991. I was up bright and early in the morning, dressed and on my way to Randy's house. I knocked on Randy's door.

"Yo, who is it?"

"It's me. Holz. Are y'all open for business?"

"Yeah, we're open for business," Randy answered. "What do you need?"

"Lemme get four dimes."

Randy opened the door and I slipped him forty dollars. He gave me four vials of crack, then we both started laughing.

"Open for business," we said out loud, as we slapped each other five. It was already past nine in the morning. Donnie urged us to hurry up so that we could make our deliveries. Donnie and Dwight quickly departed for Merrick Blvd.

"I got the keys to the wagon," I said. "Come on, let's be out."

We all piled into my father's car, each of us packing heat. We were each supplied with enough drugs to stockpile a pharmacy. Off to Far Rockaway and then to Brooklyn's Flatbush section is where we headed.

Once we arrived at our destinations, we dropped off our drugs to Gangsta in Far Rockaway and to Earl's cousin in Brooklyn. After being introduced to our workers we stood around and cracked jokes for a while in order to ease the tension. Then we asked them did they need anything like guns or beepers.

Latiefe informed them that he would be coming around every couple of days to collect our loot. He told them to make sure that they kept track of how many packages we gave them and the amount they were worth.

"I'm paying y'all $40 for every $100," Latiefe said. Being that we were done telling jokes and snapping on each other, Latiefe then sternly warned, "There's one thing I ain't gonna tolerate. I ain't tryin' to tolerate any of y'all cats coming up short with my money! I don't give a damn if y'all are only $5 short. I ain't having that. And I won't be tryin' to hear it. I'll know how much work I gave y'all, so all of y'all better come correct when it's time to collect!"

Latiefe then gave out beeper numbers of some of the members in our crew. He instructed the workers by saying, "If y'all ever run out of work, beep one of these numbers. Tell the person where y'all are at and they'll get y'all some more work. If y'all get robbed, beep one of us and tell us right away. And Yo! Word up! Word is bond! Listen real close to this. If y'all don't remember anything else that I say, remember this: when it comes time to collect the money, I don't want y'all to give the cash to nobody. Nobody but me! Me and only me! Not unless I tell y'all otherwise. Ah'ight?"

All of them nodded their heads in agreement. Then one cat who was gonna be working for us sounded like a wiseguy as he answered, "Yeah, yeah. Ah'ight, money. I'm sayin', we ain't got no problem with that. It's the same ol' same ol'. If you paying us forty beans for every hun-ed, then it's gonna be all love, kna'imean? You'll get your money. Don't worry about that."

Latiefe had been brief and to the point. He sounded very hard-nosed and serious, which was a good thing, 'cause we wanted our workers to be loyal to us. The only way that we were gonna get that loyalty and gain the proper respect from our street wise workers was if we let them know straight off the bat that we meant strictly business. Having their respect meant that they wouldn't try to run off with our drugs. It also meant that they would be very punctual with our money, making sure to never come up short.

Yo, it was basically like fear and control had to be instilled into our workers if we were going to gain their total respect. How was that fear and control going to be kept intact? One way was by giving anyone who came up short what is known as a crack smile. A crack smile is a deep cut that runs from a person's ear lobe all the way to the corner of their mouth. A crack smile along with a good butt whipping more than likely would have done the trick. If that ever proved not to be enough, then the death penalty would have been the only other surefire way to gain maximum respect from our workers.

For the record, the average age of our workers was about 19 years old. We had workers ranging from as young as 12 years old all the way up to cats who were in their early twenties. They all had to be treated the same. No one was to be treated special.

So our deliveries were made. We were on our way back home. A feeling of ecstasy could be felt flowing through the air. Dead presidents, Grant and Hamilton, would soon fill our pockets. All of the hard work had been done. Now more than ever, all we had to do was kick back and parlay.

Sold Out

Very much to my surprise, all aspects of our drug operation were going smooth. In fact, things were flowing too smooth. I kept thinking that something was bound to go wrong. I was waiting for friction to come from somewhere. Yet there had been no friction at all and the first week of business was already behind us. Were our unorthodox methods of getting into the drug trade methods of genius? Were we going to help turn Queens into the narcotics capital of America? Yes and yes.

Heaps and heaps of money filled Randy's bedroom, which by the way, was our unofficial bank. By the 5th of July we'd grossed a little more than $30,000. Of course we had to pay our workers 40%, but we were still left with more than 20,000 dollars.

Carelessly, we had let our supply of drugs reach depletion before we were able to re-up. And like we had feared it would, that in turn caused us to lose money. But hey, no way on Earth did we expect our product to sell that fast. See, the Fourth of July was the day that wiped out our inventory. Everyone and their great aunt was in New York City for the Fourth. We should have prepared better than we did for that day, simply because we knew that everyone liked to get high and party at cookouts on America's birthday.

When the Fourth of July arrived, it came with a bang. Our beepers were vibrating faster than we could light firecrackers. All of our workers needed more dope to sell. They were knocking off $500 packages left and right. And like clockwork we kept supplying our workers with whatever they needed. Unfortunately, by Friday July 5th, all of our stock was gone and the inventory shelves were barren. Latiefe had rounded up all of our money and in Randy's bedroom is where it laid.

Saturday morning, July 6th, all of Fourth Crew was in Randy's basement. We all took turns counting and feeling the cash so that things would feel more tangible and real. And boy, did it ever feel real. When it was all tabulated, we realized that we had netted $21,000. All of that money was ours to keep if we wanted.

Dwight formally announced, "This is what we made so far, and I hope y'all realize how quickly and easily and effortlessly we made this loot. Now, whoever wants to get out can take their fair share right now and step!"

At that point, with all of that green staring us in the face, nobody would have been stupid enough to back out, especially with the ease in which the money had come to us. I mean, man! We had taken a little more than ten grand and managed to turn it into $21,000 after expenses, and that was all within one week! So just imagine what the $21,000 was bound to return us.

Everyone in the crew took $100 just so that we would have pocket change. We were so happy over how much money we'd made that no one even cared about the fact that we had let our supply run out. Yet we knew that we definitely had to make a drug run uptown as quick as possible in order to keep the business afloat.

Dwight said that we might as well take a yellow cab uptown for the re-up run. He also suggested that we take a yellow cab and not a gypsy livery cab on the return trip home. Dwight had made those suggestions simply because he knew that Five-O was already hip to cats running drugs via gypsy cabs. Yellow cabs, on the other hand, were very regulated by the city and were usually reserved for a higher class of people so to speak, so no cop would ever have expected drug runners to be inside of a yellow cab.

So what exactly were we gonna purchase? That was the question on everyone's mind. Earl suggested that we try to negotiate with Mob Style and see if they would sell us a kilo for $20,000. But we all knew that even if they laced the kilo ten ways to China they would never sell us a kilo that cheap.

We desperately wanted to purchase our first kilo, because as a drug dealer, buying a kilo meant that you had stepped up to the big leagues. It was probably equivalent to a singer or a rapper having a platinum record, or an athlete getting drafted into the pros.

Anyway, we knew that we didn't have enough for a full kilo, but we figured that we would at least be able to buy three quarters of a kilo and one more pound of weed. Actually, we would be a little short in terms of having enough to buy the pound of weed, but we felt that we would be able to successfully negotiate buying the pound of weed.

Before we departed for uptown, we very carefully sorted the money into piles of fives, twenties, hundreds, and so on. We would count out five hundred dollars in cash before putting a rubber band around it. We had a little more than forty separate stacks of money. Each stack totaled five hundred dollars, and all of the money was stuffed into a book bag.

"Let's bounce," Dwight instructed as he flung the book bag on to his shoulder. Five of us had decided to go uptown. Dwight, Earl, Latiefe, Randy, and yours truly. We made our way to Kennedy Airport, which was literally ten minutes, if that much, from 234th street. We went there because that was the closest place to our block where we could find a yellow cab.

Once we arrived at the airport we saw a sea of yellow cabs with foreign drivers who were eager to get a fare. We hopped into a cab and were on our way to Harlem. On our way there we realized that we hadn't spoken to Bunny.

"It don't matter," Latiefe said. "We'll just deal with anybody we see, just as long as they're down with Mob Style."

Along the Van Wyck Expressway we drove. We talked out loud and in the open. We were so brash and cocky to the point that we didn't care if the cab driver overheard us or not.

"I can't believe that our work sold out that quick," I commented.

Earl replied, "I knew all along how much money we could make. I was trying to tell y'all last summer let's do this. But y'all kept frontin'. Didn't I tell y'all our money would turning over real quick?"

"One week, though?" I questioned with cheerful surprise.

"Yeah!" Earl replied. "And what we buy today, I don't know how long it'll take for us to get rid of it, but it shouldn't be no longer than, like, two weeks."

Randy said, "Do y'all know how paid we're gonna be after the work that we buy today gets knocked off? We're gonna have more than six figures, easily! Yo kid, I'm sayin', this is like some Scarface movie type ordeal. I can't believe it!"

"Well start believing it," Earl said, " 'cause this is big time now. This is how all of the real live cats do it."

"Yo, on the real, though. We need more spots to move this work," Dwight stated.

Latiefe informed us that Gangsta was willing to give us part of a block that he controlled in Far Rockaway. All we would have to do is give him like $6,000 a week and the spot would be ours.

"Six G's!" we said, taken aback. "That's too much loot."

"No it's not!" Latiefe defended. "Soon that's gonna be chump change for us. Plus the spot makes mad cake, and it's not that hot with Five-0."

"Well, then why is he so willing to part with it?" I asked.

"I'm sayin', it's not like he's just giving it to us. He wants six G's a week! Wouldn't you want six G's a week for barely doing nothing? I mean, six G's and you don't even have to manage the block! Come on man, that is a hustler's dream," Latiefe added.

I definitely saw his point.

"Where is this spot?" Dwight asked, sounding very Godfatherly.

"It's right across the street from the projects," Latiefe replied. "Red Fern projects."

"The projects?" we asked, sounding very intrigued.

"Yo Tee, say word? Word is bond?" I asked.

"Word is bond!" Latiefe answered. "Now I know y'all know how much business we'll get from out of that spot. $6,000, that'll be chicken feed."

I had to admit, Latiefe was right. To have a spot in the projects, or even nearby the projects for that matter, was good news. Why? Because the projects were a sure, can't-miss money maker. Yeah, the projects were designed for low-income families, but some of the people in the projects wanted to forget about their low incomes and all of the crime, poverty, and adverse conditions that were around them. So what did they do? They got high.

Who knew where they got the money to buy drugs, considering that their incomes were indeed low? But yo, that was not our concern. The only thing that we knew was what we'd learned on the street. When it came to drugs, low-income families would manage to get money from somewhere in order to support their habit, even if it meant they had to steal. Hey, that wasn't our problem, 'cause we weren't running no rehab clinic. We were in the drug business to make money, even if it meant at the expense of the less fortunate. We couldn't worry about other folks' problems. As long as they kept giving us their hard-to-come-by-money, we'd be ah'ight.

Besides, we were equal opportunity suppliers. It's not like we only sold to our people. Yo, the world would be shocked if we videotaped the drug users that came to buy drugs on Merrick Blvd. See, since Laurelton was in close proximity to predominantly white Long Island, I would be very accurate if I said that it was more of the white, Donald Trump-type businessmen and the Brady Bunch housewives that were lacing our pockets with dough more than anyone else.

Yeah, the white cats were coming across the Nassau county line and entering into Queens County's middle class black neighborhood of Laurelton, Queens in order to purchase drugs and then jet back to their prissy, good-school-district neighborhoods. We were very thankful though, because if it weren't for them, the demand for drugs wouldn't have existed outside of the projects and slums.

Finally, we'd made it uptown. The cabbie charged us ten dollars a piece. We gave him three twenty-dollar bills and told him to keep the surplus as a tip. Yeah, we had tipped him because we knew that he'd done us a big favor by actually driving to Harlem. That's something very few yellow cab drivers did, out of fear that they might get robbed.

We got out of the cab and walked toward the entrance of Bunny's building. As usual, a lot of wanna-be tough guys were standing in front of the building as well as in the building's lobby area. They were all quiet as they tried to intimidate us with hard stares. They did that because they knew we were not from Harlem or any of the other surrounding neighborhoods. Like thug-hounds, they probably smelled the borough of Queens all over us, the same way Queens thugs could smell Long Island on a Long Islander from a block away.

So what if them Harlem niggahs thought Queens niggahs weren't hard? We had heat on us and we were ready to put it on cats in their own backyard if we had to. Especially with over twenty g's on us. Yo, there was no way in hell that we were gonna get played like suckers. We had worked entirely too hard for our money to just simply let it get jacked from us.

The heads in front of the building didn't say anything to us and we made our way to the elevator. We went up to Bunny's apartment. We knew that she wasn't expecting us, but we decided to take a chance anyway. We rang her doorbell and surprisingly, she answered right away.

"What's up?" she excitedly screamed. "What are y'all doing here?"

Dwight winked his right eye, and she immediately knew why we had come to visit.

"Oh, oh," she said. "I was just about to leave, but y'all come in and sit, chill for a minute."

Randy asked her, "Bunny, you didn't go out partying last night, did you?"

"Nah," she replied. "That's why I'm already up and dressed, 'cause I'm not tired. Dwight come over here for a minute."

Bunny and Dwight talked in private in the kitchen of Bunny's apartment. Then Bunny went to her room and got her shoes. When she came back to the living room she told us that she and Dwight were stepping out.

"Yo Earl, walk with us," Dwight ordered. Earl got up and the three of them left. As for the rest of us, we raided the kitchen. Soon both of Bunny's sisters woke up. The smell of burnt pancakes must have woken them. I don't know why Randy had tried to cook pancakes. I mean, the niggah couldn't even boil water without burning it.

Bunny's sister Cheryll hollered, "What are y'all doing to my kitchen? And what the hell are y'all doing here anyway? It's like, what? One in the afternoon?"

Randy jokingly said, "Yeah, we knew that y'all would just be waking up and we wanted to see how y'all look in those short little nighties. And yes, yes, yesss," he added, "Y'all do look damn good! No doubt about that!"

"Shut up, Randy," Cheryll said as she laughed and playfully slapped him. "I'll cook y'all something to eat. Just let me take a shower and get dressed first."

"Can I take a shower with you?" Randy asked.

"Oh, of course you can baby." We all knew that she was only joking but we still lusted in awe as we watched Cheryll seductively walk off to take her shower.

In the meantime we watched television to kill time as we waited. We were watching that phony wrestling garbage, or American Gladiators, I forget. Surprisingly, Dwight, Earl, and Bunny returned rather quickly. They hadn't been gone longer than thirty minutes.

After their return we joked with Bunny for a little while longer, but we managed to leave in a somewhat hasty manner. Bunny told us that even though she was about to go out, she was still getting tired of us always coming and jetting so quickly.

To tell the truth, none of us wanted to leave, especially not Randy. He wanted to stay and wait for Cheryll to cook us some food. But we had to stay focused, and unfortunately we had to go, because we knew that another treacherous day of work lay ahead of us.

Once outside Bunny's building we hailed a cab, hopped in and told the driver where we were going. Then Earl, sounding as if he couldn't hold back his excitement happily shouted, "Yo, they gave us a ki for only $18,000! And it is straight raw! Not laced with no garbage."

"Say word? What else did y'all get?" Randy asked in an eager tone.

"We bought the pound of weed and they gave us another half a pound for nothing," Earl answered.

I figured to myself that the extra quarter of a ki and the extra half-pound of weed was sort of like a thank you from Mob Style to us. It probably was done so that they could ensure our business in the future. Not to mention that they had to know that we were on our way to being large, because after all, not many cats could knock off the retail equivalent of eight and a half ounces of coke and a pound of weed in one week like we had done. So the bottom line was Mob Style probably wanted to keep supplying water to our well.

Earl proceeded to say that he and Dwight had started to buy some heroin instead of the marijuana, but they decided against it. That was a smart move, 'cause we weren't prepared to move heroin just yet, even though we all knew that we couldn't rule it out for the future when we re-upped.

The moment we reached Randy's basement we went straight to work. Dwight sent for everyone in the crew in order for them to come help us. We entered the code 234 into everyone's beeper so that they would know exactly where we were at. But we definitely weren't going to just sit around and wait for all of the crew to arrive. There was no telling where the rest of the crew was. We started without them. Most of us assumed the same positions we had held the first time. We all worked to get our product out on the street.

Eventually, one by one, the members of our crew arrived and joined us as we prepared our drugs. It was Saturday and we knew we had to have the work ready to go before it got dark. Everyone partied on Saturday night, which of course meant that everyone would be out and about the city streets. Which meant... Well to put it bluntly, we knew any Saturday night was money in the bank and we simply couldn't afford to lose anymore money.

Before long, all of the members in our crew were in the basement. We were all working very hard. We didn't even stop to take a break like we had done previously, and boy, did we feel it. Everyone was so woozy and tired. By refusing to pause from our work, we actually slowed down our operation rather than speeding it up like we intended. We had started at about 2:30 PM and it was already a little past 8 PM. But thankfully we were finished and ready to punch out.

We were pooped, but that didn't stop us from jumping into taxis to Brooklyn and Far Rockaway to make drop-offs. As for the start of our new spot in Red Fern projects, that would have to wait until at least Monday. It was no problem though, because all Latiefe had to do was make a phone call to Gangsta and we were in there.

Donnie trooped it to Merrick Blvd. on foot and dropped off work to our workers that were on the block. Donnie loved the hard-core atmosphere of the urban streets. So much so that he would stay on Merrick and hustle alongside our workers. He sold drugs hand to hand just as they did. He said what drove him to go hand to hand was the fact that he loved the cat and mouse games he was always forced to play with the DT's. He loved the fact that the detectives couldn't catch him, and that's how he earned the nickname "Slick-Don." Although Slick-Don was going hand to hand, he never would literally have drugs on his personal possession.

Donnie always stated that the trick to hustling was to strategically place drugs inside a napkin, an old cigarette box, or anything un-useful and just leave it on the ground. If a crackhead or anyone else for that matter wanted drugs, they would simply pay Donnie or any other drug dealer for the drugs. Then they would be nonchalantly instructed as to what to pick up from off the ground. After they'd pick up the napkin or whatever, they would be off and on their way to smoke their drugs. That was done because if the police ever showed up on the scene unexpectedly, then the drugs couldn't be pinned to a specific dealer.

Our drop-offs went smooth and quick. Before we knew it, we were all back at headquarters, a.k.a 234th street. Once we were on the block, I walked to the front yard of my house and sat by myself on the front steps. Looking into the sky, I remember feeling scared like crazy. In fact, I knew that subconsciously everyone in the crew was afraid. We knew that the lifestyle that we were living was not really truly and genuinely us at all. I mean, after all, we had grown up as privileged, middle class cats that had toys, clothes, nice roofs over our heads, and food to eat whenever we wanted it.

Even though hustling was wrong, no matter how I looked at it, I could at least understand cats hustling for the fact that they'd grown up dirt poor and hungry for their entire lives. In fact, the drug game should be reserved for those type of cats simply because the streets were like the jungle and they were the lions and kings of that jungle. Middle class cats like us were nothing more than swift, highly-trained house cats that knew damn well that we needed a litter box by our side at all times. In fact, I could sense that it was just a matter of time before we would lose some of that swiftness. I was just hoping that just like house cats, if we ever lost our balance we would at least land on our feet.

It was ill, 'cause I knew this was no longer a game. We were actually doing major dirt. We were hustling on blocks that niggahs had sweated years to gain control of! We was wild, Yo!

As I sat, I remember saying to myself, *this ain't the way, Mark…Holz this ain't the way!* I sat in twisted confusion. I was in a daze….

Despite the fast lifestyle that I was starting to lead, the previous week was a good one for me. I had managed to finish writing two more of *The Elements Of A Black Man's Fist.* I wondered if mailing out those thoughts I had written down was actually gonna be worth it. I didn't know, but I decided to just write them anyway and hold on to them. I knew that with so much going on it was going to take at least until the end of the summer before I would actually finish writing about all of the elements. Would people really care, though? I thought to myself, *Probably not.* I probably wouldn't even mail them out. I mean, would it really make a difference?

Blow Up

How should I spend my cheese? Should I just blow up the spot and go buy a new car? Maybe I'll just buy mad jewelry and clothes. Then again, I should do something like save my money and invest it in stocks and bonds. Those were the thoughts that ran through my head after a big payoff. Payday had finally arrived for our clique, and what a big payday it was. We each received over three thousand dollars in cash. The good thing about it was that we still had a good supply of drugs to keep things rolling. Man, did I feel good! I was walking around with $3,000 in my pocket, and it was all my cheese to keep and do whatever with.

Saturday, July 13th was only three days away. Once again, people were gonna be coming from all over just to be in New York on that day. Jones Beach, which is located out on Long Island, would be everyone's precise destination. An event called Greekfest was to take place. No doubt about it, our crew had plans to be there. And unlike last year when we went to the event looking like straight-up street bums, this year was definitely gonna be different.

'Blowing up' was a street term that meant buying a lot of extravagant items. For 1991's Greekfest, Fourth Crew definitely planned to blow up. We all decided to go shopping. Our pockets were right, and we knew that we could go to any mall in New York and come back with just about whatever we wanted. We went everywhere: Green Acres Mall, Kings Plaza Mall, Roosevelt Field Mall, The Coliseum on Jamaica Avenue, Fifth Avenue in Manhattan, and basically everywhere else in the Big Apple that sold clothes. Our shopping spree reminded me of the way a woman liked to shop. You know, going into every store and looking at every piece of merchandise. But unlike women who entered every store only to come out with nothing new, we came out of stores with our hands full.

On our return trip home from the very hectic day of shopping, we had bags upon bags of new clothing. All of the latest trends and designer names in clothes could be found in our possession. Five-hundred-dollar gold watches, chains, medallions, rings, bracelets. You name it we bought it.

I for one had spent over twelve hundred dollars on my new gear, which consisted of every thing from silk boxers to Versace designer clothes. I could have cared less about how much I had spent. I was looking at things from the point of view that it was only our first payday and many more paydays were sure to follow. So as far I was concerned, money wasn't nothing but a thing. Very soon we each expected to see somewhere in the neighborhood of five figures in our respective pockets, with still enough left in the pot to re-up our supply. We all expected to see those five figures within a week or so.

With that money, plans to buy new cars were being discussed. Everyone had their different tastes. Latiefe wanted a BMW. Randy wanted a Honda Accord, and Kwame liked Volvos. I personally loved Jeeps and SUV's, particularly Chevrolet Blazers, and that was what I intended to buy.

After we'd arrived home from shopping, we quickly went our separate ways in order to try on our new duds. I was feeling real good about myself. My self-esteem had reached a level that I didn't think it was capable of reaching. As I modeled my new clothes in front of my mirror I had a big Kool-Aid smile plastered smack-dab across my grill. My sister Paula watched as I tried on my new threads.

"Mark, that's nice... Ooh, I like that!... Oh, that is the bomb!... Mark, that is slammin'!..." Those were the remarks that Paula made as I modeled for her.

Paula knew about the crew's drug activity. She didn't approve of it, but she also didn't cause any waves. I had already warned her not to mention to our parents what I was doing. My sister and I were very close, therefore I trusted that she would keep her mouth shut. I assured her that I wasn't gonna get mixed up in the violence that went along with the drug territory. Paula was mad cool. She didn't really have a huge problem with my illegal activities and she showed trust in me. She trusted that I knew exactly what I was into and that I knew my limitations.

None of the crew members' parents knew of our involvement with drugs. However, it would soon be hard for them not to know, especially with the way we were planning to blow up. Our parents were bound to get suspicious as to where the money was coming from, but we were determined to keep them in the dark for as long as possible. Actually, none of us really worried about our families, because we knew that they wouldn't get hurt as a result of our methods of making a good living.

The night went on and I continued to show off my new clothes to my sister. I gave her $250 and told her to do whatever she wanted with it. In my mind ,I wondered if the fringe benefits that Paula was receiving was what motivated her to keep her mouth shut. Nonetheless, I'd planned to also mail my brother $250. My brother Ronnie was still locked up. He was upstate doing his bid and waiting to be released. I knew that two hundred and fifty dollars in his commissary would be butta. It could help him get some weed or whateva he wanted while he was in the pen.

I said to my sister, "Paula, before you go back to college next semester you're gonna have a new whip. It's gonna be one of those Geo Storms, the kind that all of the girls are driving."

"Mark, you know that I can't really drive that good yet."

"So what?" I replied. "I'm paying for it."

"Hold up. Wait a minute. You mean that y'all are gonna be making that much money?"

"No doubt," I replied.

Paula smiled a sinister smile as she shook her head. Then she asked me if I wanted to go with her and Nia to a club in the City.

"Yeah, I'll go."

"OK, good. Why don't you bring Sabine along with us?"

"Nah. Uh, I don't think I can do that."

"Why not?"

"Because... Well see, you know how strict her parents are. They ain't trying to let her go out." Although that was true, I didn't want to tell Paula that we weren't together anymore. Anyway, I planned to go out for a night that was sure to be fun-filled and action packed. Going out was sure to do me some good and help me to relax.

July 13th was now upon us. We arrived at Jones Beach in true to form, Mac-daddy fashion. We had our gold on, along with our new short sets and flip-flops. We also had our haircuts freshly dipped.

Booties were literally everywhere. I mean, girls had on thong bikinis, but they might as well have had nothing on at all. Their thongs looked as if they'd taken a piece of dental floss and stuck it between their butt cheeks. But believe me, no one in our crew was complaining. To us, half-dressed, college-age females was what the Greekfest was all about and we lived for the annual event.

1991's Greekfest reminded me of the Greek Picnic which had taken place about a month before. I just hoped that this honey-filled event didn't turn out like the picnic in terms of violence and chaos. As we canvassed the sands of the beach there was a different aura or ambience that went along with us. It was like there was this invisible glow around each member in the crew. Girls were coming up to us and asking us for our phone numbers! They were asking us out on their own initiative. It was mad ill, 'cause we didn't have to do anything. Although we didn't have to, we still approached females. Our confidence was soaring. In fact, it was amazingly high, probably because not one female had tried to dis us. Not one!

The beach was packed. The Greekfest was definitely a beautiful thing. I mean, literally thousands upon thousands of women were all over the beach. Short ones, tall ones, medium ones, brown ones, dark ones, light ones, Puerto Rican ones, thick ones, skinny ones, many with nice bodies, some with ok bodies. Yo, to put it simply, it was a lustful person's paradise, or a human meat market. It really was

We walked around with both Randy and Latiefe carrying illegal cell phones. Wiggie worked the camcorder that we'd purchased specifically for the occasion. He filmed everything. He filmed me doing things that would be banned in movie theatres. He had shots of people swimming, dancing, and rhyming. Even celebrities were on our tape.

The day was truly worth living for. We ate food, drank beer and smoked weed. To put it in religious terms, we were sinning big time. But for us, that meant living it up. The Greekfest served as like a pre-celebration of our soon to come riches.

Before we knew it, the sun was beginning to shift its location in the sky and people were starting to disperse. But all that meant was that the fun was about to really begin. See, the drive home was always the best part of the Greekfest. The drive home was when everyone from the beach would be at their drunkest and highest point of the day and acting the fool.

During our ride home, people literally stopped their cars on the Meadowbrook Parkway, got out and started partying. With the traffic grid-locked and at a stand still, more and more people were getting out of their cars and joining in on the highway party. At that point, everyone was either taking pictures, filming with their camcorders, or trying to get a last minute phone number from people that they found attractive.

It was sad, but females were just out of control. And believe me when I say that it takes a lot for me to say a party was out of control. But I'm sayin', some females were so desperately trying to get attention from guys that they were literally stripping naked and yelling for everyone to come and inspect their anatomy. Others weren't as bold, so they just went topless and stood through the sunroof of their cars shaking what their mommas had given them.

The day was finally winding down, but we had had a bomb time. We had met many women and we had gotten our drink on. So as far as we were concerned, our mission had been accomplished. Miraculously there had been no gun-plays and no fights had taken place. The day turned out to be wonderful.

Sunday was payday number two, and everyone received seven thousand dollars. Those large sums of money were captivating. I can't describe in words just how good it felt to have that type of cash.

In addition to getting paid, we spent Sunday visiting some of the girls that we'd met the previous day at the beach. And man, they were throwing sex in our faces. A shortie named Tricia invited me over to her crib on Long Island. When I'd spoken to her on the phone I got her address and directions to her place. I also tried to find out what she wanted to do when we hooked up. You know, like go to the movies, a club or what have you. And yo, all I'll say, so as to not give females a bad name is... Matter of fact, I won't even repeat what Tricia told me that she wanted to do, 'cause it just wasn't respectable at all.

I couldn't believe my ears. I'm no Don Juan or nothing like that, but what was so ill was the fact that Tricia was dead up serious about what she wanted to do. When I arrived at her house we talked and watched television for a little while, but before you could blink an eye we were engaged in a very unrespectable sex act.

Again, I have to say that it was mad ill, because the cash that drugs brought into my life made it mad easy for me to sin. Although I knew everything that I was doing was wrong, I just loved my meaningless way of life. And although I loved the life, it was like something more than love was enticing me and pulling me down, causing me to want to sin.

When I returned home I told everyone about the sex ordeal that I had encountered. I learned that I wasn't the only one who had scored. Latiefe, Earl, and Erik also had fornicated with the women that they'd met at the beach. As for Dwight, J.P. and Wiggie, well they didn't believe we had had sex with some girls that we'd only known for one day. But they were determined to copy our actions, so immediately they raced each other to the phone and started making phone calls.

Those of us who had already scored were still not satisfied and we wanted more and more of the sex that we had just experienced. So we too worked the phones like telemarketers trying to contact some of the other chicken heads that we'd met at the beach. It was like a modern day Sodom and Gomorrah.

Randy and I managed to get in contact with two females from Manhattan. They were sisters, so a double date was suggested and arranged. The two sisters, who were named Whitney and Denise, suggested that we go to a club called 'Kilimanjaros', which was located on the Lower East Side.

When we arrived at the club we danced and drank liquor at the bar. But surprisingly, the overall mood of the club wasn't really hitting so we decided to bounce. My head was feeling nice from all of the liquor that I had consumed. I wasn't drunk, but I was at the tipsy stage. I was still sober enough to hear the girls say "alright," when Randy suggested that we go to a hotel.

Being that we had pockets full of cash we decided to go a hotel called 'Embassy Suites'. Embassy Suites is located near Times Square, right where Dick Clark drops the ball every New Year's Eve on T.V. The hotel was extremely expensive, but who cared? Money was definitely no object.

Continuing in our quest for sign, Whitney and I received room 715. Randy and Denise had a room on the third floor. Whitney ordered room service for the both of us, 'cause we hadn't eaten anything. Unfortunately we didn't eat the food when it arrived because, like animals in heat, we were too preoccupied with sexing each other.

The next morning I woke to the sound of my telephone ringing. It was Randy calling to tell me to tell Whitney that Denise was leaving to go home. I relayed the message to Whitney, and she too prepared herself to depart. When she was ready to leave, I paid her. I mean, I gave her one hundred dollars and asked her was that how much she charged. I mean, was that enough for her to get a cab to go home.

She told me that it was more than she charged, uh, that it was more than enough to get her home. As she departed, she told me to call her during the week. I promised her that I would and then kissed her good-bye. I knew that once the door closed behind her that I probably would never speak to Whitney again in my life. Yo, to some people, the way I was living would have been deemed straight-up foul. But to many others, if they could have lived as I was currently living, they would not have hesitated to jump at the chance.

After Whitney was out of my sight, the only thing that I had on my mind was the fact that it was July 15th. July 15th was the anniversary date for me and Sabine. Even though we weren't together, it still marked the day that we had originally became a couple. So I immediately called Sabine. Her bratty little sister Dorothy answered the phone and I had to bribe her to give Sabine the phone.

"Hello Pookie, this is Mark," I said when Sabine got on the line.

"Hi, how you doing Mark?" Sabine asked, sounding very happy to hear my voice.

I replied, "I'm fine. Happy anniversary."

Sabine laughed and said, "Happy anniversary to you too, honey."

"Sabine, can I see you today?"

"Of course you can see me. That's if you really want to see me," she added. Then she went on to tell me that she had seen me at the Greekfest.

"Well, why didn't you come speak to me?" I asked.

"Because, Mark… You looked like you had your hands full, if you know what I mean. Anyway, I won't even get into that. What time is it?"

"It's 11:30."

Although Sabine didn't know where I was calling from, she told me that she would get to my house at 2:00 in the afternoon.

"Just take a cab and I'll pay for it when you get to my house."

"OK."

I immediately called Randy's room and told him why I had to hurry like hell and make it home. He said that he would be fully dressed and ready to bounce in 15 minutes.

On our way home we each described our sexual experiences with Whitney and Denise. We were both feeling like Big Willies as we repeatedly laughed and slapped each other five.

When I reached home, I showered and went straight to the mall to buy Sabine a card and some perfume then I raced back home so that I would be back at my crib before she got there. As soon as Sabine reached my front door, I greeted her with a long kiss and then I handed her the gifts that I'd bought for her. Needless to say, she was both surprised and happy. Then we went upstairs to my room and watched a movie that I had rented. As we were watching the movie she said, "Mark, you know that I still love you, right?"

"If you say you do, then it must be true. Sabine, I hope you know that I have never stopped loving you, and I'll never stop loving you. Baby, why did we break up anyway?"

"Because, Mark..."

"Sabine, I'm going through a lot right now in terms of constantly feeling stressed out, and I need you now more than ever."

"Mark we can't totally get back with one another. At least not until you first prove to me that you ain't involved with those drugs."

Sounding as convincing as possible I explained to her that I wasn't gonna get hurt and that I wouldn't let her get caught up in what I was doing.

She responded by saying, "That's not good enough for me. Mark, you..."

"Shhhh," I said as I raised my index finger to my mouth in an attempt to interrupt her. "Don't say another word," I told her. I pressed play on my stereo and my Luther Vandross cassette came on. As Luther sang, I asked Sabine to slow dance with me for a little while. I knew that slow dancing turned her on. I started to undress her, and before I knew it we were fornicating.

I don't know why it was going through my mind, but I began wondering how my life would change if Sabine were to get pregnant by me. Actually, I would have loved that, 'cause then the two of us would have been connected in an inseparable way. Plus, it would have been cool to have a little Holz running around. Maybe a newborn baby would have persuaded me to stop sinning.

Anyway, later that day, Sabine and I went shopping. She refused to let me buy her anything. I tried as hard as I could to be her sugar daddy, but she wouldn't give in. Even on our way back home, I tried to give her ten hundred-dollar bills, but of course she refused to take it. So as the cab dropped me in front of my house and prepared to take Sabine to her house, I kissed her good-bye and I quickly stuffed one thousand dollars into her shirt pocket. She attempted to give me back the money but I wouldn't take it. She was kinda caught between a rock and a hard place, but she eventually decided to keep the money. I mean, after all, it was one thousand dollars.

"Thank you, Mark. I love you. Please be careful."

Colombian Connection

So far Latiefe had been doing his job very honorably. Everyone was getting their money exactly the way they were supposed to. Latiefe was also doing a good job at making sure money was set aside to re-up. He had managed to set aside close to fifty grand for us to make another big drug purchase, and that was something that we would soon have to do.

Earl and Dwight suggested that we stop dealing with Mob Style. They had met two Colombian drug dealers who were from the Bronx. Supposedly the two dealers had ties to some Colombian cartel. The two Colombians promised Earl and Dwight much more drugs for our money. Way more than what Mob Style could give us. They even promised Dwight and Earl heroin at a very good price.

We were all skeptical about dealing with these Colombians. None of us knew anything about them, nor did we personally know anyone who knew them or vice-versa. Why should we travel all the way to the Bronx to buy drugs and run the risk of getting robbed or busted by the cops? For all we knew, the two Colombians could have been Feds. So why run all the risks when we had a good drug connection in Harlem? No one in the crew was really big on the idea. But with Dwight and Earl's persistence and with their constant pleading, badgering, and urging, we gave in and decided to go along with their newfound Colombian connection.

"So, are yall wit' it?" Earl asked.

Reluctantly we all agreed, "Yeah, we wit' it."

"Well, we have to go up to the Bronx today, then," Earl said. "Our inventory is running real low."

Earl, Dwight, Wiggie, and Latiefe decided to make the drug run to the Bronx. Armed and with close to fifty thousand dollars in hand, the four of them left for the

Bronx. As for the rest of us, we just stayed on the block and chilled. All we could do was hope that the drug run would turn out alright.

Later that day, a girl that I'd met in Brooklyn called me. I decided to go spend some time with her to see what she was about. She lived in the Marcy Projects. When I reached her apartment I knew right away that I didn't like the atmosphere that she was living in. Nah, I didn't like it at all, but I was there, so what could I do? I couldn't just up and leave as soon as I'd arrived.

Her place was wild, to say the least. Little kids and babies scurried around her apartment, toys were everywhere, dirty dishes were in the kitchen sink, soggy corn flakes were in a bowl on the table and the bowl looked as if it had been there for hours. It was typical and reminiscent of a welfare home.

Her name was Toni. The two of us talked for a long time, over three hours, as a matter of fact. To my surprise, she was a very intelligent girl. Despite the fact that she had two kids, Toni still managed to keep up a 3.0 average at New York University. NYU is a very prestigious school, known all around the world for its high academic standards.

As she was telling me about her future plans of becoming a doctor, my beeper went off.

"Toni, can I use your phone?"

"Sure," she said as she went to retrieve her cordless phone.

Kwame's number had appeared on my beeper. After reaching him, he told me to come to his crib right away. His parents were in North Carolina visiting relatives, so his house was where we were going cut, cook and bag up our new supply. He couldn't tell me all of the details, but he told me that Dwight and the rest of them had returned from the Bronx with an enormous amount of dope.

"Ah'ight. I'll be there in about a half," I informed Kwame before ending the call.

"Toni, I'm sorry, but I gotta bounce. Something came up unexpected."

"Oh, you gotta leave so soon?" Toni sounded disappointed.

"Yeah. Like I said, something real unexpected and urgent came up. I gotta get back to Queens."

"Well, when can I come out to Queens to see you?"

I replied, "Just call me whenever you want to come."

Toni put on a pair of slippers and decided that she wanted to *walk* me downstairs and show me the way out.

"You want to *walk* me downstairs?" I asked. "Are you bugging? Let's take the elevator. I mean, you do live on the 4th floor." Actually, the distance of being on the 4th floor was not the problem. The problem was that I was scared as hell to walk down four flights of stairs. I didn't know who was bound to be lurking in the projects' staircase. I was liable to run into the projects' version of Freddy Kreuger.

"Holz," she said in a persuading manner, "just walk with me."

Reluctantly, I entered into the stairwell with her. When we arrived at the first landing, she stopped.

"You're not gonna give me a good-bye kiss?" she asked.

"Not in here I ain't! Well, I mean, I was gonna do that when we got outside."

She didn't say anything, and before I knew it, I was slobbing her down. She stopped kissing me and unzipped my pants. I was gonna stop her, 'cause I just didn't know what to think. I was really buggin' out. Like I said, I was gonna stop her, but it was too late. She was already showing me her true colors. And besides, it was feeling way too good for me to have her stop.

Toni was a real fine and healthy brown-skin young lady. I couldn't believe what she was doing, but I definitely didn't want her to stop. It was unreal! I was thinking to myself, *Oh, now I see where all of those damn kids came from.*

After we were finished we scrambled to put our clothes back on, and I lied and told her that I would definitely see her again. On my way home I came to the conclusion that the money our crew was making was working wonders for us. Sex for us was now commonplace. Whenever we wanted it we got it, from almost any female we chose.

When I reached Kwame's house everybody wanted to know what had taken me so long to get there. "Oh, I was busy," I devilishly told them.

"Well, come on. Help us get this ready," Dwight commanded.

As we worked on our drugs, Dwight told me exactly what they had purchased. He also told me how much they'd paid for it and how they were able to get it so dirt cheap. After hearing his report I was able to soundly say that our new Colombian connection was definitely a smart business move. We definitely weren't gonna deal with Mob Style anymore. The deal we struck with the Colombians was way too enticing.

I'll explain very quickly how the Colombians were able to give us drugs at bargain basement prices. See, it was alleged that the Central Intelligence Agency and the Drug Enforcement Agency were down with Nicaragua. Their alleged involvement basiclly stemmed from the U.S. wanting to help Nicaragua's Democratic Force, known as the Contras. They wanted to help them beat Nicaragua's Cuban-supported socialists, the Sandinista government, which had overthrown U.S.-backed dictator Anastasio Somoza. It was also alleged that the CIA and the DEA, who were supposed to protect U.S. citizens basically turned their heads and let narcotics funnel into America. It was alleged that they allowed drugs to be smuggled into the U.S. so that they could turn around and sell the same drugs to kingpins across the country at unbelievably cheap prices.

And of course it was alleged that after the agents sold the drugs to the kingpins throughout the United Sates, they would take their cut of the dough, and then they would send the rest of the money to help finance the Contras' military efforts. Supposedly, all this went on and the government, A.K.A certain ex-presidents, looked the other way as if they were stupid. I guess they didn't care, because the drugs and guns were only being dumped into the black communities.

Yeah, every now and then people would see on the news a story about how a huge drug bust was made. And see, stories like that were purposely reported just to make it seem as if the drug problem in America was being fought. But in fact, there was no drug problem in America. It was a corruption problem.

Anyway, back to the story at hand. Supposedly these Colombians from the Bronx were dealing directly with a DEA agent who was getting dugs that had been placed onto planes that landed in New York's Kennedy airport. Allegedly, the agent would bring the drugs to the Bronx and sell it to the Colombians. Being that the CIA and DEA agents dealt with such large quantities, it meant that they were able to sell a kilo for as little as $3,000 and still make a profit! Hell, they weren't paying anything for it. The Coca Leaf plant was a natural resource in those foreign countries, so it was nothing but huge profit all the way around.

Enter the Colombians we knew. Supposedly they paid these agents $3,000 for a kilo of coke and then they turned around and sold it to us. So that meant that if they sold it to us for anything over $3,000 they made a profit.

Similar to us, the Colombians also wanted to make huge profits, so all they had to do was beat the going street rate for a kilo of coke, which was in the $24,000 range. Even if you're not the best in math you could easily see that it wasn't hard for them to beat that $24,000 figure and eventually they would dominate the wholesale cocaine distribution in New York.

That Friday the 19th was Xavier's last day of summer classes. He called me and told me that he wanted to get drunk and party later that night. It was to be his way of celebrating all of the studying he had been doing. Xavier wanted to go back to Harlem to visit Bunny like he'd promised her he would do once school was over.

"Ah'ight, bet," I said. "I'll go to Bunny's with you."

Xavier asked me to call her and make sure that she would be home when we came. When I called to speak to Bunny, her sister answered the phone. She wanted to know why we had left so quickly the last time we were there.

"Bid'ness," I nonchalantly told her. "We had moves to make. We're bid'ness men." I went on to tell her that we were planning to come see them later that day.

"Will y'all be home?" I asked.

"Yeah, we'll be here. Just as long as y'all don't pull that same 'hi and good-bye' garbage like y'all always do. I'm sayin', I understand that y'all have to take care of business and all, but I'm sayin' y'all could still chill like y'all used to."

"Nah, I hear you, and we're definitely gonna stay for a while this time," I promised. "Is Bunny there?"

"Yeah, she's here."

"Let me speak to her real quick."

"OK, hold on a minute. Bunny! The phone." I heard Bunny in the background hollering that she had it.

"Hello," Bunny said as she took the hold of the phone.

"What's up, Bunny? This is Holz."

"Hey Holz, what's up, Boo?"

"Nothing much. I'm chillin'. Yo, Xavier and us are gonna shoot out there and come check y'all tonight if that's ah'ight with you."

"Yeah, that's cool with me," she responded. "Holz, you already know that y'all can come by and kick it whenever y'all get ready. Oh Holz, good thing that you called, 'cause that kid PI from Mob Style asked me to find out when were y'all coming back to buy some more work."

"Oh, I ain't tell you? We ain't tryin to see them niggahs no more. We're buying our joints from these Colombians up in the Bronx. But I'll explain that to you later."

"Oh, ok then," Bunny said very nonchalantly. "I'll tell him when I see him, 'cause I know he's gonna ask what's up. So I'll see y'all tonight, right?"

"Yeah, tonight," I said. "Bunny, listen. I'm gonna hit you off with some loot for helping us out, ah'ight?"

"Holz, now you know you don't have to do that. I'm good."

"Yeah, I know honey, but I'm sayin' it'll be my way of saying thank you. Does twenty five hundred sound good?"

"Holz you don't..."

"Ah'ight Bunny, I'll see you tonight," I said as I rudely interrupted her.

Later that night, Xavier, Donnie, Earl and myself decided to leave for uptown. We piled into Xavier's little blue Toyota and made our way to Harlem.

"One more semester and I'm done with school for good!" Xavier emphatically said as we drove in his ride. "Yeah, just one more semester," he exhaled. I asked Xavier had he considered attending graduate school. He said he planned to just try and land a job and work for a few years, then maybe he would consider graduate school.

When we reached Bunny's building on East 110th Street, we saw her already standing outside, chilling with some of her friends. We parked the car and walked over to her. Bunny, in a hurried type of way, took me to the side and asked, "Holz did you bring money with you?"

"Yeah," I said. "I told you that I got you. Don't worry about it. I'ma lace you."

"No, it's not that," she said, sounding kind of annoyed. "PI was bugging me and asking me why aren't y'all dealing with them anymore. I didn't tell him about the Colombians or whoever it was that you said y'all were messing with, but I mean, he was really stressing me, and I don't wanna have to keep hearing this niggah's mouth every time I'm in the street."

"Bunny, I got money on me, but not that kind of cake! I only got about four G's in my pocket."

"Yeah, ok. That's good," Bunny said, sounding kind of desperate. "He told me that the next time y'all bought from him that he would hit me off with some weed for myself, for free. I guess he's gonna try to spit game to y'all and give y'all a good deal on some more work. You know, he's probably gonna try to gas y'all and lure y'all back as customers, especially if he finds out that y'all are going somewhere else."

Being as street smart as I was, I thought to myself, *Nah Holz, something ain't right.* I couldn't figure out what it was, but for some reason I was starting to smell some kind of a rat. Was Bunny trying to set us up? I wondered. Nah, why was I bugging? There was no way in hell that she would ever do that, but I was still feeling a bit suspicious. Why all of a sudden did it seem like PI was fiendin' for us to buy some drugs? I'm sure he had many other dealers and crews that he was supplying throughout the city.

After quickly pondering over the situation I said, "Ah'ight, Bunny, listen. I'll buy something off this cat, but I'm just doing it so that you can get this weed that he promised you. You sure that he wasn't just frontin' when he told you that he was gonna hit you off?"

"Holz, I doubt that he was frontin'. But to be honest, it's not even about the free weed. I want you to talk to this niggah and let him know where y'all are at so that he won't be stressin' me."

Since I was definitely not one to be frontin' I wanted to make moves to see PI. Even though my instincts hadn't figured out what was up, I knew that I had to handle the crew's bid'ness with PI.

"OK then, let's hurry and go see that niggah," I instructed.

"Ah'ight. Good, 'cause I already told him we would be there."

Xavier, Donnie, and Earl wanted to know where Bunny and I were off to.

"We'll be right back," I told them. "Y'all just chill here for a minute and wait for us."

I was praying that the three of them wouldn't follow us upstairs, but they did. *Damn!* I thought to myself. I didn't care too much if Donnie and Earl came along, in fact it was probably better if they were with me just in case in drama jumped off, but I didn't want X to know what was up.

"Where y'all going?" Xavier asked.

Up to my friend's apartment," Bunny answered. "It won't take long. I just have to tell him something real quick. We'll be in and out."

Unfortunately, Donnie and Earl were too dull to take the hint that Bunny and I didn't want to be accompanied by them. So of course, being that Donnie and Earl had followed us, Xavier was also right on our coat tails.

When we reached the entrance to PI's apartment we were all frisked at the door.

"Yo, what's up with this?" Xavier asked, as the guy who was frisking us took a biscuit from me and a biscuit from Donnie.

"Don't worry about it, X," I said in an effort to calm him down. "I'll explain it to you later. Just chill."

Xavier was rightfully very alarmed as he asked, "Yo Holz, what the hell are y'all doing with guns? Yo, whose apartment is this? Holz, how long are we gonna be here?"

I angrily, and a bit fearfully replied, "I'll tell you later, X! Now just chill! Damn!" That was the last thing I needed was to have X nagging me like some woman. I was trying my hardest to figure out what, if anything, was about to go down. I was trying to figure out what moves I was gonna make. And at the same time I felt somewhat like a parent because I knew that if anything jumped off that I would have to make sure that X was ah'ight.

We all knew that we were about to enter a drug apartment, or should I say a drug warehouse. All of us knew that except for X. And that of course explained why he'd gotten so alarmed when we were all frisked. Xavier wasn't the only alarmed one in our clique, 'cause I could sense that Donnie and Earl also weren't too big on the idea of stepping into that apartment, especially without our burners.

We all entered the apartment amidst the sound of loud rap music that was being played in the background. From what I remember it sounded as if a Kid Capri mix tape was playing. Including the big diesels and sweaty-looking guy who had frisked us, there were four guys already in the apartment. There was also a sexy young lady inside the apartment that we didn't know.

We all were very cordially invited, in a street kind of way, to sit down on a leather couch that was in the living room. As we sat, we were all nervously looking at each other and no one was talking. A blunt was quickly rolled, sparked, and handed to Donnie. Donnie took a puff and then he proceeded to pass the blunt around for all of us to smoke. No one was really taking deep pulls on the blunt, 'cause we were all feeling very uncomfortable.

PI then called me over to him and out of the earshot of everyone else he said, "Yo Holz, what's up, man? I'm PI." He gave me a pound along with that quick ghetto hug.

"What's up, kid?" I answered. *How did he know my name?* I wondered. I mean, he never actually met me before. And why had he singled me out as the go-to guy in our crew? I guess he'd heard Xavier when Xavier had called out my name.

"So what's up? You or your boys want something to drink? Some Bacardi? Some Kristal?"

"Oh nah, we straight. Good lookin' out, though."

"Yo Holz, so on the business tip, what can I lace y'all with?"

"You talking in terms of work?" I asked.

PI, who stood at about 6'3" and two hundred and thirty pounds, looked at me as if I was stupid, then he replied, "Yeah, I'm talking in terms of work. What the hell else did y'all niggahs come here for? Especially with burners on y'all waist?"

At that point I began to think that I should have told PI to get us a drink. That way we wouldn't have been coming across as so nervous and edgy. I know that the gangster records and the gangster movies never reveal that nervous side that thugs have, but I for one was getting extremely nervous.

"Oh nah, see, I didn't come to buy nothing. I only got like four G's on me. Didn't Bunny tell you?" I questioned.

PI, who had a diamond-studded pinky ring on his right hand, slowly raised his drink to his mouth and took a sip. Then, sounding very arrogant, he sucked some air into his nose and said, "Nah potnah, she didn't tell that. So what about your boyz? They got loot on them, or what?"

"Yeah they got loot but they didn't come to buy nothing either. We just came to chill, you kna'imean? We don't want to blow up too fast and have the Feds breathing down our backs," after saying that I nervously chuckled.

"What's up, Holz? Man, y'all trying to play us or what?" PI asked, sounding as if he was truly ticked off.

At that point I was feeling mad shook. "Nah man, it ain't even like that."

PI knew he was in control and he could sense my fear as he remained quiet. Trying harder to ease the tension I reassured him, "Yeah, like I said, see, it's not even like that, you know? I mean, I'm sayin', y'all niggahs hooked us up and we ain't gonna ever forget how y'all hit us off lovely. Yeah, y'all hit us off a little something when we didn't really have nothing going on, you kna'imean? So I'm sayin', we wouldn't ever snake y'all."

In an attempt to call my bluff PI said, "Ah'ight, I hear what you sayin' kid. But yo, listen. I'll give you a kilo for four G's right now, and y'all can come back next week and I'll give y'all the same price. What's up?"

Like I said, I was shook and PI could sense it, but I knew that I couldn't just let him totally think that I was a sucker. So I added a little bass to my voice and I too donned a serious thug look. "Yo PI, I'll be straight up with you. I'll buy the kilo for four G's tonight, but that's all I'm buying. And yo, I ain't gonna stand here and lie in your face and tell you that we'll be back next week, 'cause I doubt that that's gonna happen."

"What's up? Your money ain't right or something like that?" PI inquired.

I knew that four G's for a kilo was a dynamite deal, but I also knew that the Colombians could either match or beat that price. My knowledge of what the Colombians could do for us and for just about any other drug dealer in the city is what led me to believe that PI somehow got wind of the fact that we had purchased drugs from the Colombians. That had to be why he brought his figure so low and said four thousand. He probably lost mad customers like us to the Colombians and he had to have heard that they were selling kilo's for as low as four G's.

Yeah, PI wanted to test me and see how I would react when he offered me the ki for four G's. And yeah, I could have fronted and acted all excited about the price and even made real plans to continue to buy from them if they were to promise us that price from now on. But I knew that they didn't have that kind of juice with the CIA and the DEA and that eventually they would balk on the four thousand-dollar a kilo deal. And to get PI out of Bunny's hair, I had to hold my ground and just straight up tell him what was up.

I mean hell, if he was gonna lose us as a customer and if his distribution racket was hurting because of the Colombian competition then all he had to do was start taking over other cats' retail operations and he would be fine. Actually, as I quickly thought, that was probably his only option, because I doubt that the Colombians would have even sold work to Mob Style. Mob Style was a form of competition to them.

"Nah, our money is on point. I'm just sayin'."

"Oh word," he said, as if he could read my mind. "Ah'ight. So your money is right and all you want is that one kilo? You don't want nothin' else and you won't be back for nothin' else? Come on, niggah, you know you can't get that price anywhere else on the entire East Coast! Holz, don't dis us! Man, you know we hit y'all off with like what, a free half-pound of weed and we basically gave y'all a kilo when y'all couldn't even afford to buy a full one a couple of weeks back. And this is how y'all cats from Queens turn around and front in a niggah's face? Niggah, we the hand that fed y'all and you gonna straight try to play us like that?"

Some of my fears were starting to subside and I was beginning to get a bit annoyed. I mean, the niggah was talking to me like he basically had handed everything to us in the past. He was sounding as if we had been desperate and came crawling on our hands and knees, begging for a handout. Man, we had worked our butts of to get to where we were, and the truth of the matter was that we hadn't never *asked* them for a got-damn thing for free!

I clearly over stepped my bounds as I responded to PI, "Like I already said, good looking out with that work in the past. But that's it, kid! I'm sayin', we'll see y'all, but I ain't gonna promise you that we'll be back this week. Now come on, money. Stop stressing me. Word!"

PI looked as if he had demons inside of him. He immediately reached into his waistband and pulled out a silver, twenty-two long, with the seven-inch barrel. "What!? You clown ass niggah!" is what he screamed as he fired at me.

I'll tell you, and believe me when I do, that having the barrel of a hostile gun cocked and looking you in the face is one of the most frightening experiences in the world. As soon as I saw him reaching for the gun I started sweating razor blades.

"AHHH!" I screamed as I put my hands up to ward off the bullet. The bullet struck me in my left forearm. As I tried to shield myself I had violently made a 180 degree turn and I fell very hard, face down to the floor.

As I lay motionless on the floor I was earnestly praying to God to stop the madness. I was literally terrified and about to piss on myself, but I made sure not to move. I then heard Earl yell, "Yo, what's up? What's going on?"

Bunny was screaming. X was screaming like a little girl, and I don't remember if I heard Donnie. Then it sounded like that big bodyguard-looking guy who had frisked us was telling Earl to be quiet. "Yo, money! Shut the hell up, Kid! I want all y'all to shut the hell up and be quiet!"

I heard PI ordering everybody to get face down on the floor. "Get on the floor right now! And turn over! Bunny, you too!"

In a frantic plea, Bunny asked, "PI, what's up? Baby, what are you doing? Why are y'all doing this?"

"Bunny, get on the got-damn floor!" he insanely screamed. "All y'all cats is dying right got-damn now! That's what's up!"

At that point I was in a state that was beyond total fear, but just before death. And the only thing that I could seriously think about was my Moms. I no longer felt the pain from the gunshot wound to my forearm. I would have given anything to wake up from that nightmare. I was praying that the whole episode was just a dream where I was falling, but unfortunately I knew that it was the real deal, 'cause I was too close to the ground and I hadn't woke yet. I personally testified to the term 'scared the crap out of me.' I didn't want to check, but I thought I had just violated my underwear.

"Yo, turn the stereo up as loud as it'll go," PI angrily instructed.

After the volume was raised I heard 'plunk-plunk.' Then there was a pause, which was followed by 'plunk-plunk-plunk.' Then I heard a single 'plunk.' After that, I barely heard Bunny's petite voice over the music as she screamed in terror. Then I heard 'plunk plunk' and I no longer heard Bunny screaming.

"Yo, check their pockets!" PI instructed. "I know all of them got loot. Make sure y'all get all of it! These niggahs still owe us like eight G's and they tryin' to bounce on the bill!"

"PI, what's up with this niggah? You want me to pop a cap in him, too?" someone asked.

"Oh, hell yeah!" PI answered. "Especially him! Murder all these cats."

After PI had barked the orders of execution, he started chanting, "Mo' money, mo' homicide, mo' murder!"

Bang! Bang! Bang! was what followed, along with a writhing, burning pain and two gaping holes that were now in my back. I, along with everyone else who was unfortunately in the room, had just been shot. It felt like the wounds were aimed at the back of the head, execution style.

"God, please, please, let me live," I remember quietly begging. One bullet went into my shoulder blade. The other bullet felt as if it was in my skull. But actually, it had entered the lower part of my neck, right near the base of my head. The third shot must have missed, or I just was in too much pain to feel it.

I lay as limp as an impotent man. My eyes were closed and I was in shock. My forearm and my back felt as though they were on fire. I was in extreme pain, but yet I refused to scream. Instinctively, I wanted to fight back. I was ready to grab hold of the person who was now rummaging through my pockets. I wanted that four G's that they were stealing from me, but I knew that my life was much more important than four G's. I remember thinking, *Holz, if you flinch, you're dead. Just chil., God is watching over you.*

I wouldn't let myself breathe 'cause I was too scared that they would see that and kill me. *Never say die, Holz. Never say die. Mark, don't let yourself die.* I desperately wanted to open my eyes to see what was going on. Being left in the dark by my eyelids was torture in and of itself. I was silently panicking. I felt like I was drowning and choking on my own globs of blood. I wanted to cough up the blood, but again I didn't, 'cause if I did, I knew that I would be standing face to face giving an account of my life to God.

I continued to feign dead. Then PI repeated his words from earlier, "Yo, make sure all of those cats are dead. Ah'ight?"

BANG! BANG! BANG! BANG! BANG!

I fervently started praying, *Lord, please don't let me die! Don't take my life, Lord, please!*

"Yo, you got everything outta the kitchen and the bedroom, right? Well come on. Let's get up outta this piece," PI calmly said to the rest of his boyz.

The stereo was lowered and a very *loud* silence quickly filled the room. I was still afraid to open my eyes. Certainty wasn't upon me. I thought the gunmen might still be in the apartment. I felt blood all over my body. *Why didn't they shoot me again?* I asked myself. They must have thought that they'd shot me in the head and killed me. The shot had come extremely close to my head, but fortunately it wasn't a direct hit. I knew that if I or anyone else in that apartment was gonna live, then I had to do something.

Now or never, I thought. *Get help. Holz, get outta this apartment.* As I staggered to my feet I scanned the room. My vision was very blurry. One by one, I managed to see Earl, Xavier, Donnie, Bunny, and another guy and a young lady sprawled out on the floor. Ironically, everyone had their eyes open, but it didn't look promising. They were all laying in their own bright, prostitute-red blood. Pools and pools of blood were everywhere. None of them were attempting to move. I wondered if they'd all died with their eyes open.

I tried to yell, but all that came out of my mouth was a painful and vague gargling, mixed with the blood that I was simultaneously throwing up. "Donnie... Xavier... X... Answer... me. Come.... on y'all.... Let's.... get outta here..... We gotta... hurry up." I pleaded in a weak voice.

No way on Earth did I want to believe it. I didn't want to believe that they were all dead. "Earl... get up.... Come on... y'all.... Let's go... before... they come back," I urged.

I was feeling very, very weak and dizzy. I was so weak that I dropped to my knees. Miraculously, with my blurry vision I was still able to crawl to the telephone and dial 911.

"Hello," I said.

"This is 911. What's your emergency?"

"I've been shot," I mumbled.

"Excuse me," the operator said.

"I've... We got killed... I've been shot...they're dead," I vaguely mumbled.

"Sir, did you say you've been shot?" she asked.

"Yes. I've... been... shot," I mumbled.

"Sir, what's your address? I'll send the police and an ambulance right away. Hello? Sir, are you still there?"

"Yeah."

"Sir, we need your address so that we can help you."

"East 110th... in Harlem," I whispered. With that, I had no more energy to even hold the phone. I was beyond weak. My hands were ice cold. I remember thinking of my family and of Sabine. I wondered if I would ever see them again. *Don't die, Mark! Hold on!* I pleaded with myself. At that point I closed my eyes and I blacked out.

I Don't Know

I vaguely remember being wheeled into the trauma unit. I remember opening my eyes and seeing doctors all around me, frantically trying to save me. I had all kinds of tubes and bags attached to me and needles stuck into my veins. I was face down on some type of table or stretcher. I closed my eyes and just lay there. The next thing I remember was waking up in a hospital bedroom. I didn't know what was going on. All I knew was that I was butt naked with a gown on and bandages all over my body.

No more than ten minutes had passed since I woke up and before I knew it, I had detectives asking me all kinds of questions. "Leave me alone! What's going on?" I recognized my mother and father, who were also in my room.

"Mom, what happened? What's going on?"

"Mark, you were shot," my Mom explained. "Just relax."

She instructed my father to get the detectives away from me so that I could gather my thoughts. As my room began to clear out, I started to remember what had transpired. A gruesome picture popped into my head. Bunny and Xavier and the rest of them were all sprawled out, dead on the floor.

"Mom, I wanna sleep."

"OK, Mark. Just relax. Close your eyes and go to sleep. You're OK. You'll wake back up," she promised.

During the next four days I had many visitors. Friends, relatives and people that I didn't even know had come by the hospital to see me. My room was covered with balloons, flowers, candy, and cards. On Sunday my room was filled to the brim with Fourth Crew members and associates, all of whom had managed to sneak past security guards and made their way up to my room, # 614. Fourth Crew members were the only ones I was willing to tell what actually happened. In full detail I recanted all that had happened and why I thought it happened.

Fourth Crew went on to tell me that when they heard that we'd been shot, they bugged out. They couldn't believe it. They told me that they didn't find out about the killings until Saturday afternoon. My first guess was that they'd heard about it in the news. I listened in shock as they told me that the killings never surfaced in any of the newspapers, much less appeared on the TV news.

"Word," they said. "We found out from Xavier's mom's. She was flippin' out! Yo, she was crying and screaming like she'd lost her mind. The cops that came to tell her the news couldn't control her. She just kept kicking and screaming and yelling, 'My baby! My baby! They killed my baby!'"

I suppose I shouldn't have been too surprised to find out that such a tragic incident hadn't appeared on the news. After all, who cared when blacks murdered each other? Even though it was an execution-style slaying of six people, it still wasn't worthy of making the news. To the world, black urban life wasn't worth a dime! Why? Black, that's why. If blacks were killed and it happened to be reported, it rarely was the lead story.

Just about all of the members who came to see me were visibly shaken. Dwight told me of how they'd gone on a mission throughout Harlem on Saturday night. They went in search of the perpetrators who'd shot me. He told me how they randomly licked off gunshots at any and all drug dealers that they saw. But in reality, I knew in my heart that the crew wasn't wild and brazen enough to really hunt down PI and the rest of Mob Style and shoot it out in an all-out war of revenge. Although we didn't say it, we knew that the idea of seeking real revenge was probably water under the bridge.

Dwight also told me that on that same night, Fourth Crew did a drive-by shooting and shot up Cory's house, the same Cory who killed Richie just before the start of the summer. He informed me that they also threw a Molotov Cocktail through the front window of Cory's house, which set the place ablaze. But the most shocking news to me was that Cory had been released from jail. Yup, set scott-damn-free! With all of the eyewitnesses that were at the scene of the killing, I didn't believe it. Actually, I didn't want to believe it. I didn't want to believe that the justice system would let him walk just like that.

Throwing salt on the wound, Dwight informed me that not only had Cory been released, but he had been released without ever having to post bail. Don't ask me how, 'cause I don't know. My first inclination, and probably the most accurate, was that Richie's black life just didn't mean anything to the system. The system probably just viewed him as some other worthless niggah.

Randy talked about taking the law into his own hands. "Yo. word is bond. If I see Cory on the street, I'ma kidnap and torture that niggah. I'll straight up chop his fingers off one by one, then pour gasoline on him and set him on fire. I want that niggah to feel the same pain that I'm feeling right now."

The crew was basically trying to lift my spirits as well as lift their own. Talking about how they'd gotten revenge or street justice was equivalent to a grandmother talking about how she'd received edification and encouragement from going to church and listening to the pastor preach. Well, I guess I'd only be justifying our mentality by saying, "You can't blame the clay for what the potter has made." We were products of our environment. We never benefited from a normal way of living, therefore our actions manifested themselves in abnormal ways.

Case in point: the system will never see to it that Cory does twenty-five years behind bars. The system will never catch and convict the guys who shot me and murdered my friends.

As a crew, we knew that injustices like these would go on forever. That type of abnormal thinking became normal to us. I guess it became normal for us to seek refuge in hideous acts of violence, violence in the form of violating Cory's crib, violence in the form of trying to kill every "innocent" drug dealer in Harlem, violence in the form of good ol', down home, black on black crime.

My roommate, who was a mad cool cat, had been wheeled out of the room for surgery. It was a good thing, because it meant that we didn't have to worry about someone eavesdropping on our conversations. The crew stayed in my room for hours and we discussed a million and one things. Despite all that had happened, we decided that we would continue on with our drug crusade. But obviously, we all realized that certain changes had to be made.

We were now going to pay someone to go on drug runs for us. We also were going to hire females to work for us. The females would take over the responsibility of preparing and bagging our drugs. As a crew, we were now going to be the bishops of an entire drug operation. We were gonna be like head honchos on Wall Street. You know, they're the ones who never do anything, never get dirty, but yet they call all of the shots and make the most money. So like Wall Street executives, our only job now was gonna be to collect our money. Latiefe still held that position.

After a big shooting incident like the one I lived through, we all agree that those close to us were bound to think that it was drug related. Those close to us meaning our parents and the people who lived on our block.

"So what should we do?" I asked.

Well to start, the eight of us that remained in the drug operation decided to get an apartment to share amongst ourselves. An apartment would be good, because then when we all started driving our new cars and the big money that we were gonna continue to make started becoming evident, our new neighbors, not knowing our mediocre past, wouldn't have reason to be suspicious. The apartment could also be used for our female workers to work in.

Randy was the only one in the crew who stated that he would rather just stay on the block and live with Ma Dukes. None of us gave him a hard time about his decision. We just figured it would be more room in the apartment for the rest of us, seven instead of eight. One less head to worry about.

Fourth Crew wasn't my only steady visitors. My mother and father visited me every day. With each passing day, they were growing more and more skeptical of my reasons for being shot. I would always tell them very resoundingly, "I don't know why I got shot! Listen, I was in the apartment and two guys with masks and guns came in and shot us. They ordered us to get down on the floor and they shot us. And Mom, that's all that happened. I'm sayin'! Man, y'all act like I'm hiding something. Don't y'all think I would tell y'all and the cops what happened or who did this if I knew? I mean, I do want the people who did this to get locked up! Besides, I'm just thankful that I'm alright. I'll worry about everything else when I get home."

Detectives, who were constantly in and out of my room, would always ask me to recount what had happened. "I don't know! I don't know!" That's how I repeatedly responded to their persistent questioning. Each time the DT's visited my room, they would go through this big song and dance, telling me how they would never be able to find the people who shot me and my friends unless I cooperated with them.

Yeah right, I kept thinking. I knew that I would have to get justice on my own. Street justice. See, I had a problem talking with detectives. Number one, I didn't really care for the police, and number two, I wasn't no damn rat! Even though it was my head that nearly got blown off, and even though my friends got killed, I knew that the code of the street had to be followed. I had to keep my mouth shut and under no circumstances should I, nor anyone else for that matter, be talking to the cops. That would make me the biggest hypocrite in the world. Plus, the cops get a paycheck every week, so that they can figure out crimes like the one I was a victim of. All they had to do was stop being lazy and earn their money. I'm sayin', dust for fingerprints and then run those fingerprints. Speak to people in the building and see what information they could get. And shouldn't that apartment have already been on some kind of watch list? Heck no. I wasn't gonna bail out the cops on this issue. They don't pay me a salary for that. Besides, if I was dead, then what would they have done?

In reality, those detectives wanted information so that they could make their arrest and make themselves look good. Then a month later, some judge would let the same guys that almost murdered me walk free. Yeah, right! I didn't think so. I knew that those cops could care less about me and my thug life. So why should I have cared about them? If they didn't give a damn, then I didn't give a damn!

"I don't know!" I screamed at the detectives. "And even if I did know who shot me, I wouldn't tell y'all anyway! Please, just leave me alone. I don't know what happened! I'm sayin', I don't like y'all anyway. Now, get outta here. Beat it, scram, be out, get lost, BYE!"

Talk like that not only embarrassed my parents, but it really made them suspicious. But all I knew was that I wasn't gonna cooperate. Again, I knew that I had come within a hair of being murdered, and that some of my closest friends had in fact already met God. And even though I did love them dearly, I have to reiterate that even that wasn't enough to get me to cooperate with an unjust organization. An organization that was supposed to uphold justice in all communities equally.

Sabine was also one of my many visitors. She came to see me on Monday. The moment she walked through the door she began to cry. She gave me a kiss and a hug and asked if I was alright. She was genuinely very concerned as to how I was doing. I had expected her to lash me with the third degree, along with the 'I-told-you-so's.' Astonishingly, she didn't do that at all. Not once did she mention anything about my involvement with drugs. She didn't even ask me to tell her what had happened. But I guess it wasn't too hard for her to figure out.

As she sat down next to me on my bed, I wiped away her tears. As the day went along, we talked, joked, and watched television. Visiting hours quickly came to an end and as Sabine prepared to leave, she promised to cook me many different Haitian dishes when I came home. Although I wasn't Haitian like she was, I loved the food. I knew that some good, home-cooked food would surely help me replace some of the weight that I had lost as a result of being in the hospital.

I hated for Sabine to see me all bandaged up. All I wanted was to be able to get up out of that bed and walk out of that hospital with Sabine. I knew that was very wishful thinking. I had brought this on myself, so now I had to deal with it.

Finally Wednesday came and I was well enough to leave the hospital. My left arm was in a sling. But as for the rest of my body, considering what it had been through, it was in reasonably good condition. A person would never have been able to tell that I'd been shot, not unless they happened to have seen the two scars on my back. Despite my weight loss, I felt good. The doctor told me to expect some dizzy spells at times, but he told me not to get alarmed by it. He said that the dizziness would be due to the bullet that had punctured one of my lungs before exiting my body.

My ride home from the hospital was very pleasant. I rode with my parents and my sister. It had been a long time since we all actually did something together as a family. On the way home we stopped at Burger King. I laughed to myself because it reminded me so much of the times when I was an innocent, carefree youngster. Every Sunday when I was a little kid, we as a family would always stop at Carvel or McDonalds after church, just to spend some family time together. My ride home from the hospital reminded me of those times. Deja vu, I guess.

After we left Burger King we got back in the car and didn't stop until we were home. When I stepped foot into my house, I whispered real softly, "Thank you, Lord." I knew that it was the grace of God and his spirit living in me that had actually saved me.

To myself I thought, *Man, God could have very easily and probably should have taken my life.* After all, I had taken someone's life earlier in the summer. I always said that there's a reason for everything. I knew that the reason Donnie, Earl, and Bunny had been killed was because of the Crew's involvement in so much crime and negativity.

What I couldn't understand was why did Xavier have to die? I pondered that question over and over in my head. He wasn't involved in our wrong doings. Matter of fact, neither was Bunny really involved. Donnie and Earl, yes they were intricately involved, but why then hadn't I also reaped what I'd sown? Why, up until this point, was Dwight still alive? Why was Wiggie still breathing? I mean, it was the three of us who'd actually murdered innocent people.

I couldn't figure it out. I concluded that the price we had to pay for those murders we'd committed was to suffer the pain of losing four friends. One friend had a possible college degree and a bright future ahead of him. Two other friends, victims of their environment, but yet with eternal good in their hearts and potential greatness in their minds. Still another friend, an innocent black female, full of good, one capable of bearing a leader, was also dead.

I felt like I was at a crossroads in my life. I should have been dead but I wasn't. What was the reason? The real question was, what was I gonna do with my spared life? The only reason that I could come up with for God to have saved me was that maybe through me, if I was willing, then I could help to better the world.

My hospital episode was now behind me. One thing that I could say was that at least my stint in the hospital had afforded me a lot of free time. And I used that free time to finish writing about two more elements. I was almost there…

When we reached home, I settled in nice and comfortably upstairs in my bedroom. Unfortunately, as soon as I was good and relaxed, my father called me downstairs.

"Man! Can't a brotha get some rest in this place?" I said to myself.

I stubbornly made my way to the kitchen where I saw both my father and my mother. They had that 'sitting down at the table' look about them, which had to mean that they were waiting for me to have a serious discussion. See, whenever I or any of my siblings were called to the kitchen table, it was always for a grim reason.

"Mark, sit down," my father said. "Your mother and I want to talk to you."After I'd taken my seat my father continued on. "Mark, we're concerned about you. Since we've been living here, you have been the ideal, model child. You were always very smart in school. Never once did you get into any trouble at school. We've never had a problem with you. As parents, and stop me if I'm wrong, we have always given you, your brother, and your sister whatever it was that you all wanted. We have never abused you nor have we neglected you. Mark, you know that you've always been able to come to me or your mother whenever you're having a problem, because we're always here for you, the both of us. Am I right?"

"Yes, you're right."

"I know you've never been involved in any kind of trouble before, but when you tell me you were in an apartment and someone walks in and nearly blows you away for absolutely no reason at all, I find that very hard to believe. But if that's what you say happened, I'll believe you. You've never lied to me, so why would you be lying to me now? Plus, based on your past record, as far as behavior is concerned, I don't see why I shouldn't believe you."

"Mom and Dad, I'm telling y'all. I don't know who shot me, or why they shot me. I'm not making up a story when I tell y'all that."

My mother jumped in, "Mark, this whole incident, it couldn't be connected with drugs in any way, could it?"

"No! Of course not, Ma! What makes you think that?" I was starting to feel a little pressure.

"Well, because," she said, "your sister told us that you, Randy, and the rest of your friends, Fourth Crew or whatever y'all call yourselves, had started dealing drugs or had people selling drugs for y'all or something to that effect. Is that true, Mark?"

I had to think real quick on my feet as I said, "Well, yes and no. No, I'm not involved with any drugs, and yes, some of my friends did get mixed up in the drug game. But it doesn't have nothing to do with this." Like a boxer, I was trying hard to fight my way off the ropes.

My father said, "Mark, I can't control your life. But as your father, I'm supposed to give you positive advice and proper guidance. I'm asking you to please stay away from your friends that are into that drug crap. Drugs are a two-way street. One direction is headed for jail and the other direction is headed for death. Now I believe what you told me. However, Mark, if you do decide to get caught up in that drug game, you better not let me find out about it, 'cause you'll be out of this house. I mean that! 'Cause the next thing you know, people will be after your mother and I, trying to kill us over something that you did. Don't get involved with that, Mark, and don't bring it around here if you do. Believe me when I tell you that if I find out that you're involved in that, I'll kill you my damn self! I'll make sure that I do it before someone out there on the street does."

"Daddy, don't worry. I'm not into anything negative, ok?" As I moved myself away from the table I told my parents, "Um, Mom and Dad, I know that this might sound off the wall, but I guess now is a good time to tell y'all that, well... I think that I'm gonna move out."

"What?" My mother screamed. "What are you talking about and where are you planning on moving to?"

"Well, I don't know where I'm moving to yet, but me and some of my friends have already discussed getting an apartment together."

My father said to me, "Mark, you have a probationary job with the utility company. Now suppose they lay you off? Then what?"

"Daddy, I'll manage. I think y'all are forgetting that I'm a man."

"A man? See, that's the problem with young people today. They want to grow up too quick. They want things too fast. Be patient, Mark. Patience sometimes means having to deal with long-term suffering and sacrifice. It takes time to get an apartment and things like that. But those things aren't going anywhere. They'll be there for you when you're ready for them.

You'll learn, Mark. If you wanna move out, I'm not going to stop you, but you're gonna learn the hard way. It's rough out there. Believe me when I tell you. Listen to experience when it talks to you."

"Daddy, I'm tired of being patient! I already know it's rough out there. I got shot, didn't I? It doesn't get any rougher than that. Remember one thing though, and that's that I didn't die. And you know why I didn't die? I know how to survive, that's why."

"Mark go somewhere and get out of my face," my mother said, sounding very ticked off. "Boy, when they told me you got shot I didn't know what to think. I didn't know if you were dead or alive. All I know is that my blood pressure shot up. But I don't know if I feel worse right now hearing you talk like this. You're making my pressure go up again! Boy, just go somewhere and leave me the hell alone! All this crazy nonsense you're talking, just go somewhere." As I walked up to my room I knew that it was imperative that I move out of my parents' house as soon as possible.

"Mark," my father yelled as I walked away. "You better get your black behin' back in college next semester. I mean that! A black man can't make it today without a degree. You hear me?"

"Yeah yeah," I said as I kept it moving. If only my parents knew that in the last two months I had drastically changed. I wasn't the same Mark that they'd raised from the time I was a baby. I couldn't believe that I was lying to my parents the way I was. Why didn't I just tell them the truth and ask for help? I knew that they'd be more than willing to help me.

If they only knew that I'd quit my job at the gas company a long time ago, the same job that I would have killed to get. But to hell with that job. They weren't paying me no real money anyway.

Well, it definitely was not my parent's fault that my life was turning upside down. They had done their job in terms of raising me well. It was basically all on me now. Why was I desiring to live such a jacked up life? The family element definitely hadn't gone bad and caused my life to turn this way. I was surely at a big-time crossroads. I'd probably go the wrong way, but why? I hoped to have it figured out before it was too late. Maybe society had failed me. Maybe God was now shining his light in another direction. I didn't know.

The Wake

"Mark, go see who's at the door. I think I just heard the doorbell ring," my sister yelled.

As I approached the door I asked, "Who is it?"

"It's me," Randy responded.

"Yo, what's up?" I asked as I opened the door.

"Holz, what's the matter kid? Ain't you going to the wake?"

"Yeah, I'm going."

"Dressed like that?"

"Yeah, niggah! What's wrong with the way I'm dressed?" I asked angrily. "Oh, I don't have on a suit. Is that it? Got-dammit, Randy, I'm tired of wearing that suit!"

"Okay, okay, Holz, calm down. Wear what you have on. But let's hurry up and bounce 'cause we're gonna be late. I'm driving my mother's car so we don't have to worry about a cab."

"Ah'ight, let me just tell Paula that we're bouncing. Yo, Paula! Come on, let's go! Randy's driving us."

As we climbed into the ride, my sister asked, "Mark, what's wrong with you? Have some respect. You can't go to a wake with sneakers on."

"Paula, leave me the hell alone, ah'ight?" I hollered. "I'm really not in the mood for no nonsense." I was really starting to get heated. First of all, I hated the fact that I was going to a wake, which, quite frankly, should have been my own. But to top it off, everyone was criticizing what I had on.

"I'm going to a wake for my dead homies, so to hell with that suit and tie image. They wasn't about that anyway. They were homeboys. Homeboys don't wear hard shoes and all that. I gotta stay true to the game. I'm wearing my bagging jeans, sneakers and a Polo shirt with my medallion. If people don't like what I have on, well then yo, that's too bad, 'cause they know what they can kiss!" I yelled.

"Calm down, Mark," everyone in the car pleaded.

I was really feeling testy. It was Thursday, July 25th and I was going to a wake for Xavier, Earl, and Donnie, three of my closest friends. That was the main reason for all of my bitterness. Their wake was being held simultaneously. They were all reposing at Gilmore's Funeral Home, which is located in St. Albans, Queens. The wake was scheduled to start at 6 PM.

It was now about ten minutes to six, and we were just pulling up to the funeral home. As we parked and prepared to walk through the rain and into the funeral home, I could see tons of people, both young and old. Some were crying, others were hugging. Most of the people formed little huddles. They jammed close together under umbrellas and talked amongst themselves. There was also a large police presence at the wake. Although I mostly saw uniformed police officers, I was sure that inside and outside the wake was littered with undercovers posing as mourners.

As we walked toward the funeral home I felt as though all eyes were glued on me, but I didn't care. I put my dark shades on and proceeded to B-bop my way into the funeral home. All of Fourth Crew was surrounding me as we walked in. They swarmed around me as if I was the President or a celebrity and they were Secret Service police assigned to protect me.

As I bopped into the funeral home I heard someone saying, "Yeah, that's him. He was with them when they got shot." I turned and glanced at the person but I didn't comment. Then I heard another lady ask, "Who?" Someone told her, "Him, the one with his arm in a sling."

Once inside the funeral home I signed my name and address in the guest register. I took a seat on the aisle alongside Fourth Crew. As I sat and looked toward the front of the room I saw the three coffins, but I wasn't able to see the faces of those inside the coffins. Out of nowhere I had a quick flashback of the gruesome bloody murder scene. Very clearly, as if it were right in front of me, I envisioned Earl, Donnie, and Xavier lying dead on an apartment floor in Harlem with their eyes wide open.

There was a quick memorial service, which was followed my many people sharing their memories of the deceased. But mostly everyone came just to view the bodies. As we sat in the funeral home, I felt like bursting out into laughter. I guess I was feeling that way simply because I was so scared of looking at three more of my friends in caskets. Or maybe I wanted to laugh because I was afraid of what my future held. In my mind, I was having laughs of insanity and insecurity. I kept wondering what everybody was looking at. When were people gonna stop turning around and staring at me?

As we all prepared to get out of our seats and go view the bodies, I remember thinking to myself, *This ain't like Richie's funeral. I don't even feel lightheaded or numb. I feel perfectly fine.* We walked past the three coffins, which were set up one in front of the other. I stopped at the head of each casket. I shook my head as one by one I stared at three potential great human beings. "Man!" I said. "Damn!" With as much affection as I could muster, I kissed each of my deceased friends on the forehead. "Peace," I softly whispered to each one of them, holding up my middle finger and my index finger to visually display the message of peace. Although my back was to the rest of the mourners, I knew for a fact that every eye in that place was glued to my every move.

Very calmly I turned around, stepped away from the caskets and walked out of the funeral home. I didn't want to sit back down. I had already seen enough to prove to myself that this was no dream. They were truly dead. I decided to just wait outside in the rain until the wake was over. I waited all alone with my thoughts.

"Holz, you're already used to this. And you know that this is probably the worst that it can get, I thought as I stood and smiled by myself on the steps of the funeral home. Yeah, I had to smile, because who was I fooling? I mean, I knew that it could get worse, simply because next time it might be my corpse that everyone was coming to look at. A dead me. That's a concept that I didn't think that I'd ever be able to get used to. But ironically, I kinda knew that it was one that was inevitable.

"Yeah I know," I answered to the voice inside of me that told me I should have been in one of those caskets laying stiff as a board. "Yeah, I definitely know." Tears ran down my face. I stared into the sky, which was full of misty rain, and nodded my head up and down in an effort to confirm my intuition. I knew my turn at death was lurking around the corner, yet I still couldn't muster up the courage to live right.

Later that night, well after the wake was over, all of our crew and many of our other close friends and associates gathered outside at the intersection of 234th street and 135th avenue. We gathered for our own little ghetto memorial-type service. I would say it was easily close to twenty of us huddled together in a circle. In an effort to ease the pain, we were all getting sloppy drunk. Among us we must have drunk close to a thousand ounces of malt liquor. We also smoked about a pound of bones as we reminisced about the fun times we had all had with X, Donnie, and Earl.

Randy said, "Yo, that niggah Donnie was still in high school! He was still wet behind the ears."

We all laughed and told jokes. The jokes were being told so that the mood would brighten just a little bit. I just wanted to get high like I'd never been before. I was feeling schizophrenic or bipolar or something. At times I felt angry because of my friends' deaths. Then in a split second my anger would revert back to unbridled happiness and laughter. I would laugh as though I was listening to Eddie Murphy tell jokes. Then before you knew it, my happiness would switch to sadness. I could only guess that, yes, now something was definitely mentally wrong with me. A screw or two definitely needed tightening.

Earlier that evening, after the wake was over and before we'd decided to get drunk, something came over me and I'd just felt obligated to personally speak to Xavier's Moms and Pops. They had graciously invited my sinful soul to their house. While I was at their house, I stood alone in their basement. It was an eerie and spooky feeling. In fact, I was kind of scared to be there alone. I stared at a pair of Xavier's old sneakers. The sneakers were right next to each other and facing a wall. It was so funny, because I know that I actually saw Xavier standing in that pair of sneakers. I reached out my hand to touch him, but all I felt was thin air. I could still see him, though. A single tear rolled down his right cheek and he was talking to me, but I couldn't make out his words. As he spoke, he had his hands lifted up toward the sky. He seemed as if he was desperately trying to tell me something.

I asked his spirit, "X, what's up man? Speak to me. What's up? Talk to me, dog." Then I felt a tap on my shoulder. Startled, I said, "Oh man!" Then I chuckled. "I'm sorry. I'm so sorry," I told his parents.

"That's alright, Mark," they said. They understood what I was going through.
"Everyone is having a difficult time coping with this tragedy," they told me.

Xavier's parents couldn't figure out why such a bad thing had happened. They viewed all of us in Fourth Crew, including their son, as All-American boys. They had no clue about our drug involvement.

"Mark, do you have any idea why this happened?" they asked.

I responded by looking X's parents straight in their eyes. And as sympathetic as a lying, racist Robo cop, I said, "Mr. and Mrs. Wright, first let me say that on one hand I know how fortunate I am to still be alive. But on the other hand, I wish that your son was still alive and that it was me who had passed on. It's just so sad, and I can't explain how or why my life was spared and Xavier's wasn't. But I can do everything in my power to help the police catch who did this. And I would help the police, but I just don't have any information to give them. I honestly don't have a clue as to why this happened. Honestly. We just have to remember that this is New York, and unexplainable things like this happen."

They asked me a few more probing questions, questions which I was able to shield off with adulteress-style smooth language. They told me that they were just trying to make sense out of the whole thing. They needed that feeling of closure. I continued to sympathize with them and they asked me would I be attending the funeral in the morning.

"Oh, sure. Of course I'll be there."

In actuality, I knew that I wasn't going to nobody's funeral. My mental state was damn near crazy as it was, hallucinating and what not. Going to a funeral would have made me just short of needing to be fitted for a straight jacket.

Maybe I should go to the funeral… Yeah, go… Nah, forget it, don't go. Ah man, I just felt like screaming because I was jacked up on the inside. What was wrong with me? I violently screamed to myself.

As I walked out of Xavier's yard I saw his little blue Toyota and it was the sight of his car that basically answered the question about my funeral attendance. I said, "Nah, no way am I going to that funeral. There's just no way." I thought about all of the people who were at the wake. I thought about how they had been crying, screaming, and carrying on. I thought about the multitudes of young lives that were in attendance and I knew that the response to a triple funeral service was sure to be overwhelming. "Nah, I'm not going," I said to myself.

Well, the night went on, as did our ghetto memorial service. All of us got stupid-high. More jokes were told. Highlights from the lives of X, Donnie and Earl continued to be replayed. Everyone took turns saying things like, "Yo, remember when that niggah Donnie did..." or "Oh, word! Yeah, remember when Donnie snuffed that punk niggah up on Merrick?" There were memories and stories for days that were being told, but after a while I drew tired of the whole service.

Out of nowhere and in a rage, I yelled, "Yeah, whateva, man! We gotta forget about X, Donnie, and Earl! Them niggahs is dead and they ain't coming back! Look how stupid we look. We all getting' high and drunk 'cause we can't cope with death. We should be used to this by now. This is the life we live! We live like vultures so why all of a sudden we catching feelings? Man, y'all niggahs is soft, every last one of y'all! Word!"

Everyone glared at me as if I'd lost my mind, and for a split second they were brought down from their highs as a result of my piercing, reckless words. I screamed out. "What? What are y'all looking at? Y'all know I'm right! Y'all know it! Look at y'all niggahs, eyes welling up like y'all wanna cry or something. Man, but yo! You know what? Fourth Crew and everybody else that's out on this corner right now are a bunch of soft, faggot niggahs! Word!" I shrugged my shoulders and continued. "I'm sayin'! They're dead! So what's the sense in us getting all worked up and all that?"

No one in the group was willing to bend and see things my way so I just shook my head and threw my hands up into the air. "Man, I don't know. I mean, look at y'all niggahs! I see why X, Donnie, and Earl got bodied. They got bodied because they were part of the same soft-faggot crew as y'all cats. How the hell could they let themselves die? I took mad shots and I'm still walking. WHAT! Tell me how them niggahs let themselves die. Tell me how! All of y'all dumb, black, ignorant...Man, whateva! Y'all can stay out on this corner until the sun comes up and be hung over in the morning if y'all want to. But I'm out... And yo! Nobody, and I mean nobody better come get me in the morning to go to no got damn funeral, 'cause I ain't going!"

Even after saying all of that I still had more frustration and anger to vent as I slammed my bottle of Malt Liquor onto the street, breaking the bottle and spilling its contents everywhere. Then I turned around and jogged off to my crib. When I reached my house I stormed up to my bedroom. I was madder than the devil.

"Mark what's the matter?" my sister asked out of concern.

"Leave me alone!" I barked at her.

My mother and father also wanted to know what was wrong with me.

"Nothing's wrong," I yelled as I paced back and forth in my dark room with the door locked.

My father banged on my bedroom door and he yelled for me to unlock the door. They could hear me punching walls, crying, screaming, groaning, and slamming things around. I even threw my picture of Jesus Christ against the wall, shattering the glass frame. I felt as if I was in a trance. I didn't know if I was starting to calm down or what. What I did know was that I laid on my bed breathing real hard and heavy. As I hyperventilated, I had a chrome 357 magnum to my temple.

A sympathetic voice inside of me whispered, "Pull the trigger, Holz. It's ok. Pull the trigger."

I was a split second from ending all the Drama. Bang! Only I didn't have the guts to do it.

"Mark, are you alright?" my sister asked through the door. "Mark answer me!" she pleaded.

I just lay on my bed with the gun to my head, staring into space.

July 26, 1991. One of the worst days in my life. I didn't wake up until 12:30 PM. I wondered if my parents or my sister had tried to wake me to go to the funeral. I definitely knew that none of my friends had came to get me. Or maybe they had. If they had, it was way too late now. I had already missed it. It's not that I was trying to disrespect my deceased homies, but I just wouldn't have been able to live through three eulogies, I'm sorry. A triple funeral with three open caskets was scheduled. I tried to block out the thought of the funeral I knew that everyone would want to know what had happened to me, but hey. I'd just tell them that I bugged out, and that it would have been too much for a brotha to deal with.

I proceeded to the bathroom to take a shower and to get dressed. After I was dressed I decided to go get a forty to help take away the guilt of not going to the funeral. As I walked in the rain to the corner candy store, I remembered that Bunny's wake was scheduled for later on in the afternoon. Her funeral was to be held the following day. *Oh well,* I said to myself, *I guess I won't be paying my respects to her either.* Just the thought of Bunny's corpse made me contemplate whether one forty would be enough to take away the pain. Funerals and wakes, and more funeral and more wakes. When was it all gonna end? Going to wakes and funerals was starting to become a full time job for a niggah. It was just too much to deal with.

When I got to the store I purchased a box of Newport cigarettes and decided that one forty ounce of Old

English indeed was enough. I stood in front of the store with my forty in hand. I hugged the bottle of beer and I stood amidst overcast skies. As I was sipping on my beer I looked up and saw three black hearses slowly driving east on Merrick Blvd. Following the hearses was a long procession of black limousines and cars, all with their headlights on and their windshield wipers going. The procession was heading in the direction of Long Island. I knew that those hearses were carrying my three friends. This must have been their farewell tour through the neighborhood.

As I stood and watched the seemingly endless procession, I realized that I was standing in the exact same spot where Richie had been murdered. Richie's picture and name had been drawn in a graffiti mural and I stood in front of his mural as cars continued to drive by. I poured some beer on the ground for my dead homies and I proceeded to walk back towards my house. I realized that never again would I see my three friends, so I sadly turned and took one more look at the procession. "I love y'all niggahs."

For the remainder of that black Friday I stayed by myself. On Saturday I also found myself alone. I couldn't hang with the crew. I didn't seek their company, because I was embarrassed by the way I had behaved on Thursday night.

The crew however, stayed very busy. Right after the funeral they had to prepare to go to Bunny's wake. After a night's sleep, then they would have to wake up Saturday morning and go to Bunny's funeral. All of that left no time for socializing.

The time by myself did me some good. It allotted me time to just simply think. It also afforded me some time to pray, which I did plenty of. I attempted to get closer to God, 'cause I figured that maybe only God held the key that would open the door and put an end to all of the madness. I also managed to write more on the elements.

But praying did the most for me. It really helped to bring my self-esteem back to a normal level. With my self-esteem functioning properly, I was able to accomplish more of what I wanted to do.

On Sunday I took the initiative of finding us an apartment. I went to look at an apartment complex that consisted of Co-ops. I spoke with the building manager and he told me that he was having difficulty selling most of the units, so he was willing to rent us an apartment with an option in the lease to buy it outright at a later date.

The Co-op was located on Merrick Blvd., between Baisley and Farmers Blvd.'s. It was in a nice-looking, two story brick building. The apartment itself was huge inside. There were three bedrooms, two bathrooms, a large living room, and a small kitchen. I was sure that the crew would love it. Actually, they had better like it, because I had already given the manager a huge security deposit on the place, not to mention the lies that I had to tell him. I had to lie about my age and my income. I also lied and told him that I was still working with the utility company. Although I showed him my ID card, which I'd never turned in when I quit, I sensed that the manager knew that I was into drugs. When he asked me to write a check and I told him that I didn't have a checking account, I knew that a red cocaine flag had really been raised. That's probably why he inflated the security deposit.

"You're twenty four years old with two kids and you don't have a checking account?" he asked. "Are you sure you're twenty four?" I knew he was getting suspicious so I told a joke in order to lighten the mood. It was a Johnny Carson type of joke.

"Nah, nah," I said. "See, I don't have a checking account because I'd rather deal with cash or money orders. I mean, I don't want to turn into one of those 'Rubbergate Politicians.' You know what I'm sayin'?"

"Ha ha ha ha ha," the white man laughed uncontrollably. "Oh, that's funny," he added, "real funny." Through his laughter he managed to say, "I look forward to having you as a tenant."

We proceeded to his office where I had to John Hancock all types of papers including the lease agreement. When we were done with all of the legalities, he handed me a key and told me that I could move in as soon as tomorrow. I was puzzled, because I knew that he knew that I was into something illegal, yet he still let me sign a lease and allowed me to take possession of an apartment. No credit check or reference check whatsoever. But hey I wasn't complaining. Maybe he had illegally pocketed a huge portion of the inflated security deposit. Indirectly, the manager was also benefiting from our drug money. He had to be.

Anyway, later that night I was finally able to hunt down the crew. They were all at Kwame's house. Kwame always kept the door to his crib unlocked, and basically whoever visited him would just walk right in without knocking or ringing the bell. When I walked into Kwame's crib, I didn't know what kind of greeting to expect. Surprisingly though, the Crew was happy to see me and they showed me much love.

"Big Holz!" they yelled. "What up, my niggah? Where you been at, kid?"

"I've been on the DL for a few days, kna'imean?" I said softly.

As Randy handed me something, he said, "Here Holz, we know you didn't go to the funerals, and believe me I don't want to remind you of anything, but just take this."

He handed me pamphlets that were from both funerals. Each pamphlet contained pictures of the respective deceased. The pamphlet included their birth dates and their death dates. On the inside of the pamphlet there were little biographies of their lives, along with obituaries and a passage of words.

"Good looking out," I said to Randy as I proceeded to read the passage from Xavier's pamphlet. It read:

Dear God,
I think I'm going to die.
I think that I'm going to leave this world.
Give me strength, Lord, that I might not fear.
I know, dear God, that when I leave I do not die,
That when I die I shall continue to live in Your arms.
And yet, dear Lord, my heart beats wildly. I am so
scared.
My heart breaks to be leaving those that I love so
dearly:
My family, my friends, my loves, my hopes, my
dreams…

I stared at that passage and I couldn't bear to even finish reading the poem. I said, "Yo, I'll read the rest later." I didn't want to get all emotional.

"So what's up, Holz?" Dwight asked.

"I found us an apartment, that's what's up."

Immediately everyone started asking me questions. They wanted to know where the apartment was located, how it looked and how much was the rent.

"Here's a brochure," I said as I handed Latiefe a booklet which contained information on the whole complex. "Y'all know where it's at. It's those Co-ops on Merrick, right near Farmer's," I said.

"Oh. Holz, you mean the Cinderella Co-ops?"

"Exactly," I said.

Dwight and Wiggie both agreed that it would be cool living there. For one, we wouldn't be too far removed from our original 'hood, yet we would be far enough away so the people we knew wouldn't be able to see us.

I told everyone in the Crew how much I had put down for the security deposit. "Don't worry about paying me back, though," I told them. "Y'all just worry about buying the furniture and carpet and all that."

They all agreed to lace our new crib with the most expensive furniture that money could buy. Money was no object, especially since Latiefe had just paid all of us. In fact, my money had been handed to me the moment I stepped into Kwame's house. I hadn't yet counted it, but I figured with the loss of Donnie and Earl, there would now be bigger paydays for the rest of us. Paydays were bound to be somewhere in the neighborhood of $12,000.

"When can we move in?" Erik asked.

"As early as tomorrow, but it won't make sense for us to move in tomorrow because we don't have any furniture. So as soon as we buy some furniture we're in there."

Favorite Pastimes

By the time Friday, August 2nd rolled around, we were living pretty lovely. The recent deaths were behind us and our crew was really starting to reap the benefits from our drug activity. We had moved into our apartment. We were all living there except for Randy.

Our furniture, along with our new carpet, filled our apartment. We had females constantly dropping by the crib. Our telephone rang off the hook. Never could one get time to himself. There were always people in and out of our place. The scene was always hectic. For me, I had to get use to the constant influx of people. I considered the true me to be a hermit type of a person, a Michael Jackson recluse type. All the constant coming and going wasn't me. But hey, when the dough was rolling in like it was for our crew, it was hard to maintain the life of a hermit. Plus, we had all just purchased our cars, so I was sure to always be on the go.

Tuesday of the previous week, our crew went to a used car lot on Hillside Avenue to look at some late model, fancy cars. We decided that used cars were the best and safest route for us to go. We had discussed the idea of buying "tag jobs" but we concluded that buying a stolen car would be way too risky. Besides, we had the money to buy brand new cars if we'd wanted. But we didn't.

Every one of us wanted a different type of whip. So if we went to, let's say, a BMW dealership, they would have given us a good deal, but that would have been if we were all going to buy BMW's. Plus we knew that, by law, big automobile dealerships were required to notify the IRS when cars are purchased with all cash, so we wanted to avoid all of that unnecessary nonsense.

The used car lots on Hillside Avenue had all types of makes and models which were already loaded with the extras. With more than five of us buying, we were guaranteed a bargain. And a bargain was what we got. The moment we stepped foot onto the lot, a swarm of salesmen came flying at us. No doubt, their fierce anticipation was due to the fact that we depicted society's image of drug dealers. Salesmen were eager to please us. They let us sit in cars, test drive them and thoroughly inspect them any way we pleased.

I took one of the salesmen to the side, opened up a knapsack and showed him fifty thousand dollars. Then I asked him what could he do for my friends and myself. The Arabian salesman almost came in his pants when he saw all of that green.

"Come, come, come into my office," he said with an accent. "Let's talk business. I'll show you a bargain."

In his office we sat and talked. I explained to him that eight of us were buying cars. I went on to say, "We want eight cars of our choice. I'll give you fifty G's right now if you let us walk with the cars today, and next week I'll hit you off with another thirty G's. But it has to be any eight cars of our choice."

"Sure, sure," the Arab said. "My friend, pick them out, you and your homeboys can drive them off the lot right now. I want to do business. I want you to buy cars."

I wanted to laugh in the salesman's face, to ask who had taught him about the slang word "homeboys." But on a more serious note, I wondered if I could have gotten a cheaper price. It seemed like he'd accepted my offer too quick. But it was too late to balk on the deal. I told him that we would be taking the cars that we selected to our mechanic, and if any one of the cars were a lemon, he wouldn't receive the other $30,000. He assured me that all the cars on the lot were good cars. So after some legal conversations, we all displayed our driver's licenses and the like. We signed the titles of the cars along with some other paperwork and soon after that we were off and driving with our new rides.

I said to Randy, "Yo, that salesman agreed to my offer a bit too quick. Maybe he low-balled us somehow."

Randy replied, "Nah Holz, he didn't snake us. You just have to remember one thing. Money talks and everything else walks."

As we drove away, we all laid back and donned real hard gangster leans. Our seats were reclined back as far as they could go and we drove with only one hand gripping the steering wheel. Most of our cars were already equipped with extras, such as dark tinted windows, which was a good thing to have in the hood. With new rides, now more than ever we really expected to get pulled over by the cops. The advantage to having the tint was that it negated the cops' ability to tell if the driver of the car was black or not. Tinted windows also prevented the cops from being able to tell exactly how many people were in the car.

Some of the other extras included expensive chrome rims, profile tires, sunroofs, ragtops, and spoiler kits. Of course our whips were equipped with booming, booming stereo systems. The only extra that our cars lacked were car telephones. That wasn't a problem, because we definitely planned to get them installed very soon.

The coming weekend was sure to rekindle old times. Our friend and fellow crew member, Reggie, was coming home for the weekend. It was his birthday, so the military gave him the two days' leave. Also, our other friend, Claudius, was coming home. Claudius had attended summer school at his college, which was in Wichita, Kansas. Claudius stayed there practically year round. He had to stay there and practice with his basketball team and lift weights and all of that superstar athlete stuff. Every year Claudius would only receive two weeks off in the summer. I guess it was rough being a big time college basketball star, but with the possibility of NBA riches I would definitely say it was worth the sacrifice.

So after we'd spent most of Friday cruising around town, showing off our cars and picking up women, we retired to the apartment and got high. With both Claudius and Reggie in town, we knew that we would be living it up on the weekend, so we didn't want to over do it until we hooked up with them.

The following day we arrived at Randy's crib and found Claudius and Reggie sitting in Randy's room. Our greetings were very loud and slangish.

"Yo, what up, big Claud?"

"My man, Reg! Long time no see, money. What up, kid?"

Reggie and Claudius both told us and showed us that they were mutually happy to see us and mad amp' to be back on the block.

"Got-damn, Claudius!" I shouted. "It looks like you keep getting bigger and bigger. How tall are you? You still 6'5"?"

"Yeah, I'm still six-five, 230lbs," Claudius replied. He went on to tell us how he'd been lifting weights all year and how strict his diet was, which explained his ex-convict looking image.

Randy remarked, "Reggie you getting cock-diesel too, niggah."

Latiefe replied, "Man, Reggie ain't getting diesel. All that is fat. There ain't a lick of muscle on that big, burly Haitian." We all started rolling.

"So what's been going on?" Claudius asked.

J.P. responded, "Yo kid, Fourth Crew is large now. Extremely large!" He emphasized his words as he pulled out about $2,000 in cash.

"Yeah Fourth Crew phat and you know that," I said with a big, devilish grin on my face. Then all at once we all started pulling out $100 bills by the thousands. As Claudius and Reggie looked on in astonishment the rest of us harmonized the chant, "Go Fourth, go Fourth, go Fourth."

Snapping from perplexity, Reggie asked with an eager smile, "Yo, what's up? What did y'all niggahs get into? Y'all pumping?"

"You damn right!" Latiefe said. "We're not exactly pumping per se, but we have hustlers working for us."

I added, "Yeah, we don't even live on 234th street anymore. We moved because y'all know how everyone can get into your business when you live on this block."

Dwight instructed Claudius and Reggie to go outside. When they got outside they were flabbergasted and at a loss for words. They saw all of our cars lined up one behind the other. We had driven all of our cars to the block to surprise them. All of our cars were washed, waxed, detailed, and shining. There was Dwight's Mazda MPV, Latiefe's convertible BMW 325, Wiggie's gold Acura Legend coupe, Kwame's silver Volvo, J.P.'s Jeep Wrangler, Erik's Jaguar, and although I wanted so much to get a Chevy Blazer, I had purchased a sweet Saab 9000. It just looked too good to pass up. As for Randy, he wanted to stay low key and on the humble, so like a fool he bought an inexpensive Hyundai Excel. I couldn't front, though. Randy's ride did slam because of all the extras it had on it. But in my opinion, he would have been much better off with an Infiniti Q45 or a Lexus, because that would have made our fleet complete and strictly official as far as the streets were concerned.

"Yo, this looks like 125th Street out this piece! How the hell did y'all get so large?" Claudius asked as he jumped behind the steering wheel of each whip, reminiscent of a happy little kid pretending to drive his daddy's car.

Wiggie, who by the way had yet to show that he was in mourning for his deceased brother, said, "Yo, we col' got rambunctious and blew up the spot."

We couldn't keep the car show going for too long because we were on the block. So we got in our rides and drove back to our apartment. We sat down in our plush living room. The white carpet was nice and fluffy. We had a black leather sectional couch, which went well with the fifty-inch color TV. We also had the fat CD system and magazines such as Essence and Jet on the glass coffee table.

As Reggie and Claudius toured the apartment and agreed that it was the bomb, they became curious as to where the rest of the cats in the crew were. People like Richie, Xavier, Donnie, and Earl. The room suddenly became pin-drop silent. The mood switched from eat, drink, and be merry, to dull, sad, and somber. No one said a word. Everyone looked at each other.

Actually, I was shocked that Reggie and Claudius hadn't heard the news. I mean, I would have thought that someone in their immediate families would have reached out to them and let them know about all of the deaths that had taken place. But apparently they were still in the dark.

Reggie, with an insecure smile asked, "What? Did they get locked up or something?"

"Nah, kid, them cats got mercked," Erik said.

Reggie and Claudius both ripped through the silence as they shouted, "What? You mean them niggahs is up outta here?"

Everyone's silence basically confirmed Erik's statement.

Reggie still wasn't convinced as he paced the room and waved his right hand from side to side. "Nah! Hol' up! Hol' up! Hol' up! They're dead?"

The room remained silent.

Reggie looked at each one of us individually in the face. No one blinked.

"Get outta here man! Yo, on the real. Y'all shouldn't joke like that. Y'all had me going for a second," Reggie rebuked.

"It ain't no joke. They're dead," Erik whispered.

Reggie who was getting frustrated with the silence, yelled "What the hell happened? And how come nobody got in touch with me to tell me what was up?"

Claudius began to voice his disbelief as he asked, "You mean Donnie? Donnie? Donnie? The same Donnie that lives next door to me? Slick-Don is dead?"

"Yup," Erik confirmed.

Reggie added, "Yo, y'all are straight up serious, ain't yall?"

"Yeah, Reggie. You know we wouldn't joke like that," I said.

Claudius looked to the ground and shook his head and said, "I just spoke to Donnie last month to tell him that I was coming home. Yo, I can't believe this."

With the closeness of our crew, I understood very well, just exactly how both Reggie and Claudius must have been feeling. The two of them started to cry just a little. Everyone in the room was quiet. I guess no one knew what to say. Everyone was taking their individual time out to reflect on our lost members.

"Well at least none of us are in jail," Randy bloopishly said.

Clauidus replied, "I would much rather come home and find out that all of y'all are alive and in jail than to come home and find out that four of my friends are dead! Word! Yo, how did they die, anyway?"

"What do y'all want to hear about first? Do y'all want to hear about how we got large or do y'all want to hear about X and the rest of them?" I asked.

Claudius and Reggie agreed that they would rather hear about our rise from what seemed like poverty to paradise. So in graphic detail, we all took turns telling about everything that had happened to us as a crew. We told them about the Mafia-like breakfast meetings we had and about the crime rampage that we undertook. We also explained to them exactly how our first drug purchase went down, how we paid ourselves and how our money kept turning over.

After explaining and talking about that for almost an hour, I took the initiative and explained how Richie had been killed. I also told them where it happened, why it happened and who did it. Then I went on to tell them how I had narrowly escaped death. I showed them the bullet scars that were on my body. By this time my arm was out of the sling and practically back to normal.

"Word! Donnie, X, and Earl were all right next to me," I continued to explain.

Randy threw in that Bunny too had been killed.

"You mean big butt Bunny?" Reggie asked.

"Yup, that Bunny," I replied.

Claudius responded, "Yo, I don't believe this. It sounds like some movie script or something."

J.P. started to give details on their funerals, but he was interrupted by Claudius. Claudius said that he had heard enough. He wanted to remember them as he had last seen them. He couldn't bear to hear anymore. He insisted that he see their grave sites before he went back to Kansas.

Reggie and Claudius were both bitter about the loss of their good friends. But considering the amount of lives that were lost, they took it rather well. See, they were from the 'hood, so they understood everything that went down. Like us, they knew how to cope with incidents such as death. In their minds, I know that they knew that it was just a matter of time before crime and violence had caught up with our crew. I mean, it was always right under our noses.

Reggie and Claudius' bitter feelings lingered for a while, but soon they seemed to be taking everything in stride. They were very impressed with the way we had all blown up. We each gave Claudius and Reggie $500 in cash, leaving them with $4,000 in their possession.

"You know why we gave y'all that loot?" Dwight asked.

"Nah, why?"

"Fourth Crew for life, that's why. Y'all will always be down, no matter what!"

Claudius and Reggie had never had that kind of money. They were beginning to get real excited. Even though Reggie stayed in Virginia, he was begging us to get him started in the business. We assured him that we had everything on smash and that we indeed already had a plan for him. We vowed to tell him about the plan before he left to go back to Virginia.

"Reggie, calm down, kid. You know that we're family. So if we're large, you're large. You'll be phat just like us," Latiefe promised. "Just be patient. We'll get you paid."

We reminded Reggie that he was in the military, which meant that the battle was half won. What we meant was, with Reggie being in the military, any drug involvement on his part could easily be camouflaged. He could wear his "nice-looking-proud-to-be-an-American," uniform when he was off duty, and at the same time transport drugs anywhere he pleased. What cop was gonna question a full-blooded American soldier?

Claudius also wanted in on the narcotics scene. He told us that he could easily hook up with drug dealers out in Kansas. There was a brief, deafening pause of silence in the room after Claudius had made his comment. Then the entire crew fell out onto the floor in laughter. "Kansas drug dealers? Ha ha ha ha ha."

Latiefe asked, "Yo, don't you stay in Witchita? Where the hell is that? In westbubblehut?" More balled over, belly-aching, knee jerk laughter filled the room.

Claudius laughed with us. He went on to tell us about the gangs in Kansas. He told us about the drugs and killings out there, and about the Crips and the Bloods. "It's just like New York," Claudius said. "Urban life is just about the same everywhere."

I blurted out, "Nah, hell no! No way, kid! Claudius, we're not letting you get mixed up in this. You have a full basketball scholarship, so take advantage of it. Don't blow that."

Erik added, "Even if you don't make the pros, you'll still have that degree to fall back on. Claudius, go for the NBA millions, or at least get that degree. Don't worry about the street loot. Plus, Claudius, we'll hit you off with loot, so don't worry about it. But in a few years when you're playing against Jordan and all them cats in the finals, we want front row seats right on the floor where Spike Lee and all the celebrities be at."

Claudius didn't want to listen to our advice. He pleaded with us to put him down. But we persisted in our refusal.

I added, "Claudius, on the real, this drug game ain't no joke. It'll totally jack you up. Once you get involved with this game you start to live on the edge. Best friends of yours start getting stomped out and exterminated like roaches. It ain't worth it. Claudius, when you're on the outside looking in, everything looks sweet. You start looking at the fly cars and females be throwing themselves at you and all that, but yo, it's still not worth it.

Claudius, hang with us for the next two weeks and you'll see what I'm talking about. Examine our actions, conversations and our way of thinking. I guarantee you'll see a different crew from the last time you saw us. We used to care, or at least I know I did. Now I don't even give a damn about nothing. When I tell you that I'll snap a niggah's neck in a second or I'll shoot somebody and won't lose sleep over it, believe it. Someone could walk in this room right now and blow you away and I wouldn't be phased. Not one bit. See, I already lived through it, so I'm used to it happening.

Claudius, this lifestyle will have you thinking that you're crazy! You'll stop caring about life. Not that I'm immortal or anything, but this game will have you thinking like you can't die. And I know that I won't die 'cause in my mind I honestly believe that there ain't a cat out there that's smarter than me and more ruthless than me. You know what I'm sayin? And that's how you have to think. If there is a cat iller than me and I do die at his hands, then so be it. I mean, everybody has to die one day, right?"

After I said all of that, Claudius contemplated for a little while. "Yo, I'm sayin' it's still worth it. Man, I be so broke at school I don't even be having money to go out or nothing like that. It just be hard to maintain. Just put me down. Please, y'all!"

Randy looked at Claudius in disbelief and asked, "Didn't you hear any of what Holz said? Claudius, you know Holz never used to talk all ill and sick like that. Now he's a straight-up thug niggah, and you're saying that you still want to be down? You're buggin'. You mean you would chance all of what you have just for some dead presidents? Claudius, I don't know man. Yo what are they teaching you in that college?"

Erik continued with our onslaught of Claudius. He told us "Yo, don't give in to that niggah. Yo Claudius, we ain't putting you down with this, 'cause we love you too much. Period!"

So the weekend went on. It lived up to its advanced billing. With Reggie and Claudius hanging with us we had extra fun in the sun. All weekend long we just partied, got high, and committed all kinds of sin. When

Tuesday rolled around, Claudius was still talking about the past weekend. He couldn't believe how much better our quality of life was. Tons of loot will have that kind of an effect on a brotha. Most of all, he loved the high maintenance, top notch, beautiful females that yearned to be with us.

He pointed out, "Last summer when I came home, everything was mediocre and boring. Now it's like a fantasy reel."

Dwight added, which probably enforced Claudius' illegal desires, "That's because when you came home last summer we were all broker than a joke. Now we have cash coming out of our anus, and the world is our footstool."

Later that Tuesday night, for Reggie's sake and Claudius' sake, we decided to relive some of the pastimes that had crafted us into such a tight knit family. We were all on Merrick Blvd. We had a big boom box radio and one microphone. One by one, each of us would take the mic and start freestyling. While one of us would freestyle, the rest of us would dance.

That night, while on Merrick Blvd., we all drank forties and danced. Randy had the mic in his hand and he recited his rhyme. I have to admit that Randy was talented with the mic. He had a gift to produce hype and energy in those that heard him rhyme. Probably because he had a natural B-boy's voice, coupled with the fact that when he rhymed he always said a lot of "1,2's". His rhymes always sounded phat. That night was no different. Randy had managed to set things off. He sparked all of us who were out there on the corner.

Latiefe then took the mic and said his rhyme. Latiefe thought he was the best M.C. in our crew. He had some skills, but I don't know if he was definitely the best M.C. in our crew. That was always something that we debated. I would always tell Latiefe that his rhymes were pre-written, which gave him an unfair advantage. See, true freestyling was the art of saying rhymes off the top of your head, and that's what the rest of us did. We were actually more lyrically gifted than Latiefe.

His rhyme kept the atmosphere charged, and after he finished rhyming he passed me the mic. The tape that was being played in the boom box was the 'Rising To The Top' instrumental. That beat was the Queens anthem, as far as young, New york hip=hoppers were concerned. A legendary park DJ from Queens, DJ Grandmaster Vic, was responsible for branding the 'Rising To The Top' instrumental and making the Queens anthem.

So with the Queens anthem playing in the background, I kicked my rhyme. It was dark outside and we were all standing under a streetlight, directly in front of Pop and Kim's candy. As I rhymed, people started to crowd around me. The more people that gathered around, more hyped up I got. So with all kinds of passion and enthusiasm in my voice I kicked my rhyme like this:

"Wednesday night, Uptown 1-2-5
We had to let punk niggahs know Fourth Crew was live.
In front of the Apollo
Punks tried to play us, you know.
So I pulled out the Calico and col' went Rambo.
Wet the whole block up,
Even a cop got popped,
So to avoid getting knocked I hopped
in the MPV, drove off
and boomed the Cypress Hill CD.
"How could I just kill a man?"
Yeahhh, and you know the MPV was packed,
'cause Fourth is stacked.
We were rolling phat,
low profile tires, deep dish rims
sippin' on the brew from Pop & Kim's.
The cold Old Gold had my head feeling nice.

> *I remember twice in life*
> *I was called the hot diggidy dog,*
> *And on both occasions I sent suckers to the morgue.*
> *Yeahhh, Fourth Crew will catch wreck,*
> *Snap a niggahs' neck in a sec,*
> *Step and won't give a heck,*
> *'cause we're ruthless!*
> *So bus' it, big Wiggie.*
> *Yeah, you know you're my man –*
> *Grab the mic and rip it the best you can."*

Wiggie took the mic and started rhyming. His rhyme went like this:

> *"I grab the mic from my man, big Holz,*
> *proceed to rip things just like I was told.*
> *Because I've been bus'in' funky*
> *rhymes since I was eight years old.*
> *This to me is like second nature.*
> *In the summertime we go to Six Flags Great Adventure,*
> *terrorize the park..."*

While Wiggie was rhyming, the police came and made us stop. They said we were disturbing the peace. Of course we argued with them and told them that we were just having fun. And of course, we lost that argument as they pressed us and told us to get off the Blvd. or else we would all get summonses.

To pacify the police we walked a few blocks down Merrick Blvd. and started rolling dice, another one of our favorite pastimes. We played a dice game called Ci-Lo. When playing Ci-Lo, three dice are used instead of two. Ci-Lo was much more fun than craps or 7/11 which only used two dice. In Ci-Lo the object was to roll the dice, get two dice to have the same number and the third die would be considered your point.

While we rolled, I had the bank. I was winning mad dough. There were people watching, but they didn't join in because our stakes were too high. Back in the days, when we were broke, we would roll for single dollar bills. The most we would ever roll for was five dollars. But now that we had money, we were rolling for fifties and hundreds.

We rolled for a pretty long time, then it became boring. See, back in the day, we were happy if we won two dollars or depressed even if we lost a small amount like seven dollars. But now money was no object to us, so it was easy come, easy go. It didn't matter if we won or lost, so we got bored.

After rolling Ci-Lo we went back to the Fourth Crew apartment. Claudius was petrified of the Pit-Bull that we had. He was also afraid of our other dog, which was a Rotweiler. As big as Claudius was, he had no business being afraid of the dogs, but we still locked the dogs in the bathroom so that we could all be relaxed. Once the dogs were put away, we all sat and got drunk. Still reliving our lost lifestyle, we decided to play a game that we used to play all of the time, Russian Roulette. Not the same Roulette that's played in the casinos. Our version of Roulette was played with a handgun, preferably a six-shot revolver.

All of the bullets would be emptied from the gun, except for one. With that one bullet in the gun, the revolver was spun so that we would be unable to tell when the bullet might enter the chamber. The gun was passed around the room and everyone took a turn pointing the gun at someone else, then he would pull the trigger. With a six-shot revolver, there was a slightly better than 16% chance that the bullet would enter the chamber each time a new contestant took a turn. And that unlucky person could end up dead.

We unloaded a .22 long then put one hollow point bullet inside the gun. After the bullet was loaded into the gun, we decided who would go first. Whoever was the first person to get shot at proceeded to become the next shooter, providing he didn't get hit with the bullet. After that shooter pulled the trigger, that shootee became the shooter, and so on. According to the rules, if the trigger had been pulled four times and no bullet discharged, then the revolver would be spun to relocate the bullet. It added suspense to the game. In order for the game to end, everyone had to be shot at two times. Unless of course someone was actually shot dead before the game ended.

Down the line we went, pulling the trigger. Our hearts were beating and our palms were sweating, but no one wanted to admit they were nervous. When it came time for you to get shot at, you had better not play like a sucker and try to run or quit. If you did front, you'd have to receive a five-minute beating from all of the other participants. A "five minute wreck" is what the beat down was called.

We had managed to successfully complete the first go around. The second go around started. J.P. put the gun to Erik's head. As Erik cringed and closed his eyes, J.P. pulled the trigger… Click! Nothing. Then Erik took the gun and put it to Latiefe's temple. Latiefe was stone-faced and didn't flinch. Erik pulled the trigger… Click! No bullet discharged. Everyone released a sigh after each attempt. Two more attempts were made, and both of them came up empty. So Randy spun the revolver. Now it was my turn to be shot at. Randy put the gun to my head. I was eerie, feeling as though my best friend was about to kill me. I sat in the chair as still as I could. There was a split second of silence.

"Hol' up! Hol' up! Chill!" I screamed just as Randy was about to pull the trigger. "I ain't doing it! I'm out!"

"Yo Holz, you're a sucker! Word!" Everyone yelled, "Five minute wreck!"

I tried to bounce as they charged at me, but they caught me and started pounding on my body. I broke loose and ran out of the apartment. I ran all the way out into the street. When they caught up to me, they beat me some more. I screamed in pain, but it was kind of funny at the same time.

"Let me explain," I yelled as I laughed. "Just let me explain," I pleaded for mercy.

"Nah, there ain't no explaining! Your five minutes ain't up yet, niggah!"

After about ten minutes I was still getting a whipping and my body was throbbing in pain. Randy stepped in to stop the melee and he said, "Holz, if I pull this trigger and a bullet doesn't come out, you're gonna get wrecked some more."

Randy pointed the gun straight into the air towards the dark night sky. It was a night where every star in the sky could be seen. He pulled the trigger. Kaboom! The sound of the gun filled the night's air. We saw the flame exit the gun along with the bullet. Everyone was startled because no one actually expected the gun to go off.

I yelled, "Yo, what the …!" I thought about how close I had came to being shot in the head by my best friend. "Yo!"

Ten Thirteen

One of the best times of the week was upon us. Wednesday night, August 7th. Fourth Crew went on yet another venture to Harlem. Nah, we didn't go to buy drugs or anything like that. We went to the world famous Apollo Theater. Like any other Wednesday night, the scene outside of the Apollo after amateur night had concluded was frenzied. People were everywhere.

On that night of August 7th, Fourth Crew stood out in the crowd like shining stars. We had an inflated sense of pride and self-esteem. We now belonged. For the first time we didn't travel to the Apollo in a little Toyota or in a beat up station wagon. Nor did we travel there on the subway. We weren't all squished into one car resembling a can of sardines.

No, none of that. The day that we had long envisioned was finally here. We traveled to the Apollo in cars worth thousands. Each of our eight whips carried no more than four men. We all drove in a convoy one behind the other. We looked like the president and his entourage being escorted into town. My Saab was leading the pack. The letters F.O.U.R.T.H C.R.E.W were printed on both sides of all of our cars. The letters were black on top of a chrome background.

As we circled 125th Street, everybody clocked us. We were dressed to the T. Our gold was blazin' and our ice was shining. After circling around the block a number of times, we decided to park and floss in front of our cars. Females stared at us as we stood in front of our cars. The same females that wouldn't give us the time of day just two short months ago were now captivated by our presence.

Yeah, we kicked game to some of the females who had dissed us weeks before. I knew that they didn't remember us, but boy, did we remember them. As we conversed with them, we played high post. We looked away as we talked to them, not giving them our full attention. After all, we were fly and we knew it. We saw in their eyes that they wanted our phone numbers or they at least wanted us to ask them for their numbers. Ha!

They sure weren't going to get what they wanted. Rooted somewhere deep in their minds were their schemes of benefiting from the money we appeared to have. Fortunately, we had pulled and filed the cards on those gold-digging, high maintenance chicks a long time ago. After they finally realized that we weren't going to ask them for their numbers they took the initiative. They wrote down their numbers and handed them to us.

"Ha!" we chuckled as we ripped up the little pieces of paper that they handed us. "Next!" we would yell as we prepared to dis some more women.

We didn't play like big Willies all night, though. We did give our phone numbers out and we took phone numbers, but only from a select few females who hadn't dissed us before. Other guys, of course, were insanely jealous of us. But who the hell cared? We blasted our car stereos into the wee hours of the night and had all types of fun.

After we'd left the Apollo and returned to our apartment, we laughed and discussed everything that had happened. And our discussion carried one common theme, what a drastic difference life was now that we had loot.

The next night was Thursday. And during the summer of 1991, Thursday nights had developed into a big night for urban New Yorkers. A club called the Red Zone was open on Thursday nights. Club promoter Sean "Puff Daddy" Combs had the spot on Thursdays, and he dubbed it Daddy's Night. Everybody who was anybody could be found at the Red Zone on Daddy's Night. Like most New

York hot spots, the Red Zone was frequented by many rap stars.

Every Thursday night our crew had to represent and make an appearance at the Red Zone. We had to be there simply because that was the place to be. The Red Zone contained the ghetto type of atmosphere that we lived for. Whenever we would go to the Red Zone we would wait on long lines to get in, just as everyone else would. Even the A- list celebrities had to wait on line. That's how packed the club would always be. After waiting on line we would pay our $10.00 entrance fee and then we would be inside the nightclub. After we'd passed through the metal detectors and were frisked, of course.

Every week the music inside the club would be on point. Heads would lose their minds when MC's like Biz Markie or KRS ONE would rip the mic and start freestyling over some ill break beat or whateva. All of the best DJ's in New York showed their stuff at the Red Zone. DJ's like Kid Capri, Red Alert, and Funkmaster Flex. The Red Zone would always be so rammed that you could hardly move around, much less get busy on the dance floor. But in essence, that's what made it fun. I would get high just thinking about how much fun the Red Zone generated. Inside the club, we would smoke our weed, parlay at the bar, dance and have a good time.

On that Thursday at the Red Zone, the response that we were getting from females continued on the up and up. Everybody wanted a piece of our action. I knew that once the summer came to an end the club would definitely lose some of its pizzazz, but until it did, you could expect to see Fourth Crew in the joint every Thursday night.

Friday night, Latiefe, Randy, and I sat in Randy's room counting cheese and discussing what we thought should be Fourth Crew's next moves as far as our drug business went. As we counted and conversed, Latiefe expressed that he was getting bored with all of our newfound riches. I related to what Latiefe was expressing. It was like once you have something that you've never had but always wanted, you're like, "Oh, it's not all that I thought it would be."

Latiefe said, "Yo, if we do like we did before we had loot, then new ways of flipping our loot will automatically come to us."

Randy didn't understand what Latiefe was talking about. He was about to ask Latiefe a question, but I beat him to the punch. "Yeah," I said in response to Latiefe. "Let's go uptown and play some ball until the sun comes up. We could put on them Harlem cats at that park with all the lights."

"You mean Rucker Park?" Randy asked.

"Yeah, the Rucker. Yo, wouldn't it be fun if someone organized a midnight basketball league? That way we could spend our spare time constructively, you know, just ballin' in the park."

Randy added, "Word, that would be the move." Then he reminded us of the nighttime basketball tournament that the drug dealers used to run. The tournament was SNIFF.

"Didn't someone get killed in that tournament?" I asked.

"Yeah," Randy replied, "I think it was the referee that got mercked. He made a bad call near the end of the game or something like that."

"Yeah yo, you can't make no bad calls and expect to live," I said.

Randy added, "Especially when cats are betting $50,000 on a game! You got- damn right you can't make no bad calls."

Latiefe, sounding very disgusted, interrupted and said, "What the hell are y'all talking about? I'm not talking about us going to play no damn basketball! Can't y'all understand what I'm sayin'? I'm bored. I want to jack a niggah! You know what I'm sayin'? Let's rob some sucker! Y'all wit' it or what? Come on, we'll steal a car, rob a niggah and laugh, you kna'imean?"

I was thinking to myself, "Latiefe, you sound so pathetic."

Then I said out loud, "For what? Latiefe, why should we steal a car and rob somebody? We already got loot! When we were broke it was a different story."

Latiefe informed me, "Why? Because we're thugs, that's why! Whatchu mean, it's a different story? I'm sayin', let's just do it for fun Man, y'all niggahs is mad boring! And y'all are supposed to be some thugs niggahs?"

Everyone was quiet for about thirty seconds. We were trying to figure out exactly what we should do with our idle time. Randy broke the silence and said, "Ah'ight, whateva. I'm wit' it. Let's go have some fun."

Also sounding very lethargic, I sucked my teeth like a Jamaican and said, "Ah'ight. But I'm only doing it if we steal a Blazer."

"Yeah, alright," Latiefe replied, sounding very eager to step into sin. "That ain't no problem. Let's be out before y'all softy-moist niggahs change y'all mind."

Later that night the three of us canvassed the neighborhood of Laurelton. We were looking for a Chevy Blazer. It didn't matter what year the Blazer was, because all of the models looked the same. We walked through the dark streets dressed in the latest fashions. We weren't wearing the quote-unquote preppie type fashions. Instead we were wearing the hoodlum fashions, saggy jeans and all.

As we walked down 228th Street we came upon a 1987 Blazer. "Lets do it!" Latiefe said as he barked his orders.

At that point I was a little skeptical because the Blazer was parked in someone's driveway. "Yo we can't mess with that one," I loudly whispered. "We gotta find one that's parked on the curb. It's easier access. Plus this piece could have an alarm or whateva. If they look out their window they'll either start shooting, or they'll be calling the cops, or both."

With the sound of crickets in the background, Latiefe whispered back, "Holz, stop being a sucker. Come on, we're taking this one while we got the chance. Trust me, we ain't gonna get caught."

With that, Randy quickly proceeded to break the driver's side window of the Blazer. I unlocked the door and got in, then opened the other door and allowed Latiefe and Randy to jump in.

"Hurry and start the car, Holz!" Latiefe loudly whispered.

"I can't," I said in a panicked tone. "I'm having trouble with this pulley. I don't know what's up."

"Man, move the hell out of the way and let me do it!" Latiefe quietly barked.

We switched positions and Latiefe snatched the pulley and screwdriver out of my hand. In seconds he had the car started. He backed it out of the driveway and we were off.

After we had driven two blocks or so away from the house, Latiefe stopped the car so that we could clean out some of the glass that was inside. When we were done with that I retook the position as driver and we were again off and driving in search of our first victim. As we drove I instructed Latiefe, "Yo, don't turn that radio on. The system is probably too loud, and I ain't trying to get stopped in this damn car!"

As I realized that we were actually cruising in a stolen car, it was like a brick had hit me, and I couldn't believe it. Was I just totally stupid or what? "Man what are we doing in this car?" I asked. "This whole thing is stupid! What the hell are we doing?"

Randy yelled from the back seat, "Holz, just shut up and drive. And yo, turn that radio on. We ain't getting caught. We're just having fun. You tell me how the hell are we gonna have fun with no music? We're just going for a little joyride. What's up? You scared or something? Besides, I'm sayin', I'll kill somebody tonight before I go to jail, word up!"

Randy, who was carrying the gun that we planned to use in our robbery, reached into the front of the car and cranked the music up. The Blazer was now booming. Everyone could hear us coming from at least two or three blocks away as we drove along the streets of Queens.

I abruptly turned the radio off and said, "It's too late at night for that. If it was daylight then yeah we could blast it, but not now. We'll attract way too much attention."

We drove and drove through just about every town in Queens; South Ozone Park, Howard Beach, Astoria, St. Albans, Hollis, Jamaica, Corona, everywhere. Latiefe asked, "Why is it so dead tonight? Ain't nobody outside. Where the hell is everybody? We've been driving for too long. Yo, forget that waiting for the perfect victim. Man, the next person that we see we're sticking them up. I'm just itching to jack somebody. I ain't having no fun yet. This driving and driving and driving is boring!"

In an effort to speed things up so that I could go home and get some sleep I eagerly said, "Bet! The next person we see, 'cause it's too late for this nonsense. I could be laid up knocking Kendra's boots right about now, but instead I'm driving around with y'all clowns. Ain't nobody out here on the street 'cause everybody is in the crib 'sleep."

As we continued to drive I became suspicious of a car that was trailing in back of us. *It must be following us,* I thought to myself. I had remembered seeing it about seven or eight turns ago. In the tone of a kid that was about to get into trouble, I said to Randy and Latiefe, "Yo, don't both of y'all look now, but I think Five-O is following us."

Latiefe who was sitting in the passenger seat immediately turned his head like a fool. "Yo kid, that is Five-O!" Latiefe emphatically proclaimed.

"Got-damn!" I screamed as I simultaneously rammed my fist against the dashboard. "I told y'all dumb niggahs! See, this whole idea was stupid! Latiefe, why the hell did you turn around? Now we definitely look suspicious."

"Holz, shut the hell up! I been listening to you crying like a girl all night long and now is definitely not the time for more of your crying!" Latiefe yelled.

Tensions were on edge as Randy yelled from the back seat, "Yo, why don't both of y'all niggahs shut the hell up? Y'all are arguing like women and the cops are following us. Just shutup and be quiet. We gotta see how we gonna get out of this. Now Holz, just relax and drive. Don't switch lanes or nothing like that."

"You sure that's Five-O?" I asked.

Sounding kind of nervous, Latiefe said, "Hell yeah. Those are the same two DT's that stopped me once before. Everybody in Queens knows what kind of unmarked car they drive. Besides, it's 2:30 in the morning. There ain't no other cars out here."

Randy informed us, "Yo, we gotta get outta this car. Holz, this is what you do. Make a right turn, and if they turn with us I want you to immediately turn the lights off and floor this thing."

For some reason I felt relaxed. I mean, under the circumstances I should have been pissing in my pants, but I wasn't nervous at all. Although the cops were following us, I felt as though we weren't gonna get caught. I followed Randy's instructions and made the right turn. And as expected, the detectives made the turn with us.

"Go Holz, go! Floor this piece!" Randy screamed.

I played counselor as I calmly said, "Yo, just chill. They're not gonna pull us over."

Latiefe yelled, "Yes they are! Yo Holz, lose them!"

"Yo, we're gonna get caught if I try to outrun them. This big truck ain't fast enough."

Randy instructed, "Well just drive this thing as fast as you can. I need some way to throw this gun out the window. I ain't trying to get bagged with this gun on me."

Latiefe informed me that he had an ounce of coke on him, which of course only stood to make matters much worse. By the second, things were falling apart for us.

"Yo Holz," Latiefe said, "I gotta get rid of this work! Lose those pigs so that I can throw this work out the window. If we get caught for a stolen car we'll get off, but if we get caught with a gun and drugs, we're going up north."

"OK, OK. Ah'ight, check it. I'ma make another turn, and if they turn with me, I'm gonna pull over and get out and ask them for directions like I'm lost."

In disbelief Randy screamed out, "Man, are you crazy? If that ain't the most jack-ass backwards move! That won't work. Don't you know that they probably already know this car is stolen? With all that damn noise we made in the driveway, the people in that house probably saw us taxing their jeep and called the cops. All I know is that if we go to jail because you didn't try to outrun these pigs, man, I'm gonna hold your butt cheeks open for the cat that rapes you."

I remained silent as I turned onto Springfield Blvd. In the daytime, Springfield Blvd. was always crowded with cars. But at night there were certain stretches along Springfield Blvd. that were usually deserted. I drove down the Blvd. and the cops were still tailing us. I pulled over to the curb.

"Got-damn it! Holz, what the hell are you doing? Drive this car! We still dirty! We didn't get rid of the heat or the blow." Latiefe sounded like he'd lost his mind.

"Just chill! I'm gonna play it off like I'm using the pay phone. If they step to me, I'll talk us out of any trouble."

Latiefe clenched his teeth and uttered, "Oh my God! What the …. That's not gonna work! Yo, I can't belive that we're gonna go to jail because of this niggah. Yo Holz, drive this car."

"I can't do that," I said. "I already pulled to the side and it'll definitely look too suspicious if I all of a sudden pull off and start driving again."

"Well yo, do this. Just sit in the car, because you know that they're gonna stop right behind us. As soon as they get out of their car and start approaching our car, that's when you hit the accelerator. That'll give us enough time to dump this gun and these drugs. Plus if we have to, we would even have enough time drive a few blocks and then get out and run on foot." Randy sounded anxious.

"Nah, nah. Trust me. I got this this," I said as I prepared to step out of the truck.

Just as I was stepping out of the Blazer, the cops pulled up right behind us. They put their red flashing light onto the dashboard of their car to let us know that they indeed were cops.

I could hear the sound of thumping hearts coming from inside the stolen Blazer.

I calmly proceeded to walk to the pay phone. The phone was located on the corners of Springfield Blvd. and Westgate Ave., right in front of Montebello Park. As I picked up the telephone's receiver, one of the detectives said to me, "Put the phone down right now."

The other DT shined his flashlight into the truck so that he could see exactly who was inside. The one near me showed me his badge, announcing that he was detective Mark Schienbart and that his partner was named Darryl Gates. They were with the 105th police precinct.

"Oh, word," I said sounding very cheery, "Your name is Mark? That's my name. What a coincidence."

Unfortunately he didn't appreciate my conversation starter. "Oh, that's nice," he replied. "So Mark, let me see some papers. Do you have a driver's license?"

By this time the other detective had come over to where I was standing.

"Detective Daryll Gates," he introduced himself. To my surprise, he sounded somewhat polite.

"Do you have a registration and insurance card for that vehicle?"

Quickly thinking on my feet, I answered, "Yes, I do. It's in the glove compartment. Do you wanna see it?"

Detective Schienbart responded with his voice full of arrogance. "Yes, we would love to see it. But first I want to see your driver's license."

I showed him my license. He examined it real close, and I guess he wanted to test to see if it was authentic or not because he started with a quick line of questioning.

"What street do you live on?" he asked.

"234th street," I responded.

"How tall are you?"

"I'm six feet."

"What's your eye color?"

"Brown."

"What's your date of birth?"

"June 14th."

Finally he stopped with the quick line of questions which were designed to try to see if I would slip up and to see if I came across as nervous.

"OK, Mr. Holsey, now lets see the registration, if you don't mind."

I was desperately trying to think of a way to buy us some time. I was willing to try anything in order to have us avoid being arrested.

"Can I use the phone first?" I asked. "I mean, that is why I pulled over."

"No, you can't use the got-damn phone! Now let me see the friggin' reggie and the friggin' insurance card!" the cop yelled. Don't ask me what the heck friggin' means, but apparently it is some type of white slang, because angry white men are always using it.

Anyway, still trying to buy some time, I added, "But it's a very important phone call." I reached for the phone and begged, trying my best to sound like a white boy. "Oh c'mon, it'll only take a second."

The cop got blood red from anger as he told me, "Look, you little black nigger! You and your nigger friends will be making phone calls from jail if you don't let me see the registration and the insurance card right now!"

The detectives had us and they knew it. Their actions were so cocky it made me sick to my stomach. Other than calling me a nigger, they were being way too polite. In the past, even when we hadn't done anything wrong and they pulled us over, they would still harass us. They would throw us on the floor and all of that. Now it was different. They hadn't even asked Latiefe and Randy to get out of the car. I supposed that they wanted to savor the arrests that they were about to make.

Again, for some strange reason, I still wasn't nervous as I should have been. But I would be lying if I said that my heart rate didn't increase. Reality was quickly setting in, because I knew that I was running out of both time and excuses. I walked to the passenger side of the Blazer in an attempt to reach into the window. The DT was breathing right on my back with his hand near his gun. I was about to pretend as though I was reaching into the glove compartment for the paperwork. I wisely paused and explained to the detective, "Look, please don't shoot me or anything. I'm just gonna slowly reach into the glove compartment for the paperwork, ah'ight?"

The detective didn't respond, but took two steps back, so I took that as an OK to proceed. When I stuck my head in the car Latiefe nervously whispered, "Yo Holz, what's up man? What did they say?"

"Nothing. They didn't say nothin' yet. They want the paperwork. But yo, they got us. They know that they got us," I quickly whispered back.

Just as I was about to pull away from the window, Randy, who was sitting in the back seat whispered back to me, "Holz, on the ah'ight?"

"Ah'ight," I replied as I looked Randy straight into his eyes, trying my hardest to use ESP. I backed away from the Blazer and spoke to the cop. "Yo, um, I don't know. My pops must have taken the registration and the insurance card out of the car this morning, 'cause I can't find it."

"Oh, is that right?" the two white DT's asked sarcastically.

"Yeah, that has to be it," I said as if I was trying to win an Academy award for 'Most Convincing Thug in a Street Drama.'

"Mr. Holsey, this car was reported stolen about an hour ago. And it's registered to a Mrs. Jackson. You, of course, wouldn't know anything about that, now would you?"

There was a pause for a moment. Dead silence. I thought about bolting and running for my life and my freedom. I contemplated hitting one of the cops in the mouth with the phone receiver, but it was too late for that.

"Alright, get up against the gate and assume the position. Play time is over!"

I tried to keep both of the cops' attention on myself. I figured that if I was at least able to keep them distracted that would give Randy and Latiefe a chance to get away. There was no sense in all of us going to jail.

"Nah, nah! I'm tired of this harassment! I ain't assuming no position! What! What!" I yelled in an attempt to show up both cops.

"Get your hands up behind your head and spread your legs apart right now!" Gates yelled as he kicked my legs apart and pushed me against a fence. The other DT was on his walkie-talkie. I guess he was asking for a squad car to assist them in the arrest. I mean, after all, it was three of us that they had to haul in.

As I was being frisked I purposely continued to resist. Again, I was hoping to at least free Randy and Latiefe. I couldn't believe they hadn't bounced by now. I didn't know what the hell they were doing, but they were blowing their chance.

"Yo money, you don't gotta be grabbing all up on my nuts like that! I'm clean! I ain't got nothing on me, damn! Y'all cats be buggin'!"

These cops were way too confident. In fact, they were forgetting that they were cops, probably because they knew they were about to make a big arrest. They probably only made the rank of detective based on the color of their white skin, 'cause man, they were so dumb with their tactics. With my back to the Blazer and my face rammed against a park fence, Gates ordered, "Pull your pants down. I wanna see what's under your ball sac."

"What?" I replied. Even with all of my years of being harassed, that remark was a new one for me.

"What the hell is under your balls? You got crack rocks? Let me know now!" Gates barked. By this time Schienbart was off of his walkie-talkie and he joined in on the crusade. He proceeded to sift through my belongings that DT Gates had taken from my pockets, which by this time were on the ground.

Schienbart asked, "Where did you get all of this money from?" I kept silent.

Then Schienbart said, "Cuff him."

"Handcuff me for what?" I demanded to know. "What did I do?"

They asked me again, "Where did you get all of this cash from?"

With my fingers interlocked in place behind my head, I turned slightly and looked at the cop. "I worked for it. I work for the utility company. Can't a black man have a job? Or is that also against the law?" As I said that, I glanced at Latiefe. It looked as if he had winked his eye at me, but it was dark and kind of hard to see with the glare from the street light. I turned my head back towards the fence.

"Yeah, right!" one of the cops yelled while he slapped me upside my head. "No job pays an 18-year-old nigger that kind of money."

While he was saying that racist mumbojumbo, I counted in my head, *One thousand and one, one thousand and two, one thousand and three...* I finished counting.

As soon as I reached one thousand and three I heard either Latiefe or Randy make a hissing sound, sort of like when you're flirting with the opposite sex. "Spsss, pssss, sssps."

Being with the crew day in and day out for so many years, and based on my intuition, I knew at that moment to just hit the ground. Right after the last "Sssps", I instantly and violently dropped to the concrete and covered my head with my arms. I was sort of curled up in the fetal position. As I lay balled up on the ground I heard the massive sound of shattering glass, followed by the sound of rapid gunfire. The gunfire sounded, "Rat tat tat tat tat tat tat tat tat tat tat tat tat tat!"

The gun that was being fired sounded as if it was just spitting out bullets and wouldn't stop. I felt a thump on my body. I cautiously peeked and saw that it was one of the detectives. He'd fallen on top of me after being shot. I tried to look to my left and I saw the other detective, Darryl Gates, fall to the ground!

As the sound of gunfire was still rapidly erupting I could hear Schienbart grimacing in pain as he continue to lay on top of me, sort of acting as my human proof vest. As I lay underneath him, I didn't know who it was that was doing the shooting. I couldn't tell whether it was Randy or Latiefe. And to tell you the truth, I really didn't care who was pulling the trigger I just knew to concentrate on keeping myself covered up and I hoped that I didn't catch a bullet. The detective still had bullets entering into his body as he lay on top of me.

Finally, after about ten seconds, which actually felt more like ten minutes, the gunfire had stopped. There was nothing but dead silence. I felt like I was in a scene from a Rambo movie.

"Yo Holz, you ah'ight? Holz, get up man. Come on. Get in the car."

I couldn't tell if I was still alive, but I had no time to pinch myself because this was definitely real-life, big time drama. I pushed the cop's body off of me. I got up and quickly examined the gruesome scene. The whole right side rear passenger window of the Blazer was gone. Then I saw two white detectives, bloodier than ever and laying face first on the pavement. Their bodies were riddled with bullet holes. They looked as though they were cardboard someone had used for target practice. Spaghetti sauce-like blood spilled out of their bodies. Some of their blood had managed to get on to my body.

"Come on, Holz! What the hell are you looking at? Let's go! We have to be out! Now get in the car!" Latiefe yelled.

I screamed back, "Nah. No! Oh hell, no! I ain't leaving yet! I'm getting mines! It's time for the big payback." After saying that I sort of slipped into a sadistic rage. I yelled as I kicked DT Schienbart in the face. I repeatedly yelled and kicked him in the face and ribs. His blood got all over my pants and sneakers. I didn't care though, because

I knew that he was just about dead. But the pig still had enough energy though to try and grab hold of my leg.

"Yo, get off of me!" I yelled. Then I kicked him three more times. Each time that I kicked him I would yell out, "Ugh!" The sound helped me expel the maximum amount of strength that my body could dish out. I got up real close to Schienbart's earlobe and I hollered, "Don't you ever try to arrest me! Ugh!" Then I kicked him again. "That's for all those times y'all harassed us for no reason at all. Ugh! How does that feel? Ugh! You dumb pig! Thha. I just spit in your face. Get up, punk! Thha. I spit on you again. Arent't you gonna arrest me?"

Latiefe pleaded, "Holz, come on and get in the car or you're gettin' left! We ain't got time for this!"

"Go ahead and leave me 'cause I ain't finished with these pigs yet. Ugh!" I yelled as I went running and kicked the other officer square in the nose. "You don't look so bad. Ugh! Here's another! Ugh!" I let loose a barrage of punches to his face. I threw those punches with every ounce of energy that was inside my body. "Thha thha thha thha," I spit in his face until I couldn't spit no more. I kicked him numerous times, making sure that I broke some of his ribs. I reached and picked up a stick that was nearby and I rapidly and repeatedly whacked detective Darryll Gates with the stick. Then I performed the two deadliest sins that could be dealt to the self- proclaimed god-like men. I took the 9mm pistol that Bates was carrying. I also took his badge from around his neck.

"I got your badge! I got your gun! And you know what? You ain't much without a gun or a badge! Come on, knuckle up now! What?" I yelled. "Get up, punk! Spread your legs, get your hands over your head! Drop all of your drugs on the ground right now! Lift up your nut sac. You don't got no crack, do you? Tell me now and I'll make it easier on you. Ugh! Ugh! Ugh!" I grunted as I whipped the officer with his own gun.

"Holz, I'll shoot you right now if you don't get in this truck!" Randy screamed as he pointed his gun in my direction.

Breathing hard and heavy, I said to Randy and Latiefe, "Yo, I thought we was doing this to have fun. What's wrong? Y'all ain't having fun yet?"

I hit Gates. "Didn't I tell you to get up? Ugh! That's for Eleanor Bumpers. Ugh! That's for Phillip Pannell."

I ran back to the other officer and whacked him in the mouth with the gun. "That's for Michael Stewart. Ugh!" I hit him again. "That's for me and all of my homeboyz. Ugh! And that's for my boy Rodney King out in Los Angeles."

Randy again pointed the gun out of the missing window and he hollered with renewed anger and conviction, "Holz, come on! I hear sirens!"

I ignored him and I took the wallet out of Schienbart's pocket. "Is this your wife?" I asked. "Is it? Answer me! She looks good. I think I'll leave now and go pay her a visit. I want you and your partner to think about that while the two of y'all rot in hell! And think about all the people you've harassed over the years." I spit in the detectives' faces and then I quickly gathered all of my money and ID that was still on the ground. I ran a few feet to the Blazer with the DT's gun in my hand. My adrenaline was racing.

As I put the car in drive and violently peeled off screeching rubber, Randy let his gun off, aiming it in the direction of the detectives. He did that to ensure that the two detectives were dead. Then he stuck his head out of the window and screamed in ecstasy, "Woooooo!"

Latiefe scolded me. "Holz, we could've got bagged! Why did you put on that show for so long?"

"Forget that, man!" I said, still breathing heavy. After realizing what had just transpired, I was now more nervous than ever. Panting, I continued, "Yo, that... That was my one shining moment in time! You... You only get one shot in life and I had to take advantage of my one shot... Yo kid, did you see how I slaughtered those pigs? Yo, I took his gun! I beat a DT and took his badge and his gun! Ha ha ha."

Latiefe instructed me to hurry and go back to 228th, where we had stolen the car from. So when we reached 228th Street, which was about a minute from where we'd shot the detectives, we parked the car about two blocks away from the actual house that we had stolen it from. We all hopped out of the truck and proceeded to run non-stop for six blocks until we reached Randy's basement on 234th street. In his basement we all sat huffing and puffing. I had to pull off all of my clothes and sneakers because of the blood that was on them. I placed the soiled clothes that still had warm detective blood on them inside a plastic garbage bag and Randy gave me some of his gear to put on.

When we had all caught our breath I said, "Yo Randy, you are a wild cat, yo! Kid, you just murdered two poh-leeces!"

Randy sounded nervous as he proudly replied, "Yeah, I just killed two rednecks! I guess I'm a racist now. But you know what? I don't care, 'cause every black person in America has to be a racist, you know?"

Randy continued, "Police ain't nobody. They ain't God, but they be trying to play like they God. So I just made sure that we had no other gods before our God. 'Cause see, you know that they was about to make us bow down to them, word! And yo, I ain't bowing down to no other gods. Matter of fact, what y'all just witnessed is called reverse brutality. I call it homeboy brutality."

We all burst out into laughter and dance as we started reciting the rap songs 'F the_Police,' and '911 is a Joke.' Latiefe, who also sounded slightly nervous but at the same time relieved and excited said, "Holz, you ducked in the nick of time, 'cause if you had waited one more second, Randy would have popped a cap in your back. Word! But yo, I can't front. At first I thought that he had shot you."

"Yo, word is bond," I said. "Randy, are you crazy niggah? That Calico ain't no joke. It seems like it be spitting out like three or four rounds per second. It's much iller than an AK-47."

Randy boasted, "You saw how I maimed those white cops? I col' snuffed the life right out of them! Now that's what you call a Ten-Thirteen." Ten-Thirteen is a code, used by the cops to relay on their radios and walkie-talkies that they need immediate assistance because they are either getting their butt kicked or they are in serious danger.

Latiefe informed me, "Yo, Holz, right after I made that hissing sound, both of the detectives turned around and they were staring right at the Calico. Yo, you should have seen the look on their faces. They looked as pale as a ghost and as shook as I don't know what!"

I interrupted joyfully, "Yes! So they saw it coming, right? They knew that they were about to die, right?"

"You damn right they saw it coming," Randy said. "I don't know if you heard me, but right before I pulled the trigger I yelled 'surprise!' And then I let them have it. Ha!"

"Randy, you are definitely the wildest and illest niggah that I know! Do you know what you just did?"

"Hell, yeah, I know what I just did," Randy proclaimed with conviction. "I just took two lives, two police officers' lives." After a pause Randy said in a more serious tone, "But yo, on the serious tip, all jokes aside, I don't know about y'all, but I'm outta here tomorrow. I'm going down to Virginia for a while and I'ma just chill until things calm down. I gotta hide out."

"Hide out for what?" I asked.

Randy replied, "What do you mean, for what? I'm sayin'! I'm outta here until everything calms down. 'Cause when New York City finds out that two detectives were murdered, man, listen! There's gonna be cops everywhere. They won't stop paying all of Five-O overtime until they catch me. Y'all know that whenever a cop gets shot they always catch the person that pulled the trigger. So imagine what they'll do now, and how hard they're gonna come after me. Man, I whacked two poh-leeces, Mafia style at that. I basically left two DT's laying dead on the curb and full of bullet holes. They got better laws to protect animals from that type of treatment. Man, when you kill a cop they hunt you down forever if they have to. But eventually they get you."

After Randy finished venting, Latiefe spoke up. "We're not gonna get caught, so we don't even have to worry about that. But Randy, if you leave town we all would have to leave town. Just because you pulled the trigger, that doesn't mean that me and Holz are innocent. If I get caught, I'm going up for Murder One. And it's the same deal for Holz if he gets bagged, because we're both accomplices to the crime."

"Yo, kill all of that 'going up for Murder One' garbage! We ain't getting locked up. End of discussion," I assured.

Randy asked, "Y'all sounding all confident, but how do y'all really know that we won't get bagged? Come on. I'm telling y'all, let's just go to Hampton, Virginia for a minute and we'll bounce back to New York after the storm clouds pass. I'm telling y'all there will be cops everywhere in New York searching for us and eventually they'll get us."

Getting kind of annoyed with Randy's fears, I yelled, "Randy! The only way that we can get caught is if we start opening our mouths and telling everybody what we did. Hell, the cops ain't God! You be seeing on the news how they caught this person or that person. But unless they see you doing the crime, the only way that they can catch anybody is through tips that they get. And they get those tips from people that overheard cats running their mouths about the crime. Think about it. How the hell else can they catch a person? The only other way that they can catch a person is if the fugitive turns himself in or if there were witnesses to the crime.

Randy, I'm not gonna rat you out, because if I did then I'd get locked up too. Tee ain't saying nothing. You're not gonna turn yourself in. Nobody but the three of us knows what happened. The boulevard was empty. There were no witnesses. The cops can't trace the car back to us because it was stolen. We got all the bases covered, kid. You see what I'm sayin', Randy?"

Seeming a bit more sure about the situation, Randy replied, "Yeah, I hear you Holz, but yo, don't nobody open their mouth about this! When everybody starts talking about it, just play along with the conversation. Don't be saying that we did this and that. We ain't trying to big ourselves up on this. I hope y'all understand me. I mean, don't y'all say nothing! N-O-T-H-I-N-G! Don't tell nobody, not even the people in our crew. 'Till the day we die, only us and God will know who killed those two pigs."

We all agreed to stay tight lipped. Latiefe said, "Ah'ight, bet. Let's put our hands together on this." So as our hands touched one another's, I instructed everyone to look into each others' eyes. Then we all closed our eyes and I uttered, "Fourth Crew 'till the day we die." We were confirming our faithfulness to secrecy.

After a slight pause our eyes reopened. I advised the fellas, Latiefe in particular, that it would be best if we all slept at Randy's crib, and in the morning we would jet over to the apartment. Before we departed to take showers, Latiefe said, "Hey, listen. We were out at Long Beach boardwalk by ourselves tonight from 1 AM until 6 this morning, ok?"

Randy and I both replied, "OK."

Then Latiefe added, "Just the three of us; me, you, and Holz. We went there to just talk and chill."

"No doubt," Randy and I responded.

Stool Pigeon

"Oh man! What the hell is that smell? Randy, did you break wind?"

"Holz, that's probably the toe jam on your smelly feet," Latiefe interjected.

I was pissed off because Randy was always farting in his sleep. And when I say fart, I am not talking about no ordinary fart. His farts were always lethal. Whenever he farted, it was always time to open up all of the windows and doors and turn on the fan to push the smell out. Unfortunately it was Randy's smelly fart that woke us up from some well-needed sleep. Not to mention the fact that the phone had also been ringing off the hook all morning long. It was doing it now as I wiped the cold out of my eyes.

"Randy, get up and answer the phone! And go wipe your butt when you're done. You probably stained your underwear with that fart," I grouchily said.

Randy, who sounded a bit nervous said, "Nah man, you get up and answer it."

I made my way across the room to answer the phone, and sounding like an angry bear I yelled a sharp, "Hello!"

The voice on the other end asked, "Yo, who is this? Is this Holz?"

"Yeah, this is Holz. What's up? Who's this? Oh, yo, this is you, Dwight?"

"Yeah. Yo Holz, where the hell y'all niggahs been at? I've been callin' there all morning. But yo, did y'all hear about the two DT's that got killed on Springfield last night?"

"What? Nah! Where did you hear that?"

"Yo, it was on like every TV channel and every radio station this morning. You know, it was one of those 'We interrupt this program to bring you this special report.'"

In an attempt to come across more convincing, I turned my head away from the phone and yelled, "Yo Randy, yo Tee! Dwight just told me that two DT's got killed on Springfield last night!"

Returning to the phone I added, "Yo, Dee, that's ill man!"

Dwight replied, "Yeah, I know. Now our business is gonna be hurtin' big time. Man, why the hell they have to kill those cops around here? That's the last thing we needed. Now there's gonna be swarms of cops everywhere on the street. The TNT narcotics cops ain't gonna let us sleep until they catch who murdered those cops."

"Yeah yeah, that's true Dwight. Yo listen, I'ma go buy the newspaper and see if the story is in there. We'll be at the apartment later on today, ah'ight? So I'll check you later."

"Ah'ight Holz, chill."

"Damn! Dee heard about it already?" Randy asked.

I responded, "Yeah, what did you expect?"

"Man, I don't know," Randy replied. "I really don't know, y'all."

In an attempt to ease the fears in the room, I reassured everyone that we wasn't gonna get caught. I let them know that we couldn't go tip toeing around and acting all nervous and scared. We just had to be ourselves. "We can't be constantly watching our backs and always looking over our shoulders for the police. If someone knocks on our door we can't be getting all nervous and peeking out of the window and all of that, 'cause it won't be the police. We ain't getting caught."

Latiefe, sounding as if he was tired of being lectured, said, "Yeah, OK, Holz. We know that we're not getting caught. Now what exactly did Dwight say to you?"

"Nothing really," I replied. "He just asked me had I heard about what happened to the two detectives. He told me that it was on every news channel and every radio station. I played it off like I hadn't heard about it, and yo, I played it off good, 'cause I told him that I was gonna go buy the paper so that I could read about it. Yeah, and he was telling me how he thinks that the narcotics task force will be breathing on all of Laurelton's neck so we won't be able to make any money until this thing cools down."

Latiefe and Randy sat and pondered, but they didn't say anything. Latiefe broke the silence by finally saying, "I don't know about y'all, but I really don't care about this whole cop killing thing and I ain't even trying to think about it no more. I mean, all I know is that in a minute, I'm gonna get so high and blunted and drunk and do whateva. Word!"

Latiefe had a good idea in terms of his plans to get blunted. As for me though, I was just tired. I was tired for good reason. Killing two cops in the wee hours of the night would drain most people. And I guess that I was probably more mentally drained as opposed to being physically drained. So I decided to go back to the apartment and just chill for the day. Randy decided to do the same. I guess that we were all mentally drained after the grotesquely grueling night. We all needed some quiet time by ourselves.

Later that day, as I lay in my bed at the apartment, I didn't know if I was slipping into depression or what. I was trying to get some sleep but I just couldn't fall into a deep sleep. I was tossing and turning and I kept waking up like every ten minutes, so I finally decided to do something that I hadn't done in weeks, which was pray.

I prayed, "Dear Lord, please let me, my mother, my brother, my father, my sister, Sabine, and those that are still alive in Fourth Crew be alright. Look after us, Lord. Please. Lord, forgive me for all of the wrongs that I have done. God, you are all-knowing. Lord, please understand that evil is not truly in my heart. Please forgive me, Lord. God, what is up with my life? Why all the nonsense? Lord, please lead me away from this. Without You, without Your help, I'm lost and I know that. Lord, please help me. In your Son's name I pray. Amen."

After that prayer I was out like a light. When I woke up later on in the day, all I did was watch movies and talk on the phone. The next couple of days went pretty much the same. I just stayed home watching television and talking on the phone. I had spoken to my sister and I promised her that I would come by the house and see her that upcoming Saturday.

Wednesday night, we of course visited the Apollo. Also, Latiefe had paid all of us that Wednesday. $7,000 in cash is what we each received. I personally was surprised to receive so much money, especially with the increase in narcotics cops that had been on the street during the past four days. I decided that I was going to hold on to the loot that I had, just in case things got real shaky and slow, or if we abruptly went out of business.

It was Thursday, August 15th when I got a beep on my pager from Dwight. He beeped me to tell me that we were all going to meet at the Red Zone later that night. He also informed me that the crew had to have a meeting in order to discuss and examine our goings on. We would discuss everything at the club, in the VIP section.

The day flew by. Before I knew it, I was preparing to go to the club. I had made plans to arrive there real early, but as usual, my plans fell through and I wound up getting to the Red Zone pretty late, 11:30 PM to be exact. The line to get in the club was so long that it stretched and wrapped around the corner of the building. Fortunately, I knew someone that was already on the line and they were pretty close to the entrance. I knew that cutting them on the line would save me at least an hour of waiting time, so I paid them in order to let me skip in front of them.

As I waited to get frisked, I saw cops everywhere. I smirked to myself as I thought, *If they only knew who I was and what I had done. Only if they knew, ha, but they don't have a clue.* And just to amuse myself, I rubbed up as close to cops as I could. And the amazing thing was that they didn't even arrest me.

When I finally made my way fully inside the club, I searched frantically for Fourth Crew. I searched high and low throughout the crowded club. DJ Funkmaster Flex was on the turntables and the music was bangin'. Everyone in the house was rockin'. The place was deafening. Brand Nubians, a hot rap group, was slated to perform. Luckily I'd made it inside the club in time to see them perform. As they got ready to come on stage I was able to spot Latiefe. He was with the rest of the crew, and they were all at the bar looking real expensive and sippin' on drinks.

I yelled, "Fourth Crew's in the howze! Hey yo, what up?"

"Yo, big Holz, what's up, my niggah? Where the hell you been?"

I responded, "I'm sayin', I had some personal business to take care. Plus, I thought that y'all told me that y'all would be in the VIP section, and now I find y'all at the bar. Man, look! Don't question me."

All of a sudden there was a big roar from the crowd as Brand Nubians came to the stage. The crowd went into a frenzy. Brand Nubians performed their hit song called 'Slow Down.'

The beginning of the song went like this; "Slow down, slow slow slow down!"

As I, along with the whole crowd, recited the song simultaneously with Brand Nubians, Randy grabbed me by my shoulder and stopped me from dancing. "Yo Holz…"

"Yeah, what's up?" I yelled, trying to speak over the loud music. It was like a zoo inside the club so Randy and I were forced to almost scream directly into each other's ears.

He asked me, "Yo, Latiefe paid you yesterday, right?"

"Yeah, why? What's up?"

"I wanna know how much you got."

"He gave me seven G's. That's what everybody got."

Randy's light-skin face turned blood red as he said, "Oh, word? That's how much all of y'all got? Yo, I'ma kill that short little snake!"

I screamed, "Whoa! Randy, what's up? What happened?"

"He only gave me two G's, that's what happened! He told me that things were going slow because of too many undercovers on the street."

I put both of my palms face up as I told Randy, "Yo, I don't know. All I know is that he gave me seven thousand dollars. But Randy, whateva you do, don't confront Latiefe in a hostile manner, 'cause you know how his temper is."

Randy, looking even redder, screamed, "I don't give a damn about his temper. He's gonna see my temper. I'ma handle my bi'ness right now. He owes me five G's and he better have it on him tonight or I'ma be all up in his butt right in this club." Randy walked over to Latiefe. I was praying that he wouldn't start a commotion. I followed right behind Randy. When he reached Latiefe, he didn't waste anytime.

"Yo, Tee, why you trying to play me like I'm a herb or somethin'?"

Latiefe, who looked surprised, asked "What the hell are you talking about?"

"Don't play stupid, Latiefe. You know exactly what I'm talking about. You tryin' to herb me. You gave Holz and everybody else seven G's and you only gave me two G's, tryin'a tell me some garbage about business is slow! What's the deal, kid? You know I ain't no sucka'. Now give me my got-damn loot or I'll murder you right now. Word is bond!"

Latiefe's fuse had been lit. His war juices immediately started flowing out of his mouth. "What? Yo, hol' up! Hol' the hell up! First of all, who are you raising your voice to? That's number one. And number two, I wanna see you murder me."

There was about a three-second pause in the action before Latiefe sucked his teeth and walked away. He violently pulled out a fat wad of money and threw it in Randy's direction. Needless to say, that money-throwing incident had caught many of the clubgoers' attention as people began scrambling to pick up the 100's, 50's, and 20's that were floating all over the place.

In the 'hood if someone throws money at you it is considered a sign of blatant disrespect, and that had to be what led Randy to totally ignore the money that Latiefe had just thrown at him. Randy rushed toward Latiefe as if he was a lion stalking its prey.

Latiefe stopped dead in his track, turned around and gave an instructional warning, "Yo, if you want some more loot, I just gave it to you! Pick it up off the floor since you want it so bad. But I tell you this, you betta step with that hard-rock gangsta nonsense, 'cause word is bond, Randy, I'll buss a cap in you! Matter of fact, man, listen. I must be trippin' or something because I already paid you your seven G's just like everybody else, so get out of my face! What the hell? Are you tryin' to extort me or something? Man, Randy, there are too many ladies standing around up in this club, so don't try to be mista big cheese up in here."

Randy yelled, "Man, I don't care about these whores up in here! Do you have my money or not?"

"What money, niggah?" Latiefe yelled as he stared into Randy's grill. "You better pick that loot up off the ground and get out of my face, word!"

Randy angrily replied, "Niggah, I ain't picking up a got-damn thing off the ground. I ain't your ho! Ahh, man! Yo, you better have that dough in the crib or I'm sayin'."

Latiefe nonchalantly laughed and said, "Yo, are you threatenin' me? I paid you your loot and you ain't getting nothing else from me. Now move from in front of me. I'm tryin'a watch the show." Latiefe calmly lifted his drink to his mouth and took a sip of it.

At that moment, Randy, all in one big sweeping motion, backed up, made a fist and clocked Latiefe, sending both him and his drink crashing to the floor. He quickly pounced on top of Latiefe and commenced to punching like a Mike Tyson lunatic.

Dwight, Wiggie, and I tried to pull Randy off of Latiefe, but we couldn't. Randy was in a black rage or something. I had never seen Randy get that angry before. I knew that he was upset about the money, but I didn't understand why he was so angry. I mean, he knew that our money was easy come easy go. It wasn't like he wasn't gonna get his loot. But maybe he was just thinking about the principle of what Latiefe had done, or maybe he was unleashing stress from all that had been going on in our lives.

Finally, we manged to pull Randy off of Latiefe. Latiefe's nose was bloodied and his clothes were dirty. "Randy, I'ma kill you! Word is bond, I'ma kill you!" Latiefe threatened as we held him back.

Randy, looking as cocky as a heavy-breathing person could look, said, "Shut up, punk! And go wipe your nose!"

As the rest of our crew tried to keep Randy and Latiefe separated, girls looked on and screamed as globs of blood trickled out of Latiefe's nose. That one quick little squabble managed to trigger off the crowd, and in turn caused a lot of pushing and shoving. Then someone fired two shots into the direction of the crowd, which sent everyone, including us, running for the exits. Randy and Latiefe had just ruined a fun night for the entire metropolitan area.

After we'd all made it safely to our respective cars, everyone in the crew wanted to know just exactly what had caused Randy to want to kick Latiefe's butt. Randy explained, showboating like Muhammad Ali after a prize fight. "He tried to play me like a roach! You don't play around with somebody's livelihood, especially mines. Cats on the street die behind that. You kna'imean? So I had to bring it to him!"

At that point none of us knew where Latiefe was. His car was gone. We figured that he was ah'ight. He was probably just upset and embarrassed so he left without speaking to anyone. In a way, I wished that Latiefe had not bounced because all of that civil war crap had to be squashed. He and Randy and all of us needed to talk out the entire thing right there outside the club.

As we prepared to depart, Dwight said, "Tomorrow, Randy, you and Tee are gonna squash this! Our crew is too close for this crap. We were suppose to talk about our operation tonight, but we'll just take care of it tomorrow."

"Man, I ain't squashing a got-damn thing. Five G's ain't five dollars. I want my money. I never did trust that niggah. I knew something like this was gonna happen. I knew it! He'll cut your throat if you let him, that snake, con artist bastard."

"Ah'ight chill, Randy. We'll get you your money, ah'ight, man?

Randy didn't respond.

The next day rolled around and Latiefe was still missing in action. No one had seen nor heard from him since the night of the fight. Yeah, Latiefe was MIA throught the entire day, until later that night when he burst into the apartment happier than a pig in slop. He was smiling from ear to ear. When he walked through the door, we all looked at him as if he was a ghost or something.

"Hey hey hey," Latiefe said, trying to imitate the infamous line from the old television show 'What's Happening?'

Kinda surprised to see Latiefe in such a good mood, we all replied, "What's up?"

Latiefe responded, "Oh, I'm chillin'. I'm good. Yo, where's my man Randy at?"

Erik answered, "He's at Susan's house."

Latiefe replied, "Oh word, that's cool. Yo, did y'all buy anything to eat?"

"Yeah, there's something in the kitchen," Erik advised.

I was confused and didn't know exactly what to make of Latiefe's happy go lucky mood. As I departed for my bed I informed the crew, "Yo, I'm outta here. I gotta get some sleep."

Latiefe questioned, "Holz, why you going to bed so early for?"

"Because I'm going to see my sister in the morning and I know if I go out tonight then I won't wanna wake up in the morning."

I stuck true to my word, and the next morning I was at my parents' house at about 11 AM. "What's up sis'?" I rhetorically asked as I hugged her and gave her a kiss on the cheek. "How you been?" I asked.

"I've been alright," she replied. "How about you?"

"Chillin', just chillin'."

"Mark, you stayin' out of trouble?"

"Of course."

"So what's new, Mark?"

"Nothing really. It's just the same ol' same ol'. I'm trying to make enough money so that I can just go to school and concentrate totally on my school work."

Sounding encouraged, my sister questioned, "Oh, you're going back to college in September?"

"Hopefully."

"Well Mark, you better make up your mind real quick, because registration ends in a week. The fall semester starts in like another two weeks."

"I don't know. I'll probably just skip this semester."
Sounding discouraged, Paula pleaded, "Mark, please try to finish school. We need more positive brothers in this world."

"I am, Paula. I'm gonna finish just for you. I'ma get that degree because I love you and I know how important it is to you, to Sabine, and to Daddy. If that's what y'all want, then that is what I'll do."

"Mark, don't do it for me or for anybody else. Do it for yourself and for society. Plus, Mark, you really don't need money in order to go to school. You'll make all the money that you wanna make as soon as you get out of school. OK?"

Trying to change the subject I asked, "Where's everybody at?"

"Daddy's at work and Mommy's working a double shift. Nia just left a few minutes ago."

"I probably won't be here when Mom and Dad get home, but make sure that you tell them that I love them and that I'm ok. Matter of fact, here. Take this 800 dollars and give it to them."

Paula informed me that my parents were sure to object to the gift.

"I know, but just give it to them anyway, even if they don't take it. Alright? But listen, I'm gonna go up to my room for a while and reminisce. Do you still want me to take you shopping for clothes?"

"Yeah."

"OK, we'll bounce in a few minutes. You didn't tell me whether or not you like my car."

"Oh yeah, that's right. I forgot that you bought a car. I'll look at it right after I put these clothes in the washing machine."

"Yeah, you can look out the front window and you'll be able to see it. It's the gray Saab that's parked right in front of our house. I'll be upstairs in my room laying down."

"Alright, let me go in the basement and take care of these clothes, then I'll look and see if your car is all of that, the way you say it is."

As I lay upstairs in my room I couldn't help but think about all of the peace and tranquility that I'd forgone. "Why did I give all of this up? Home cooked meals every night, clean surroundings, a nice, warm, loving family. Why did I trade in all of this for the way that I'm now living? Maybe I'm just stupid, or a psycho. No, no, I'm a hoodlum. Better yet, I'm a thug. Mark, you've been called those names for as long as you can remember, so you might as well believe it and continue trying to live up to it."

I continued to just melt in the sense of peace that I was experiencing in my old room. My old bed felt so good. I had to stop reminiscing because it was starting to make me feel like a punk. So I didn't focus my thoughts on anything, I just laid there.

As I laid in my bed, just about to doze off, I heard the sound of my sister yelling and screaming as if she was being attacked.

"Mark! Mark! Look! Come downstairs, hurry up and look! Look outside!"

I jumped up and darted downstairs. I hadn't a clue what was going on. "What happened? What's going on?"

The first thing I thought was that somebody must have been trying to steal my car, so I asked, "Is it my car?"

Paula responded, "No, no, look out the window!"

I pushed the curtains away from my living room window so that I could see exactly what was going on. What in the world was my sister being so hyper about? As soon as I was able to focus my eyes on what it was that was causing all of the hype I yelled out "Holy ....!"

I was in disbelief. Although I now had a pretty good idea as to what was happening, I still asked myself the question, "Yo, what in the world is going on?"

With my brown eyes wide open I scanned the block. All I could see were police and more police. 234th Street was filled with emergency service police. There were big police trucks that looked as though they could carry every SWAT team in this country. There were unmarked police cars, police dogs, auxiliary police, tons of ambulances, and an uncountable number of patrol cars that crowded the somewhat narrow block. Two helicopters were hovering above the houses. I even saw the local TV news vans.

"Mark, what's going on?" my sister asked.

"I don't know," I quickly answered.

"Mark, who are they looking for? It looks like they're watching Randy's house."

Randy's house was directly across the street from my parents' home. I could see everything that was going on.

"Yeah Paula, they are at Randy's crib. Yo, I have to get out of here! Where's the key to the back door?"

"What do you mean you have to get out of here? What happened? Are they looking for you or something?"

"Paula, I don't have time to stand here and talk, OK? Now hurry up and go get me the damn key!" I yelled.

"What did y'all do?" my sister demanded to know.

I snatched the key from her hand as I explained to her, "We didn't do nothin'. I'm outta here. If the cops come looking for me, I want you to tell them that you haven't seen me."

My sister yelled in frustration, "Mark!"

"OK?... I'm out."

At that moment the picture of the two detectives laying on the ground in a pool of blood flashed through my head. "Oh no!" I said, as my heart started to pound faster and faster.

My sister warned, "If they're after you, you can't leave this house or they'll definitely catch you."

My sister and I had been thinking the exact same thing, but I tried to play it off. "They ain't after me!"

What am I gonna do? I frantically paced the living room floor trying to come up with an idea. I sat on the couch and planted my face into the palms of both of my hands. *Think, Mark. Think.* Actually, I was way too nervous to think rationally. My heart was beating very furiously, I had nothing but pure adrenaline flowing through my veins. I was grabbing at my hair, trying to calm down.

As my sister peeked out of the window, I yelled inside of my head, *Holz stop being a sucker! Calm down right now!* My nerves started to fall a notch. Then I thought, *Why am I worried? They're not coming after me, or else they would already be surrounding my crib, too.* I was scared like crazy but I didn't care.

"Forget this! Come on, Paula!" I barked.

My sister asked, "Mark, what is wrong with you? What are you talking about? Where are we going?"

I screamed, "Let's go outside and watch like the rest of the nosy neighbors are doing!"

"I'm perfectly fine right here. I'll look from the window where it's nice and safe. And you better not leave this house, 'cause they could start shooting or whatever. Don't go out there."

"I don't give a damn if they start shooting." I said. I got a gun, too."

I boldly opened my front door and stood on my front steps, watching as the drama unfolded. If they were after me, well then they sure could have had me. I stared at the movie-like action. I didn't want to believe it, but I knew that they were after Randy.

I said to myself, *Holz if they come out of that house with Randy, take your gun and pop at least one of those pigs. Let them have it! If you die, you die, but you can't let your boy go to jail. Smoke them jokers. No conscience, Mark. No conscience. You're Fourth Crew 'till the day you die. Don't front.*

There I stood on my steps, ready to give my life as a ransom for my homeboy. I was filled and ready to pour out all kinds of nervous energy. I waited and waited for the police to commence with their police tactics. It seemed as if the police were taking forever to make their move. But the long wait for something to unfold did me a lot of good. It allowed me to return back to my normal self.

Be sensible, I told myself. H*ow the hell are you gonna shoot a cop when there's a million other pigs around? They'll put so many holes in you that you wouldn't even be able to have an open casket funeral.*

As the two helicopters drew closer to the land they made a heck of a lot of noise. Then suddenly there was a lot of movement in the street. The movie-like drama was about to unfold. Cops started running around, some began to take aim, others began to take cover. By this time, every news camera in the city was on our block. Cameramen went to work, as did the photographers. My heart rate shot up because I knew something was about to happen. Neighbors anxiously waited for the climax.

At that point in time Randy emerged from the side entrance of his house. He was stereotypically dressed for this role. His pants were hanging off of him, revealing his boxer shorts. He looked as if he had a sack of doo-doo in his pants. To spice up his thug character he had a huge gold chain on, not to mention the gold caps that were in his mouth.

As Randy walked from the side of his house, heading toward the street, he was in full view of everyone. But he didn't walk alone. He walked with his hands cuffed behind his back. He also had two detectives right by his side. One detective walked and held Randy's left arm while the other detective held his right. Randy didn't look the least bit worried or embarrassed. As he walked and prepared to enter into one of the patrol cars, he donned a serious B-Boy/Gangster limp. He was walking as though he was the toughest thing since nails. He bopped and bopped and at the same time he chewed on a piece of green bubble gum.

Just before he sat down in the patrol car he spit at a news reporter and tried to kick a photographer. It was at that point that he was pushed head first into the back seat of the patrol car where he sat for about five minutes. As he sat, the media swarmed in on the car, similar to the way fans swarm a limo when Michael Jackson is inside. The herd of reporters all wanted to get some type of comment from, or picture of Mr. Randy Allen.

Randy's mom, his brothers, and sisters all looked on in disbelief. His mom was crying and screaming. With her Caribbean accent she wailed, "He didn't do it! He didn't do any*ting*! Let my baby go. Where are you taking him?"

Neighbors watched in astonishment. Some were whispering to each other. This, by far, was one of, if not the most dramatic episodes that 234th Street had ever seen.

Oh no! I thought to myself. *They caught him. They actually caught him!* I couldn't believe it. I yelled out Randy's name as loud as I could. "Randy! Randy!" I screamed to the top of my lungs. "Yo, Randy!"

Finally I managed to get his attention. He peered out of the car window. With my right hand I made the letter

Y in sign language. With my thumb extending to my ear and my pinkie extending to the front of my mouth I was trying to convey to Randy that I wanted him to call me.

"Call me!" I yelled. "Call the crib! Call the crib!" Randy nodded his head up and down then he was whisked away, along with a caravan of police cars that served as escorts. He was probably on his way to the precinct and then he would surely end up at central booking.

The block started to clear up a bit. The helicopters were gone before I could blink. Bystanders and the rest of the police started to disperse. I turned around and went back into my house where I found my sister in tears.

"What did he do, Mark? Why did they need all of those cops to arrest him?"

"I don't know what he did. But whateva they think it is, he probably didn't do it. Yo Paula, Randy is the man, though! Did you see how he bopped in front of those TV cameras? He was proud as hell! He wasn't like all of those other fake thugs that get arrested and then try to hide their faces from the news cameras. Nah, none of that! Randy walked proud with those handcuffs on. He was full of ballsiness. And he was definitely representing Fourth Crew to the fullest. Did you see that cat?"

In disbelief my sister questioned, "What are you talking about? And why are you so proud? What is wrong with you? Randy is in trouble! Big trouble! They don't come with all of those cops for nothing. And that makes you happy? You lost me somewhere."

I realized that Paula just didn't get it. "Do you still wanna go shopping? Yes or no?"

"No!" she harshly snapped.

"Ah'ight cool, 'cause I gots to be out. I'll be by here to see you before you go back to school. When do you have to go back again? About two to three weeks or something like that, right?"

"Yes Mark," my sister answered, sounding very defeated.

"OK, I'ma see you then. Bye. Paula, stop crying. Randy's gonna be ah'ight. This ain't nothing but a G thang. Do I look worried? Did Randy look upset? No.So stop crying. What are you crying for?"

I kissed my sister good-bye and darted out of the house. I quickly jumped into my car and sped over to our apartment. When I arrived at the apartment I burst in yelling, "Yo yo yo! Randy just got pinched!"

"What?" Dwight asked.

I repeated myself. "Randy just got bagged! He got arrested! Five-O came to his crib and snatched him up. Yo, it was ill! I mean, a whole swarm of poh-leece flooded the block outside his joint. They were rollin' about four hundred deep. Cops were in helicopters, on rooftops, they had the k-9 units and all that. It looked like every cop in the city was on 234th Street.

Dwight asked, "But for what? What did he do?"

"I don't know," I said, focusing my eyes on Latiefe. "I don't know, yo. But yo, every TV station and their mother was out there, so it has to be on TV."

Dwight quickly instructed Wiggie to move from in front of the TV and turn it on. No sooner had Wiggie completed his task than we saw Randy's body bopping across the TV screen. With the volume turned up on the TV, words from the anchorwoman's mouth echoed through the room. "Today, police ended a week-long manhunt for a suspect in one of the city's most gripping, grueling, and devastating crimes ever. The police arrested a suspect, allegedly believed to be the gunman who gunned down and murdered two New York city detectives last week on a Queens street. Police arrested 20- year- old Randolph Allen this afternoon at his home in Queens. Police were led to the suspect by an anonymous tip, supplied to them, apparently, by an eyewitness to the horrific shooting. The witnesses' name is being withheld at this time.

Police apparently surprised Mr. Allen, who hampered their efforts in arresting him, by holding his younger brother hostage for some time in the basement of his family's two-story home.

Police are also believed to have recovered the weapon which which was used to slay the two detectives. A Calico automatic gun is believed to be the murder weapon. Two other guns were recovered in the basement, along with a large amount of cash. The amount of cash is not yet known at this point in time. Neighbors that we interviewed from the quiet middle class block in Laurelton were shocked by the arrest. The alleged suspect was said to be an ideal young man, one with promise and no previous felony arrest record.

So agin, to recap the latest development in a story that has gripped this city over the last week, police have arrested the alleged gunman believed to be the killer of two detectives that were gunned down last week in Queens. Police are said to be still searching for at least one more suspect in the case. Mr Allen is being held in custody and is being questioned by police as we speak. At this time there is no word on whether bail will be set. We'll have more details on this tonight at eleven."

"Yo, turn that garbage off!" I ordered as everyone else sat in disbelief.

Erik yelled, "Yo, how did they bag Randy for that? I know he didn't do it, 'cause he would have told us about something that ill."

Wiggie agreed, "Word, he would've at least told one of us. Man, this is all jacked up! Of all people, why did they arrest Randy for this, yo? I'm really trippin' off of this, because if they can arrest Randy for this that means they can arrest anybody they want to for whatever they want to."

Dwight tried to put a grasp on all of the shock. "Ah'ight, y'all. We just have to find out the truth about what happened so that we can see how to figure out this whole thing. We gotta speak to Randy's Moms and see if they give him bail or not. And if they do, no matter how much it is, we're gonna have to do whatever we have to do to come up with the bail money."

Erik pessimistically added that although it was Randy's first major offense, he was skeptical about anyone getting bail after murdering two cops in cold blood.

While the crew mulled things over, I quietly pulled Latiefe to the side and nervously whispered, "I think we're next. We're getting locked up too."

"No we're not," Latiefe confidently whispered back.

Anxiously I asked, "Why not? Are you thinking like I'm thinking, as far as skipping town?"

"Nah, we don't have to do that. The cops won't catch us. Trust me."

"Tee, how do you know that? That's exactly what I told Randy, and look at him. He got knocked."

Latiefe began softly chuckling. "What the hell is so funny?" I angrily whispered.

Still smiling, Latiefe replied, "Nothing. It's just that I know how Randy got caught and that's why I know we can't get bagged."

I made sure not to raise my voice above the loud whisperas I asked, "What? I'm sayin', Tee, how did he get bagged? Speak to me."

Latiefe's giggles had just about turned to laughter as he tried to calm down and explain. "OK, OK, Holz, calm down. I'll tell you."

After another quick chuckle, Latiefe continued, "Now Holz, you know how my temper is, right? I mean, you know how quick I am to get upset? Last week when Randy played me out at the Red Zone, I got pissed off."

Starting to realize where this might be going, I said in a very serious tone, "No! Latiefe, wait! Wait a minute. Don't tell me that you ratted on your boy!"

"Yeah, Holz. I told...but...but I didn't mean for him to actually get caught."

"Man, what do you mean, you didn't mean for him to get caught? You go and sing like a canary-rat-stool-pigeon and you didn't expect for him to get caught? Latiefe, that's your boy! Randy was down with all of us from day one. We've all known each since we were three years old. Three years old, man! Latiefe, what the.... How could you rat Randy out like that?" I was really stunned.I felt like unleashing tears of anger and frustration.

All of a sudden, sounding repentent and nervous, Latiefe said, "Holz, I'm sorry man. I was just upset and you know how I get. Man, after I left the club that night, I drove around for a while trying to calm down, but I couldn't. Randy shouldn't have played me out like that. We were both wrong."

"Latiefe, so what if he played you! Why did you short him his cut of the money? We're all in this drug thing together. You don't jerk nobody in the crew out of their money. See, I knew that this drug thing was gonna do us up somehow. I knew it! I knew it! I knew it! Latiefe, man, I don't know...So what did you do? You just marched into the police station and told the cops that Randy did the killings? What's the deal? What's up?"

I guess in an attempt to appear sorrowful, Latiefe bowed his head as he said, "Nah, see, that night after I left the club I saw this sign. Well actually, it was on a billboard or something. I don't know, but anyway, the sign stated that the police would pay $10,000 for information leading to the arrest and conviction of anyone killing a New York City Cop. Holz, I had to call! I was so ticked off and vexed that night, and after I made that call I felt more relieved and more at ease. I felt like I was on top!"

"Why didn't you just punch a wall? Or kick somebody? Or fight somebody? I mean, you could have done anything like that. But Latiefe, the bottom line is that you don't rat on your boy like that. Matter of fact, you don't rat on anybody. That's the code of the streets and you know that. Ah, man! You know that Randy ain't gonna see light for maybe fifty years? Two dead cops! Man, he might get double life. If they had the death penalty in New York, he would probably be headed straight for death row. And for $10,000! Latiefe, you didn't want the money, did you? No, my fault. $20,000. I forgot it was two cops, so the hero's reward is doubled. 20 G's. Do you know how quick we could've made that? Latiefe, tell me what makes you think that they're even gonna give you the 20 G's anyway? Remember one thing. They have to not only arrest Randy, they have to convict him before you would get your money. And that could be like six months to maybe even a year from now. In that time, who knows? Randy could be dead. Or he could beat the charges. Slim chance on that happening, but if he does beat the rap you, won't even get the 20 G's."

Latiefe interrupted. "Holz, you know what? I could care less about the ten thousand or twenty thousand dollars or whateva it is. All I'm sayin' is Randy embarrassed me in front of females, and for what? If we use your same logic, then that means that Randy embarrassed me for only $5,000! He didn't care, so why should I care?"

"You still don't get it, do you? You just don't get it! Yo, I ain't even gonna try to figure you out no more. What's done is done. And to be honest, I hate you for this. I mean, you still my man and all, but ratting on your boy, singing like a stool pigeon, dropping dime, I don't know. Latiefe, all I'm sayin' is you better watch out, 'cause I know that those police tip hotlines don't make you give your name, they give you an I.D. number and all that 'protect the witness' bull. But you can bet on one thing. Randy is gonna talk. He ain't gonna do time in the clink by himself. He's in the joint right now! And you better believe that when they start questioning him and threatening him and putting all kinds of pressure on him that he's gonna drop dime, especially if they work out some kinda plea bargain with the District Attorney. Me and you will be looking at more time than he is."

Although Latiefe knew what I was saying made a lot of sense he tried to down play it. "Randy won't drop dime. You know and I know that he won't. We're still Fourth Crew for life! Besides, Randy will never even know who told on him. Even though we had that little squirmish, if I personally told Randy that I ratted him out, he wouldn't believe it. He'd just believe that it was a very smart police department that nabbed him. Plus, after today you probably won't see me anymore, 'cause I'm outta here. I can't stick around. I mean, it's time for a change."

After a pause in his speech, Latiefe laughed and said, "As a matter of fact, you know what? You're right. Randy isn't as stupid as he looks. He just might rat us out. But yo, like I said, I'm outta here. It's time to start all over." Latiefe started laughing like this was all a game, just one big joke.

I interrupted his laughter by angrily instructing, "So then leave, man! I'll take over the money from now on. I'm sayin'! Man, where the heck are you gonna go anyway?"

"I don't know."

"Do you need me to send you your loot or what?"

"Nah Holz, I'll be ah'ight. With the changes that I plan to make, I won't even be worrying about loot and women and stuff like that."

"Yeah ah'ight, man. Whateva. But wherever you go, just remember, Fourth Crew for life. Even though you are wrong, you still my man for life. And yo, I'm gonna still keep my mouth shut about our part in the killings."

Latiefe reached to grasp my hand and pull me close for a quick ghetto hug. "Yeah, yeah, Holz. Do that. And Holz, do me a favor kid, don't ever let anybody know that I ratted on Randy. But if it happens to come up when you speak to Big Randy, tell him that I'm sorry."

Jail House Talk

Many days had passed since Randy had been arrested. I hadn't spoken to him since he'd been locked up and neither had anyone else in the crew. I just wished he would call me. I prayed regularly that he'd maintain his sanity throughout his ordeal.

With Latiefe out of sight, it was now my responsibility to collect the loot. No one had seen or heard from Latiefe. I guess he was making good on his promise to bounce and start life over somewhere else. With all that we had gone through in order to get where we were, I couldn't believe that Latiefe would just walk away from it all just like that.

Lately I had been thinking thoughts like, *Yo, what is going on?* I mean, the crew was shrinking with each passing day. Our drug business was hurting due to the increased police presence, which hadn't died down even though Randy had been arrested. With whatever money I was making, I had been trying to save it for Randy's bail. I didn't even know if they had given him a bail, but I knew that if he was fortunate enough to have a bail that it was bound to be a tremendous amount. Regardless of the amount, with the other crew members chipping in, I was sure that we'd raise whatever amount was necessary.

But even just trying to pull the crew together for a cause like raising Randy's bail would prove to be hard work. It was like Dwight, Wiggie, J.P., and all of them didn't even really care that Randy was locked up. Then again, caring was not in our repertoire of feelings. We were B-Boys. But for real, it was like the rest of the crew was going on with life as if everything was normal. I guess though, considering everything, things were pretty much status quo. But I mean, the crew wasn't even questioning Latiefe's whereabouts.

At times, man, I would just be sitting and thinking about my life, and more specifically, thinking about how screwed up it was. I just wanted the drama to end. Word.

More days went by without any word from Randy. Finally an operator called asking if I would accept the charges from Rikers Island Correctional Facility.

I very eagerly replied, "Yeah, yeah, yeah, I'll accept the charges."

The operator said, "Thank you. One moment please."

After a clicking sound I heard Randy say, "Hello." Man, that was the best sound that I'd heard in weeks. It was like I'd been hit with a shot of caffeine.

"Big Ran! Is that you kid? What's up, dog? What the hell took you so long to call a niggah?"

Randy replied in a low monotone that wasn't nearly as excited as mine, "Yo, I'm sayin', I'm on Rikers Island just tryin' to hold it down. Yo Holz, I'm on Rikers man! It ain't no joke in this piece. It's mad hectic up in here, word! I'm sorry that it took me so long to call y'all, but whenever I did get to a phone I would have to call my moms or my pops."

"Yo Randy, you ain't gotta apologize or nothing like that. I mean, I understand where you resting and all that. I was just crazy worried. Word! Yo, where exactly are you at?"

"I'm in C-74. Some people call it 'The Bing.' But you can't come check me until Monday. Don't ask me why. There's just some bull going on in here. You know?"

"Yeah, I'm digging you."

"Holz, this jail is way overcrowded, so I'm only allowed visitors on Mondays and Tuesdays."

"Yeah, that's cool. But you ah'ight though, right?"

"Yeah, I'm chillin', man. But I ain't exactly smiling on Rikers Island, you know what I'm sayin'?"

"Yeah, I know. Listen, Randy did they give you bail?"

Randy answered with a renewed spark of life to his voice as he replied, "Yeah. And yo, you won't believe it, kid. It's like God laced me lovely. They only set my bail at $100,000! That's what I've been talking to my Moms about. Her and my Pops are going to take out a second mortgage on the crib. But even with that, all they could come up with was about $60,000. The lawyer fees are hitting them lovely. But it's ah'ight, though, 'cause I'm sayin', my lawyer is mad smart, so it's definitely worth paying him his loot. But yo, Holz, try to get me up outta this joint! I can't take it being in here."

I assured Randy, "We'll get up the rest of the money for you. Don't worry."

"Ah'ight, Holz. And yo, don't forget to come see me on Monday. I need you, kid. Word! When you come I'll tell you the dirt that went down with me and my bail and all of that. Ah'ight?"

"Yeah, no doubt. I'll be there on Monday. 'The Bing', right?"

"Yeah, that's where I'm at. Holz... Like I said, I need you man."

"Randy, I'ma hold you down. I'll be there, kid. Peace out," I said as I hesitantly hung up the phone.

Time to get busy, I told myself. I had to get on top of our workers to make sure that they were selling the work right and efficiently. We couldn't afford to let sales slip any further. Not at this crucial time. No way. I had to convince myself to take care of business. *You're the CEO, Holz. Run this operation correctly."*

Frantic was the best word to describe my life over the next few days. Trying to raise Randy's bail money had me hustling like a maniac. But after taking a step back and examining everything, I realized that things had worked out pretty cool. I mean, with all my hard work and all, before I knew it, it was Monday.

On Monday I was off to Rikers Island to see Randy. No one else in the crew was around to go with me to visit him, which I thought was a damn shame. But then again, they probably wouldn't have gone even if they were around. It seemed like almost overnight, but just that quick, it was like the crew was all about self. Every man for himself. Unfortunately there was not much that I could do about that. All I was sayin' was that it was just mad foul that Randy's so called "boys" wouldn't even come peep him while he was in the joint. I'm sayin'...

I got in my car and was able to make it to Rikers Island in about half an hour. After arriving, showing my identification and being treated like a prisoner by the correction officers, not to mention passing through many metal detectors and waiting on this long line, I was finally soon gonna be able to talk to Randy face to face. The correction officers brought me to this big room that was filled with desks and with other visitors and inmates.

I sat down at a desk and waited for Randy to come out. After about ten minutes or so, he emerged in a bright orange jail jumpsuit with some black Reebok sneakers, minus the laces. He walked over to me, bopping like a true thug, and sat down right in front of me. As he slapped my hand, he smilingly asked, "What's up, big Holz? My mellow, my man!"

"I don't know. You tell me, Baby Pa."

"I'm just reacting, that's all. I'm trying not to think. I'm just reacting, you know? Yo Holz, let me tell you kid, this place ain't no joke. This is just a holding jail for cats waiting to go to trial, but yo! Woo! This ain't no state or federal penitentiary, but it's still wild in this joint."

Noticing all the bruises on Randy's grill I asked, "Have you been brawling?"

"No. Why?"

"Because your face looks like it's kind of puffy and bruised."

"Oh. Nah, that's not from in here.That's from the day that I got arrested. See, the cops took me back to the precinct and they beat me like a slave! Yo Holz, I'm talking about a Kunta Kente type butt whipping. First of all, they had me in this dimly lit room. They kept my hands cuffed behind my back while I sat in a chair. I didn't want to talk because I didn't have a lawyer with me, and I'm sayin', I wasn't trying to incriminate myself, you kna'imean?"

"Yeah," I replied.

Randy continued on, "So yeah, like I said, they had me in this room and I was sitting in a chair with my hands cuffed behind me and yo! Holz, they beat the crap out of me. I really thought I was gonna die. It got to the point where I was just numb from all of the blows. Yo, I had to talk. They told me that if I didn't admit to killing the two DT's that they would murder me. And I believed them, so I just let it out. They wanted all kinds of details, but I couldn't even speak because I was in so much pain and my mouth was all bloody and swollen.

Then when I admitted to them that I didn't do it alone, they really let me have it. They tried hard as hell to make me tell them who else was with me. But Holz, as God is my witness, they would have had to kill me before I would've ever ratted on any of y'all. I was like, 'yo, I guess I'ma meet God tonight, 'cause I ain't a punk like that.' I would never drop dime on y'all, you kna'imean?"

"Man, Randy, you should have ratted on us."

"What?"

"You should've told," I repeated while bowing my head.

"Holz, what the hell are you talking about? I got caught, y'all didn't. I'm gonna do my time like a man. My name ain't Michael Jackson. I don't sing on niggahs, word! You know I don't get down like that. I did the crime, now I gotta do the time."

I repeated myself, this time with a little more emphasis. "Randy, all I'm sayin' is that you should've ratted us out. I would probably be better off in here. Matter of fact, all of us would be better off in the big house. This is where we belong."

"I don't understand," Randy said. "'Cause man, Holz, I haven't even been in here that long and already I've seen guys get raped until they bled. Yo, it's ill. Talk about fights. It's like the WWF up in here all day long. Blacks vs. Blacks, Puerto Ricans vs. Blacks, Whites vs. Mexicans. The other day I saw a correction officer get slashed with a homemade weapon. The food sucks. It's overcrowded. Holz, I'm constantly watching my back. You can't tell me that you'd rather be in here or that you're better off in here.That's bull! You think our crew acts like troglodytes? Man, imagine being locked up in here for years. How do you think you would respond? I tell you one thing. Your response would be much worse than the one that got you in here.

Jail, the process needs to be revamped. This place doesn't rehabilitate, it makes you degenerate. It desecrates you, caging human beings up like wild animals. How can a person come out of here and fit back into society if his mind hasn't been exercised, exercised to rid the wrong that was in him? All this place does is help bring out the wrong that's in a person. Jail fosters evil. It sets you up to walk through a revolving door. Since I've been in here the only thing that I've allowed myself to think about is the harsh realities that go along with being locked up. Holz, 'The

Man' is making mad money off of us. But yo, I can't even speak on this system anymore 'cause I might get enraged and slaughter somebody in this prison."

I finally got a chance to speak. "Yo Randy, look at all of these black people in here. What are we doing?"

"Yeah, I know. It's jacked up, ain't it? But Holz, I'm in here, too. And I'm not even sure if I really feel remorseful. Because I know if I had more clips that night, I would have shot those cops some more. The only thing that stopped me is that I ran out of bullets. That's the only thing that stopped me!"

"Randy, I'm feeling you. You just an ill nooka! You caught mad wreck that night. You was like our man Larry Davis. You maimed those DT's like you was a homicidal juggernaut. Man, Randy, you're an American hero. Don't let nobody tell you different. Ah'ight?"

Randy laughed. "I don't know about being no American hero, but I know that I am definitely ghetto fabulous. You should see how much love and respect cats is giving me up in here because I killed those two pigs."

I continued, "Ahh, 'ghetto fabulous.' I like that kid. But yo, remember that night when I was pulling away from the curb and you yelled out the window and then you let the gun go off? Ha ha ha. Randy, I'm telling you man, only an all-American ghetto fabulous niggah hero could have done that! Nah, better yet, you're gonna be a ghetto celebrity."

"I don't know if I'm a ghetto celebrity, but what you just said about me letting off those last few bullets, that's what I'm talking about. That's when I ran out of bullets. I wanted to make sure that those DT's were dead! Holz man, after all of those times they had harassed us in the past, man it was only right. It was like, bang bang bang! Yo, I'm telling you, them bullets felt real good leaving my hand. Yo Holz, one bullet hit th DT right square in his head! Boom! It was mad funny. Did you see it? His straight blonde hair stood up on top of his head like he'd been electrocuted. He looked like a white Don King or somethin'. Then his brains just spilled out. Oh, it was a beautiful thing! Ha ha ha. Holz, I saw his brains! Did you see that? I saw his brains!"

"Yeah, I saw it... Randy listen."

Randy interrupted, "No, wait a minute, Holz. Let me finish."

Randy talked and talked. I'd never known him to be such a talker. "Remember that Bernhard Geotz thing where he shot, I think, four or five black guys? He shot them because he 'thought' he was gonna get robbed. What kinda crap is that? And yo, the cat got off! Holz, he beat all the charges except for the gun charge! Now if he got off, then I know that I better get off."

I added, "Yeah, Randy. I remember that."

"Holz, he didn't kill any of those guys. I think he left one of them paralyzed. But still, it was cold-blooded attempted murder, so how did he get off? No, no. I'm wrong. He did maybe six months to a year for the illegal gun, or for weapons possession. Something like that. I don't exactly remember. But if that's not bull, I don't know what is. I mean picture me trying to get off by telling a jury, 'Oh I thought that I was gonna get harassed by the cops, therefore I shot them.' Now doesn't that sound ridiculous? Yet if you scope it out, my case would be just as strong as Bernhard Geotz, for the simple reason that cops do harass us and brutalize us on a constant basis. So every time they pull us over I feel like I might lose my life at their hands."

Realizing his point I said, "Word! Yo, Randy that's true. When you think about it, that's a good point."

Randy added, "I know, man. Right? It's true, and I know it's a good point! But I would never get off with a weak defense like that. You know why? 'Cause number one, I'm black, and number two, cops can do no wrong. A cop's life is no better than my life or your life. A cop is a human being just like you and me, only he's got a badge. Their life isn't better than Richie's life, Xavier's life or no one's. God creates all of us equal. So why if you kill a cop, it's basically an automatic 25 years, no questions asked? Not to mention that they'll make sure that they catch you in about two weeks. When they caught that guy Cory who killed Richie, they let him out of jail, in what, six or seven days? It's ridiculous, Holz! Remember when those drug dealers shot that cop over in South Jamaica, Queens?"

"Yeah, he was guarding somebody's house, right?"

"Yeah, that's the one. Remember how quick they caught the guys who killed that particular cop? And where are those niggahs at now? Them niggahs is upstate doing hard time. And I won't even mention the deal with Larry Davis. Holz, they go after cop killers because society thinks one of the worst things that a human being can do is murder a cop. The only reason society thinks like that is because they look at that dark blue uniform. When they see that uniform and that badge they see the greatest human being that ever walked the face of the Earth. They put cops right up there alongside Jesus. They see a good, clean and wholesome, apple pie, red, white, and blue, white picket fence, home in the suburbs American who can do no wrong. You see, they never look into the lives of a cop outside of their job. If they did, then chances are they wouldn't care if a cop got shot or not."

"Randy, I think exactly like you think. Everything that you're saying, I've already thought about over and over."

Randy continued venting. "Holz, society doesn't care if we get shot or killed, because they think that we are all sub-human. They think we're all thieves, murderers and rapists. Yet if you look back on our peoples' true history, you'll be able to examine all of the greatness. See, everybody forgets about that and they focus on the grave conditions that exist now. That's why somebody could shoot me and kill me in cold blood and get away with it. That's why I'm in this joint right now. If society did change their mindset, if they started looking into our personal lives, finding out what we're capable of achieving in terms of bettering this world, they wouldn't allow us to kill ourselves the way we do. They would ensure that our killers are vigorously sought after, tried, convicted, and crucified the same way cop killers are."

"Come on, Randy, be for real! You're talking about the same society that praises soldiers for killing thousands of innocent people, then turns around and looks down on me or you for killing one or two corrupt cops."

Randy agreed. "I know, Holz, it's the same society that praises and looks up to John Gotti, then turns around and hates Al Sharpton. Go figure."

I started to laugh as I said, "Yeah, what's the deal with that Randy?"

"Holz, I don't know, but you know what? It doesn't matter anyway, 'cause we can't change nothing. Matter of fact, I'm tired of talking about this. Talking about society changing for us, man, it's just a waste of our good energy. So what else is up, Holz? What's been going on since I've been in here?"

"Everything, Randy. Everything! First off, I think the crew is finished. Everybody's out for themselves."

Randy showed concern. "Yeah, how is the crew doing? What's up with Latiefe? Has anybody seen him?"

I informed Randy, "Yeah, we saw him the day after you and him had that little scrap inside of the Red Zone. We saw him maybe once or twice after that night. Then he told me that he wasn't gonna be around anymore. He said he was leaving but he wouldn't tell me where he was going. He just said something about starting his life over."

"He probably moved in with his girl Esther in her apartment in Brooklyn."

"Maybe, but I don't know. It's like he just disappeared. He don't even collect the dough for us anymore. He doesn't come to receive any money from us. It was all his choice to give everything up. Don't ask me why. But yo, all I know is that the other day two girls came by the apartment looking for Latiefe. Both of them were like two months pregnant. I was like, I didn't know what to tell them. I think they needed some loot, but yo, what was I gonna do for them? I guess that means that there will just be two more babies brought up in this world without a father."

Randy, sounding kind of disgusted said, "That's crazy."

I added, "Yo, you remember when Earl was alive and how he cared for his little daughter? People could say what they wanted to about Earl, but at least he took care of his responsibilities. He was always there for his daughter."

Randy nodded in agreement.

"Oh! Guess what, kid?"

"What?" Randy asked.

"The other day I beat the daylights out of Jamal. I'm talking about a major beat down."

"Which Jamal?"

"You know, the one that sells for us. That niggah came up short on like two thousand dollars. Now how do you come up short by that much?"

"He kept the loot for self." Randy reasoned. "He didn't come up short. You know he didn't."

"Yeah, I know that. He probably figured that he could get over on me being that Latiefe had stopped collecting the loot. But yo, I ain't stupid. I ain't no sucka. I beat that niggah down! I'm talking, I cut him on his face and he bled like a leaky faucet. He was straight leaking right in the middle of the street. I was gonna kill him, but I just beat him with a baseball bat instead. I figured that killing him would have been too easy, so I tried my hardest to break both of his knees. Man, I hope he slipped into a coma and is in ICU somewhere. I was already stressed. I mean, here I am trying and working my hardest to get up your bail money, then this niggah is gonna come up short? I was like, if that's not bringing a death wish on yourself…"

I continued on, "Dwight told me that I should watch my back because he said that Montana was close to Jamal. Plus Montanan doesn't like it when someone other than himself hurts one of his workers, especially if he didn't give the order. Hurt drug dealers in his crew basically equals lower sales for him."

"Holz, you gotta chill. You can't just be doing niggahs like that. Plus you don't want Montana to find out that we had his boys working for us on the low."

"Man, I don't even care! I mean, I think Montana is gonna find out anyway. Especially now, considering how everybody's cash is starting to get real thin. Montana is bound to find out, because everything always comes out in the wash. You kna'imean? But whateva. I mean, I can't worry about that."

Randy warned, "Just be careful. Niggahs will snake you and cut your throat in a second. So just watch out for his hit man, that niggah Be-Bo. Monatana ain't necessarily the type of cat that will kill you. He just hires ruthless cats to do it for him."

"Yeah, yeah, I know. That niggah Be-Bo, he be doing all of Montana's hits. I know exactly who that niggah is. But Randy, I can't be walking on thin ice and eggshells. I gots to do my thing. And believe me, we'll have you up outta this piece by next week."

Randy reminded me that his birthday was on September third and that he wanted more than anything to be home for his birthday. I promised him that he wouldn't be in the joint on his 21st birthday. Then I explained to him that the only thing that he'd missed out on since he'd been locked up was this spot that was out in New Jersey called

The Rink. It was a roller skating rink that everyone went to on Tuesday nights. Randy wasn't too disappointed on missing out on The Rink. He said based on the way that I had described the atmosphere it sounded like the same ol' same ol'. He was right.

"Yo Holz, I gotta tell you the story."

"What story?"

Randy went on to explain. "Yo, after I got caught in the okey doke, I told you how Five-O took me back to the precinct and waxed my behin'. Right?"

"Yeah."

"Well, my face was so jacked up with bruises that there was no way that the D.A. was gonna bring me into a courtroom and have me formally arraigned on charges. See, the D.A. knew that every TV camera in the city had had me on tape when I got bagged. The D.A. also knew that there were no blemishes on my grill when I was being led into the police car. So after the cops had beat me down, my lawyer took pictures of my grill and my body and all that. My lawyer took the pictures to the D.A. and he told the D.A. that if they didn't delay the arraignment that he was gonna bring the city up on police brutality charges. 'Cause how else could my face and body have gotten so jacked up like that? Especially when the actual precinct mug shot pictures that they took of me showed no cuts or black eyes or bruises.

The D.A. was caught between a rock and a hard place. He knew that we had no defense going into this whole case, but he didn't want this police brutality thing to cause the prosecution trouble in getting a conviction. The D.A wants to get re-elected, and he knows people always remember the high profile and high publicity cases. So needless to say he wanted to make sure that he built an open and shut case. See if I walk, the city will go crazy and the D.A. won't stand a chance of getting re-elected. Now with brutality in the picture, things changed. He knew that my lawyer could play that up in a million different ways. And like I said, the D.A. was stuck. See, taking certain mitigating circumstances into account, by law the system can't hold anyone no longer than like five or six days unless they have been formally charged. If they do hold someone without formally charging them, then by law they technically have to let the person go, scott free, no matter what the crime is. My lawyer kind of sparked a pre-trial plea bargain behind that technicality.

My lawyer knew that it would take longer than the five or six days for my face to heal, so he told the D.A. that I would be willing to waive my allotted time to be formally charged if they would agree to give me a substantially reduced bail. And if they didn't agree to our terms, he was gonna go public with my charges against the police department. Yo, the D.A. took the bait. They had no choice but to bite. But being that this case is so highly publicized, they couldn't let anyone know that I was given a bail, especially a bail that's so low. So the deal is that if I come up with the loot then I walk outta here mad quiet in some kind of disguise, and nobody will know. Only thing is that I will be on house arrest until my trial starts.

Yo Holz, I was like, whateva. Just as long as I ain't gotta sit up behind these bars. Yo B, God looked out lovely, because otherwise I wasn't seeing no kind of bail. I just hope that my lawyer can work the same kind of magic for my trial when it comes. But somehow between now and then, we'll figure something out."

I couldn't really respond to Randy's story, because the correction officers had informed us that Randy had used up his allotted visiting time. So as Randy and I both stood and prepared to venture on our separate paths, we embraced and said good-bye I felt something in that hug. It was as though that was the last time I would see Randy.

"Yo Randy, I'll have you outta here real soon. Just be cool and hold tight. Ah'ight?"

"Ah'ight, Holz. I'm depending on you. Yo, check on my mother for me. Make sure that she's ah'ight."

"No problem, duke. See ya."

Randy strolled off and yelled, "FOURTH CREW!" His voice literally echoed throughout the prison.

Revelation

September 3, 1991. Randy's birthday, and he was coming home. Even if it was just until his trial started, at least he'd be home for his birthday. Over the last few days I'd split my time between gathering up the rest of the loot for Randy and sitting with Randy's father discussing his son's future. We talked about everything. I knew that Mr. Allen wasn't so naïve as to not know exactly where the bail money for Randy was coming from. Still, he never questioned me about it.

I accompanied Randy's father to his lawyer's office. I'd never learned more about the legal system than I learned in just two visits to this sharp Philadelphia lawyer's office. Randy's lawyer was about six feet tall, medium build with dark hair and dark eyes. Of course he was white, but he was as sharp as a whip. He knew every legal loophole in the book.

On my second visit to the law office, Randy's father informed the lawyer that he had come up with the rest of the bail money. His lawyer immediately got on the phone and spoke to whomever and then he spoke privately with Randy's Pops. I hadn't a clue as to what was going on.

Then in his thick Jamaican accent, Randy's father, who seemed elated, told me that there was some legal stuff that had to go on in terms of posting Randy's bail, but he asked me if I could meet Randy at six pm to take him home. I had no problem with picking him up. However, I just didn't understand why he didn't pick up Randy himself. I didn't ask any questions. I simply went along with the plan.

Later that evening, when I got to Rikers Island, I was instructed by correction officers where to wait for

Randy. I waited in a huge parking lot. Randy was taking forever to come out. In fact, I had to be waiting a few hours up until this point. I didn't know if something had gone wrong or what. I started to think that maybe the media had gotten wind of what was going on. All I knew was that I had been waiting for close to two hours for Randy to be released.

Before I knew it, I'd dozed off in my car, only to be awakened by the sound of a bus with a very bad muffler system. The automatic gate that led to the parking lot began to open. The bus drove up to the gate and stopped. After about a minute or so, Randy stepped off the bus. The door to the bus closed and the bus drove off, leaving behind a thick cloud of black pollution. When the pollution cloud had disappeared, Randy, who had on a hat and some shades was still standing and looking around as if he were lost.

I jumped out of my car and yelled to him. "Yo, Randy, over here, kid!"

When Randy recognized me he quickly jogged over to where I was standing.

"Big Holz, what's up, kid?"

"It's your birthday, that's what's up," I said as Randy and I embraced. "You wanna drive?"

Without answering me, Randy took the keys and we were out. Randy told me that he wanted to get off of Rikers Island as quickly as possible. He feared that this was all some sort of a dream and that he would soon awake only to find himself back behind bars. I could relate to his sense of urgency so I helped him navigate his way home.

When we finally made it to the Grand Central Parkway, Randy realized that he in fact wasn't dreaming as he said, "Yo Holz I am a free man." I simply smiled and watched as Randy basked in his glory.

Then he went on, "I just want to get home and take a nice bath. And after that I'm gonna sit back, relax, and eat a nice, home cooked meal."

So with Randy behind the steering wheel, we drove toward Lauerlton. It was now dark outside. Darkness had been appearing quicker and quicker with each passing day, a sign that the summer would soon be behind us. The hot, steamy, blistering weather of July and August was also behind us. Man oh man, was this ever a buck wild summer or what? During the summer of 1991 I had experienced everything imaginable that a human being could experience. Thank God I was still alive.

I lowered the music all the way down and said to Randy, "Yo, remember back when Richie got killed? Remember how we cared so much at that time?"

"Yeah, I remember. But now it's like, whateva. But yo, didn't I tell you back then that a lot of brothas were gonna die this summer? I knew it! But it's ah'ight, though, 'cause I don't think that it can get no worse than it has been."

"Yes it can get worse. Trust me."

Randy replied, "Nah, I know it can get worse, but I just try to believe that it can't. Because humans shouldn't have to live the way we do. I mean, look at us. It's like our lives are made for the movies or something. I tell you one thing, this life that we live definitely ain't Hollywood. This life that we live is straight up as real as it gets. It's like this paper chasing lifestyle is just one big urban massacre."

"Randy, at the beginning of this year, when all of Fourth Crew was driving to Times Square to watch the ball drop, what did we do?"

Randy answered, "We all paused, bowed our heads and prayed to God and asked him to watch over us this year."

"Yup, and you know what? That's why me and you are still alive right now. We're alive because of God, the creator of all things."

Randy looked at me and nodded in agreement. "Tell me about it."

Then Randy challenged me to end the lost lifestyle that we'd been living. He reminded me that we both had brains and that we were not using them. I told him that with the way everything had been going down that it looked as though it was just gonna be me and him anyway. No more Fourth Crew. Yeah, from now on it was going to be me and Randy, doing something positive with our lives, like opening up a restaurant or whatever.

"Holz, realistically though, I'm facing a double homicide rap. Who am I fooling? My life is over!"

"Stop thinking like that! We're gonna deal with your whole trial and all of that. We have brains. All we have to do is use them. With our brains and with God we can overcome anything, including a double homicide rap." Randy remained silent.

After I reminded Randy to get off at the next exit, he looked at me and said, "Holz, I remember where to get off. I wasn't in jail that long." Then, very sarcastically, Randy recited, "I get off here, then I make a right at the light, then I make a left at the next light."

"Go to hell, niggah," I joked.

After a minute or so of silence, Randy yelled, "There it is, Holz! 234th Street! Thank you Lord for getting me home. I'm back on the block! Yesss!"

"Randy, hold up, hold up. Stop at the corner. I'ma run in the store real quick and buy some brew."

"Yeah, ah'ight."

As I got out of the car I felt rain starting to come down. "Damn!" I said, "it's starting to rain."

When I came out of the store and made my way back to the car I asked, "Randy, you didn't want anything, right?"

Randy replied, "Nah, I'm straight. It's my first day home. I can't be smelling like alcohol when I walk into my house. My Moms will flip."

It was pretty close to 10:00 pm. Randy and I had decided to park the car and sit until I was finished drinking my beer. We were parked right in front of the spot where Richie had been killed. We sat a block and a half away from Randy's house. The rain started to come down a little harder.

I commented, "I'm glad it's raining, at least it can cool things off."

"Man, forget that! It's my birthday. It can't be raining on my birthday."

Switching subjects, I asked, "Randy, are you still gonna take the test to become a cop?"

Randy laughed, "Yeah, if they let me take it. The job pays alright."

I knew that joke time was over and it was time to drop the bombshell. I braced myself as I said, "Yo, I got something to tell you that's gonna shock the hell out of you."

Randy calmly asked, "What? What is it?"

"Now Randy, believe me when I tell you this, because I wouldn't play with you about something like this."

"What is it?" Randy raised his voice.

"You wanna know how you got bagged by the cops? Latiefe dropped dime, that's how."

"What?" Randy screamed.

As I looked Randy in his face I said, "Word to Richie, he ratted on you, B."

After a long pause, Randy gathered himself and asked, "Holz you ain't joking, are you?"

"No. I'm dead serious."

Randy sighed and said, "My own man? Nah, Latiefe's my man. He wouldn't do something like that."

I remained quiet and after another long pause Randy continued. "Then again, I don't know. Yo Holz, I know he didn't do it over that little fight that we had in the Red Zone."

I was feeling like I had to do something. I wanted to tell Randy that I was lying, but I wasn't lying, so I nonchalantly said, "Yup, that's exactly why he told."

"Nah, it's more than that," Randy said defensively. "Trust me. It's more than that."

Randy was in deep thought. Then he said, "Yo, whateva man! I could get all worked up about it. I could try to hunt Latiefe down and kill him, but what good would that do? Like I was telling you before, I have to start living a step above that. I have to start loving myself. But it's hard to love myself, Holz. It's hard to love anything because it seems like love doesn't last. You know what I say? I say to hell with love and all of that other nonsense. If a person wants to be successful in life, all he has to do is prepare for the worst and fear the good. Holz, when things are going good in my life, I have to start fearing it, 'cause when things are going good, something bad has to go along with it. It has to!

I just got released from jail. And that's a good thing. But I'm afraid of that. I'm afraid simply because I know that before the night is over with, something bad is going to happen to me. Like Five-O is probably gonna show up at my crib tonight and haul me back off to jail. But whatever bad thing that does happen, it won't matter, because actually I'll be expecting it to happen. I'm telling you, kid, watch. Five-O will show up at the crib tonight with a new warrant, kna'imean?"

"Yo Randy, I moved to Queens when I was about three years old. In my head I can still see you walking across the street innocently, coming to play with me. That was only fifteen years ago and it's like, where did all of that innocence go? Remember when we played little league together? G.I.Joes? Atari? All of that. But now it's like that was in another lifetime. But yo, those were the good times...Yo, I'm gonna give you a word and you give me the first word that comes into your mind, ah'ight?"

"Ah'ight," Randy replied.

"Money." --- "Corrupting."

"Women." --- "Whores."

"Education." --- "Overrated."

"Guns." --- "Power."

"People." --- "Ha ha."

"Drugs." --- "Government."

"Trust." --- "Nobody."

"Future." --- "Bleak."

"Life." --- "Hectic."

"God." --- "Almighty."

"Jesus." --- "Michaelangelo."

"Death." --- "Inevitable."

"Ah'ight, game over. You're right about trust nobody. I know I don't trust anybody. How can I, when I don't even trust myself? That's like when people ask me do I love so and so? I used to say, yes I love 'em. I used to even believe that I loved certain people. But now I realize that I don't love nobody. Again, it's like, how can I love someone else when I don't even love myself? They say 'to know me is to love me,' and then I hear people saying that they want the black on black violence to stop 'cause they love us. But Randy, how can they love us if they don't even know who we really are? The biggest part of knowing us begins with being able to relate to us. You know?"

"Holz, I'm feeling what you're sayin', but yo, it's pouring out this piece. Let's be out." As Randy prepared to put the car in drive so that we could make our way down the block he asked, "Yo Holz, who was that in that Jeep that just drove by?"

"Oh, that's Tony from up the block. See, that niggah is chillin' and he ain't do half of the dirt that we did. He was telling me that he took two semesters off from school so he could work and save for his college tuition, which is what he did, and he had enough dough left over so he bought that fat ride. Yo, I be regretting that I didn't just do things like that instead of being so impatient and chasing the glitter. But then again, I tried to do things that way. You know, the straight and narrow, but no one would let me. Everybody had something negative to say. I know I shouldn't care about other people's opinions but it's hard to just block things out and focus."

"Holz, you can't care what other people think about you. You just have to believe in yourself. Don't even sweat what they think. They can't judge you. Only God can judge you. Plus they don't really know you anyway, which means they don't love you, so why listen to 'em?"

"Yeah, I hear you. But yo, enough of this politickin'. This beer is starting to mess my head up. You sure you don't want any?"

"Nah, I'm cool. Yo, let's be out. It's starting to fog up in this piece."

Randy gently pressed on the gas pedal to pull away from the curb, but then he quickly had to jam on the brakes to avoid hitting someone who had darted in front of the car. What happened next transpired in about five to ten seconds.

"Yo what the...! Who the hell? Yo Holz, what's wrong with that niggah?"

As I realized who had darted out in front of the car I said, "Yo, that's Montana's car parked alongside of us. Oh, yo! Randy, look out! NO!" As I closed my eyes and ducked, I braced for the worst to happen. I heard *boom boom boom.* Glass had shattered. My entire body was near the floor mats of the car, trying to squeeze underneath the dashboard. I felt as if Mike Tyson had hit me with a body blow and knocked the wind out of me.

There was a second or two of silence. Then I heard the sound of screeching tires peeling off the road. I opened my eyes and saw Randy sitting slumped, bloody, and limp.

"Ah, man! Hahhh... Randy! Randy! You ah'ight?" Randy didn't say a word.

I urgently asked again, "Randy, you ah'ight, kid?' Again I got no answer and I pleaded, "Oh, Lord. Oh no. Help me. Somebody help me! Please Lord, help me! Somebody."

Montana's hit-man had just pumped two shotgun blasts into Randy's chest and one into my back. Finally Randy tried to speak, which at least let me know that he was still alive. He struggled to ask, "Holz, why'd he shoot me? What did I do? Help me, Holz."

I felt as if I was living the episode with Richie all over again. I was more worried about Randy's well being than my own. I could barely breathe, but I managed to frantically holler for someone to help my dying friend. I was in shock. I knew that I couldn't waste too much time because I saw how bad Randy looked as he coughed up huge globs of blood.

He continually asked me to help him, so I quickly got a grip of myself. Clutching my ribs with my right hand, I reached across my body and opened the passenger door to my Saab. In unbearable pain, I trekked out into the rain and quickly made it to the driver's side of the car. I ripped the door open and shoved Randy's blood drenched torso into the passenger's seat.

I was mad nervous and I couldn't think which way to go to get to the nearest hospital. I spun the car around and decided to go to Mary Immaculate Hospital, which was near Jamaica Avenue, about ten minutes away. I sped off in the rain, driving as fast as I could down Merrick Blvd.

The streets were slick and rain was hitting me in the face through the shattered window.

I tried to ease Randy's fears as I assured him, "I'm gonna get you there, Randy. We're almost there. Just hold tight." I plowed the accelerator to the floor like Mario Andretti, and man, I mean I was really moving! It was like I had no regard for the other cars that were on the road. I kept glancing at Randy. I was trying to talk to him to keep him calm. He looked as if he were getting weaker by the second. "God please! Please, please God," I kept uttering as I'd suddenly became extra holy.

Adrenaline had taken over my body, but at this point the adrenaline was really beginning to wear off. I could not breathe at all. I had to literally reach my head out of the window and gasp for air. My entire body felt as if it was trembling and I began to get dizzy. I took my eyes off of the road and stared at Randy as he sat amongst the shattered pieces of glass. Then I don't know what came over me.

"God, no. No!" I yelled as I felt agony and tears beginning to form inside of me. I realized that Randy was no longer in the car with me. His spirit had left his body. Everything that was inside of me felt as if it had suddenly left me also. I had to laugh in order to keep myself from literally freakin' out. I felt very nauseous and jittery, not to mention helpless. I didn't know how to react.

I violently slammed on the brakes, which caused my car to spin out and do a 360. Then I skidded sideways for about a block before coming to a complete stop. I just sat there in the middle of a busy intersection. Cars slowly drove by and rubbernecked in order to see what kind of maniac was behind the wheel of my car. Other cars viciously blew their horns and cursed at me, telling me to get the hell off of the road and all other kinds of profane suggestions. But I blocked them out. I was beyond weak. I was crying and laughing at the same time as I looked at Randy's butchered body.

With no more energy, I stepped on the gas pedal and I slowly began to drive. I was totally disoriented and didn't realize that I was headed back toward Laurelton. As I drove, I was hearing what sounded like Randy's voice, pleading and saying, "No Holz, take me to the hospital, please!"

But before I knew it I had blacked out and lost control of the car. My Saab slowly rolled head on into a utility pole. With smoke coming from beneath the crunched hood, my motionless body lay limp and slumped over the steering wheel. The horn was blaring into the rainy, overcast sky.

And just like that, one buckshot to my back had ended it all.

■■

Looking back, I realize that the bullet from Be-Bo's shotgun was beyond painful. However, comparatively speaking, the pain didn't last very long. It was like, in a flash, I had been transformed. I saw and felt my soul leaving my shell, and it was transported into a new body, a body that wasn't made of flesh. I didn't have emotions, because I was outside of my flesh. I guess that's why I wasn't afraid. Then before I knew it I was kneeled before the most beautiful spirit that I had ever seen. It had to be Jesus.

Jesus spoke with so much compassion and love as he touched me. He told me that before the creation of the world he knew me. He explained that He longed to be with me. Then He revealed to me all that I had done with my life and with the talents that He had given me. And I couldn't help but to be completely humbled as I bowed at His feet. If I was still in my flesh, I would have begun to cry.

"Lord, please forgive me," I begged.

The Lord calmly explained that although He knew of me and that I knew of Him, I truly never knew Him.

"But Lord, I always prayed to You and I even went to church at times. I do know You! I believe in You! You are the son of God."

Then the Lord revealed to me exactly why I was gonna be eternally punished. He explained that although I was gonna be punished for the wrong that I'd done, I was also gonna be punished for having never obeyed the Gospel. The Gospel contained the fact that Jesus had lowered himself and become a human so that He could sympathize with us and understand the trials that we face on Earth. The Gospel also contained the fact that Jesus had given His life as a sacrifice so that we might live with Him forever.

Realizing my fate, I earnestly began to beg. "But Lord, I do believe in You. I know that You gave Your life for me, and that's why I love You."

Jesus told me that if I'd really loved him, then when I was on Earth I would have repented and been baptized for the forgiveness of my sins and proceeded to live as sanctified a life as possible. "That," He said, "would have been truly obeying the Gospel. Then, and only then, would you have known Me."

Then Jesus departed from my sight, and an angel came and tapped me on the shoulder. "Come, let me show you something."

The angel showed me what looked like Paradise, but human words couldn't explain the beauty of what I saw. It made the Hawaiian Islands look like Harlem or Compton. It was bugged, because at every funeral that I'd ever been to in my lifetime, the deceased person was always spoken of in terms of having gone on to "A better place." Yet there weren't too many people that I knew from my lifetime on Earth that were in that garden of serenity that the angel was showing me. But yo, people that were in that Paradise looked as if they didn't have a care in the world. The streets looked like they were made of gold and the people were sitting back, kicking it with God. Nobody was working or anything. Nobody was worrying about paper chasing.

Then the angel showed me what looked like a lake of fire and burning sulfur. There was complete darkness, and all I heard were pleas for help. People sounded as if they were agonizing and suffering. Again, it was indescribable in human terms, but it looked as if everything was on fire and melting. A scorching, hot, unquenchable fire is the best way to describe the fire. It seemed as if the people were experiencing extreme pain from the fire. Pain that would not and could not go away. I realized that almost everyone that I knew from my life on Earth was in that lake of fire and suffering.

Then the Lord re-appeared and said to me, "Away from me, you evildoer!" And with that, I too was added to the lake of fire. What made matters worse was that I could see the people on the other side of this great chasm. They were enjoying God's splendor. Yeah, the people in Paradise could also see us, but they couldn't feel for us, because on their side of the chasm there was no place for tears.

In the lake of fire I also saw the one known as the Devil. He was where I was. All the people where I was, suffering along with me, realized that we were there because while on Earth we had been deceived by the Devil to do wrong. We had been deceived just as Eve had been deceived. We all wanted to unleash anger at the Devil for having deceived us. But what good would it have done? The suffering and pain that we all were feeling would be forever. We weren't capable of increasing the agony. Plus, when we really looked at the whole picture, yeah, Satan had deceived us, but he had never forced us to do anything. All of us that were in the lake of fire had willingly chose to do what was wrong.

It was bugged, because as I continued to feel the intense pain and suffering, not once did I think about driving a nice car. Not once did I think about needing large amounts of cash in order to impress women. Not once did I think about flossing on 125th street. Not once did I think about sex. Not once did I think about smoking weed or getting drunk. Not once did I think about going to the Red Zone or to the Jones Beach Greekfest to chase women and do all kinds of things that shouldn't be done. Not once did I think about rolling dice or just hanging out on street corners. The reason that I didn't think of such things was because there was only one thought on my mind, and that thought was evident, as I pleaded with the angel, "Please just send me a drop of water for the tip of my tongue. Please... The pain is just too great. I can't take this heat."

To my plea, the angel calmly responded, "It is impossible for that to happen. Remember when you were on Earth you lived as you wanted to. Never denying yourself anything. Now you will be denied the goodness of the Lord forever and ever."

I continued to plead. "OK, but will you please send someone to warn the people that I love who are still on Earth? I don't want anyone to experience this torture."

The angel replied, "That someone you are talking about has already been there. His name is Jesus Christ. Besides, they have their Bibles, the word of God. That is all that they need. All they have to do is open it up and read it and they will know how to avoid what you are experiencing."

Then the angel revealed one last thing to me. On the other side of the chasm I saw Latiefe being cradled in the bosom of the Lord. I was totally dumbfounded. But the angel explained that what I was witnessing was a revelation of what was to come of Latiefe's life in the future. He revealed to me how Latiefe had turned his life around and obeyed Acts 2:38, as had many others that were once lost. Acts 2:38 stated, "Repent and be baptized, every one of you, in the name of Jesus Christ for the forgiveness of your sins. And you will receive the gift of the Holy Spirit."

The angel's last words to me were, "Mark Holsey, or Holz, as they called you in the other life, everyone experiences a physical death. But woe to those who experience what is known as the second death, or spiritual death. That is what you are experiencing, and what you will continue to experience for an eternity. The second death is separation from God. The second death isn't temporary, like the physical death that you experienced when you got shot. Holz, those who obey Acts 2:38 will never experience the second death, because they will live forever with God in Paradise."

Then it was made even more crystal clear to me why my fate was sealed and just. I was allowed to open the Bible and read any passage that I chose. Not ironic at all was the fact that I turned to Romans 1:28-32, which reads:

Furthermore, since you did not think it worthwhile to retain the knowledge of God, he gave you over to a depraved mind, to do what ought not to be done. You have become filled with every kind of wickedness, evil, greed, and depravity. You are full of envy, murder, drunkenness, sexual immorality, strife, deceit, and malice. You are a gossip, slanderer, God hater, insolent, arrogant and boastful, you invent ways of doing evil; You disobey your parents, you are senseless, faithless, heartless, ruthless. Although you know God's righteous decree that those who do such things deserve death, you not only continue to do these very things but you also approve of those who practice them.

Dictionary

Amp - 1. Charged 2. Extremely excited
Ayyite – 1. Alright 2. O.K.
B – 1. A good friend 2. A buddy 3. A pal
Baller – 1. A person with a lot of money and nice material things
Baby Pa – 1. Good friend 2. A buddy 3. A pal
Bagged – 1. Arrested 2. To get locked up
B-Boy - 1. Someone that is street wise and tough 2. A hoodlum 3. A thug
Big Up – 1. To acknowledge 2. Give praise
Big Willies - 1. A lavish person 2. Someone that appears to have a lot of money 3. A high roller
Binis- 1. Business
Biscuit – 1. A gun
Blazin' - 1. Extremely stylish 2. Very high quality
Blunt - 1. A cigar wrapping that is filled with marijuana for the intentions to be smoked
Blow up - 1. To become extravagant 2. To start displaying a lavish lifestyle
Bodied - 1. Killed 2. Murdered 3. To be a victim of homicide
Bomb – 1. Exquisite 2. Nice 3. Lavish
Bounce. 1. To leave 2. To depart 3. To exit
Boyz - 1. Boys 2. Guys 3. Gentlemen
Burner – 1. A gun
Butta - 1. Extremely nice 2. Denotes fine quality
Buss - 1. To shoot 2. To fire a bullet from a gun
Buss a Cap – 1. To fire a bullet from a gun
Cake – 1. Cash 2. Money
Cats – 1. Guys 2. People 3. Hoodlums 4. Men
Car Jack – 1. The act of face to face robbing a person of their car
Cheese - 1. Cash 2. Money
Chicken Head - 1. A bimbo 2. A woman that lacks common sense 3. An airhead
Chop Shop - 1. A black market operation that buys stolen cars and strips the cars and resells the parts to the unknowing public
Chromed Out – 1. A car that has very expensive chrome rims
Cipher – 1. A group of people standing in a circle having a discussion
Clink - 1. Jail 2. Prison

Cock Diesel – 1. A person with really big muscles
Crazy - 1. A large quantity 2. A big amount of something
Cream - 1. Cash 2. Money
Crib - 1. House 2. Place of rest
Dead Presidents – 1. Money 2. Cash
Diggidy - 1. Doubt
Dis – 1. Disrespect
Dough - 1. Cash 2. Money
Down Low - 1. To keep something quiet or secret 2. To keep to ones' self 3. To hideout
Drop-Dime – 1. To tell on a person 2. To tattletale
DT's – 1. Detectives 2. Undercover police officers
Duke – 1. Dude 2.Guy 3. Person 4. friend
Fat – 1. Extremely nice quality 2. Lavish
Feds - 1. FBI
Fella - 1. Guys 2. People 3. Men 4. Hoodlum
Five O – 1. The police 2. Cops 3. Detectives 4. Undercover police officers
Flip – 1. To double or increase by more than double 2. To get upset
Flipping - 1. To double one's money mostly by illegal means
Flossin' - 1. To show off 2. To boast 3. To brag
Fly - 1. Something that is nice 2. Pleasing
Forties – 1. Forty ounce bottles of Malt Liquor
Freestyling – 1. To speak lyrics, as from a rap song, from off of the top of a person's head, or lyrics that were not previously prepared or memorized
Freshly Dipped – 1. A person that looks very stylish 2. A person with expensive clothes
Frontin' - 1. To not go through with a plan of action 2.To not follow through due to fear
Front - 1. (See definition for Frontin')
G's - 1. Thousands of dollars (one G equals one thousand dollars)
Gangster Lean - 1. The sitting style when driving a car, characterized by sitting with one's body leaning in an exaggerated manner to one side of the car while one's arm is extended straight out and only one hand grips the steering wheel.
G Thang – 1. Gangster thing
Gonna - 1. Going to
Grill - 1. A person's face
Heat - 1. A gun

Heads - 1. Guys 2. People 3. Men 4. Hoodlum
Herb - 1. A whimp
Hiccup Juice – 1. Liquor 2. Beer
High Post - 1. A very cool or relaxed manner
Homeboys - 1. Very close friends or associates from the neighborhood 2. Long time pals
Homey - 1. (See definition for Homeboys)
Hood - 1. Neighborhood
Hot – 1. To denote an area that has a very high police presence 2. Stylish 3. Nice
Hustling – 1. Selling Drugs 2. Doing illegal activity 3. Striving hard to get money by nay or various means
Ice – 1. Diamonds
Ice Shining - 1. Very high quality diamonds that shine
Ill - 1. Nasty 2. Ruthless 3. Shocking 4. Explicit 5. No joke
Jack - 1. To rob a person 2. To forcefully steal something
Joint - 1. A gun 2. Jail 3. Material things 4. A relatively small amount of marijuana that has been rolled and is ready to be smoked
Kee (Key) – 1. Denotes a Kilo of Cocaine
Kick It - 1. To relax and just talk 2. To do nothing but pleasurable things
Kids - 1. Guys 2. People 3. Men 4. Hoodlum
Knaaimean - 1. Do you know what I mean? 2. Do you understand?
Knocking Boots - 1. Having sex
Knocking It Off - 1. Selling drugs
Lace - 1. To mix drugs with something else, such as Baking Soda 2. Something very extravagant
Lamped - 1. To just relax 2. To be at ease 3. Standing around with nothing to do
Leaking - 1. Bleeding
Licked Off Shots - 1. To shoot off a gun
Live - 1. A person that is very wild and daring 2. A noisy person
Loot - 1. Money
Mad – 1. A large quantity 2. A big amount of something
Ma' Dukes - 1. A person's biological mother
Mercked – 1. Killed 2. Murdered
Money - 1. A person 2. A guy 3. Cash
Nah-Nah - 1. Sex 2. A females vagina
Niggah - 1. A friend 2. A close associate 3. Reference to a male person in a non-derogatory manner

No Diggidy - 1. No doubt
Nooka - 1. Same as Niggah (See definition for niggah)
Off The Hook - 1. Out of this world 2. Unbelievable
Okey Doke - 1. A freak thing
On Point - 1. Something or someone that is very organized
2. The opposite of a flimsy operation
Package - 1. A certain amount or denomination of illegal retail
drugs that are ready to be distributed and or sold.
Packin' - 1. Carrying a gun 2. A well endowed woman or
man
Paper - 1. Money 2. Cash
Packin' - 1. Carrying a gun
Phat - 1. Stylish 2.Very nice 3.Good
Pigs – 1. Cops
Pinched - 1. To get arrested
Player - 1. A man that has a lot of women 2. A gigolo 3. A
womanizer
Politickin' - 1. Denotes much friendly talk and actions 2.
Creating a free spirited atmosphere
Pop A Cap In Him – 1. To Shoot a person
Potnah - 1. To sarcastically label someone as your partner or
associate
Pusha – 1. Drug dealer 2. Dope seller
Pound Of Bones – 1. A lot of marijuana
Pump – 1. To sell drugs
Pump Shotty - 1. A shot gun
Pulley - 1. A device or toll which is used in car thefts
Rammed - 1. A place that is filled with a lot of people
Rat – 1. Someone who tells on another person
Rip The Mic - 1. To take hold of a microphone and shout very
powerful and hype lyrics.
Rollin' – 1. Living extremely lavish 2. Someone who is making
a lot of money
Run It – 1. To forcefully demand or rob a person's possessions
Shook - 1. A person that is very scared 2. A very nervous
person
Shotty - 1. A shotgun
Slammin' – 1. Very nice 2. Outstanding (Mike Tyson's house
is slammin')
Sleep - 1. To take someone or a certain situation very lightly
and nonchalantly
Smash - 1. Something that is number one 2. Hype
Snake - 1. A backstabber 2. To double cross someone

Solid - 1. To do or owe someone a favor
Stepping To Someone – 1. To approach someone in a hostile or confrontational manner
Strapped – 1. Carrying a gun   2. Out of cash
Swiss Chessed Up - 1. A person or thing that has been shot numerous times.   2. Full of bullet holes.
Sucker – 1. Someone with no heart or no backbone   2. Someone that is not brave: scared; soft.
Tag Jobs - 1. Stolen cars in which the vehicle identification number has been changed so that the car can be re-registered and sold to the public
Taxing – 1. A large quantity   2. A big amount of something
The Bomb – 1. Very nice   2. Outstanding (Mike Tyson's house is the bomb)
The Man - 1. A person with very high stature or in a powerful position   2. One with a lot of respect on the street.   3. Someone held in high esteem   4. The government   5. The police
Treed Up - 1. A person that is high from smoking marijuana
Up North – 1. State prison   2. To go to jail   3. One that is in jail
Wet - 1. To get shot   2. To bleed
Whateva – 1. Whatever
Whip - 1. A car
Whipped – 1. A person that is head over heels for a woman and will do anything to please her
Wit' - 1. With
Word - 1. To confirm something
Word Is Bond - 1. A person's word is true and can be trusted   2. A person's word has integrity behind it
Work – 1. Drugs

Other Meanings:

Larry Davis - 1. A notorious New York City street crime legend

The following are the names of victims of police brutality:
Eleanor Bumpers
Phillip Pannell
Michael Stewart
Rodney King

About The Author:

Mark Anthony is the author of two novels's, <u>**Paper Chasers**</u>, which is his first novel, and <u>**Dogism**</u>, which is his second novel. He is an entrepreneur and an honors graduate of Iona College, in New Rochelle, NY. Mark Anthony resides in Queens, NY along with his wife Sabine and their son and daughter. Mark has a vivid and real life capturing storytelling style that keeps readers anxiously turning the pages of his books.